"Have dinner with me."

Her jaw clenched—he hadn't even framed it as a question. "No." She gave the word all the finality she could muster.

"Because of the chair?"

"Not because of the chair—because we are currently working together on a school matter."

He leaned back. "It's because of the chair."

Heather planted her hands on the table. "It's because of the arrogant, pushy man *in* the chair." She let out a breath and began putting the notebook back into her handbag. "I was just trying to be nice, to celebrate all the good you've done with Simon, but I should have known it'd get like this. I'll walk back to school, thanks."

Max put his hands up. "Okay, okay. I'll take it down a notch. Let's have pie and coffee and talk about Simon, and I'll keep my dinner plans with Alex and JJ and pretend this never happened."

She glared at him. "You were going to ditch Alex and JJ for dinner?"

"Well, not really. I was pretty sure you'd say no."

Heather put one hand to her forehead. "You are absolutely impossible. You should come with a warning label."

ALLIE PLEITER

A Heart to Heal
&
Saved by the Fireman

⬧HARLEQUIN® LOVE INSPIRED®CLASSICS

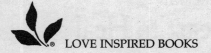 LOVE INSPIRED BOOKS

Recycling programs
for this product may
not exist in your area.

ISBN-13: 978-1-335-23256-4

A Heart to Heal & Saved by the Fireman

Copyright © 2019 by Harlequin Books S.A.

The publisher acknowledges the copyright holder
of the individual works as follows:

A Heart to Heal
Copyright © 2014 by Alyse Stanko Pleiter

Saved by the Fireman
Copyright © 2014 by Alyse Stanko Pleiter

CONTENTS

A HEART TO HEAL   7

SAVED BY THE FIREMAN   243

Allie Pleiter, an award-winning author and RITA® Award finalist, writes both fiction and nonfiction. Her passion for knitting shows up in many of her books and all over her life. Entirely too fond of French macarons and lemon meringue pie, Allie spends her days writing books and avoiding housework. Allie grew up in Connecticut, holds a BS in speech from Northwestern University and lives near Chicago, Illinois.

Books by Allie Pleiter

Love Inspired

Matrimony Valley

His Surprise Son
Snowbound with the Best Man

Blue Thorn Ranch

The Texas Rancher's Return
Coming Home to Texas
The Texan's Second Chance
The Bull Rider's Homecoming
The Texas Rancher's New Family

Lone Star Cowboy League: Boys Ranch

The Rancher's Texas Twins

Lone Star Cowboy League

A Ranger for the Holidays

Visit the Author Profile page at Harlequin.com for more titles.

A HEART TO HEAL

The light shines in the darkness,
and the darkness has not overcome it.
—*John* 1:5

To Jeff
And he knows why.

Acknowledgments

Some stories beg relentlessly to be told,
even if it poses a challenge. My thanks to
Erin Kinahan for sharing her experience of life in a
wheelchair with me, and for the ongoing assistance
of Dr. David Chen from the Rehabilitation Institute
of Chicago for his medical expertise. I also owe
a debt of thanks to author and wheelchair rugby
star Mark Zupan for his frank and compelling
memoir, *Gimp*, which helped me to understand Max's
experience. If any of the medical or disability facts
of this book are incorrect, the fault lies with me
and not with any of these generous experts.

Chapter One

High school guidance counselor Heather Browning was twenty minutes into The Backup Plan and regretting it already.

Principal Margot Thomas seemed to agree. "That's who you called to help Simon?"

Simon Williams, the frail but brilliant freshman boy who was Heather's biggest concern this year, had already become the target of a senior thug. "It's still August. We're two days into the school year," Heather admitted. "I thought I'd have more time than this to get Simon settled before anyone bothered him." But that wasn't the way it had turned out. Her initial goal—help Simon find some friends who would be protective camouflage against getting noticed by bullies—hadn't worked fast enough.

The principal looked out the school window at that "backup plan" as he appeared in the parking lot. A boxy black car with flames painted on the side pulled into the handicapped-accessible parking space. Max Jones had arrived.

"This afternoon at lunch, Jason Kikowitz decided

Simon was sitting too close to the 'varsity table.' Evidently he grabbed the back of Simon's wheelchair and spun him around, knocking most of Simon's books out of his backpack."

"Sounds like our Kikowitz," Margot commiserated. "I'll be glad when that boy graduates—*if* he graduates."

"Simon spun around fast enough to whack Jason in the shins with the footrest of his wheelchair. It must've hurt, because evidently Jason hopped around on one foot and swore a blue streak in front of the lunch monitor."

Margot gave the sigh of the weary. "Lovely."

"At least it gave Simon a chance to get away. For now. You know Kikowitz," Heather explained, feeling less and less sure of her course of action. "He's likely to lay into Simon every day this week, even if I give him twenty detentions."

The older woman looked at Heather with determination in her eyes. "You know I'll back you up on those even if Coach Mullen gives me grief."

Heather was grateful for Margot Thomas every single day. The principal was an outstanding administrator who cared enough to address problems head-on, even when it meant things got sticky. "Thanks, but you and I both know detentions don't stop Kikowitz. What we need is help for Simon, and the assistance agency couldn't come through with a proper mentor until next month. We don't have that long, so I called JJ." JJ was Heather's friend and Max's sister. And Max Jones, or "Hot Wheels," as a local magazine had dubbed him during their coverage of his highly publicized injury and recovery, was quite possibly the last thing Simon Williams needed. Even if he was the only other resident of Gordon Falls who used a wheelchair, Max seemed to be everything Heather didn't want Simon to be rolled up into one defiant renegade.

The foolishness of calling on him struck her anew as she spied the HTWELZ2 license plate on the car. "Help me, Margot. I need wisdom and calm and I recruited a rolling tornado. Tell him I've been called into a meeting and that we don't need a mentor anymore. I've made a huge mistake, and I don't want Simon to pay for it."

Margot leaned back against the windowsill. "I won't tell him any such thing. I think I want to see how this turns out."

"I don't." Heather rested her forehead in her open hand.

Together Heather and Margot watched Max perform the complicated task of extracting his wheelchair—black with flames on it that matched his car—and settling himself into it. He was athletic, graceful even, and managed to look casual, as if the process were no more taxing than tying a shoe. He wore blue jeans, expensive sneakers and a gray T-shirt with the words *Ramp it up, baby* running across his chest. It was easy to see that his shoulders and biceps carried most of his weight—his arms were toned and outdoor tan. His large hands boasted black leather driving gloves, and his mussed dirty-blond hair framed a strong face. Heather thought he needed a shave, not to mention a haircut and probably half a dozen diplomacy lessons. "Honestly," she told her boss as Max started toward the ramp that led up the stairs to the school entrance, "that guy looks a far cry from an appropriate mentor for an impressionable teenager."

"He's a key executive at Adventure Access, which

is supposed to be a fast-rising company in the adaptive recreation business. If they put faith in him," offered the principal, sounding as if she was grasping at straws and not a little bit amused, "maybe he's not as bad as…he looks."

"Oh, I expect he's worse," Heather moaned. JJ's husband, Alex Cushman, ran that fast-rising adaptive recreation company and had drafted Max as their spokesperson and development consultant. It wasn't hard to see why. Max Jones had been so handsome, daring, arrogant and flamboyant before he'd injured himself that he'd been chosen for a nationally televised reality television show featuring adventure sports. As cruel chance would have it, he'd gotten hurt on that TV show during a risky night climb. Yet looking at him now, it seemed as if his disability barely slowed him down.

"Simon will probably adore him," Margot offered.

"That's exactly what I'm afraid of," Heather moaned. "Nothing good can come from pairing that boy with that man."

Kids were not his thing. Not before, not now.

As he rolled up the ramp to the Gordon Falls High School entrance, Max had to wonder how he'd let JJ talk him into this. If the GFHS teachers knew the kind of tyrant he'd been in high school, they'd be barring the doors.

Only they wouldn't have to. Just take out the ramp and he couldn't get inside no matter how hard he tried. While he'd worked on the development of all kinds of adaptive gear in his new position at Adventure Access, even those top innovators hadn't yet come up with a wheelchair that could climb stairs.

Still, Max remembered the "special" kids from his high school days—not that long ago, for crying out loud—and how they'd been treated. It stuck in his gut that he'd been as mean as the next guy to kids who used wheelchairs or crutches or were in *those* classes. Max had done lots of crazy and regrettable things in high school, but those moments of picking on the weaker kids, the different kids—those gnawed at him now. He'd only said yes to this stint as a "mentor" because JJ seemed to think it might make up for some of his past crimes.

It's four weeks with a gawky fifteen-year-old—I've faced far worse, Max assured himself as he punched the assistive-entrance button and listened to the door whoosh open in front of him. At least schools usually had all the adaptations right. He'd had to sit there feeling stupid the other week when a restaurant had to literally move four tables in order to let him sit down with JJ and have lunch. Then the server had asked JJ what her "special friend" would like to eat. The nerve of some people! He'd given the server such a loud piece of his mind that they'd comped his lunch just to get him out of the place.

He rolled into the entrance, marveling at how high school was still high school. The bang of lockers, the smattering of posters for dances and sporting events, the echo of shouts from a distant gymnasium—it all flung Max's mind back to those years. Hockey team. Prom. Working on his first car. Life was one big game back then, a never-ending stream of escapades, pranks and good times. He'd loved high school, been a master of the school scene—the social side of it, that was. Academics weren't ever his thing, though he'd managed to graduate just fine, despite a few...dozen...trips to the principal's office.

Funny that it was his first stop now—or rather, the guidance counselor's office, which was practically the same thing.

"I'm Max Jones, here to see Heather Browning." Max swallowed his annoyance that he was calling toward a counter over which he could not see. Well over six feet when he could stand, he was especially annoyed by tall counters now that he navigated the world from about three feet lower.

A gray-haired lady—school secretaries evidently hadn't changed one bit since his varsity days—popped up from behind the blue Formica to peer at him over the top of her glasses. "Mr. Jones?" She did the double take Max always enjoyed. Somehow people never expected to see a guy in a wheelchair looking like him, and he got a kick out of leveraging the "Hot Wheels" persona to challenge their assumptions.

Max flicked an Adventure Access business card up onto the counter—shiny black with flames along the bottom with his name and title, Company Spokesman and Adaptive Gear Development Specialist, screaming out in yellow letters. "In the flesh and on the roll."

Her wrinkled eyes popped wide for a moment, then narrowed in suspicion. "Is she expecting you?"

"Yes, I am" came a female voice from behind Max.

Max spun around and sucked in a breath. The high school guidance counselors he remembered didn't look like *that*. Maybe this wouldn't be such a rough gig after all. "Well, hello, Ms. Browning." He didn't even try to hide the pleasant surprise in his voice. Where had JJ been hiding this "friend"? If he'd had a counselor like Heather Browning trying to lure him into higher education, he'd be working on his PhD by now. She had fantastic hair—long, honey-colored curls tumbled down to her shoulders in a wave. Bottle-green eyes that—well, okay, they were currently scowling a bit at him, but he could handle that. People scowled at him all the time, and he much preferred it to the diverted glances of pity that some people threw him. Pulling off his driving glove, Max extended a hand. "I am most definitely pleased to meet you."

"Thanks for coming." He could tell she only barely meant it. He probably shouldn't have squealed his tires pulling into the parking lot like that.

"Anything for JJ," Max said as they went into her office. It was filled with all the stuff one would expect of a helping professional—inspirational quotes, pretty pictures, plants and pottery. The only surprising thing was a "flock" of various flamingo figurines on her bookshelf and a metal flamingo statue-ish thingy on her desk. Max picked it up and inspected it. "I'm surprised we haven't met before."

Ms. Browning plucked the metal bird from his hands, returned it to its perch on her desk and sat down. She crossed her arms. "We have. This summer at the church picnic."

He remembered that picnic as a rather boring affair, all happy community fried chicken and potato salad. Nice, if you liked that sort of thing, which he didn't.

"Mr. Jones, if you—"

"Max," he corrected.

"Max," she relented. "I want to state one thing right

off. This is a serious time commitment, and I'm sure you're very busy. If you don't have the time to give Simon the attention he needs, I'll completely understand."

"Hang on." Max felt his stomach tighten at the low expectation expressed in her words. "I'm willing to make the time. Only I'm not really sure how you go about making freshman year of high school *not* hard, if you know what I mean. That's sort of how it goes, isn't it?"

"I'd like to think we can do better than that. A senior boy—Jason Kikowitz—has made Simon a target of sorts, and it's going to take more than a stack of detention slips to set things right."

"Kikowitz?" Max chuckled; the name brought up an instant vision of a thick-necked linebacker with a crew cut and four like-size friends. "Why do the thugs always have names like Kikowitz?"

She didn't seem to appreciate his commentary. "I want Simon to learn the right way to stand up for himself while I get Mr. Kikowitz to change his thinking."

"Only Simon can't stand up for himself, can he? Wheelchair. That's the whole problem, isn't it?" People always talked around the wheelchair—the elephant in the room—and Max liked to make them face it outright. It made everything easier after that, even if it took an off-color joke to get there.

She flushed and broke eye contact. "It's part of the problem, yes."

"It's lots of the problem, I'd guess. Look, I'm in a chair. I get that. It's part of who I am now, and pretending I'm just like you isn't going to help anyone. It doesn't bug me, so don't let it bug you. I can take you out dancing if I wanted to, so I should be able to help this Simon kid hold his own."

"You cannot take me out dancing."

It was clear she wasn't the type to like a joke. "Well, not in the usual sense, but there's a guy in Chicago building an exoskeleton thingy that—"

"This is not a social meeting. Are we clear?"

She really did know how to suck all the fun out of a room.

"Crystal clear, Ms. Browning." She was too stiff to even match his invitation to use first names. He'd have to work on that. "What is it, exactly, that you think Simon needs?"

"Well, I'd have to say social confidence. He's led a fairly sheltered life because of his condition, but he's brilliant…"

"The geeks always are."

She sat back in her chair. "Can you at least *try* to do this on a professional level?"

Max made a show of folding his hands obediently in his lap. "Okay, Counselor Browning. Simon needs some base-level social skills and maybe enough confidence to know high school is survivable. Have I got it?"

She seemed to appreciate that. "Yes, in a manner of speaking."

"And you're thinking you need something just a little out of the ordinary to solve the problem, right?"

"Well, I…"

"Hey, you called me, not the nice bland people from social services."

That probably wasn't a smart crack to make to someone in guidance counseling. Her eyes narrowed. "Yes, well, the nice, *appropriate* people from social services were not available. This isn't how I normally operate. It's only fair to tell you you're not my first choice."

Max could only smile. "Alternative. Well, I'd have to say that's exactly my specialty."

Chapter Two

Max hadn't really expected Appropriate Ms. Browning to go for the idea of a pickup basketball game—especially one with the twist he had in mind—but she surprised him by agreeing to book the school auxiliary gym. Two days later, Max found himself whistling as his basketball made a perfect arc, rolled dramatically around the rim and then settled obediently through the net. "Jones nails it from behind the line with seconds to spare."

His sister, JJ, palmed a ball against one hip. "Nice shot."

Max turned to face her. "Let me see you do one."

JJ nodded and dribbled the ball, getting ready to best her little brother. "No," Max corrected. "From the chair." He pointed toward the three armless, low-backed sports wheelchairs that sat against the wall. He'd decided even before he was out of the parking lot the other day that the best way to meet Simon Williams was a pickup game of wheelchair basketball. The boys-against-girls element, with he and Simon facing

JJ and Heather Browning? Well, that had been a brilliant afterthought.

JJ paused for a moment, shot Max the look years of sibling rivalry had perfected and sauntered over to the chair. After settling in, she wheeled toward him in a wobbly line, smirking. "Not so hard."

"Really?" Max teased, rocking back to pop a wheelie in his chair. "I've been waiting to smoke you on the court for months."

She laughed, trying to bounce the ball until it got away from her. "Just like you smoked me on the ski slope?"

Max shot over to scoop up the ball and passed it back to her. "Worse. Okay, try a shot."

JJ missed by a mile. "This is going to be harder than I thought."

Max grabbed the ball, dribbled up to the basket and sunk another one in. "Actually, this is going to be a lot more fun than I thought. Me and Simon should wipe the floor with you *girls*."

"Simon *and I*" came Heather's voice from the gym door. "And don't get too confident. You will get a fair fight from us *ladies*."

Max groaned, JJ smirked and the kid who had to be Simon Williams had the good sense to look a little baffled by whatever he'd just gotten himself into. The boy was spindly thin and a bit pale. His glasses sat a little crooked on his face, and a 1970s haircut didn't help his overall lack of style. Still, his sharp blue eyes and goofy grin made him oddly likable.

Max caught the kid's eye and lamented, "Teacher types."

"Yeah." The boy's response was noncommittal and

soft. He'd expected the boy's smile to widen, but it had all but disappeared.

Shy, skinny and unsure of himself—Max remembered the years when he used to eat kids like this for breakfast. It wasn't a comfortable memory. He wheeled over to Simon and pointed to the line of chairs. "Can you transfer into that sports chair by yourself? I guessed on your size but I think it's close enough." Heather had given him some basic medical info on Simon's cerebral palsy—a condition that mostly left his legs too unstable to support him for more than a few steps.

"Uh-huh." Again, a small voice lacking any stitch of confidence. Max began to wonder if the kid had ever played any sport, ever. He looked as if his family hardly let him outside in the sunshine. Max pretended to be adjusting his gloves while he watched Simon slowly maneuver from his larger daily chair to the smaller, lower sports chair. It was a relief to see that he could do it by himself. The kid's steps were gangly and poorly controlled, but while Max had met other cerebral palsy patients with very spastic movements all over their bodies, Simon's seemed to be confined to his legs. He had the upper-body control to have some fun in a sports chair, yet he looked as if he'd never seen one. If he'd never known speed, this chair would be a barrel of fun. Somehow, he doubted this kid had ever seen much fun.

Whose fault was that? His shy personality? Or overprotective parents? Well, that drought was going to end today. The thought of introducing the boy to agility sparked a faint foreign glow of satisfaction that caught Max up short.

JJ noticed his reaction. She raised an eyebrow in inquiry as Simon finished settling himself into his seat. "What?"

"I think I just got a bit of an Alex rush." Max knew he'd regret admitting that to his sister. His boss—Alex Cushman, JJ's husband—was always going on and on about the charge he got from taking people out of their comfort zones into new adventures.

"Not all about the new toys anymore?" Her tone was teasing, but JJ's eyes were warm. That girl was so stuck on her new husband it was like a nonstop valentine to be with either one of them.

"No, it's still about the new toys." Max popped another wheelie and executed a tight circle around his sister. He turned his attention back to Simon, now sitting next to a delightfully baffled Heather as the two of them explored the gear. "What do you think?"

"They're crooked," Simon offered in a sheepish voice as he pointed to the wheels. Unlike the straight-up-and-down wheels of his daily chair, this chair's wheels tilted toward the middle.

"Nah, they're *cambered*. Gives you stability and agility. You can turn fast on these. Try it."

Max watched as Simon, JJ and Heather made circles in their chairs. Slow, careful circles. Max growled and came up behind JJ to give her a hefty shove. She shot forward, yelping, and then managed to turn herself around in a respectably quick U-turn. "Cut that out, Max!"

"Quit being snails, the lot of you. These things are made for speed. Use 'em!" He angled up next to Simon, who looked as if someone needed to give him permission to keep breathing. "Race ya."

"Huh?"

"First one to the end of the gym and back gets ice cream."

Simon just looked at him. Who'd been keeping this poor kid under glass? Max chose to ignore the uncertainty written on the boy's face and pretend his silence was a bargaining tactic.

"Okay, then, two ice creams and you get a three-second lead," he conceded. Max allowed himself a sly wink at the guidance counselor. "Ms. Browning said she'd buy."

"I never..."

Simon started pushing on his wheels. Max whooped. "One...two...three!"

A sweaty, crazy hour later, Heather had fed every dollar bill and coin she had into the school vending machine as she, Max, JJ and Simon sat on the school's front steps eating ice cream.

"There's a whole basketball league," Max explained to Simon. "And hockey. I've even seen a ski team." She watched Max look Simon up and down. "You're kinda skinny for the hockey thing, but I saw the way you shot today. Wouldn't take long for you to hold your own pretty nicely on the court."

"You outshot *me*," JJ offered, licking chocolate off her fingers.

"I've always had a chair." Simon said it as if it was a weak excuse. The embarrassed tone in his voice burrowed into Heather's heart and made her want to send Jason Kikowitz to Mars.

A red van pulled up, and Heather saw Brian Williams wave his hand out the driver's side window.

"My dad's here," Simon said, tossing his last wrapper into the trash bin and angling toward the wheelchair ramp. At the top of the incline, he paused. "Thanks, Mr. Jones. That was fun."

"Max," Max corrected, making a funny face. "Nobody calls me Mr. Jones. Want to go sailing next week?"

Heather watched Simon's response. His eyes lit up for a moment, then darkened a bit as he heard the door click open and the *whrrr* of the lift extending out of his parents' van. "I don't think my folks would go for it." Simon's lack of optimism stung. Heather knew that despite his spot on the Gordon Falls Volunteer Fire Department—or maybe because of it—Simon's dad was a highly protective father. She'd had a highly protective dad herself—she'd had her own share of medical challenges in high school—but even she had reservations about how far Brian Williams went to keep his son away from any kind of risk.

Max had caught the boy's disappointment. He waved at the van. "They'll say yes. Can I come meet them?"

"Um…maybe next time," Simon said, quickly darting down the ramp.

"Hey, slow down there, Speedy!" Simon's dad called as the lift platform rattled onto the ground. "Watch that crack there or your wheel might get stuck. You've got to take your time on ramps, remember?"

Heather heard Max mutter a few unkind words under his breath. JJ got to her feet. "Speaking of speed, my shift starts in half an hour and I've got to run home first." She gave Heather a hug, then pecked her brother on the cheek and snatched up the sweatshirt she'd been sitting on. "Dinner still on for next Thursday?"

"You bet," Max said, still staring as Simon was swallowed up by the van's mechanism. His irritation jutted out in all directions, sharp and prickly. "Does he know how much he's holding Simon back?" Max nearly growled. "Have you talked to him about it?"

"Hey," she said. "Cut the dad a little slack here, will you?"

"You know what half of Simon's problem is?" Max jutted a finger at the van as it pulled away. "*That*. I was trying to figure out what made Simon such a walking ball of shy and I just got my answer."

Heather swallowed her own frustration. People were shy for lots of reasons, not just fatherly protectiveness. "So after two hours with the boy, you've got him all figured out? Is that it?"

"It doesn't take a PhD in counseling to figure out they keep that kid under lock and key. He's afraid of his own shadow, and somebody had to teach him that."

"Aren't you coming down awfully hard on someone you hardly even know?"

"Simon's not sick. Okay, his legs don't work so hot, but I get how that goes. He could be so much stronger than he is. He could be doing so much *more*."

It needed saying. "He's not you, Max. Not everyone needs to come at this full throttle." When that just made him frown, Heather tried a different tack. "What were you like in high school?"

"A whole lot different than that. Even as a freshman."

"I can imagine that."

Max shook out the mane of shaggy dirty-blond hair that gave him such a rugged look. He was tanned and muscular—the furthest thing imaginable from Simon's pale, thin features—with mischievous eyes and a smile Heather expected made girls swoon back in high school. She found his not-quite-yet-cleaned-up-bad-boy persona as infuriating as it was intriguing. Max Jones just didn't add up the way he ought to, and she didn't know what to do with that.

Max tossed an ice-cream wrapper into the trash bin with all the precision he'd shown on the basketball court. "Truth is," he said, his voice losing the edge it had held a moment ago, "I was a lot closer to the Kikowitzes of the world than to geeky kids like Simon." He shot Heather a guilty glance. "Let's just say I've shoved my share of kids into lockers. And, okay, I'm not especially proud of it, but I think I'd rather be that than go through life like Simon."

Heather tried to picture a teenage Max prowling the halls of GFHS, picking on kids and collecting detention slips. It didn't take much imagination. "Football team? Motorcycles?"

He laughed, and Heather reminded herself how such charming smiles shouldn't always be trusted. Sometimes those dashing ways covered some pretty devastating weaknesses. "No," he corrected her. "Basketball and my dad's old Thunderbird. Well, before I rolled it my junior year, that is."

"You were a terror in high school." She nodded over to the black car with flames and the HTWELZ2 license plate. "It boggles the mind."

"Very funny. You have no idea how much work it takes to make a car like that look so cool. No way was I going to drive around in some suburban-housewife minivan." He looked at her, hard. "I'm still the guy I was, and if people can't take that it comes in a wheeled version now, it's their problem."

It was an admirable thought, but his words came with such a defiant edge that Heather wondered how many times a week Max chewed someone's head off for an ill-phrased remark or just plain ignorance about life with a disability. Bitterness did that to some men. "Maybe that's just it. Maybe Simon hasn't figured out who he is yet. I had no idea who I was in high school— I just bumbled around most of the time trying to stay out of the sights of all those mean cheerleader types." She borrowed Max's measurement. "I suppose I'd say I was a lot closer to Simon than thugs like Kikowitz."

"Thugs like me?" Again the disarming smile, the penitent hoodlum with his hand over his heart.

"I don't know too many thugs who would round up a bunch of wheelchairs to play basketball with a geeky kid and two hapless ladies." She was going to say *girls,* but hadn't she chided Max for the label earlier?

"Don't call my sister *hapless*. She was in the army, you know." He wheeled a careless arc around the front walkway, ending up a foot or two closer to her than his earlier position. "So let me guess—4-H Club? Junior Librarians of America? Church choir?" He did not list them with any admiration—that was certain.

"Art, mostly. I kept to myself a lot. And not choir, but church youth group."

"I knew it." Max executed a spin while he rolled his head back. "One of *those*."

"Hey, cut that out. I had a…good time in high school." That was at least partially true. Some of high school had been great, but she'd learned her sophomore year what Simon already knew: high school wasn't kind to sick or injured kids.

Max stopped his maneuvers. "No, you didn't."

Heather froze.

"Girls who had awesome times in high school do not come back as guidance counselors. You want to help people. And you want to help people because you don't want anyone to go through what you did."

"Where do you get off making assumptions like that?"

Max threw his hands in the air. "Hey, don't get all up about it. Do you know how many physical therapists I've had since my accident? How many counselors and docs? Pretty soon it gets easy to recognize the type, that's all."

"Oh, yes, JJ told me you used to tear through a therapist a week back at the beginning. A paragon of empathy." That wasn't particularly fair to throw back at him, but for Heather, his attitude struck an old nerve. "Look—" she forced herself to soften her voice when Max's eyes grew hard and dark "—I want you to help Simon, and I think you might actually be able to. But not if you dump him into some labeled box based on your own experience. Simon's had his disability his entire life—he's never known anything different. You need to respect who he is, not who you want him to be, or this will never work."

Max didn't reply at first. He looked down, fiddling with a joint on his chair. "Okay, I get it." When he raised his eyes again, the edge in his features was replaced by something else. Determination? She couldn't quite tell. "What do you want to happen from all this?"

"What do you mean?"

"I don't know if you want Simon to be happy, to be less of a target or to be able to punch Kikowitz out. What's the end goal here?"

She thought carefully before she answered. "I want Simon not to be afraid of who he is or what Kikowitz might do to him. He's brilliant, you know. Simon's one of the smartest kids at our school. I want him to enjoy coming here, not dread it."

Max didn't appear to have an immediate answer to that. After what she hoped was a thoughtful pause, he said, "You want him to be able to take risks?"

"He needs a few outlets, I'll admit that."

Max pivoted to face her. "Then we go sailing. You, me and Simon on Saturday afternoon. That way we both can convince the geek there's more to life than Math Club."

"Don't call him a geek. And how did you know Simon was in Math Club?"

"*Puh-lease.* I saw two calculators in his backpack. The dock behind Jones River Sports, two o'clock. You're in charge of permission slips and snacks."

Heather tucked her hands into her pockets. "Who said you could take over here?"

"Eleven therapists," he called as he started down the ramp, clicking the remote starter on his car to send it roaring to life as he descended. "Actually twelve, if you count the one who lasted ten minutes. And four nurses. And there was an intern at Adventure Access who—"

"Okay!" Heather shouted as Max somehow made the engine rev before he even got into the car. "I get the picture."

Chapter Three

Max checked his watch again Saturday afternoon. Since when did he get nervous about stuff like this? Chronically late, he didn't have a leg to stand on—if he could stand—about anyone's punctuality. Still, Simon's dad seemed like the guy to show up ten minutes early, not twenty minutes late. And where was Heather? He wheeled the length of the dock again, needlessly checking the ropes that tied the *Sea Legs* to the dock, frustrated with how much he'd managed to invest in one kid's sailing lesson.

It was the look in Simon's eyes that did him in. That heartbreaking eagerness at the mention of going sailing nearly instantly squashed by a dad's harping voice. Parents were hard enough to take at that age as it was. To have all that other stuff loaded on top, then compounded by kids like Kikowitz?

Kids like he'd been?

The faces of all the kids he'd ever bullied had haunted him last night. He saw Simon's face every time he shut his eyes, and it was making him crazy. Sleepless, fidgety and just plain nuts.

The sound of tires on gravel hit his ears, and he looked up, expecting the Williamses' big red van. Instead, a small tan sedan pulled into the parking area and Heather climbed out of the nondescript little car. Shoulders slumped, head slightly down, Heather's body broadcast what he'd begun to suspect: Simon wasn't showing.

His understanding—and annoyance—must have been clear on his face, for all Heather said when she walked onto to the dock was "I'm sorry."

Max grunted. It was a better choice than the nasty language currently running in his head.

"I've been on the phone with Brian Williams, trying to convince him Simon would be safe, but—"

"But hooligans like Max Jones can't be trusted with his precious son—oh, I can just hear the speech."

She set down the loudly patterned tote bag she was carrying and eased onto the dock's little bench. "It's not about you."

"Oh, not all about me, but I can just imagine what Simon's dad thinks of someone like me." He flipped open the equipment locker's lid and tossed the third life jacket back inside.

He was picking up the second one when she put out a hand to stop him. "So I guess we're not going, huh?" Disappointment tinged her words.

Max looked up, life jacket still in his hand, surprised. "No, we can still go." He'd just assumed she'd ditch the day with Simon not coming. Sail alone, just with her? He'd have to go so *slow* and be so *nice*.

"I sort of want to know how this whole rigging works." She gestured toward the specially modified sailboat, covering her tracks with a "professional curiosity" that didn't quite pass muster. She frowned and crossed her arms when she reached the back of the boat. "*Sea Legs?* Really?"

"I thought that was particularly clever, actually. Much better than my first choice."

Her brows knotted together. "I'm almost afraid to ask."

"The *Crip Ship*. JJ thought that a bit confrontational."

Heather laughed. "Max Jones? Confrontational? Imagine my surprise."

Max spread his arms. "Got me where I am today." He tossed her the life jacket. "Hop in. I'll hand over your bag and cast us off." Wheeling over to the bag, he picked it up. It weighed a ton. "There had better be decent snacks in here."

"Homemade brownies, watermelon and some of the firehouse root beer."

Max handed over the bag as he rolled on board after her. "Someone ought to call Simon and tell him what he's missing." He pulled the ramp up and stowed it in its special spot alongside the keel.

"I think he knows." Heather's voice sounded like he felt. Disappointed and not a little miffed. "This would have been so good for him."

Max liked the way that sounded. Ever since he'd wheeled into Heather's office, he'd gotten the vibe from her that he was a poor substitute for whatever mentor she'd had in mind. It bugged him that Heather hadn't judged him capable of helping someone. Then again, no one was more surprised than him that he'd even cared to take the whole thing on.

He pointed to the bowline. "Undo that knot and pull the line aboard, will you?"

While she climbed up to the front of the boat, Max transferred himself from his chair and into the swiveling seat on rails that allowed him to move freely about the boat. It wasn't a particularly graceful maneuver, and he preferred having her attention diverted elsewhere. Once settled, he collapsed his wheelchair and stowed it in a compartment. Pulling the jib tight, Max felt the singular, blissful sensation of the boat under way. Even before his injury, nothing felt like pulling out onto the river. Now that gravity was often his enemy, the river gave him even more freedom to unwind his nerves. *Sea Legs* may be a mildly tacky joke to some, but it was actually close to how he saw the boat. Anything that gave Max speed and movement gave him life. They counterbalanced all the parts of his life that had become slow and cumbersome since falling from that cliff a little over a year ago.

In a matter of minutes, *Sea Legs* was under way, slicing her way through the Gordon River and catching the perfect breeze that blew through the warm September afternoon. Heading upriver and upwind, he angled the boat toward the opposite shore, ready to "tack" back and forth as the craft moved against the current and into the wind. He watched Heather settle into one of the seats closer to the bow, the breeze tumbling through her hair.

"You're different here than at school," he offered, liking how she angled her face up toward the sunshine. "Not so serious."

She shot him a look. "I take my job seriously. Don't you?"

Max shrugged and tightened up a line. "I don't have a serious job. I'm…enthusiastic about it, but Adventure Access is about making fun, so it's not the kind of job you ought to take seriously."

Heather brought her knees up and hugged them. He found himself staring at her bright pink toenails peeking out of the blue thong sandals she wore. Funny the details that don't come out at the office. Max spent a lot of time noticing feet—now that his weren't much use—and she had ridiculously cute toes that wiggled when she realized he was staring at them.

"Are you serious about anything?" she asked, shifting to tuck her legs underneath her and blushing. Some part of Max was highly entertained that he'd made her blush. What kind of woman wore sensible clear polish on her nails but bright pink on her hidden toes?

"I've been seriously injured. Been listed in 'serious condition' at Lincoln General." He tied off the line. "And I've been in serious trouble lots of times."

She looked more disappointed than annoyed. "What does it take to get a straight answer out of you?"

That was a loaded question. His boss and now brother-in-law, Alex Cushman, had asked pretty much the same thing before bringing him on board at Adventure Access. Nobody seemed willing to take a smart aleck at his word these days—they all wanted to see some deep and serious version of him, as if what he'd been through didn't supply enough credentials. "It takes a straight question. Duck, by the way—we're coming about and the boom is going to come across the boat."

"Okay," she said as she ducked. "Straight question. What did it feel like?"

It was obvious what she meant by "it." "When you

cut to the chase, you really cut to the chase, huh?" He
had a couple of stock answers to insensitive questions
like that—mostly asked by curious kids who didn't
know better or adults who only wanted gory, tragic
details—but opted against using them. He'd asked her
for a straight question, after all. He just hadn't counted
on "straight" going to "serious."

"You don't have to tell me. It's none of my business."

"No." Max was surprised to find he didn't feel any
of the irritation that kind of question generally raised.
He actually wanted to tell her. It must be some kind of
empathetic-counselor trick. "It's okay. But it's not especially pretty."

She didn't reply, just leaned one elbow on the bow
behind her and looked ready to listen. So he told her.

"I wanted to die."

Heather swallowed hard. Max said it so matter-of-
factly. As if *I wanted to die* was like *my left shoulder
hurt.* All her counselor training left her no response to
his casual attitude.

He actually laughed—a dark half laugh, but still, it
sounded wildly inappropriate to her—and she cringed
at the sound. "That's horrible," she said, not exactly
sure if she meant his feelings that night or his disturbing attitude now.

"Horrible, tragic, devastating—pick your sad word.
I've heard them all. Everybody was being so kind and
vague and optimistic, but it didn't fool me. People get
that look in their eyes, you know? The one they cover
up in a second but you still catch it?"

She did know, but she didn't say anything.

"I think I knew right when I fell that something really serious had happened, but I don't remember hardly anything from that night. I don't remember the helicopter ride—which is rotten, by the way, because I think that would have been cool—or the hospital or surgery or really anything until about a day later. And even my memories from those first days are sort of blurry." Max pivoted the seat and shifted a bit down the rails, adjusting his position as the boat picked up a bit of speed. Heather felt the wind lift her hair and the sun warm her shoulders. It was easy to see why Max craved time on this boat.

"The first thing I clearly remember," he went on, his voice still remarkably conversational, "is waking up in the middle of the night and trying to get up out of bed—I think I wanted to go find JJ or something. That was the moment when I really, truly figured out that I couldn't feel my legs. Like the world just stopped at my hips." He pretended to busy himself with some adjustment to the rigging, but even without a counseling degree, Heather could've seen he couldn't look her in the eye while talking about the trauma. His eyes darted everywhere around the boat but at her, and she could see how hard his hands gripped the tiller. Why even pretend this was an easy memory? What had made her think it would be a good idea to ask?

Max cleared his throat and shifted. "I remember pinching my thigh, hard, and feeling nothing. Zip. Nada. Then all the tubes and nurses and Mom showing up clicked in my head, and I knew. Alone, in the dark, I just *knew*. And I decided it would be better if I stopped breathing, right there and then. It was like I didn't even have enough life left in me to get mad. I was hollow, empty…just gone, like my legs."

He ventured a glance up at her, and she felt the severity in his eyes as fiercely as if he'd grabbed her hand. "So that's what it was like. *Lousy*'s not really a strong enough word, if you get what I mean."

She had a way-more-than-lousy memory like that. The scars running down her left hip and thigh shouted memories that made her feel hollow and "just gone." Only she couldn't brandish them like Max did. There had been another man in her life, years back, who pushed his pain out onto the world like that. Mike had forced his illness on people, daring them to cope with the nasty details, almost looking down on her when she couldn't do it that way. Heather could count the number of people who had seen her scarred leg on the fingers of one hand. "I'm sorry," she whispered, not knowing how else to respond.

Max shook his head, his sardonic smile mocking her compassion. "You know, everybody says that. I've got enough I'm-sorrys to fill this river twice over. That always struck me as funny, 'cause it never accomplishes anything."

"Oh, yes, you make it clear no one's allowed to feel sorry for you." That came out a bit sharper than she'd planned, but some part of her was having trouble swallowing Max's nonstop bravado. Sure, he laughed off his huge trauma—and looked down on anyone else who couldn't do the same—but he wasn't fooling anyone. He thought all that casual charm hid his dark edge, but it didn't. Not to her.

"I don't think Simon wants people feeling sorry for him, either. I think half his problem comes from how much people coddle him." Max waved his hand around the boat. "See anything life threatening here? Any deep, dark dangers?"

"Only one, and he's just as dangerous on land."

Max jutted a finger at her. "See? That's *exactly* what I'm talking about. Would you make a crack like that at Simon? Would you give him the respect of thinking him strong enough to take it?"

"Simon is a fifteen-year-old boy who's sick."

"No," Max nearly shouted, jerking a line in tighter so the boat picked up speed. "He's *not* sick. That's just it, Heather—he's not sick any more than I am. Okay, his legs don't work right. My legs don't work at all, but I can do almost anything I want, while he…" Max growled and slid the seat so fast down the rails that Heather felt the whole boat shake when the chair locked into a new position. "Simon and I have been texting each other since the basketball game. His mom cuts up his meat, for crying out loud. The only thing limiting him is his parents. If he's having social problems, it's their fault."

"That's not fair! My mom had to help me like that after I got hurt, and—" Heather snapped her mouth shut, beyond angry with herself for letting that slip. She angled away from Max, pretending—uselessly—to look out over the water while he took the boat into another turn. She couldn't go anywhere; she was trapped on this boat with Max Jones and an admission she'd give anything to take back right now. The silence on board was so thick she felt paralyzed herself.

He stayed quiet the whole way across the river, which surprised her. She'd expected Max to pry the rest of the story out of her, but he didn't. She felt him looking at her, sensed his gaze even though she kept her eyes on the river.

Finally, as he turned the boat around again, Heather dared to look his way. His whole face had changed. His face showed warmth and understanding, not the defiance that seemed to be his constant expression. "What happened?" An hour ago, she wouldn't have believed Max capable of such a tender tone.

She didn't like the idea of his knowing the details. Those were private. But Max Jones needed to know he was not the only person on earth to suffer a life-changing accident. And out here on the water, Heather felt as if the secret could be safely contained. "I was burned. In an accident. My junior year of high school." Even those vague details made her feel wildly exposed, and she hugged her knees again, clutching the scarred thigh close and away from the world. "And whether or not you think it's *useless,* I'm still very, very sorry it happened."

She expected him to press her for details, but Max seemed to sense she'd taken a huge step in admitting just the basic facts. He didn't pry or challenge her need for privacy; he just let her be quiet amid the wind and water. When they pulled the boat up to the dock a peaceful hour later, Heather conceded that there might be more to Max Jones than she'd realized.

Chapter Four

Jeannie Owens adjusted the gift basket's ribbon Monday afternoon with an artist's touch before pushing it across the counter to Heather. "That ought to do the parents' night fund-raising auction proud, don't you think?"

"Sure."

The Sweet Treats candy-shop owner furrowed her brow. "I was hoping for a more enthusiastic reaction. My chocolate-covered caramels are supposed to be sought after, not barely tolerated."

Heather knew very well how "sought after" Jeannie's caramels were. Too well, if her bathroom scale was any indication. "Sorry. This is fabulous—it's even bigger than last year's."

"But…" Jeannie cued, raising one eyebrow in concern rather than judgment.

Heather sighed. "It's not you or the candy. I'm just preoccupied, I guess."

"Trouble at school?" Heather knew Jeannie's son had encountered his share of problems freshman year at GFHS. While the school had tried to offer guidance, the real solution had come from Fire Marshal Chad Owens, who'd not only befriended Jeannie's son, Nick, but fallen for Jeannie herself. Nick was now an exemplary senior and one of Heather's favorite happy endings for this graduating class.

"I'm worried about Simon Williams. Actually, I'm worried about what Jason Kikowitz might do to Simon Williams." She usually made it a point not to give names when talking about school issues, but Jeannie had particular insight regarding a bully's influence on a boy facing problems.

Heather watched Jeannie try to place Simon's name. It was no effort to place Jason's—everyone who had a student at GFHS knew who "that Kikowitz boy" was. "Williams...Brian Williams's boy? Chad said Brian was all huffed about something that happened at school. Now it makes sense." Her eyes filled with compassion. "As if high school isn't hard enough. To have to do it in a wheelchair must feel impossible."

"Simon'll make it. He's such a good kid. Unsure of himself, but so smart."

"But a target for guys like Kikowitz, I'm sure." Jeannie pulled the top off a large glass jar on her counter that was filled with her signature chocolate-covered caramels and tilted the opening toward Heather. "You've got your hands full. That deserves one on the house."

Heather couldn't help but pull a caramel from the jar, sure she would regret it later. Even if Jeannie campaigned that the world's problems could be solved with enough sugar and chocolate, Heather's hips put up valid resistance to the idea. "He's got so much potential. I care a lot about this one. Too much, maybe."

"No such thing," Jeannie said, sliding the canister back into place. "Don't you ever stop caring too much—it's what makes you so good at what you do." Jeannie had a vibrancy about her that Heather loved. And she had a great family despite knowing a lot of trials in her life. Sure, Heather came into Sweet Treats for the chocolate, but she came in just as much for the friendship and support. "I wondered about him when the family moved in over the summer," Jeannie went on. "Chad says Brian is a terrific father. Really engaged and involved."

"He's devoted to Simon—no doubt about it. Only I think this year is going to be a challenge."

"Jason Kikowitz is good at that." Jeannie polished off the last of her caramel and licked the lingering chocolate off her fingers.

"More than that, actually."

"What do you mean?"

"Well, you remember how hard it is to loosen up on the reins when your child enters high school." That was a nicer way of putting it than Max's *he needs to back off.* "I think Mr. and Mrs. Williams are going to have a tough time granting Simon the independence to make his own mistakes, especially with the fine start Kikowitz has supplied." It was hard for most parents to strike that balance—Heather's voice mail and email filled every September with parents trying too hard to manage their kids' high school experiences—but doubly so in Simon's case.

Jeannie's face softened. "It's the hardest thing in the world. Which is why the world needs you. Have you decided how you're going to help Simon?"

"Actually, JJ came up with the idea to have Max mentor him."

Jeannie raised both her eyebrows. "Chad mentioned JJ told him something about a basketball game?" Her expression appeared hopeful. "That sounds fun." Yes, well, Jeannie had always been famous for her unflinching optimism.

"It was…sort of. He and Simon certainly seemed to connect, but let's just say I have doubts Max will be much of a calming influence."

"Calm?" Jeannie laughed. "Max Jones hasn't been calm a day in his life. Did you see his car? Nick was drooling over the flame paint job the other day."

The car. Everyone in Gordon Falls knew that car and had an opinion of both its look-at-me paint and its here-I-come roar. "Yep. Can't miss it—that's for sure."

Jeannie leaned on the counter with both elbows. "Well, I understand why you're worried, but you never know. Max might surprise you."

"He's already been a surprise—and not necessarily the good kind." She hadn't expected Simon to take to Max so strongly, nor had she expected Max to take a shine to Simon with the strength that he had. Of course, she'd wanted to put a halt to the thing at first, but there was something about the combination of Max and Simon that wouldn't let her give up on the pair just yet. Maybe it had something to do with the way Simon had laughed in triumph at the end of their basketball game. She got the sense he didn't laugh like that very often.

Jeannie came out from behind the counter to sit on one of the sunny yellow window-seat cushions that lined one side of her shop. "I can't help thinking it takes someone like Max to stand up to someone like Kikowitz."

"That's just it," Heather agreed.

"Then again," Jeannie went on, "if I had to pick someone just as likely to make everything worse, it might be Max."

"And *that's* just it." Heather sat down beside Jeannie. "Sure, Simon thinks he's terrific right now. He looks cool. He talks up a great game. But I don't really know him—he seems all swagger and no substance. Max could have too much influence—and all the wrong kind—on a kid like that."

"Alex puts a lot of faith in him, and I don't think Alex would do that if he didn't see something in Max that was more than just a snazzy paint job. He's willing to help, right? Can't be all that bad if he's at least willing to lend a hand."

The memory of Max's thundering muffler as it roared out of the school parking lot gave Heather enough reason to doubt Jeannie's optimism. "I'm not so sure. Max is very…sure of himself. Actually, he's arrogant, confrontational and rather tactless."

Jeannie wound one piece of hair around a finger, thinking. "Maybe Max is exactly the kind of guy Simon needs. What boy wouldn't want to know you can be in a wheelchair and still be that cool? I know he's a bit over-the-top, but Nick thinks he's 'sick'—and evidently that's a compliment." Jeannie laughed. "He's not exactly hard to look at, and all those adventures he goes on…"

"He's a walking…*rolling* barrel of 'look at me.' He's so busy shoving his circumstances in your face that he forgets you're even in the room." Max wasn't the first man in her life to be so busy being a cause that he'd forgotten how to be a person. She wasn't eager to re-peat the experience.

Jeannie pushed off the wall and headed toward the cash register as a knot of giggling girls pushed into the store. "Well, I'll give him one thing."

Heather settled her handbag higher on her shoulder and picked up the massive gift basket. "What?"

"He knows how to get a rise out of you."

Tuesday afternoon, Max rolled into Heather's office in response to a phone-message summons.

"It's one-thirty." She scowled at the big white stan-dard-issue school clock on her wall when he arrived. "I asked you to come by in the morning. It was kind of urgent."

"I had an appointment. I got here as soon as I could afterward." Normally he didn't mention the dozens of monthly medical visits his condition required, but he wanted her to know life wasn't all fun and games for him, even if he was in the fun-and-games business. "My neurologist is a nice guy but not nice enough to ditch just because you need backup."

She didn't seem capable of pulling off a mean face. "Who says I need backup?"

"It doesn't take a rocket scientist to know your voice mail is probably chock-full of worried calls from Brian Williams today. Come on—I saw that one coming a mile off. Has he asked you to keep me away from his precious impressionable son yet?"

He'd nailed it; he could see it in her eyes. "Do you have to ride the man so hard? He cares about his son."

He wheeled farther into her office. She'd moved her guest chair to the side to accommodate his chair. That settled somewhere soft in the back of his brain. "It's been my experience that there's a very thin line between care and smother. Especially when you're fifteen. Did you see Simon's eyes when his father pulled up after the basketball game? Did you hear how even the school ramp made Pops nervous?"

Heather leaned one elbow on her desk. "How long, exactly, has it been since you were fifteen?"

He didn't want to give her the satisfaction of a number. "A while."

"Well, then, think back a while and remember that every student his age—disability or not—is mortified by everything their parents do. It's practically rule number one in the high schooler's handbook."

"Hey, you just made a joke." He angled himself around to dig a hand into the bag he kept attached to the back of his chair.

She narrowed her eyes at him. "Really?" Heather was just so much fun to tick off, Max suspected he was going to get in trouble here far faster than his usual rate—which was pretty fast as it was.

"Well—" he found what he was looking for and pulled it out of the bag "—it just makes it easier to give you this." Scooting up to her desk, he planted a bright pink rubber duck made to look like a flamingo on top of her files. It made a ridiculous squeaking sound as he did so, its little black rubber sunglasses squishing in on its hooked flamingo beak before inflating back into shape. Normally he wasn't the gift type—barely remembering birthdays and such—but this had caught his eye in the hospital gift shop. The tone of her voice mail had made it clear Brian Williams had clouded up and rained all over her morning, and he'd wanted to cheer her up. "It's a flamingo rubber duck, which is kind of a joke when you think about it." When she looked genuinely startled, he added, "For your collection. And for not getting here until now."

She reached for it, and he could see she was holding back a smile. "You know, a phone call to let me know your time frame would have been all I needed." Her words were all *you shouldn't have* but her eyes were *I love it.* How did someone so transparent make any headway with predators like teenagers?

She placed the flamingo-duck right next to the one he'd toyed with at their first meeting. "Yes, Mr. Williams expressed his concern."

"Is that teacher-speak for *he chewed my ear off?*"

"Let's just say I think it will take more than rubber waterfowl to bring Mr. Williams around. He was curious…suspicious, actually, that you clearly did not include him in your sailing invitation. That, more than any physical danger, is what kept Simon off your boat Saturday."

Max didn't like where this was heading. "He's jealous?"

"Could you be serious for one minute here? Schools have to tread carefully where and how we let adults alone with students. And there are really good reasons—really awful ones, actually—why those rules are in place. He's in the right here, Max. I should have never okayed that boat outing."

Max had no patience for this kind of red-tape stupidity. "You've gotta be kidding me. You were going along. Brian Williams knows who I am. He works with my sister. I'm not some creep off the train from the big bad city."

Heather sat back in her chair. "Do you want to help Simon or not?"

"Yes!" He didn't even have to think about the answer. Simon's eyes had been haunting him all weekend. He was like a walking poster child for everything Adventure Access was about—giving people with disabilities the chance to be regular people and have the kinds of fun that everyone craved. Max didn't just want to help Simon; some part of him *needed* to help the little guy.

That clearly wasn't the answer she was expecting. Wow, did she really think he'd walk away just because Daddy got hot under the collar? That bugged him more than Williams's unfounded suspicions.

"Then we've got to work within the boundaries here. Simon's dad sees him as vulnerable, and he's not all wrong. This is hard for any parent, much less one with as much to worry about as Brian Williams has on his plate."

She was right, of course. Some part of him recognized that. He'd gone in full blast, letting Williams's perfectly natural responses get under his skin because of how much *he* hated being coddled. And while she was eons better now, hadn't his own mother been ten times worse than Brian Williams when he was first injured? "Yeah." He owed her at least that much of an acknowledgment.

"If it helps, I think he really should go out on your boat. It's a beautiful boat, and it's fascinating to watch how it works and you work on it. It's just not the right starting point. Basketball? Now, that was a good first step for a lot of reasons. Can we think of something else like that? Something that can take place here on school property?"

"Williams is going to supervise, isn't he?"

"Yes." Her eyes flicked down at the admission. "He's asked to be present." She looked up. "Think you can play nice here?"

Normally, Max's reply to a request like that would have been a resounding *Not on your life!* Only it was as if Simon's pleading eyes watched him even though the kid wasn't even in the room. "How are you at Ping-Pong?"

That smile could have made him buy twelve flamingo-ducks in rainbow colors. "I happen to be pretty good. Thursday afternoon?"

He could move his marketing-team meeting. It'd mean he would have to get up an hour earlier than normal—something he only did in the most dire circumstances—but he'd do it. "Let me make a few calls."

Chapter Five

"Got 'em!"

Heather watched in amazement Thursday afternoon as Simon edged his chair in front of his father to nail the match's winning shot. In the last half of the game, Simon had seemed to come alive right before her eyes, showing a determination and enthusiasm she'd not ever seen from him. It was the first time she could use the phrase *young man* to describe Simon. Lots of boys made the transition from "boy" to "young man" in their first year of high school, but she'd never seen the transformation happen quite so dramatically.

Max had noticed the change, as well; she could tell by the way he caught her eye in between volleys or when Simon made a particularly spectacular shot. Simon wasn't the only one making surprising changes right in front of her. Max had gone out of his way to "play nice" with Brian Williams. Right down to the nondescript polo shirt instead of his usual T-shirt bearing a wild message. She'd spent the first game trying not to notice what the light blue color did for Max's eyes. JJ had told her Max had rolled up in a tux for her wedding, and suddenly she wanted to see the pictures of what that looked like. Max Jones, for all his edgy attire, cleaned up *very* nice.

"Hey, Dad, watch this!"

Heather gasped as Simon made an attempt to pop one of the wild wheelies Max was known for—and succeeded only in toppling himself out of the chair. Mr. Williams let out a "Don't do that!" and flew out of his own chair—for everyone had to play in chairs again to even the odds—grabbing Simon's arm before Heather even had a chance to blink.

"I'm fine!" Simon declared, pulling his arm out of his father's grasp. The air in the gym suddenly thickened. Heather didn't know quite what to do.

Max did. In a matter of seconds, Max spun over next to Simon and proceeded to catapult himself out of his own chair. Now there were two people on the ground, with Heather and Mr. Williams standing in shock beside them.

"Didn't that hurt?" Simon asked, as stunned as anyone else in the room.

"Not if I can't feel anything below my waist. Of course, I wouldn't advise this as a general practice, but it's easier to show you how to get up than to sit there and explain it."

"I can help him get up," Mr. Williams interjected, reaching between Max and Simon.

"No, Dad," Simon protested. "Let me see how Max does this."

Mr. Williams looked ready to object, but Heather walked over and gently touched his elbow. "Let him try," she whispered, seeing the panic in the father's eyes. "You can step in if he gets in trouble."

"What do I do?" Simon was as cool as a cucumber and obviously not a bit hurt.

"First—" Max winked "—you find somewhere else for the people around you to look because this isn't pretty. Point out a flower or a puppy or something."

Simon managed a wry grin. "They're staring right at us."

"Well." Max elbowed Simon as if being sprawled out on the gym floor were all part of the plan. "Think of something."

Simon pointed clear across the gym. "Hey, Dad, could you go get the Ping-Pong ball where it landed over in the corner?"

Mr. Williams did not look as if he cared for this one bit. Heather offered him an encouraging smile, eyebrows raised in a silent invitation to just play along.

The pause before Mr. Williams said, "Sure, son," felt excruciating. He pinched the bridge of his nose as he stepped away from Max and Simon and walked across the gym floor.

As she followed Mr. Williams, swallowing the urge to turn and look at whatever it was Max was teaching Simon, she heard the smile in Max's voice as he instructed, "Okay, pull your chair over here and put your left hand up on this."

She walked in the direction Simon had pointed, catching Mr. Williams's eye one more time. "I know that was hard," she said, keenly aware that she truly had no idea how hard it might have been.

Brian Williams was trying; she had to give him that. He wanted to turn and watch as badly as Heather did— it was all over his face—but he made a show of searching for the little white ball both of them quickly realized wasn't anywhere near where Simon had sent them.

After he heard Max's overloud, "There you go, back upright," Heather turned and threw up her hands in mock failure, inwardly delighted at the beaming and seated Simon—right next to a seated and slightly winded Max. Something hummed under her ribs as she realized what it had cost Max to toss himself out of his chair like that.

"Hey, look, Dad—the ball was right here all the time."

Did Simon actually just wink?

"No kidding," Mr. Williams said, his voice a mixture of emotions Heather couldn't quite read. Was he proud of his son? Or annoyed at being "played"?

"Yeah. And I'm fine," Simon repeated.

"Upright and awesome." Max held up a fist and Simon bumped it in the universal high school sign of victory and admiration. "Only, I'd hold back on the wheelies till you get better at them. Knocks the cool right out of the whole thing if you tumble like we just did."

"True." Simon looked at Max. "We still beat you."

Max pasted a dejected look on his face. "You and your dad creamed me and Ms. Browning. I'm not used to losing—we'd better find something else to play next time where I can be sure I'll win."

"Then it can't be chess," Mr. Williams offered. "He beats me every time."

Surely this would bring some crack about chess's geek factor. Max probably stuffed the Chess Club into lockers on a weekly basis in high school. Heather saw the barb come across his face, then watched as he swallowed whatever wisecrack was on the tip of his tongue. "Not really my thing, chess. But I'll think of something and run it by Ms. Browning and your dad before I set it up, okay?"

Heather had to work to keep her mouth from dropping open. Somehow she was sure Max Jones never sought approval for anything—he definitely seemed more like the "do what you want and apologize later if you get caught" type. Was Max doing a little maturing of his own?

After they'd packed up the equipment and walked Simon and his dad to their car—and Max had gotten a lot of mileage out of a "walk you to your car" bit— Heather found herself at a loss for how to deal with this new side of Max.

She knew where to start, at least. Sitting down on the short wall that framed the school steps, she folded her hands in her lap. "Thank you."

"For what?" His face told her he knew exactly for what.

"I want to say for behaving, but that doesn't sound very good." She fiddled with her watch, suddenly finding his eyes a little too intense. "You know what you did back there. I just want you to know I appreciate it."

"You mean launching myself onto the floor so Simon wouldn't feel like a train wreck? That was kind of fun, actually. Although, I expect I'll find a few bruises in the morning."

"Did it hurt?" The minute the words left her mouth, they felt like the most insensitive thing she could have picked to ask.

Max held her gaze for a moment—something that made her insides buzz. The man had astounding, expressive eyes. "It's okay to ask stuff like that, you know. I don't mind. If I think you're stepping over the line, believe me, I'll tell you." He shifted in his chair. "No, it didn't hurt. Nothing hurts. I'm deadweight from the waist down. But it also means I can't tell if I've hurt myself, so flinging myself out of chairs isn't the smartest thing I could be doing. That was more of an impulse."

"It was a good one—I mean, provided you didn't get hurt. Did you see Simon's eyes?"

"Couldn't miss it. Kid lit up like a firecracker. Do you think that's the first time he's told his dad to back off a bit?" Max was as excited about Simon's confidence level as she was.

"Could be. And you found an appropriate way to make that happen."

He got that heart-slayer gleam in his eyes again. "Look at me, Mr. Appropriate. Who knew I had it in me?"

She hadn't. Up until today, Heather had worried that he would grow bored and skip out on Simon in a matter of days. Looking at him now, she could see his investment in Simon was surprising even him. "You did a great thing today. I hope you know that." Before she could think better of it, she nodded toward his shirt. "You even dressed for the occasion."

"You noticed." He preened the collar on his polo shirt, grinning. "Had to dig deep in the closet for this. Not a lot of call for business-casual attire at Adventure Access."

"Not a suit-and-tie kind of office?"

"Are you kidding? This counts for formal wear at AA."

The visage of a tuxedoed Max at the wedding where Alex married Max's sister popped back up in her imagination. *He must have had ladies lined up at his feet when he could walk.*

The horrid nature of that thought shot through her— what an awful, terrible thing to think! Why was Max Jones such a mental minefield for her good sense?

"Okay, what was that?"

She hated that he noticed. "Nothing."

He pointed at her. "You just had a cripple thought."

"A *what?*"

"Aw, come on—you think I can't tell? Someone has a thought, usually to do with my paralysis, that they think is totally awful and cruel, usually because it is, and their face goes all screwy like yours just did. I call them 'cripple thoughts,' because that's the most offensive word for what I am."

She felt horrendously exposed. Guilty and trapped. What on earth was she supposed to do? Why did Max feel as if he had to shove the awkwardness in everyone's face like this?

"Look, just get over it, okay? It's easier if you admit this is weird. I hate tiptoeing around the issue. You had a cripple thought. It's gonna happen. I'm used to it. I can see it a mile off."

Heather launched up off the wall. "Why do you do that? It was a terrible thing to think and I'm already ashamed of myself, so why are you making me feel so bad about it when you were just so incredibly nice to Simon?"

Max spun around to follow her. "There. See? You can yell at me for being a jerk just like any other guy. Glad we got that out of the way."

She turned to look at him. "You're awful—you know that?" But, she had to admit, the tension had just evaporated. Crude as it was, he was breaking down her misconceptions about him one at a time. Ten minutes ago she would not have felt free to tell him he was awful. He'd sensed her pity even before she had, and he'd called her on it because he didn't want pity from her. Or anyone.

"*Awful* is a personal specialty. Just don't sugarcoat things for me on account of my wheels, okay? I can take just about anything but that." He motioned to the wall again, silently asking her to sit down so they could be eye to eye again. Heather was coming to realize how important that courtesy was to him.

"So," he said, rubbing his hands together, "how about we start that part over?"

Heather cleared her throat. She would do as he asked; she would treat him as she would treat any other person who had just done something incredibly nice for Simon. "Can I buy you a cup of coffee and a slice of pie at Karl's to show my appreciation?"

It was fun to be the one surprising him for once. He wasn't expecting that. "Celebrate our little victory over helicopter dad?"

Heather rolled her eyes. "When you put it that way…"

"No. I mean, I won't put it that way. Which means yes. Yes to coffee. If you're buying."

"I am."

"Only if I drive."

How had she known there'd be a catch to his yes? "You drive?"

"Yep. If you're willing to ride in the flaming toaster, I'll know you really mean it."

"Is *everything* a test with you?"

There was that glint again. "Only the good stuff."

She might regret this. "I'll go get my handbag—since I'm paying and all." She walked toward the door, then turned around again. "The *flaming toaster?*"

"JJ's name. Fits."

She didn't know what to say. *I feel that a lot around you,* she thought as she pulled the door open and went inside.

Max punched JJ's number into his cell phone the minute the school door shut behind Heather.

"Hi there," she answered. "I just put the steaks into the marinade."

"I might not make dinner. I don't have a ton of time to talk, but I'm heading out for coffee with Heather Browning."

Silence greeted his news.

"Look, we can have dinner tomorrow night, right?"

Another long pause. "Max, don't."

Oh, she was a master of the big-sister tone of conviction. "What?"

"You promised me you wouldn't get personal with Heather. She's a friend. You were helping her out. Now you're going to go all Max on her, aren't you?" Max could practically hear her stabbing the steaks with a sharp fork over the phone.

"I'm not doing anything. She invited me out for coffee. A friendly celebration over something good that happened with Simon."

"You don't know how to do friendly, Max. Please don't get into this with Heather."

Now she was getting annoying. "Get into what, exactly?" Sure, Max had left a long line of broken hearts in his wake before his accident, but he hadn't exactly boasted a stuffed social calendar since. "So now that I'm in a wheelchair, the entire female gender is off-limits?"

"You can date anyone you like, Max, as long as it's not Heather."

"Who said I was even dating Heather? Or planning to date her? Jumping to a few conclusions, aren't you?" Max kept one eye on the door. "You're out of line here, JJ."

There was a pause on her end of the line. "I just don't want you...well...you know."

"Wow. Your confidence in me staggers the mind. It's pie and coffee at Karl's, for crying out loud. And she asked. Give me a little credit here."

"Credit or not, you're still blowing Alex and me off for dinner. We've been planning this for two weeks."

She was right about that much. Between her shifts at the firehouse and Alex's schedule, getting together was proving nearly impossible lately. "What if I came by at seven—would that work?"

"Yes. I'd like that." After a moment she added, "I miss you, Max. I used to see you all the time and now—"

"Hey. We're still Max and JJ. Besides, you've got that spiffy new groom to keep you occupied."

"That spiffy new groom also happens to be your boss. Have you considered you were just trying to ditch your boss, too?"

"I'm trying to help a kid out, JJ. That's all this is."

"Look, I just want you to steer clear of Heather in the date department. You know your track record. She's a friend. This could get all kinds of weird, you know?"

It bugged Max that his own sister thought of him as toxic in the boyfriend department. Sure, he wasn't a master of solid relationships, and all her cautiousness hinted at a seriously painful past, but that didn't mean he couldn't be a decent human being over a slice of pie. "It's just coffee, JJ. I gotta go."

"Be nice, Max. Nice? Do you remember how?"

Chapter Six

Max hit the remote-control button that slowly opened the double doors on his adapted Honda Element. Heather was surprised to see the pair of doors open from the middle like French doors, but it made sense given the large opening they formed.

"Ta-da!" Max imitated a trumpet fanfare as if the gates to his castle were being raised. He was always cracking jokes. Max was like a kid that way—ramping up the wisecracks when he was nervous or uncomfortable. The mechanized ramp unfolded, making the drawbridge metaphor a little more apt, and Max waved her on board with a grandiose gesture. "Ladies first. You get to ride like I'm your chauffeur this time. I can put in the passenger seat with a little more notice, but right now my chair goes there. Although I'll warn you, it's not the cleanest car in the world. Just shove everything over on the backseat and make room for yourself."

She walked up the ramp, surprised to see the backseats were a little higher than the front seats. It made her feel like a spectator instead of a passenger; an odd sensation. True to Max's warning, Heather had to move

three T-shirts, a fast-food bag and a pair of sports magazines over to make a spot to sit. Max rolled on board
and went through the process of securing his chair
where the passenger seat usually went, then shifted
himself into the driver's seat and rotated it into position.

"It's amazing," Heather said, watching the adaptations. It was both interesting and a little unnerving to
be in his car. She couldn't remember the last time she'd
even been in the backseat of a car, much less one as
tricked out as this.

Max caught her eye in the rearview mirror. "You
didn't think I'd drive a minivan, did you?"

"No, the paint job pretty much gives your taste in
cars away." He turned the ignition, sending a deafen-
ing blast of loud music through the car.

"Sorry!" he hollered as he quickly lowered the vol-
ume. "I like it loud." The engine roared to life, loud
enough without the music. He really was like a teenage boy in too many ways.

He grinned and adopted a terrible highbrow accent.
"To Karl's, madam?"

"Yes, please." She watched in fascination as he
worked the hand controls that pulled the car out and
into gear. "Was it hard to learn to drive?"

"The hand controls?" Max called over his shoulder.
"Not really. I just think of it like a real-live video game.
I took out a mailbox my first week, but it's been smooth
sailing since then. I had more accidents with my old
walking car than I've had with this one."

It was a matter of minutes before he pulled up into
the accessible spot around the corner from Karl's Koffee. "I get all the best spots at the mall," he said, doing
a spot-on imitation of a teenage girl as he hit the button

to reopen the automated doors. She climbed out, then waited on the sidewalk for him to shift into his chair and come down the ramp.

"This is where it gets a bit tricky. Karl's front has steps, so I get to use the secret entrance."

"That sounds fun," she replied.

His eyes darkened a bit. "You'd think, but not really. You can meet me around front if you'd like."

She didn't know if this was another of those diversionary tactics like he'd coached Simon to use or a true invitation. She decided to see Karl's from his point of view. "I'll go for what's behind door number two."

Max's smile was pleased but cautious. They went around to the back of the establishment, where Max hit a doorbell. After about a minute, Karl, the friendly older man who owned the place, pushed open the door. "Maxwell! Saw that boat out on the river the other day—pretty spiffy. It's good to see ya, son. Gimme a second to clear the decks."

Heather felt a twinge of guilt as Karl went back inside. "I didn't even think about the front steps before I suggested Karl's. I'm sorry."

"Don't be." Max almost looked as though he meant it. Was he really okay with her choice, or was he using this as a lesson in how challenging Gordon Falls could be for him? "I was a regular here back before I got hurt, and I've always liked the place. He just has to move a few things to give me a clear shot to the front. He's always good about it, but…." Max finished the thought with weary eyes rather than words. "I can get in easier at Café Homestead, but I like their pie better here. You gave me an excuse to make the extra effort."

"Me, too. Everyone always goes there for pie, but I think it's better here."

The door reopened. "Okay, all set. Corner table's all waiting."

"You rate the corner table at Karl's?" Heather asked. It was always taken when she came here, and it was a favorite spot with the best view out the window.

"Sort of," Max admitted. "It's the only place I fit, so it's a backhanded benefit. Evidently you get a free coffee if Karl has to move you to make room for me." He said it with a cheerful tone Heather didn't fully believe.

He had good reason. Heather was astounded how much effort it took to get Max through the back of the coffeehouse, around the existing tables and settled in the corner spot. It made her feel terrible at how easily she breezed in whenever she felt like it.

"Don't go all pity party on me." He sent her a dismissive grin, tossing back his tousled hair. "I get seated first on the airplane, and if we ever go to Disney World I can get you on Space Mountain without waiting in line. This is nothing. I'm used to it."

She sat back in her chair. "Why did you ever say yes to here if you knew it would be such a hassle?"

"Because it's where you wanted to go." He peered toward the chalkboard that held Karl's daily offerings. "And like you said, the pie is good here. Besides, I like Karl and I don't get to see him as much. They have blueberry today. Awesome." When she stared at him, he added, "Don't you ever do things that are a hassle just because you want to do them?"

Heather thought of the fifty-minute drive she made to her preferred hairstylist. "I suppose I do."

"So, are we just pie celebrating, or did today's victories rate pie a la mode?"

His eyes could stop a train when he smiled like that. "Oh, definitely with ice cream." Karl had walked up, so when Max nodded in her direction, she said, "Dutch apple pie a la mode and coffee, Karl."

Karl wrote on the little green notepad he always used. "And what about you, Hot Wheels?"

"Blueberry. With ice cream. And coffee."

Karl scribbled, then tucked the notepad into his apron pocket. "Done and done. Coming right up, kids."

Heather laughed. "Kids?"

Max looked after the old man as he limped away. "Karl's hip isn't doing so good. Age. I guess to him we're all kids. He told me once that he has a grand-daughter about our age, but I've never met her."

"He didn't try to set you up?" Max was handsome and Karl poked his nose in everyone's business.

Max shot her a look that belonged on a pirate. "Would *you* set me up with your granddaughter?"

She laughed at the way he could make fun of himself so easily. "Well, now that you mention it, I suppose I'd hesitate. You drive a flaming toaster, after all."

He laughed, as well, but Heather caught something in the way Max looked at the man. "How long has your dad been gone? JJ told me he passed away, but I never did ask her much more."

"Years." Max tapped his chair. "It's probably for the best. I don't think Pops would have handled this too well. My dad was hard-core military. A 'walk it off' kind of guy who even had trouble when JJ wouldn't re-up after all she'd been through. This isn't a 'walk it off' kind of thing, if you'll pardon the pun."

Heather decided she would try a different approach. "Why do you make so many jokes about it?"

"Why wouldn't I?"

"Well, it's just that you say it doesn't matter, but you make it matter all the time by making cracks about it. Dark, on-the-edge-of-not-quite-so-funny cracks."

Max put both elbows on the table and pasted an enthralled look on his face. "No, really, counselor, tell me straight-out what you think my issues are."

"Close your mouth, son. She's pretty, but she's already sitting with you" came Karl's voice over Heather's shoulder as he put down the two slices of pie. "Don't try so hard."

"This is school related," Heather felt compelled to point out, waiting for Max to back her up.

"Could have fooled me." Karl nudged Max's shoulder. "Nice going, Hot Wheels."

Heather remembered the one reason she didn't come to Karl's more often—it was ground zero for the local gossip chain. Why hadn't she remembered that if she showed up at Karl's with Max, it would take about seventeen minutes for folks to start making inferences? She pulled a notebook out of her handbag and put it on the table with a pen.

"Oh, that'll throw them off for sure," Max whispered loudly.

"You weren't helping."

"It's Karl."

"No, it's everybody. They're staring."

"I'm in a wheelchair with flames painted on the sides. Of course they're staring." He was baiting her, and worse yet, he was enjoying it. "Look." He leaned in. "They could actually be staring for other reasons, but

I'm so used to the stares I'd probably never even realize it. You want to go? I'll take you back to school. But I don't think we're going to die from overexposure here."

She felt cornered. If she didn't go, people might start linking her with Max Jones, and she definitely wasn't ready for that. If she did go, she'd look as if she was ashamed to be seen in public with him—or maybe with anyone in a wheelchair—and that wasn't appropriate... or true, either.

Max cut off the end of his slice with his fork. "Okay, my turn. Why do you weird out when people notice you?"

"I don't."

"You do."

"I don't crave attention the way you do, if that's what you're saying."

Max scooped up the piece of pie and put it into his mouth. "Nope, you can't make this one about me. A fine-looking lady shouldn't work so hard to be invisible." He pointed at Heather with his fork. "Somebody or something taught you to want to hide like that. You've got issues."

She gave him her best "I am in control of this conversation" look. "You are making a lot of assumptions here, Mr. Jones."

He cocked his head to one side. "Have dinner with me."

Her jaw clenched—he hadn't even framed it as a question. "We're already eating pie."

"I've always thought dessert first was a fine culinary strategy. Let's have dinner."

"No." She gave the word all the finality she could

muster. She should have known he'd push too hard at anything he did—why not at her?

"Because of the chair?"

"Stop that. I said no. And not because of the chair, but because we are currently working together on a school matter."

He leaned back. "It's because of the chair."

Heather planted her hands on the table. "It's because of the arrogant, pushy man *in* the chair." She let out a breath and began putting the notebook back into her handbag. "I was just trying to be nice, to celebrate all the good you've done with Simon, but I should have known it'd get like this. I'll walk back to school, thanks."

Max put his hands up. "Okay, okay. I'll take it down a notch."

"Or three."

"Fine, I'll take it down four notches. We did good with Simon. Let's have pie and coffee and talk about Simon and I'll keep my dinner plans with Alex and JJ and pretend this never happened."

She glared at him. "You were going to ditch Alex and JJ for dinner?"

"Well, not really. I was pretty sure you'd say no."

Heather put one hand to her forehead. "You are absolutely impossible. You should come with a warning label."

Just then a preschool girl wobbled up, pointing at the flames on the side of his chair. As Max was raising a hand to wave hello, the mom rushed up, gushed out an embarrassed apology and pulled the child away.

His gaze followed the child, who craned her neck around against her mother's tug to look again at Max. "I already do."

Max wheeled up alongside the current national Paralympic cycling champion. Max had flown down to Atlanta Friday afternoon to attend a track-and-field event AA had eyes on sponsoring next year. "Man," he puffed, wheezing so hard he could barely see the competitor. "You...are...fast."

Luke Sullivan looked as if he could have done another ten laps. "Six medals to prove it." He snagged the hem of his T-shirt and used it to wipe his sweating forehead. The guy looked nearly military—lean, muscular, buzz-cut hair. Max thought the guy could probably take on half of JJ's old army unit sitting down. Sullivan had just won yet another race—his third of the day. "You have some skills there—for an amateur, I mean. With a little training, you could hold your own."

Before working with Adventure Access and their sponsorship of para-athletic events around the country, Max never even knew there were professional athletes like Luke. The guy was impressive. "I'm not the dedicated type. I'll stick to the flashier side—no pesky results to worry about."

"There's flash enough on my end of the deal," Luke boasted. "You'll see at the sponsors' dinner Sunday night." He gave a knowing smirk. "Lots of ladies."

That was a business perk Alex hadn't discussed. "Shame I've got a four-o'clock flight Sunday. Remind me to stay over till Monday next time."

Luke rolled his massive shoulders and started wheeling toward the equipment trailers. "Yeah, the competition is fun, but the pity perks are outstanding."

Max caught up with him. "The what?"

"Aw, come on—you know what I mean. The rehab nurses. The physical therapists. All those *helping professionals*." He gave the last two words a locker-room tone of voice, and Max's mild shock must have shown on his face. "You're, what, fourteen months out? Injured last summer, wasn't it?"

"July. And what's that got to do with anything?"

Luke pulled up closer. "How many dates have you had since then?"

Max suddenly wasn't interested in playing notch-on-the-post with this guy. Not that he was a long-term-relationship guy himself, but he hadn't realized a legend like Luke Sullivan took the phrase "wheeling womanizer" to a new level. "Enough." Was Sullivan for real? JJ lectured him on taking Heather to dinner when there were guys like *this* rolling around the world?

Luke's chuckle of disbelief annoyed Max. "Yeah, just like I thought. Not one, huh? You need to play to your strengths, Jones. Pity perks are all we get around here. Don't go believing that rehab nonsense about rich, full lives with all the same things we'd have had before the chair. We're out of that race—you don't see too many of us rolling down the aisle."

Max halted his wheels, a bit stunned. Of all the guys in chairs to garner a full social life, Sullivan should top the list. "Wait a minute—you've been in a chair for, what, six years?"

"Seven and a half."

"And you're telling me no woman has ever gone out with you for just—"

Sullivan cut him off with a laugh and waved his hand as if the thought were ludicrous. "Pity perks are all you get, dude. Best to own up to that now."

"But…"

Luke angled to face Max. "Sure, there are the ones that talk a great game. Acceptance, accessibility—oh, the social workers are really good at that one—and they'll stick with you for a little while. Then you get sick or they want to go on vacation somewhere you can't go, or worse yet, their family gets wind of it. Then it's bye-bye."

Max was sorry he could still feel enough of his gut for it to knot. "Don't mess with me. Come on, you're like G.I. Joe in a chair. If somebody like you only gets dates out of pity, what hope is there for the rest of us?"

"That's just it, dude. There isn't any hope. Don't get sucked in. In the end, you're just the compassion merit badge. And it feels like being dropped a mile. You want my advice? Don't even try to do the relationship thing. It doesn't work."

It was the first time Max had ever found anyone more cynical than himself, and it wasn't a pretty sight. "That's harsh, man."

"Better to know now. Relationships do not work out for guys like us. Let me guess—your rehab therapist told you not to start a serious relationship for the first year, right?"

Max tried to remember the speech he'd received and mostly ignored. "Well, yeah. I figured it wouldn't be all that easy, but I didn't take myself totally out of the market. I mean, there have to be women who can handle this." His thoughts went to Heather and the bright future she'd painted for Simon. She thought it possible.

"No," Luke said with a dark certainty Max practically felt run cold down the back of his neck. "Only women who *think* they can. And everybody finds out how ugly that can get." Luke pulled up to his regular chair and shifted himself out of the racing model with a strength and agility Max had to admire. The guy was the best in the world, and an Adonis on wheels to boot. If anybody knew the rules of the game, it was Luke Sullivan. "Sorry to be the bearer of grim news, but better you know now. It just isn't possible." With a bump of his fist on Max's shoulder, Luke wheeled off in the direction of the athlete's tent.

The entire concept of Adventure Access was that anything was possible for someone with a disability. Well, almost anything. Then again, Max knew that JJ had a bucketload of veteran friends whose marriages and relationships hadn't survived the injuries soldiers brought home. Granted, he hadn't been at this very long, but now that he thought about it, he hadn't run into one happily married man in a chair. He'd just figured they weren't into the sports and outdoor pursuits AA sponsored—the company had a decidedly young demographic—but what if they weren't out there at all? What if Luke was right?

Luke Sullivan, you're pretty much a jerk, aren't you? Max thought bitterly. Luke couldn't be right. The guy's paralysis just started at his heart, that was all. He'd known men who attacked their dating life with that "take no prisoners" attitude—he'd been one himself, for crying out loud. Max decided he no longer admired Luke Sullivan very much—the guy's handicap went a lot further than his legs.

Until he remembered something an old friend of

his had said—one of the many friends who had fallen
by the wayside, unable to cope with the new world of
"Max on Wheels"—that now rang disturbingly true:
*Sometimes it's the jerks who say out loud what we all
wish weren't true.*

Chapter Seven

Max wasn't back in town more than twenty-four hours before JJ insisted he come with her and Alex to attend the funeral of Mort Wingate, an older guy in town who'd been sick for a while.

"I know who Mort is…was…but it's not like I was close to the guy," Max argued with JJ outside the church entrance.

"That doesn't matter," JJ retorted. "You know his daughter, Melba, and her husband, Clark, and this is as much about them as it is about Mort." JJ went all motherly on Max, an odd soft tone in her voice as she found something to brush off his shoulder. "This is how community works, Max. Everybody's there for everybody else."

His sister and her new husband had really made Gordon Falls home in a way that even he hadn't, although he'd lived there longer. In fact, JJ had been house-sitting for him when she'd first met Alex, who'd been on a sabbatical of sorts in Gordon Falls. They'd met, they'd become friends, they'd grown close…and then they'd watched it all fall apart thanks to Max's injury.

Adventure Access was born from the ashes of Adventure Gear, Alex's old company that had made the new, experimental climbing line from which Max had fallen. Anger, blame and guilt had separated Alex and JJ for a time in the aftermath, but they'd worked it all out.

As for himself, Max had long stopped caring whether the injury was the result of faulty equipment or his own recklessness. JJ would say that was God's healing. To Max, it simply didn't seem worth the energy to point fingers now that all that business had been settled. Especially since Alex and JJ looked so happy that Max could almost believe the stuff JJ spouted about how God had worked that whole mess for good.

That was easy to believe when the "for good" had really changed your life "for good." Sure, his job at Adventure Access was far better than anything he'd done before the accident, but it didn't quite even out in Max's view, nor could he really believe that it would. It had all left him on not very friendly terms with God, which was why it made him so antsy to be wheeling into the Gordon Falls Community Church for this funeral.

"There's a spot for chairs up front," Alex said, knowing Max hadn't set foot in the sanctuary despite living in Gordon Falls for nearly two years.

"Up front? Can't the newbies sit in the back?"

"What, so you can cut out early?" JJ chided. "Come on—I promise it won't hurt."

The church was packed. Max couldn't help but wonder—if he hadn't survived his fall, would his funeral have been packed the pews like this? Max mostly avoided pondering the reason why he was still here. For a few seconds there with Simon, however, he'd felt a glimmer of what he supposed Alex would call "purpose." He

certainly was doing good at Adventure Access—people
told him every day how he changed their perceptions
of what was possible after an injury like his. That was
satisfying to hear, but it wasn't the kind of thing a guy
could build a life on. What Luke Sullivan did accomplished the same thing, but Max had no desire to end
up a bitter, manipulative skeptic like Sullivan, even if it
did mean a packed social schedule.

"You're here," Heather Browning said with a disturbing air of surprise as she walked up the church
aisle. She looked over at JJ. "Can I sit with you all?"

"Sure," Max said before JJ had a chance to respond,
rolling his chair back a bit to give her access to the pew
next to him. Maybe church wasn't so boring, after all.
When she'd settled into her seat, he leaned over and
whispered, "Melba is friends with you and JJ, isn't
she?"

Heather nodded. "She's had a long go of taking care
of Mort. Clark, too." She motioned to where Melba;
her husband, the fire chief, Clark Bradens; and some
other people still stood in the back of the sanctuary.
"It's so sad."

"Never seen a happy funeral."

Heather looked up. "Oh, I have."

"A happy funeral? Isn't that sort of an oxymoron?"

The organ music softened, signaling the start of the
service. "Not really. I'll tell you after the service."

For a church service, Max had to admit it wasn't that
bad. Heather had a sweet singing voice, so he didn't
mind that he didn't know any of the songs, because it
gave him a chance to listen to her. Pastor Allen wasn't
half-bad for a minister type—he actually seemed pretty
down-to-earth. He talked about death as heading home

to a place where all the mental and physical limitations Mort had endured late in life would be gone, where he'd be reunited with his late wife, where he'd finally see the God who loved him face-to-face. Allen made it sound as if he looked forward to his time to go, even though JJ talked all the time about his family and the strength of his friendships.

When Clark stood up and read a letter Melba had written, there was barely a dry eye in the room. When a group of older woman from the church walked up and draped Mort's casket with a stunning moss-green blanket of sorts, even Max got a lump in his throat thinking of the prayer shawl the same ladies had given him. His was black with flames on it—just like his car—and while he'd never admit it to anyone, it was one of his prized possessions. Power of prayer or no, the thing always seemed to make him feel better whenever he pulled it over his lap or shoulders. The gift had been the first evidence of the Gordon Falls community he'd seen. And now Mort had been given his last. He hadn't thought that kind of stuff ever really happened anymore.

"That was beautiful, wasn't it?" Heather asked when she closed the hymnal after the final song. She wore a pretty sky-colored dress that fluttered in the breeze coming through the open church windows. The sun coming through the stained glass cast her hair in a myriad of colors. She—and Alex and JJ for that matter—looked so at home in the church where he still felt like an intruder. Or worse yet, an impostor. He couldn't seem to drum up whatever it was that Alex and JJ and now even Heather obviously got from the place.

"Yeah," he agreed, meaning it. "It was really nice. I

hadn't realized all the history Mort had with the town."
Max had been in a hurry to leave the Ohio suburb of his
youth, and while folks had been nothing but friendly
when he'd opened the boat and cabin rental business
here, he hadn't felt the deep connection other people
seemed to make. Not yet at least, but he could feel the
edges of it starting to catch.

"Want to get some coffee and say hello? Simon and
his dad are over there with Melba and Clark." Heather
pointed to the large meeting room, where people were
gathering and chatting.

"Max!" Simon shouted and waved. The boy's enthusiasm caught in the back of Max's throat. "I saw you
earlier. Hey, guess what?"

Max wheeled up to him, offering him a fist bump
and a smile that didn't need any forcing at all. "What?"

"I'm joining the Ping-Pong Club. Ms. Browning
talked to the teacher and everything."

Heather's smile was wide and downright adorable.
"It was Simon's idea. Mr. Jackson said yes in a heartbeat."

Simon angled up beside Max. "Bailey Morton is in
the Ping-Pong Club." He said the girl's name with the
flat-out hormonal fascination only high school boys
could achieve.

"Cute, huh?"

Simon sighed. "Way out of my league."

"Cut that out!" Max pulled back in mock shock, then
leaned in to whisper, "Don't sell yourself short. Chicks
dig the wheels."

The resulting look on Simon's face was priceless—
until the scowl on Mr. Williams's face shut down
the conspiracy. "An academic club is a good idea for

Simon, don't you think?" It was clear Mr. Williams had something closer to Math Club or Chess Club in mind.

"The way he smoked us last time, I think Simon has awesome prospects in the Ping-Pong Club." Max pointed at Simon. "I gave you my cell number last time, so you keep me posted on your progress." Just because he couldn't help himself, he winked and added, "On all fronts. Text me. Anytime."

Simon grinned. "You got it."

Heather, who had acquired two cups of coffee, nodded toward some chairs lined up along the wall. He liked that she intuitively looked for ways to get them at eye level with each other without him having to ask her to do so. Not everyone caught on to how hard it was to keep craning his neck up all the time.

"Do you even realize what you've done for that boy?" she asked, handing the cup to him as she sat down. She actually teared up a bit as she stared back at Simon, and the look in her eyes lodged sharp and sweet in Max's chest.

He didn't really know how to respond. "He's a good kid. Just...unsure, I suppose."

"He thinks the world of you. You know that."

He cleared his throat, her glistening eyes again catching him up short. "Oh, people used to think a lot of things about me and what I did, but that kind of admiration hasn't ever really entered the picture."

"It's a gift, Max. A trust, really." She cast her eyes back at Simon. "Just promise me you'll take care with it, okay?" Heather took her passion for her work to a personal level Max hadn't ever seen. It was as if these kids were her own kids; she cared that much.

"Yeah, sure. I get that." He took a sip of coffee, needing to break the intensity of the moment. "I'm choking in this tie. Let's go get some air."

Heather stepped onto the path that led from Gordon Falls Community Church down toward the town's picturesque riverbank. She'd always found nature's beauty to be the best balm for the soul after something as heavy as a funeral, and it was clear to see Max wasn't at ease inside the church.

"So," Max said as he negotiated a corner with an effortless grace, "you said you were going to tell me about a happy funeral."

"I did, didn't I?"

"I'll give you this much—Mort's did feel happier than I expected. But I'm still skeptical."

"It was my grandmother's funeral service," Heather answered. She cast her memory back to the brisk October morning when Mom had laid her extraordinary mother to rest. "She had the best funeral I've ever attended. It was like a big, thankful celebration. She even made us have cake. She said she wanted it to be like an enormous party for her graduation into heaven. She was an amazing woman, my Grannie Annie."

Max eyebrow shot up at the name. "Grannie Annie? Really?"

Grannie Annie would have had a field day with the jaded look in Max's eyes. "Oh, she was a great lady. I hope I'm just like her at that age—she lived until she was eighty-seven and sharp as a tack all the way until the end. Mom used to say Grannie Annie squeezed every drop out of life every day." Heather hugged her chest, Grannie Annie's musical voice and lively eyes coming to mind. "If it weren't for her help after my accident, I don't know how I'd ever have made it through."

Max put out a hand to stop her walking. "How were you burned? Where?" He motioned to the stone wall that ran along the sidewalk. "I mean, if you're okay with telling me."

She wasn't. She wasn't ever really comfortable with telling anyone about that year—it let people in too close once they knew. Still, Max had told her about his own injury; it didn't seem fair to hold out just because it was hard. She swallowed.

"It looks like you've made a fine recovery, but I have no business prying if you don't want to talk about it. I of all people get how that feels."

"No, it just…it's hard to talk about. Exactly because I look fine. I mean I feel fine, but…well, *recovery* doesn't really seem to be the right word." The words weren't coming, so she decided it was easier to show him. She walked over to the low wall he'd pointed out, satisfied it wasn't in wide view, and sat down. Max wheeled over next to her. With a deep breath, Heather lifted the long hem of her skirt to just above her left knee, where the scars started.

She was glad he didn't say anything. He didn't do that awful sucking in of breath, that unedited reaction she imagined most people would have to the nasty visual of her scarred leg. She let the hem fall back, suddenly aware of all the feeling that had left that part of her body. The swath of numb, tough scar tissue and skin graft the doctors had called such a victory. Most days she was grateful—she knew lots of other burn patients who had it far worse and she still had a fair amount of mobility in that hip. Other days she felt damaged and discarded no matter how much her faith told her otherwise.

"What did that to you?" he said softly.

"Oil."

"That sounds awful. I'm sorry."

Did he realize he'd just said the very thing he disliked other people saying about his accident? He sounded sincere, and she was glad he didn't try to crack a joke. There weren't jokes to make about this, ever.

"I worked at a fried-chicken place in high school. One night a drunk driver—a senior from my own school, in fact—plowed through the front windows. Lots of people were hurt, and while no one lost their lives, I was standing in front of the deep fryers when they…" She never could quite come up with the right verb for what had happened. But the sound? The glass crunching and people screaming and the horrible hissing before she blacked out? She could describe that down to the last terrible detail.

"I woke up in a burn unit with all kinds of patches and pads and drugs dripping into IVs. I missed most of my junior year between all the surgeries and infections, but I walked down the aisle to get my diploma."

"Your grandmother took care of you?"

"Not the way you'd think. My mom saw to most of my care. My dad, well, he didn't handle the whole thing well. He wanted to see somebody pay for ruining his precious little girl, and he sort of let that crusade swallow him whole. Grannie Annie found ways to keep me happy, to keep me from making my whole life about my left leg."

Max was quiet for a long time before he said, "I was your dad, at first. I let my accident swallow me for a while. I wanted someone to pay." He wasn't siding with her dad; he was confessing his own downward spiral. "You might have read about it in the papers. I wasn't exactly keeping a low profile."

She nodded, the lump in her throat too big to let words past. She knew he'd been bitter. JJ had told her some of it, and Max had managed to get himself into the papers and the media for a variety of less-than-healthy behaviors in the early months after his accident. It was what had kept her from calling Max to help with Simon in the first place. She realized, looking at him now, that she'd projected a lot of her dad onto Max because of how they'd both reacted to a tragedy. The men in her life until now had left her with scars and numbness in places Max couldn't see. She'd vowed to only let people into her life who fought against bitterness, not those who succumbed to it. She wasn't completely sure yet which of those Max Jones was.

"Where are your mom and dad now?"

She picked a small stone up from the path beside her feet and fiddled with it. "They split up my sophomore year in college. Dad couldn't put the battle-ax down and Mom couldn't heal both him and me at the same time. I spent the summer of my freshman year home from college at Grannie Annie's because they were fighting so much by then."

"What happened to the guy who hit the store?"

Oh, that was the million-dollar question, the thing that had turned Dad into the person he became—and in some ways had turned her into the person she became. "Not enough, really. He had rich, powerful parents who hired supersmart lawyers. They managed to pull in a question of mechanical failure despite the guy's blood-alcohol level. Eventually, he pleaded into a deal that got him out in no time. I think that's what got to Dad most of all." Heather dared a look up into Max's face. All the smart aleck was gone. Just the intensity of his eyes was left, warm where they had been defensive. She touched her left leg. "I got the life sentence and he got off easy. Hard to swallow, if you know what I mean."

"I'm sorry." It was almost a whisper, and Max looked down at his hands for a moment. "I'm sorry, and that isn't useless, is it?"

Something unfurled in Heather's defenses. A tiny piece of her—one that had started blooming larger at the Ping-Pong match—dared to believe that maybe Max wasn't here by mistake. Maybe Max was exactly who Simon needed.

And maybe more than just Simon.

Chapter Eight

❧

"You were really good in there." Alex grinned as he and Max got into the elevator after an important work presentation Wednesday morning.

"Thanks." Max pushed the button for the ground floor. "They weren't too hard a crowd to win over."

"Maybe so, and you know persuasion is a specialty of mine, but I don't think we'd have gotten that much buy-in to the concept if you weren't in the room. I'm still just the guy with the good idea, but you're the guy who proves it works." Alex leaned back against the elevator wall. "I'm glad you're on board. Just saying." After a second he added, "Do you miss the boat biz?"

Max's boat and cottage rental business in Gordon Falls had barely been getting by when he was injured. Now JJ mostly ran it—and ran it well—when she wasn't at the volunteer fire department. "I can still dip my toes back in the water when I need to. And I've got the *Sea Legs,* which is more fun than my desk any day. Besides, the business is doing better under your wife's management than it ever did under mine. She's an outstanding employee."

Alex raised an eyebrow. "I thought JJ was a full partner now."

She was. "I just get a kick out of calling her an employee. She's not anymore, but, you know, I just can't seem to remember that." Max tapped his head. "Blocked neural pathways or something."

"Uh-huh." Alex checked his watch. "I've got another meeting at two, but you want to grab some lunch? There was a café in the lobby and presentations always make me hungry."

Max noticed a familiar look in Alex's eyes. The one that signaled "a conversation." Trouble was, Max hadn't quite figured out if the look meant a brother-in-law conversation or an employee conversation. "Sure, I could eat. If I can get in there okay."

"I scoped it out on the way in," Alex admitted, which told Max this meal wasn't as spontaneous as it had sounded. "You'll be fine." Most places in larger cities and towns, that was true—the world was becoming a more accessible place every day. But Gordon Falls and other historic small towns still held their share of challenges. The Gordon Falls Community Church hadn't had a decent wheelchair ramp until last year.

"So," Alex said carefully once they'd settled in with a pair of hefty sandwiches, "JJ is worried about you."

Max snickered. "JJ's always worried about me."

"Let me rephrase that." Alex pinched the bridge of his nose. "JJ is worried about you and Heather Browning."

"I've already been given the full speech, Alex." Max rolled his eyes. "I don't need it from you, too."

"Hey." Alex put up his hands. "I'm actually on your side here. But you know JJ. Friendships are hard for her, and she is worried you'll mess things up with Heather. You can't blame her, given your previous track record."

"I haven't dated anyone since the accident. I've been a very good little injured boy." His words had a little more edge than was perhaps necessary, but this was a sore spot. "If I wanted to be mothered, I'd have moved back to Ohio." Max ripped open his bag of chips. "Go arrange for JJ to meet Luke Sullivan. The guy's a predator on wheels. Gave me a really *inspirational* speech about the leverage of pity when scoring with the ladies. You can tell JJ she has nothing to worry about from me."

The look of surprise on Alex's face was satisfying. People held Sullivan up as a beacon of inspiration. Max had half a mind to let a few things slip to the media about what a boor the guy really was, only he didn't have the heart to shoot any bad press toward Paralympic sports.

"Charming. Remind me to take him off my list of potential spokespersons. Just proves there can a jerk factor in any business, hmm?" Alex took a bite, but he was still forming a conversation—Max could see the next question percolating behind his boss's eyes. "So you want to tell me what exactly *is* going on between you and Heather? I saw you walking out of the church service with her, and that was a pretty wide grin you were wearing for a guy who just got dragged into a funeral."

Max still hadn't decided how much he wanted to get into this with Alex. "I get a kick out of helping her help Simon. You ought to understand how that feels."

"Oh, I do. I get that. But Simon wasn't out on the riverbank for half an hour with you. And Simon hasn't prompted you to ditch dinner with us—well, not yet anyway. I'm glad you showed that night, but it would have helped if you hadn't outlawed any conversation regarding Heather at dinner. JJ thinks you're hiding something from her. You know how she gets." Alex pointed at Max with the straw of his soda. "*Are* you hiding a relationship with Heather?"

Max put his sandwich down hard enough to tumble the bread off one side. "I do not have a relationship with Heather Browning."

Alex was fully engaged now, in that communication mode that made him an unstoppable force. "Do you *want* a relationship with Heather Browning?"

Just because he needed to stall, Max said, "Is that really any of your business if I do?"

"Not at all. But I'm going to ask anyway. She's not really what I'd pick as your type."

"I like her." He felt safe admitting that—JJ had probably already guessed that much. "Only the timing is way off."

"Sort of." Given the terrible timing of Alex and JJ's meeting, the argument didn't hold much weight with Alex. "Maybe not, if she's really special."

"To tell you the truth, I'd be better if I liked her a little less, because I'm not quite sure how to…do this whole thing…on wheels, that is. In case you haven't noticed, I come with a whole lot of extra baggage now."

"Everybody's got baggage. Yours is just easier to see."

Alex's words brought the image of Heather's scarred leg to mind. She was still among the walking wounded, only no one saw her pain or recognized her fear. "I can barely cope with all the stuff involved in my condition. How am I supposed to ask someone else to take it on?"

"What if she's strong enough to take it on?" Alex sat back in his chair. "Look at how she champions Simon Williams's cause. I think if anyone could make it work, it'd be someone like her."

He couldn't help but think of Sullivan's words, *They only think they can.* "I don't want to get far into this and find out it won't work. I'd like to think I'm done with breaking ladies' hearts." That was only half-true; a tiny newfound part of him was worried it was *his* heart that would end up broken. He'd been dumped for being a jerk so many times it had almost become a painless game. The thought of someone—especially someone like Heather—breaking it off with him not because he was a jerk, but because of his broken body? That was too harsh to risk. Sullivan was right about one thing: Heather would try so hard to make it work that it would go all the way to the bitter end before she'd admit she wasn't up to the challenge.

"You know," Alex suggested, emphasizing his point with a pickle spear, "you could try something totally un-Max here."

"What would that be?"

"Go slow."

"Ha. Funny."

"This may be exactly what you need. Have you ever thought about that? You can't slam through the gears on this one. You have to take it one little bit at a time. That's completely new territory for you. In a lot of ways."

Max couldn't decide if having Alex in favor of this relationship—and it wasn't a relationship yet—was a good thing or a bad thing. Alex was staring at him with narrow, assessing eyes, as if he were some kind of puzzle to solve, some new project to tackle. The scrutiny was a little unnerving.

"You really like her, don't you?"

Max decided he couldn't fight Alex, JJ, Brian Williams and gravity all at the same time. "Yeah," he admitted. "There's something about her. She sticks with me even when I don't want her to, you know?"

Alex gave him a wily smile. "Yeah, I do know how that feels. When do you see her next?"

Max tried to keep the anticipation from his voice. "Tonight, but it's school business."

"That's good. Go slow. But keep me posted."

Well, Heather thought as she pulled up to the address Max had given her, *at least I know why he said to bring gloves and a sweater.* The parking lot of the County Ice Arena was full for a Wednesday night in September, but she had no trouble picking out a certain boxy black car in one of the handicapped parking spaces.

"Are we watching hockey?" she asked Max as he met her at the door.

He dismissed her question with a wave, rolling into the building. "Nah. Girls don't like hockey."

"I know many *women* who enjoy a good hockey game." She couldn't tell if he persisted with using *girl* because he forgot she didn't like it or because he remembered her irritation.

"But you're not one of them, are you?" His eyes held a bit of mischief.

"Actually, no. Which brings me back to my original question. What are we doing here?"

"That's not your original question." Max held up a correcting finger as he swerved his chair around a corner past the skate rental booth. "Your original question was are we watching hockey. No, we are not watching hockey. We are *playing* hockey."

Heather stopped walking.

Max noticed and swiveled around. "Kiddie-sitting-down hockey, actually. Okay, well, the technical name is sled hockey, but c'mon, a five-year-old could do this. You'll be fine. And then you can give Brian Williams a firsthand account of how Simon will survive intact when he joins us next time."

Heather didn't see how hockey, a sport famous for erupting in tooth-shattering fistfights, would pass the Brian Williams safety standards. Still, she followed Max around to the far corner of the rink, where a section had been cordoned off with a pair of goals and some devices that did indeed look like sleds. A pair of miniature hockey sticks—not more than a foot high— sat in each of the sleds. "You're serious."

Max wheeled past a rink employee, giving the man a high five as he rolled by. "Thanks, Henry."

"Anytime, Max." Henry looked up and gave Heather an enthusiastic but toothless smile. "Hiya, sweetie."

"Hello there." Heather tried to make her wave casual, but it ended up feeling more like a hyperactive flailing than any kind of greeting.

Henry put his hands on his hips. "You ain't never done this before, have you? Look at you—you're a tiny thing, aren't ya?" He chuckled. "This ought to be fun to watch."

"Cut it out, Henry. This is professional. Ms. Browning is from the high school and we're looking at recreational options for a student."

Heather's eyebrows shot up at the formal choice of vocabulary. While his words were professional, Max's expression was decidedly personal.

"Uh-huh." Henry's skepticism was hard to miss. "That's right." He grinned again and pointed at Heather. "You watch out for him, now. He's a tricky one."

"I've caught on to that," Heather replied. "Exactly how does this work?"

Max zipped up the fleece jacket he wore—she hadn't noticed until now that it bore the emblem of Chicago's NHL team, the Blackhawks—and pulled a pair of gloves from the pockets. "Pretty much the way it looks. Only getting into the sled might be a touch easier for you than it is for me." With no more explanation than that, Max rolled his chair out onto a ramped section of carpeting laid out next to the two sleds. With the same athletic prowess she'd seen at their first meeting, he maneuvered himself out of the chair and into the long, low sled, lifting his legs into place. "There are usually special gloves and helmets, but we're not going to get that complicated today. I'll show them to you, though, so you can report back to Mr. Williams on the abundance of safety equipment. Come on—get in." He motioned to the second sled as he began strapping his legs in place.

Max was right; it was pretty obvious how the whole setup worked. Given what a terrible skater she was in the standing position, this felt slightly less perilous— if one ignored the Max element of any activity. She buckled the strap that went over her lap and pulled on her gloves. "Like this?"

"You know—" Max grinned "—I never thought I'd use the word *cute* in a hockey setting. Watch the other end of the sticks. They've got little teeth on them."

"Why?"

"So you can do this." With a trick worthy of a rock-and-roll drummer, he twirled the sticks in the air and then sunk them into the ice so that the teeth gripped. Then he pushed off and went sliding down the rink toward the goal at the other end.

Heather took a breath, set her sticks on either side of her and pushed. It wasn't as hard as she thought to send her sled across the ice, and she found it much more fun to be daring without the constant fear of falling. They played politely at first, gently skidding the soft, light puck back and forth. As her comfort and ability increased, the game dissolved into a fun frenzy of yelling and cheering, egging each other on to spectacular shots and daring defenses. Each goal scored—and she managed to score her fair share—took the game to a new exuberance...until she tipped over after attempting to cut off Max's shot at the goal.

"Watch your hands," Max said, a bit out of breath as he pulled up next to her, facing the opposite direction. "Give me one arm and I'll help you up."

The rescue brought him precariously close, their shoulders touching as he gripped her upper body to upright the sled. Once up, they were facing each other at very close range. Heather looked up and got an unsettlingly close look at his eyes. They were an intriguing hazel—not quite brown, but neither gray nor green, either. They fit his personality—expressive, unclassifiable and a bit dark around the edges. She'd always thought of him as physically strong, but today Heather *felt* that strength. He lifted her as if she were a feather.

Max pulled off one glove, reached up and brushed some ice flakes off her cheek. His touch fluttered through her, her breath short from more than just the marvelous energy of the game. Heather grew warm despite the rink's chill. He was attractive in a perilous sort of way, knowing what she knew about him. JJ had bemoaned Max's past trail of broken hearts, and right now she could see why a woman would believe anything he said up this close. From a distance he was all flash and sharp edges, but this proximity offered Heather a glimpse of something completely different. She saw a jumbled man just trying to figure out how to put his life back together. Wondering, seeking, cautious behind all his cavalier bravado. He was much easier to dismiss from a distance, but so magnetic up close.

He did not move his fingers from where they brushed her cheek. He did not take his grip from her shoulder. He didn't back off one tiny bit. "You okay?" he asked, his voice quiet and rough.

That was the real question, wasn't it? Being so near to him felt both nice and precarious at the same time. He understood her, accepted things about her other people couldn't hope to understand. And yet she wasn't ready to trust him to keep those things safe and unharmed. "I just lost my balance for a moment." It was true in more ways than one.

"But you're okay?"

"Fine." Her answer came out as more of a squeak than a word.

"Liar." She wasn't anything close to fine, and they both knew it. He took his hand from her cheek, and she felt the loss in more than the rush of cold air against her skin. "I don't…know…what to do here. I'm not sure where this goes, or if it goes anywhere. My balance is sort of…off, too, if you know what I mean."

"I do."

"JJ doesn't want me anywhere near you. Outside of school, that is."

Heather managed a nervous laugh. "She told me I should steer clear of you. That you would try something and I shouldn't fall for it."

He became the little brother just then, embarrassed by his big sister, his smirk disarming. "You fell all by yourself there, kiddo." There was a spot on his own hair where flakes of ice from their scuffle had settled like snow, and she longed to reach out and brush it off. She wondered whether his wavy hair was soft or coarse. He finally broke his gaze and looked down, fiddling with one of the strap buckles on the sled. "I'm still figuring out how all this goes together. I used to be…well, let's just say JJ had good reason to warn you off. I just don't know if all this—" he waved his hand over his legs "—makes it better or worse, or even if it's possible."

"Of course it's possible." She replied so fast it rang like a platitude. Suddenly it felt like both the right answer and the wrong answer. "I mean, you should be—"

"Please." A bit of the edge returned to his voice as he cut her off. "I can't bear to hear the 'full and happy life' speech. Not from you." His bitterness pushed all the warmth from the air between them.

"It's more complicated, but that doesn't make it impossible."

Max eased their sleds apart. "Alex would tell you climbing Mount Everest is complicated but not impossible, but that doesn't mean everyone should do it."

Chapter Nine

Max tried to "go slow," staying away from school for the next two days, not returning until his next meeting with Simon after school Friday. They played one-on-one basketball and talked about the prospects of hockey.

In the parking lot after the game, Simon tried on one of the hockey gloves Max had given him to test. "How'd it happen?"

Max looked up from the sled he was putting into his van. He'd brought it to show Simon, hoping it would further convince him to come play hockey sometime soon. Simon was clearly interested, but with ice, sharp blades and the potential for aggressive play, it was going to be an uphill battle with Mr. Williams. "How'd I get my dashing good looks?"

"No." Simon looked sheepish. "You know…"

Max pushed the sled fully into the van and turned to face Simon. He was surprised it had taken Simon this long to ask. "You mean how'd I get my wheels?"

"Yeah. You haven't ever told me about your accident."

Handing him the other glove of the pair, Max hit the

button that shut the van door. "You haven't asked me. I figured when you wanted to know, you'd ask." He looked at Simon. Once the kid's face grew into those big blue eyes and he grew his hair out a little longer, Simon could swing some serious charm. Despite the shyness, the boy was genuinely curious about things, and that made him a good listener. "It doesn't have to be the first thing everyone knows about you, you know. It's a part of you—a big part—but not all of you."

They wheeled together to the stretch of grass beside the school parking lot. "I always see it in people's eyes, you know?" Simon said. "Like they need to ask but think I'll be upset if they do." He shrugged. "I'm kinda used to my condition—it's not like it's a whole new tragedy or anything."

Whole new tragedy. Max was sick enough of people referring to what happened to him as "a tragedy." What must a lifetime of that feel like? People usually experienced cerebral palsy from birth, so it wasn't as if Simon knew anything different, but still. No one's life should be branded a tragedy. Not anyone who was fifteen, at least. "That's why I like little kids," Max offered. "They just ask you what they want to know, right out."

Simon nodded. "Then their parents get all freaky and shush them."

Max rolled his eyes. "Tell me about it. Happened to me the other day at Karl's. Right in front of Heath... Ms. Browning."

That made Simon's eyes pop. "How do you get into Karl's?"

Like any coffee shop anywhere, Karl's was a favorite high school hangout. It stuck in Max's gut that Simon considered it off-limits. He leaned in toward the boy.

"You ring the bell at the back door and Karl lets you in through the kitchen. Then he gets you the corner table 'cause it's the only place guys like you and I fit. Anybody he has to move gets a free coffee, so everybody wins. You and I should go sometime. I'll show you the ropes."

Simon looked as if that would make his week, much less his day. "Man, I'd like that." He looked down, fiddling with one of the gloves. "So you and Ms. Browning, huh?"

Max was an idiot for thinking it wouldn't come to this at some point. "Well, I don't know yet. We're sort of trying to figure it out."

Simon laughed. "What's to figure out? She's a girl. She's pretty."

"She's the school counselor and I'm kind of here in an official capacity. Plus, things are kind of tricky in the dating department for those of us of the wheeled persuasion." Remembering Luke Sullivan, Max felt compelled to add, "Not impossible, just different." He gave Simon a companionable nudge to the arm of his chair. "So, who do you like?"

Simon actually blushed. Max suddenly felt a hundred years old, all mentor-ish and falsely wise. "Well, there's Bailey."

"Oh, from the Ping-Pong Club, right?"

"Yeah." Simon angled to face Max and moaned, "Only, it's like all she can see is the chair, you know?"

Max put his elbows on his knees, leaning in like a two-man football huddle. "So you gotta show her the great guy *in* the chair. I won't lie to you—it'll take time and some serious charm, but I think you're up to it."

"A guy like you, maybe."

"And a guy like you. Don't count yourself out of the running just because you roll. That's what I always say."

"Are you in the running with Ms. Browning?"

"I should tell you that such a question is none of your business." The statement got the "yeah, right" look from Simon that Max would have expected. "But the truth is I'm trying to keep it strictly official with Ms. Browning for reasons that don't have anything to do with you and me or school."

"Like what?" Simon was not going to let him get away with an avoidance like that.

How could he explain this on a level a fifteen-year-old would understand? Max took the sunglasses off the top of his head and folded them into his shirt pocket just to buy himself time to think. "You, you've been in a chair your whole life, right? None of that is new for you. The high school part is new, but not the chair part. Me, I'm still figuring out the chair part. Everything I thought I wanted from life is a bit different now. Some of it's better, some of it not so much. At first, I thought they were being jerks down at the hospital when they told me not to get into any serious relationships for a year. Now I think maybe that's not such bad advice."

"And you think if you got into it with Ms. Browning, it'd get serious?"

Well, now, that was pretty perceptive for a fifteen-year-old. It *would* get serious—fast—if he "got into it" with Heather. And while he'd tell anyone it was to spare Heather any heartbreak, some still-wounded little part of him was out-and-out terrified it'd be *his* heart lying shredded on the ground when she walked away. "I think that's a question we won't get to answer." Just to change the subject, he pointed at Simon. "Hey, wait a minute.

This was supposed to be the hair-raising story of my spinal cord's untimely demise, not a romance novel. And why don't you already know this one? Didn't you read about me in the papers?"

The boy smirked. "Well, I looked you up on the internet, if that's what you're asking."

"So you know the basics. I let the cameras on *Wide Wild World* get to me and I got stupid. I rappelled down that cliff face a lot faster than I ought to have 'cause I wanted to look cool. I took a lot less care than was smart 'cause I thought I was invincible. The show used gear they weren't supposed to—stuff that hadn't finished going through the testing phases—and the people who ought to have been paying attention weren't. There was a lot of finger-pointing afterward—lots of it by me, to be honest—but none of that matters much now. Plenty of blame to go around, if you know what I'm saying, but my spine didn't really care who whacked it against that scaffold."

"Did it hurt?"

It was the question everyone always asked, which he found funny, since the result of his injury was that he could no longer feel. "Probably. I don't remember the actual fall or any of the next day. I've seen the fall— they had it on tape, since it was TV—but I've only watched it once." That had been a mistake. His doctors had advised against it, but he'd found he couldn't resist once he knew the tape existed. Still, Max would have rather not had that image of his flopping, twisting body burned into his memory like that. It was one of the few things in life he truly regretted. "Not really something I want to relive, you know. But once I was awake and aware of the world again, did it hurt? Not

in the way you'd think. Not the 'ouch' kind of pain."
He thumped a fist to his heart. "Pain comes in more
ways than one, huh?"

"Yeah. I get that." Commiseration darkened Simon's
features, and his eyes flicked down to the gloves for a
moment. "Do you think about it? A lot, I mean?"

"My accident?" Max got the sense that wasn't Simon's real question.

"No, just…do you think…about…like what it would
be like if it never happened?"

Simon wasn't asking how; Simon was asking why.
Big stuff. Max wished Heather were there, thinking she
was better positioned to answer those kinds of questions. Then again, who better than he? He shifted un-
comfortably under the unsettling notion that Simon
hadn't come into his life by accident. "All the time,
buddy. All the time."

Simon looked relieved. Max remembered the fire-
storm of doubts that plagued any teenager, and his heart
twisted for the kid.

"The thing is, everybody thinks like that. Sure, yours
and my what-ifs are a little bigger and more dramatic,
but every single person wonders why things happen the
way they did. Alex wonders why his company crashed
the way it did. Melba Bradens wonders why her dad
got so sick. JJ wonders why some people died over in
Afghanistan and others came away fine." He felt way
out of his depth when the notion came to him to add,
"It's why people go to church. To figure that stuff out."

"I haven't seen you in church other than the funeral.
Do you go?"

JJ would be snickering right now if she were there.
Just the other night she'd tried the ploy of "Simon is

looking up to you" to get him back to church. Max hedged. "Not as much as I should."

Simon took on a mischievous smile. "Our youth group has a Friends Night next week. You should come."

Max was glad to have a way to dodge that one. "Do I look like a high school student to you?"

Simon's smile turned smug. "It's not for students. We're supposed to bring an adult we admire." The kid's eyes fairly proclaimed, *Back out of that one—I dare you.*

Nailed. JJ would howl with laughter when he told her. "You'll be sorry when I steal all your dates."

"Ha! Not a chance." A car horn sounded from the parking lot. "Mom's here. I'll text you the info."

"Show her the gloves," Max called as Simon wheeled toward the opening van door. "And the website I told you about."

Simon gave Max a thumbs-up as he spun his chair onto the van ramp. The kid had the most irresistible smile. Who knew the scrawny little nerd would get to him like that?

Heather's heart did an unsettling little flip when Max's number came up on her desk phone. They'd both stuck strictly to email since that afternoon at the ice rink, although he'd taken to suggesting several ideas for Simon and forwarding articles he'd found at work. Did he realize how invested he'd become in Simon?

Did he have any idea how much his investment charmed her? Heather had tried so hard not to like Max Jones, and he'd managed to tear down every objection she had. More than once in her prayer journal,

Max's name had been written down under the things for which she gave thanks.

She smiled as she held the receiver to her ear. "Hi there, Max."

"You've gotta help me. I don't know how to get out of this one."

The possible circumstances of Max Jones in trouble was a pretty wide world. "Out of what?"

"Youth group."

That sounded like a good story. Heather leaned back in her chair, wrapping the handset's cord around her finger. "I'll need more details than that to offer assistance." The Williamses went to GFCC just like she did, so she could guess what all this was about. She was even an adviser to the youth group. Still, she wanted to hear Max's explanation.

"Evidently there's this thing at church where kids bring friends. Adult friends. Simon sort of invited me."

Heather felt herself smile. "Congratulations. It's a big honor to be invited to Friends Night at GFCC."

There was a pause on the other end of the line. "This isn't really my thing. I don't...you know...*go* to church."

He really was worked up about it. "JJ said you used to."

"I also used to drink chocolate milk, but I don't do that anymore since my voice changed." Another pause. "I don't want to let Simon think I'm something I'm not."

"It's Friends Night, Max, not Deep Spiritual Advisers night. There isn't a test at the end. There's cake, if I remember correctly." After a second, she softened her voice to add, "You should go."

No reply.

"It'd be good for both of you." Heather sat up to lean

on her desk. "You still believe in God, don't you?" Because that sounded like such a loaded question, she added, "You haven't gone off and joined some kind of creepy cult that lures in impressionable young men in wheelchairs?"

The tone of his voice changed. "Well, yeah. I mean the God part, not the creepy-cult part. I just… Look, I don't think I'm the churchy Friends Night type. I'll look…dumb. They probably all wear sweater vests and do crosswords and knitting."

She was sure Max was kidding. Mostly. "Max, your sister and brother-in-law go to that church. I go to that church. All three of us have been invited to Friends Night at one time or another, and there's not a crossword or a sweater vest among us. Although there is some knitting—which reminds me, can you meet me at the church on Tuesday at ten? There's someone I'd like you to meet. And she's *definitely* not whatever it is you think 'church ladies' are like."

"That sounds like institutionalist propaganda to me." The edge was finally gone from his voice.

"I'll buy you pie afterward. At Karl's. If you survive the trauma, that is. I'm pretty sure one of the kids invited Violet to Friends Night, so now after this you'll know someone else."

"And if I hate it?"

No one in Gordon Falls hated Violet Sharpton. It wasn't humanly possible. "If you hate it—which you won't—I'll help you get out of Friends Night with Simon. Deal?"

"Ms. Browning, you drive a hard bargain."

"And you drive a minivan with a flame paint job."

It was fun to banter with him. She hadn't felt this play-ful in a long time.

"Don't you call my wicked-cool Honda a minivan."

"Goodbye, Max."

"So long, counselor. Keep those teen herds of rag-ing hormones in line."

He signed off, and she laughed. She was beginning to really enjoy the continual surprise that was Max Jones.

Chapter Ten

Max didn't make it to the church until ten-fifteen. He wasn't in a rush to meet whoever it was Heather thought he ought to meet. Just outside the church door, Max tried one last stalling tactic. "This is a dumb idea."

Heather and Melba Bradens—Heather had evidently brought reinforcements so he'd be outnumbered—crossed their hands over their chests like a pair of clucking mothers. "No, it's not. It's sweet," Heather said.

"It'd be fun for the knitters to meet you. And besides, I've had a lousy eight days, so you have to humor me." Melba yanked the door open. "Griever's choice." She walked through the doors.

Max looked at Heather. "Did she really just say 'griever's choice'?"

Heather cocked her head to one side. "Just humor her, okay? The way I hear it, you used to be the kind of guy who rushed into a room full of women."

"Ladies' night on Rush Street is one thing. The old ladies' church knitting circle is quite another."

"Melba's invited JJ and me to join," Heather teased. "We're not old ladies."

JJ had mentioned something about learning to knit. Max had visions of chunky ski hats in scary colors and scarves that itched. Still, he had to admit the black-with-flames prayer-blanket thing this group had made him was pretty cool. Regardless, Max was sure he was rolling into one of the most regrettable hours of his life.

"Ladies, I want you to meet Max Jones."

A chorus of hellos greeted him from a circle of women—remarkably, not all of them old and quite a few he recognized—sitting in the church parlor and knitting.

"Max Jones. Hot Wheels—isn't that what they call you?" A sparkly-eyed older woman he vaguely recognized aimed a pointy stick at him. "I knit your prayer shawl, honey. Had fun with it, too. Only I don't suppose you call it a shawl, now, do you?"

"I don't call it much of anything," he replied, liking her immediately despite his earlier resistance. "Except maybe warm and fuzzy."

"Violet did an amazing job, didn't she?"

"Warm and fuzzy but black with flames," she boasted. "That was a pretty tall order." He wheeled over and offered her a handshake, pleased when she didn't hesitate for a moment. "Violet Sharpton. I'm afraid I don't have a nifty nickname like yourself, but Violet's done me right all these years, so I can't complain." Violet winked at Melba. "You weren't kidding. He really is a looker."

Max withdrew his hand and decided maybe this was a dumb idea after all. "Thanks. I mean for the blanket thing. It matches my car and everything."

"Hard to miss that car," said a slightly younger woman Max remembered seeing around the firehouse.

"Chad's made a few jokes about needing to douse it." The remark told him that must be Jeannie Owens, the fire marshal's wife, who ran the candy shop. More than a few baskets of her sweets had ended up in his hospital room.

"I'm rather surprised you came back to Gordon Falls, son." The oldest of the group eyed him over her glasses. "Kind of quiet for the likes of you, isn't it?"

"JJ and Alex are here. My job is nearby. There wasn't a reason to leave." Max dared a quick look at Heather. "Besides, the people are nice."

His quick glance did not go unnoticed. The old lady darted her eyes back and forth between Heather and Max, making a host of assumptions that showed on her face. "So they are."

"Stop it, Marge," Violet chimed in, swatting the assuming lady's hand. She returned her attention to Max, still boasting a knowing smile. "Marge and I got free coffee off of you two coming into Karl's the other day." She turned to the group. "Did you know Karl gives you a free drink if he has to move you so Max can have the corner table?"

Another woman looked up from her knitting. "Why don't we all go over to Karl's after this, sit in the corner table and then Max can come in? We'll all get free coffee."

Jeannie Owens laughed. "That's our Tina. Always looking for a bargain."

These weren't like any old knitting ladies in rocking chairs Max had ever met. "I don't think it works that way. Since I owe you, however, how about I bring you a pie one of these days? A payment for the blanket."

"Oh, we don't accept payment," Marge said. "And I

saw in a magazine that it can be called a 'throw.'" Her eyes lit up. "Hey, that means it's a 'flame throw.' Isn't there something called a flame throw?"

Jeannie, who had barely stopped, erupted into laughter again. "That's a flamethrow*er*, Marge. If you had a teenage son with a video-game system, you'd know these kinds of things."

Violet nudged Marge in the elbow. "There is a handsome man offering to bring us pie and you're discouraging him? Did you take your pills this morning?"

"You here to learn to knit?" Tina looked a bit too pleased at the prospect.

Thankfully, Melba stepped in. "I just wanted to make sure you got to meet Max and he got to meet you." She looked at Max. "We don't always get to meet the recipients of our prayer shawls, and you have to admit, yours was pretty special."

"JJ loves hers," Max felt compelled to offer. "My mom, too. It was a really nice thing to do."

"You're a really nice young man for saying so," Violet said. "If you'd like to learn, come in anytime. Melba taught most of us, so we like beginners."

Max didn't think his image could withstand the addition of yarn and needles. "I think I'll stick to bringing you pie."

"Maybe we can start up a club at the high school," Heather offered.

"We can look into it," Melba said. After a second, she added, "I need a new project."

Violet immediately wrapped Melba in a giant hug. "Oh, we know you do, dear. How are you holding up?"

"I'm okay," Melba said, sinking down onto the couch and grabbing a tissue from the box on the coffee table.

Heather caught Max's eye. "How about Max and I get going and leave you to the yarn and such?"

Melba looked up from dabbing her eyes. "Thanks for stopping in. Heather, I mean it about you joining."

"Once summer comes, I'm yours. You only got me this morning because parent-teacher conferences are tomorrow." She picked her handbag up off the chair where she'd laid it to run her hands through the pile of fluffy shawls. "These aren't hard to make, really?"

"Not unless you want one like Max's. The ordinary ones are just knit and purl, and even my granddaughter has learned how to do that much."

"Thanks again, ladies." Max was surprised to find out how much he truly meant it. He'd never met people this warm and friendly in the city. For all the architectural obstacles it threw in his way, Gordon Falls was worth the effort.

As Max chuckled and turned out the door, Violet called, "See you around, Hot Wheels!" He heard her voice continue from the room behind him as the door closed. "Hot Wheels. It's just too much fun to say that. I think I want a nickname."

"Violet will be there for Friends Night. She's been invited to every one, I think," Heather offered as she and Max left the church building. "She's a fabulous role model for the kids."

Max cast a glance back at the church door. "She's certainly not like any grandmother I've ever met. That's one spunky lady."

"She reminds me a lot of my Grannie Annie. Only Grannie Annie was a little softer around the edges. More the home-baked-cookies, cuddle-on-the-couch type rather than Violet's brand of high-voltage." She raised an eyebrow at Max. "You two might become great friends, you know. She's got a bit of the rebel in her, and she's taken to you—that's for sure." Max got an odd look on his face at that remark. "What?"

He brushed her concern off, busying himself with something on one of his wheels.

Heather stepped in front of him. "No, really, Max, what? Did I say something wrong?"

"No. It's not that. It's just...well, you're gonna think this is stupid. Only I can't help looking at Violet and wondering how I might have turned out with someone like her in my life. Mom didn't know what to do with me. Dad just found me disappointing. And my grandma? She was too irritated with the rest of the world to even pay attention. I don't know why I just invited myself to such an all-out pity party, but..."

It made so much sense. Max would hardly be the first person to develop an over-the-top personality just because it was the only way to get anyone in his family to notice him. JJ hadn't ever talked about her family much, only how her father's military career made it hard for him to understand JJ's difficulties serving in combat. "Your dad was quite the commander, wasn't he?"

He started heading for his car again. "We didn't call him 'General Jones' for nothing. I wore my hair long in high school just because it drove him nuts. To say we didn't get along would be putting it mildly."

"That's why you care so much about the way Simon's father treats him, isn't it?"

That earned her a sharp look. "You're not going all counselor on me now, are you? I've got a menu of shrinks to choose from back at rehab. I'm not in the market for more."

She put a hand on Max's shoulder. "It's not bad that you care about Simon. I'm really glad that you do. Kids pick up on that kind of thing instantly—they know if you really care or if you're just going through the motions. I'm sorry you didn't have a Violet or a Grannie Annie in your life, but don't you think it's amazing that you get to be that for someone like Simon?"

She could almost watch his defenses rise up to cover the deep truth of those words. "I'm no Violet Sharpton." He sloughed off her comments, hitting the remote button that opened his car doors. "Don't blow this up into more than it is."

"You're more like her than you know, Max. I'd have never believed this at first, but I think you're just what Simon needs—most of the time." She still wasn't convinced Max wouldn't go a step too far one of these days. Then again, how many times had Violet done something that made everyone groan? And still, there wasn't a single person in Gordon Falls who didn't love her or want her around when things got tough. Max had that gift. There was something deeply enthralling about how he hurled himself into the world. He just hadn't tempered it with much wisdom yet. With time, would he?

She couldn't answer that question, and that jolted a small wave of panic through her chest. Max Jones was exciting and energizing to be with, but that unfocused energy also made him dangerous. As Max's smile made her heart flutter a bit, Heather knew the danger wasn't just for Simon. He ran his hand over hers for just a second before he got into his car, and the tingle told Heather just how much she'd begun to fall for Max Jones. *Oh, Lord, guard my heart. This is either going to be wonderful or awful, and I'm scared already.*

Chapter Eleven

Max was spending a quiet Wednesday night trying not to think of Heather Browning, previewing a new Adventure Access video and going over some of JJ's files from the cabin-rental business when his cell phone went off. He flipped it over and pushed the speaker-phone button when he saw Simon Williams's name on the screen. "Hey, Simon, what's up?"

"I hate him!"

"Slow down there, big guy—hate who?"

"Who do you think?" Simon's voice was a tsunami of teenage anger. "I hate him like I've never hated anything."

Max picked up the phone and switched off the speaker function. "You mean your dad?"

"He treats me like I'm a total baby. It's so embarrassing."

"You're fifteen. Your parents are supposed to be embarrassing when you're fifteen." Max had the disturbing thought that JJ would be fainting to hear him offer such advice. Dad and he had been about as compatible as snowballs and campfires in high school.

"I thought you'd understand!"

The accusation stung. He did understand. He was supposed to be the one guy who *could* understand. "No, I get it. I do. Where are you?"

"I'm in your driveway. By your car."

It was almost nine o'clock at night on a Wednesday. "You're here? For crying out loud, why didn't you just come to the door?"

"I couldn't figure out which cabin was yours." Max could believe it. Simon sounded mixed-up enough to not know his left from his right.

"Look for the ramp. It's the one right in front of you as you leave the parking lot. Number Four. I'll throw the porch light on for you." Max ended the call, tossed the phone into his lap and wheeled toward the door. He snapped on the light and pulled the door open to find a red-eyed, scowling Simon.

"Hi."

Max pushed back to give Simon room to come in. "Hi yourself. How'd you get here?"

"I walked." He managed a sour smile. "Well, you know. It's not that far and mostly downhill."

"I can't believe I'm playing the grown-up here, but do your folks know where you are?"

"I hope they don't. They're at school, at parent-teacher conferences." His eyes narrowed to angry slits. "They got me a sitter."

"A what?"

"Someone to stay with me so they could both go to the conferences. I'm fifteen years old and they hired a babysitter. Can you believe it?"

Max didn't know what to think, except that said sitter, whoever he or she was, was likely calling the high school in hysterical fits right about now. He was going to have to handle this very carefully. "How'd you sneak out?"

"Candace was so engrossed on her phone it wasn't hard. She's not too bright, so I left the door open just to drop a hint."

Max nodded toward the kitchen. "Want a soda while we talk this though?"

"Sure."

Max chose his words carefully as he reached into the fridge. "I agree the sitter was lame, but she and your parents are probably freaking out right about now, don't you think?"

Simon softened a bit. "I s'pose."

"So." Max slid a soda across the kitchen table to the boy. "How about I call Heather and she can go find your mom and dad at school and talk them down off the ledge? Otherwise, I expect we'll be hearing police sirens roaming through town in ten minutes. She can hold them off for a bit while you and I figure out your next step. Sound like a plan you can live with?"

"Okay."

Max punched in the listing for Heather's cell. She picked up after half a ring, her voice tight with panic. "Max? Do you—"

He didn't let her endure another second of worry. "It's okay," he cut in. "Simon is here. He's safe, just mad." He thought Simon had some good justification, but now wasn't the time to get into that. "He just showed up at my door about five minutes ago."

"Oh, thank goodness." He could hear shouting in the background as Heather turned her voice from the phone to address what had to be Mr. and Mrs. Williams. "He's safe—we know where he is." A woman began to cry.

"You've got to buy me twenty minutes, okay? Simon and I need to talk this through."

Mr. Williams's voice bellowed, "Where is he?" over Heather's line.

"Max, I—" she cautioned.

"The kid needs someone to listen to him, Heather. And that won't be Mom and Dad right now. You know that. Just do what you can and I'll call you back as soon as the air is clear." He ended the call before she could say anything else. If she succeeded, he might stand a chance of keeping Simon from boiling over. If she failed, Simon's parents would be breaking down his door in five minutes anyway.

Max wheeled over to the table, flipping the pop tab on his own soda with what he hoped looked like calm. "I bought you as much time as I could, Simon, but it isn't much. Why don't you tell me what's been going on?"

"They treat me like I'm five. I could be driving next year, but they don't even let me alone yet. Worst of all, this time they hired a *girl from school* to come stay with me. A junior, even. This'll be all over school by second period tomorrow. You know it will." Simon let his head drop into one hand. "I'll never live this down."

Max took a swig of his soda to buy himself time to craft a calm answer. What Simon described would have been social homicide back in his day, and he didn't think that much had changed about high school. "Was she cute?"

Simon looked up. "You're kidding me."

"Just looking for the silver lining here. Was she cute?

Did she know she was essentially babysitting?" Max hoped Simon's parents were smart enough to call it something else, but it wasn't likely.

"She was okay. She made a half-baked attempt at getting math tutoring from me, but she found her phone a lot more interesting, if you know what I mean."

"Tutoring, huh? Simon, there might be a way to salvage this. A freshman guy tutoring a junior girl is a pretty good gig. Your mom and dad would have been smarter to work this out with you ahead of time, but there's a chance we can keep this from disaster. What did you say her name was?"

"Candace Norden."

"Do you know her cell number?"

Simon rolled his eyes. "Do I look like the kind of guy who can get a junior cheerleader's phone number?"

"Then we'd better pull Heather in on this. Okay if I call Ms. Browning again?"

"Do I have to talk to my parents?"

Max sighed. "Not yet if you don't want to. But if we want Candace's cooperation on this, we ought to let her know you slipped out on her and that you're okay. If we can get everyone to agree on the story that you were tutoring her, I think we can save this. Although it could mean you might actually have to tutor her, so it helps that she's cute and a cheerleader, right?"

Simon shot Max a "you don't really think this is gonna work?" look, but he nodded.

Heather again picked up right away. Max gave a quick account of the situation and his plan to rescue Simon's social standing. Heather agreed it was worth a shot and got Candace's cell-phone number from Simon's parents, who seemed to have calmed down a little but not enough. At least they weren't breaking down his door. "Try to give me thirty minutes, Heather. See if you can get them to agree to work with Simon instead of stuffing bad plans down his throat."

As soon as he hung up with Heather, Max dialed Candace. He put on his most charming tone of voice, the one that had broken hearts back in the day. "Hey, is this Candace?"

"Who are you? Do you know where Simon Williams is?" She sounded upset, and Max took that as a good thing.

"This is Max Jones. Simon's right here, Candace. Things have gone a little haywire tonight, and I'm trying to sort it all out. Do you have a car?"

"Yeah."

"Simon is at my house. I live at the Gordon Cottages down by the river. Number Four. Can you meet Simon and me here so I can explain? It's okay—his parents know he's here now and you can call Ms. Browning at the school if you want her to confirm everything."

"No, it's okay. You're the other guy in a wheelchair, right? I know who you are. Give me ten minutes. Simon's okay and everything, right?"

"He's fine. And make it five if you can." Max hung up the phone and looked at Simon. "You know, I remember a time when *you* were 'the other guy in a wheelchair.' Now it's me. And she's worried about you. This might actually work out."

"I don't see how it can."

"It's simple. We charm Candace into agreeing that she was there tonight for math tutoring, which will probably involve you helping her score at least a B on her next test. Then we tackle the hard part of enlight-

ening your folks that there might be less socially de-
structive ways of handling this stuff. Then you agree
not to go AWOL like that again. It was understandable
but totally counterproductive. You do know what—"

"I know what *counterproductive* means," Simon cut
in. "But I was so mad. How could they possibly think
that was okay?"

"They're parents. High school freaks parents out.
And your parents? Well, they seem especially…freak-
able."

"You've got that right."

Max offered a smile. "Go hit the bathroom and wash
your face. There's a girl coming over soon."

Two long hours later, Heather stood on Max's porch,
waving goodbye to the Williams family as they headed
home after a difficult evening for everyone. She turned
her eyes to Max, who looked equally exhausted. "What
a night. At least they were speaking to each other when
they left."

"I feel for that kid. He's got a long battle to become
his own person." Max looked up at her. "Do you think
they understood him at all tonight?"

She leaned against one of the porch railings. "I want
to think they did. Her more than him, I think. Usually
it's the moms who can't ease up on the supervision, but
it seems to be Brian who's the hoverer in that family."

"Firefighters tend to have a wide protective streak
in them. JJ babied me a bit at first after my accident,
and she's not even my mom." Max rolled his shoulders,
looking weary from the intense conversation they'd all
just had. "I'd forgotten how brutal high school can be.
I sure hope this works. Simon is right—if this got out,

he'd never live it down. I can't believe they don't feel like they can leave him alone. He's fifteen and pretty capable."

"Maybe after tonight they'll start figuring out how to give him some freedom. But he's going to have to keep from pulling another disappearing act." She walked over to Max. "Thank you for saving the day."

Max rubbed his neck. "I'm not sure I saved anything yet."

"You persuaded Candace to help out. You got them talking to each other about what Simon needs. That's huge."

"Yeah, but you're the one who kept them from shouting at each other. And me. Well, mostly."

Some shouting had definitely taken place. Brian Williams had harbored suspicions that Max had put Simon up to his escape, but Heather had managed to convince him that wasn't true. "You're a good man, Max Jones. Do you know that?"

"Don't kid yourself."

"I think God knew what He was doing when He put you in Simon's life. He cut off my access to the other mentor because He knew you were the man who would understand and bond with Simon."

Max flung his hands wide. "I'm the only other guy in a chair for miles. There's no grand design here, Heather."

Had life shaken his faith that far? She'd thought she'd seen more than this dismissal back at Mort Wingate's funeral. "You can't really mean that. You can't tell me you don't believe God spared you, or that He spared you for no good reason."

Max swiveled away from her. "Most days I don't

think God spared me much of anything. I hear all the stuff JJ says to me, but I can't really swallow God loving me enough to snap my spine."

She'd never heard such dark words from him. "So you've no faith? None at all? Even after something like tonight happens?" She hadn't realized until tonight how much she was yearning to take things further with Max. He'd been a dangerous prospect before, but the way he'd talked to her after the funeral told her there was so much more running under the flashy exterior. Without faith—or a hope of faith—she couldn't begin to risk it.

He must have heard the catch in her voice, for he turned back to face her. "I don't know if it's gone or jumbled or what. I know I could have—maybe *should* have—died when I fell. I know my accident brought Alex and JJ together, and I see all the good that's come out of it. I'm glad I can help Simon. But..."

"But what?"

Such a shadow of pain crossed Max's eyes that Heather felt it like a slash to her chest. "But I'm still broken."

Heather came down onto her knees in front of him. "Oh, Max, we're all broken. You, me, Simon, the Williamses—all of us."

"I know there's a part of you that thinks I'm the same as any other man, Heather, but it's a load of—"

She grabbed his hand and shook it. "You're *not* the same as any other man. No other man could have done what you did tonight with Simon. Could you have done what you did tonight, what you've done all month, before you fell?"

He pulled back away from her. "I wouldn't have *had* to do any of this if I hadn't fallen. Can't you see that?

I'm not you. I'm still angry. I'm angry at God for letting any of it happen at all, even if JJ got Alex out of it. 'Cause you know what? I'm selfish enough to wish it all hadn't happened. I hate that it happened. I don't want to make the best of it. I want to walk. There. I said it. Are you happy?"

Heather sank down to sit on the porch, wounded. JJ was right: Max still really was "too much of a mess to mess with." She wanted to shout *No!* in answer to his question, but the word couldn't find its way beyond the massive lump in her throat.

Her silence seemed to break his anger, and he covered his face with one hand. "I'm…sorry. That wasn't fair. I didn't mean to hurt you." He slammed his hand on the porch rail next to him. "Hurting you is the absolute last thing I want to do."

"Faith doesn't deny pain exists. Pain—and your pain is huge and real—means that you need faith just to keep going."

"How do you do it?" There was a seeking desperation in his voice.

"I don't. I can't. I just beg God to do it in me, for me, because I'm still a mess on the inside. It just shows less with me. Only you can still see it. I know you can."

The Max she'd first met had looked as if he could do anything. The Max who stared back at her now looked as if faith was far out of his reach. If she knew anything, she knew that wasn't true. "I'm not as strong as you think I am, Max."

"Sure you are." His voice held a sad resignation. "You're amazing."

Heather didn't know where the courage to do so came from, but she grabbed the footrest of his chair and pulled it toward her. "I mean I'm not strong enough to do this without faith. I've got mine, but I need to know you've got yours." He kept his hands on the wheels at first, not letting her pull, but then slowly let go.

"I don't know where mine went." All his famous bravado left him, and Heather's heart cracked open.

She pulled him closer. "So let's go look for it. You and me. Because I don't think God dropped you, Max Jones. I think He caught you just in time."

He looked at her for a long, soft moment. She could see him fighting the shadows of doubt, feel the man he was wrestle with the man he could be. She was shaking inside, deeply scared, but she would not allow herself to back away or break his gaze.

He brought one hand to her face, trailing the curve of her cheek with the same tenderness he had at the ice rink. She felt the same swirling sensation, her hands clutching the front rails of his chair to keep her balance. Without a word, he moved to hold her face in both hands, looking down at her with a powerful air of wonder. The whole world held its breath as she rose up to meet his kiss.

Max was light and careful, as if the kiss were stolen rather than freely given. Yet the way the kiss made her feel was anything but light; it was deep and daring in a way Heather had not thought she could experience. She'd tried to tell herself Max was troubled and cocky and careless, but her heart refused to accept that outer shell as truth. The Max she could see underneath was also strong and seeking and full of courage. God could do amazing things with Max if he would only let Him back in all the places he'd shut Him out.

She sent her hands sliding up his arms as he wrapped

one hand around her waist. The kiss was perfection, tender, passionate, exquisitely slow. She let one hand wander into his hair, marveling at the touch of it.

His sigh rumbled low and smooth like his car engine. "Whoa," he said, pulling her hand from his hair. "You'd better not do that."

She smiled. "I've wanted to touch your hair for days."

He took her hands and placed them on his chair's armrests. "Ms. Browning—" he cleared his throat in a mock-professional manner "—every male of the species has a weak spot. A place where if you touch them just the right way, they can't even think straight."

Her grin widened.

"Now you know mine. Be careful with such powerful knowledge."

She flushed at the sparkle in his eyes. "Does that mean I have to tell you mine?"

Now his eyes fairly smoldered. "I think I already know." With that, he reached out and feathered her cheek again, producing such a head-spinning sensation that Heather had to fight to keep her eyes open. "I promise not to use it against you."

With a slippery, falling feeling, Heather realized she wished he would.

Chapter Twelve

Mrs. Williams hadn't gotten any more sleep than Heather had, and she looked it. There had been a message waiting on Heather's voice mail, time-stamped just after dawn, asking for a meeting. "Just you and me. I thought we ought to talk," Mrs. Williams had said in a soft and weary voice.

"How are things with Simon?" Heather gestured toward the guest chair in her office.

"Difficult." She chose the word with care.

"If teenagers are anything, it's difficult." Heather came around to pull up the second guest chair so that they could sit side by side with no formal desk between them. "If it makes you feel any better, I thought last night ended well, considering the circumstances. I've seen much, much worse over much, much less."

"Simon's never done anything like that, ever." Hurt coated her words.

"He's finding his way in a new, wider world. They make lots of mistakes at this age. Did he talk to you this morning?"

Mrs. Williams winced. "Barely."

"Sometimes 'barely' is all you get with boys his age. It's a rough ride, but if you can just keep the communication flowing, I know you'll get through it. Simon is an amazing young man. He copes with things other kids his age couldn't handle, and he's making good choices." Given last night's escapades, she felt compelled to add, "Mostly." She put a hand on Mrs. Williams's arm. "What can I do to help you?"

The woman looked as if she had rehearsed these questions since dawn. "What kind of man is Max Jones, really? And how much influence does he have over my Simon?"

Heather sighed. "I know you have reservations about Mr. Jones. He certainly has his share of faults. But you ought to know that I think Max was a large part of why last night wasn't a disaster."

Mrs. Williams ran one hand through her hair. "I don't think Brian sees it that way."

"I wouldn't expect him to. Simon has been trying on a lot of new independence since he met Max, and I'm sure that hasn't been comfortable for you and your husband. Only—" Heather leaned in "—I think it's really important for someone Simon's age to have another adult—one that isn't Mom or Dad—to turn to. Simon needs someone who understands what life is like in a wheelchair, and I can't help him with that. None of the teachers here can."

Mrs. Williams's expression softened a bit. Heather's heart twisted for the woman—she couldn't even begin to imagine the strain of parenting someone like Simon. She'd seen what her personal trauma—minor and fleeting compared to Simon's—had done to her own parents.

"You're doing an outstanding job with Simon—please believe that. Last night only proves he's a normal teenager, not that you are faulty parents."

She managed a weak smile. "Thank you."

"So, hopefully, you can see why I'm really grateful Simon has Max. Try to see it as a good thing that Simon went to Max last night. Try to be grateful Max helped your son when Simon was angry enough to make a choice we all might be regretting this morning."

Mrs. Williams bit her lip. "Simon idolizes Max. He'd do whatever Max told him to do. I'm sure you can see how unnerving that is for us. Max seems so—" she looked for a polite term for what Heather knew she was thinking "—wild. The car, the hair, the risky sports…" She finally gave up and blurted out, "We don't want Simon to end up like that."

Heather folded her hands. It was going to take a little work to keep her personal opinion out of this professional conversation. "Max hasn't let his limitations stop him from doing anything he sets his mind to. These are good things. They're things I know you want Simon to learn. Sure, he's a bit…outrageous, but that's because he thinks for himself and isn't afraid to be different. That's the most important value Simon can learn, and I don't think it will mean Simon will become someone who doesn't hold the values you've taught him. In short, Mrs. Williams, I think you can trust Max Jones. He's earned my trust and Simon's, and if you give him a chance, I believe he'll earn yours."

"Well…" She stood up to leave, still not looking especially convinced. In fact, her expression told Heather she was sure trusting Max Jones would lead to a Simon with ripped jeans, spiked hair and an adaptive motor-cycle—if such a thing even existed.

Heather stood up, as well. "May I suggest something?"

"Yes."

"Try not to let last night limit the time Simon and Max spend together in the next week or so. Simon's going to need to talk through what happened, what he felt and the choices everyone made. The more he understands his own feelings, the better he'll be able to tell you what he needs and wants. A little more communication will go a long way to keeping stunts like last night from happening again." She touched Mrs. Williams's elbow and offered her a warm smile. "Although he *is* a teenage boy. I can guarantee you it won't all be smooth sailing. I have high hopes for Simon, and I think you should, too. Even with last night's drama."

"I'm glad you think so." She turned to leave. The slump of her shoulders left Heather wondering if she'd been remotely successful in comforting this poor parent.

"Please keep in touch. Any questions at all, I'm available. And I'll let you know if I see anything that concerns me."

"Thank you." With a small nod, Mrs. Williams left the administrative offices. Heather would have liked it better if she hadn't clutched her handbag so tightly as she walked down the hall, but she couldn't really fault Mrs. Williams. Parenting in high school was a harrowing business—mostly because being in high school was a harrowing business. She knew that better than anyone.

Margot Thomas stood in her doorway and waved Heather inside. "I heard."

Heather put a hand to her forehead as she walked into Margot's office. "Rough stuff all around. I think everyone's okay, though."

Margot sat down on her desk. "Did you see this coming?"

Collapsing into Margot's guest chair, Heather replied, "Yes and no. I figured Simon would eventually do something to brandish his independence, but not this soon. To be honest, I'm just a bit thankful it wasn't something on school grounds, where Simon's parents could project the blame on us. Everyone could have behaved better, but there's a part of me that can't blame Simon for pushing back against a babysitter at his age."

"Did he really get all the way from his house to Jones's cottages by himself?"

"Evidently it's not that far and all downhill." Heather smirked. "Who knew?" She felt her smirk dissolve into a weary sigh. "I'm just so glad Max was there for him."

Margot leaned back in her chair. "Heather, I want you to understand that I'm speaking as your friend, not your principal, when I ask, just what is your relationship with Max Jones?"

Heather held the woman's eyes for a moment, unsure of her own answer.

"I couldn't help but notice that your admiration of him seemed to go beyond the professional."

Heather gripped the chair arms. "I…"

Margot raised a hand "Hang on—I'm not saying that's bad. Neither of you have done anything wrong. I'm just saying we might need to take a little extra care here. You just made some pretty big promises on

Jones's behalf to Mrs. Williams, and I just want to make sure you spoke as a counselor, not a young woman who's spent a lot of time with a very charismatic man." The older woman's words were cautious, but her eyes held a mother's twinkle. Margot had stopped just short of setting Heather up on several dates over the past two years.

"I do trust Max. I do think he's good for Simon. And I do think Mrs. Williams can trust him."

Margot took her glasses off. "Why?"

"I thought you said you heard what I said. I think Max is making the most of his life despite what's happened to him. I think he represents all kinds of possibilities to Simon right now, and that's a good thing. And okay, yes, I think Simon's parents need to learn to loosen up a bit, and Max can show Simon how to help that happen. In ways that don't involve sneaking out and rolling across town."

Margot didn't reply, but her eyes narrowed to say she didn't entirely agree.

"What?"

"I'm not so sure that was the counselor talking. A counselor might be pushing for moderation, for small steps of independence that can build trust and bringing in someone that would be a slam dunk for parental approval. That does not describe Max Jones."

"No, he's not the obvious choice, but Simon needs someone daring."

Margot leaned in. "Does Simon? Or do you?"

JJ poked her head through a life ring labeled Jones River Sports. "Max Jones saves the day. Never thought I'd hear that." Max and JJ were storing some of the warm-season gear away for the winter after he got home from work Thursday night.

Max fastened the straps on another life jacket and tossed it into the wire bin at the back of his storage shed. "Where'd you hear such nonsense, anyway?"

"Brian Williams."

Max spun around. "Brian Williams said that?"

"Well," JJ amended, "Brian Williams explained a situation that could be interpreted as you saving the day. I don't think he shared the view. He doesn't like you very much, actually. Some part of him still thinks you put Simon up to his escape."

"I didn't." Max deposited the last life jacket from JJ and shut the bin's lid. "But I can't say I wouldn't have done the same in his place. A babysitter? At his age?"

JJ started bringing oars in off the dock. "Brian never leaves Simon alone. Never has, from what I gather. It's a bit over-the-top, but can you blame him?"

Max grabbed the oars out of JJ's hands. "As a matter of fact, I can. They're smothering him. Next time he's going to have to do something twice as dramatic to pull free, and who knows what'll happen?"

JJ upended a bucket and sat down on it. "What really happened last night?"

"You just told me you knew the whole story." Max slid the oars into a barrel.

"I mean after Simon left. There's something you aren't telling me."

Max looked JJ square in the eye. "None of your business."

"It *is* my business if it has to do with you and my friend. Heather looked just like you do now." She wiped her hands off on a nearby towel and tightened her ponytail elastic. "Look, I know I said I wasn't for you two getting into it, but come on—something is going on. It's obvious."

JJ was military. Trying to keep secrets from her was about as effective as the huge green flood doors that sat at the end of town—they worked for a while but eventually things seeped through the cracks. "I like her. And if last night's kiss was any indication, I think she likes me. I asked her out to dinner tomorrow night. So, yes, something is going on."

JJ's eyes popped at his blatant disclosure of facts. "You kissed her?"

"Actually, I think she kissed me. But it turned entirely mutual very quickly. And close your mouth, sis. It's not like I'm twelve."

"Heather kissed you? First?" Her shock was rather annoying.

Max headed for the door. "See, this is why I didn't want to tell you." An oar landed in the doorway to block his path. "Cut that out. You're not getting any more details. I'll try to behave myself, if that's what you're worried about." He angled to face her. "Believe it or not, I'd actually like to do right by the woman this time. If that's okay by you."

JJ looked satisfyingly aghast. "Yeah, I suppose."

"Why don't you just try to be happy for me? I may have just cleaned up my act, after all. Stranger things have happened."

JJ sat back against the wall, squinting at him as if he was a puzzle she couldn't quite solve. "I was just thinking the same thing." She pulled the blocking oar toward her, her expression softening. "She could be really good for you, Max. And you might just be good for her. Don't mess this one up. Not this one."

"No," Max said, holding her gaze. "Not this one."

Chapter Thirteen

$\sim$

Max could not remember the last time he was this nervous. An actual date. Was he ready for this? Did he even know how to do this? *You used to be fantastic at this,* he told his reflection in the rearview mirror as he pulled up to Heather's apartment Friday night. *This is just fantastic Max on wheels, remember?*

It wasn't true. No matter how he tried to talk himself out of it, Heather wasn't just any girl. Something in him had come completely unwound when he'd kissed her, something he wasn't quite ready to let loose. *Imagine that—me not ready to let loose on something.* He ran his hands through his hair one last time. *Get a grip, Jones. You used to be so much smoother than this.*

He pulled up Heather's number on his cell phone and called.

"Hi." She picked up right away, a bit breathless. Her anticipation zinged through him. How long had it been since he'd felt the wonderful buzz of a first date? Startled, Max realized he'd kissed Heather before he'd started dating her. That was a first. Taking the time to get to know a woman before he dated her wasn't the usual Max Jones style.

"I'd come to your door, but that might set us back another twenty minutes." He tried to make a joke of it, but the fact that Heather's apartment was a second-story walk-up stung just a little bit too much.

"I'll be down in a jiffy." Max craned his neck up to see her waving out her front window.

Max clicked his phone off and then checked again to see that the passenger seat was set in right. He had no intention of making Heather ride in the back tonight.

She pulled open the door to her building and paused in the light of the entrance. Max wondered if her breath hitched the way his just did. For years JJ had lectured him on the difference between "a hot girl" and "a beautiful woman"—and it had just sunk in. Heather was beautiful. Not just in the way she filled out the peach-colored dress she wore or the way her hair swung about her shoulders, but in who she was and the light in her eyes. The pain in her eyes, too. She was so much braver than she gave herself credit for, so much stronger than she realized. And this amazing woman was about to get into his car and have dinner with him. Him, the guy in a chair. Tonight, just about anything seemed possible.

It bugged him that he couldn't open the door for her. She didn't seem to mind, easing herself into the passenger seat and smiling at him. "You said to dress up a bit—is this okay?" She tucked a strand of hair behind her ear.

Okay didn't even begin to describe how she looked. "You look incredible." Every ounce of cool aloofness left his voice, and he found he didn't care.

She flushed, and Max felt a glow settle under his ribs. "You look pretty good yourself. You should look beyond your T-shirt collection more often." She fastened her seat belt. "Where are we going?"

Max had chosen the restaurant with care. "The Black Swan."

Her eyes went wide. "The Black Swan? Can you get in there?" As if she realized the discomfort of that question, she backpedaled. "Of course you can get in there, right?"

It was too late. The dent in Max's confidence had already been made. Well, they were both new at this—no one could expect a completely smooth ride tonight. "I called and checked. Besides, they legally have to have a way for me to enter. Although I did get the feeling they don't do a lot of wheel traffic." In fact, the maître d', Jeremy, had been effusively confident—something Max had learned to take as a warning sign. He'd almost switched restaurants after the phone conversation, but The Black Swan was the nicest restaurant in town and he wanted to do tonight right.

He pulled into the handicapped spot right out front. "I'm probably the only person in Gordon Falls who never had to complain about how hard it is to get a parking spot on Tyler Street on a Friday night."

She laughed, but a tiny bit too much.

"They've got a ramp that fits over the front stair. Why don't you go in and let the maître d' know we're here while I get out of the car?"

He was pleased she didn't seem fazed by the request. "Sure thing."

She slipped out of the car, and with a mild rush Max noted her scent in the wake. Something flowery with a little bit of vanilla. It made him want to get her close to him and take deep breaths until his head spun. *Easy, boy. Take your time with this one.*

By the time he'd come out of the car, he saw Heather looking frazzled while a pair of busboys fumbled with a metal ramp. "I don't think they've used this before," she told him with a cringe.

"Really?" Max forced the frustration from his voice, trying to sound as if this sort of thing happened every day—which, unfortunately, it did. "Whatever gave you that idea?" Thankfully, the model in question was one he had seen before. He rolled up and pointed to the end at the bottom of the stair. "It goes the other way, boys. The lip goes on top. Slip the pins in before you put it back down and everything will be just fine." He raised one eyebrow to Heather. "We ought to hint at a free dessert for this."

A small crowd of people had gathered on the sidewalk to see what the fuss was about. Heather bit her lip and clutched her handbag. "It's fine," he assured her, touching her elbow. "Just minor logistics."

She flashed him a too-wide smile. "Sure." She was trying so hard.

Normally, Max enjoyed making an entrance. He was jazzed to be able to show the good people of Gordon Falls that a guy on wheels could take a lady out for a nice evening. Fine dining wasn't always his thing—no one could call him a "foodie" unless Dellio's burgers counted as cuisine—but he knew his way around an upscale table like The Black Swan. As long as the maître d' didn't—

"Good evening, ma'am."

—direct all his comments toward Heather. Right here, right now, was the absolute worst part about being in a chair. The people who looked down on him. Not just physically—he'd long since stopped letting sight lines bother him—but figuratively. As if the loss of leg function implied loss of brain function.

"Jeremy," Max cut in perhaps more sharply than was necessary, "I believe we have reservations under Jones for seven o'clock? You and I talked on the phone this afternoon?"

Jeremy had the good sense to look sheepish. "Of course."

"You might want to have a talk with those two working the ramp out front. They don't seem to have any idea what they're doing, and I'd like to exit the place in one piece when we're done."

"Certainly." The guy shot a questioning look at Heather, as if to say, *Is he for real?* Or perhaps it was *I had no idea.* The evening would go better if he gave poor Jeremy the benefit of the doubt.

That generosity lasted until Jeremy showed them to a table way off to the side of the restaurant. With no view of the river and entirely too near the kitchen. He tapped Jeremy's elbow and gestured for him to bend down—knowing that it only made Jeremy more uncomfortable. "I distinctly remember us discussing a table overlooking the river. This is kind of a special occasion. Can we do a little better?" He kept his words kind but put enough bite in them to let Jeremy know he meant business.

Jeremy's furtive glance around the restaurant soured Max's stomach. He held the maître d's gaze and then nodded toward an empty table for two beside the big beautiful windows now framing a dramatic fall sunset.

"Max," Heather whispered, "it's okay."

"No," Max insisted. "It's not." He looked straight at Jeremy. "Do we have a problem?"

"No, sir. I don't believe we do. Give me just a minute."

If Jeremy had just kept to his word and cleared a path to the table Max had requested, they would not have had to make the scene of asking two people to stand momentarily and move their chairs aside. Max thought about clueing Jeremy in to Karl's free-coffee policy, but he decided against it. Heather was turning four shades of pink next to him, nearly squinting her eyes shut as the server pulled out her chair and settled her into the lovely table overlooking the river.

"Did you have to do that?" She cringed when the server left.

"Actually, I did. It's always hard to wake people up to their misconceptions the first time, but I want to be able to take you here anytime I want and be able to request a table like any other patron." He softened his voice. "This is my world, Heather. Very few things are easy. And I get a lot of stares."

When she looked down, he reached across the table to take her hand. "But staring at you is very easy. You look fantastic. Really. Can we forget about Monsieur Idiot back there and have a nice dinner?"

He could literally see her choose to be brave. Could other people see her swallow that desire to hide, or was it just him? He usually loved his role as "human ice-breaker," nearly relished the rolling wake-up call his life had become, but knowing the attention made her uncomfortable tainted the experience for him.

Well, what do you know? Max Jones finally cares about someone else ahead of himself. Talk about your wake-up calls.

* * *

The man's eyes could steal the air from the room.

When Max looked at her like that, Heather fairly tingled. He was this force of energy, this freight train of courage and conviction that never seemed to let anything stop him. She was ready to believe that Max was moving past the bitter anger of his initial response to his injuries. He would be—in many ways already was—a conqueror who tackled one obstacle after another. A man to admire.

A man who was showing off tonight. If Max Jones loved to do anything, it was show off. Normally, she didn't care much for such theatrics, but the fact that he was showing off for her? It peeled off her reluctance one charming smirk at a time.

"Oh, hey, in all the tussle I almost forgot." He reached into his pocket and pulled out a ridiculously small gift bag. She recognized the pink and yellow from Jeannie Owen's candy store, and smiled at the vision of Max Jones shopping in all that sugarcoated fluff. Jeannie must have had a field day with Max.

"What's this?"

"Open it."

Heather tugged on the tissue until a small, fat marzipan flamingo and a handful of other chocolates emerged. The gift was just like Max, touching and a little bit outrageous at the same time. "A candy flamingo?"

"I saw it in her window yesterday and I couldn't resist. I remembered the one from your desk the day we met." Those last words took on a glowing tone she couldn't ignore. "You thought I was nothing but trouble that day."

Heather held his eyes a moment. "I was wrong."

His smile was smoldering. "Oh, I'm still trouble."

"You're a fine man. You're an insp—"

His hand shot up. "Please don't say *inspiration*. I hate it when people call me an inspiration. I'm just making the best of the hand I was dealt."

Why did he always sell himself short on something genuine like that when he was so quick to boast about things that didn't really matter? "I admire you, and you can't stop me." She'd meant it to come out lightly, but the truth of her growing feelings shone through instead.

Now it was his turn to stare into her eyes. "It's not your admiration I'm looking for." His eyes glanced away for a second, and he licked his lips. Was he nervous? The realization made her heart flip-flop. "I'm just a man, Heather. Like every other guy out there, only with a pair of wheels."

She took his hand. His fingers were roughened from all the time they spent pushing his wheels, but they were warm and she could feel all the power he gained from them. "You are not like every other guy out there." She spoke slowly, sincerely. "And I'm glad."

He interlaced his fingers with hers, his thumb running distractingly down the side of her hand. "Well, I hope you're as hungry as you are happy, because I plan for us to eat well tonight."

He relaxed into the evening as the meal progressed, the sharp comments falling off into something that felt much more like deep conversation. She loved watching the hard shell peel off him, enjoyed asking questions that coaxed the more tenderhearted man she'd glimpsed on his porch that night to come back out. He spent so much energy coping, pushing and blazing trails in the world that it was as if he'd forgotten how to just be. The Max on parade was flashy and fun, but the offstage version was a quieter, doubting, near poet of a guy who was quickly stealing her heart.

A jazz combo had started up earlier on the restaurant's outdoor patio, the velvety tones perfectly matching the still-warm indigo evening. "Can you really take me dancing?" she asked as she finished off the last of her chocolate cake dessert.

"Ooh, the lady remembers my offer."

"We did have a rather unforgettable first meeting."

Max put his napkin on the table and signaled the server. "We've had a few memorable moments since then. So you want to dance, do you?"

She felt her face flush. "I'm not really sure how... you...do that."

His eyes grew downright mischievous. "You worried you're going to have to lead?"

Suddenly, there was no adventure she wanted more than to dance with Max, however he managed to do it. "I don't think you know how to follow anyone, Max Jones."

He paid the bill and nodded toward the door. "We're going to have to go down by the river, but I think you can still hear the band."

She gave him a suspicious look. "Are you trying to get me alone?"

"That's a grand idea, but mostly I just need a little more space than your average prom date."

Thankfully, the pair of busboys had left the ramp in its correct position, so Max rolled easily out of the restaurant—after two more people had to shift out of his way. Once they were out, he turned the corner and said with a dashing grin, "Hop on."

"What?"

"You ever ride a grocery cart in the supermarket?"

"Sure, but…"

He tapped his knees. "Same thing, only different."

Heather didn't think it was anything like any grocery cart ride she'd ever taken. "Can you…hold me?"

"I'm not made of glass, darlin', and holding you is the whole idea. I'll be just fine."

Feeling a bit ridiculous, Heather climbed gingerly onto Max's lap. "Keep your hands in your lap and lean to one side a bit so I can see where we're going." She followed his instructions, and Max coasted the downhill slope of the street like a carnival ride, going slow enough to make her feel safe but just fast enough to tug a small squeal from her as he turned onto the short stretch of concrete that spread under the patio of The Black Swan. Music and light spilled out into the night, creating their own little dance floor.

The music flowed into a lazy samba, and Max hoisted her out of his chair as if she weighed nothing at all. Keeping one hand on her elbow, he spun her to face him, then took each of her hands in his. "I pull— you push." Sure enough, she began to move with Max, pushing apart and pulling together like dancing partners. He spun her, and she laughed. "See? You're a natural."

Emboldened, Heather lifted up her arm, and Max deftly spun underneath it, catching her waist as he went by and sending her twirling in the opposite direction. Back and forth, spinning in small arcs and big dramatic circles, she enjoyed the dance more than she'd ever have imagined. Max knew how to pull fun from life like no other man she'd met. All the awkwardness of the earlier hours melted away in the lure of his eyes and the strength of his hands.

"Put your foot here," he coached, nodding to one of his footrests. She tucked her toe in next to his as he pulled one of her hands to his shoulder. She raised herself up on tiptoe beside Max on his footrest, the other foot extended out behind her in a playful pirouette. Max spun her around, making her feel like the tiny ballerina on her childhood music box, twirling under the stars in a dazzling finish as the music ended.

Heather curled, slowly and effortlessly, into Max's lap as if it was the most natural place in all the world to be. He tilted his chin up toward her; the colored lights of the patio above them played across his face and shoulders, lighting the unchecked affection in his eyes. She moved closer, watching her hair tumble around his features until it curtained the moment when her lips met his.

The kiss was sweet and urgent at the same time. It wasn't a hungry, devouring kind of kiss, but, while it was slow and soft, it was still driven by a need to be close and closer still. Awe. That was what she felt in Max's kiss. The starstruck wonder that they'd ever met at all. It coupled with her own astonishment that he met such a deep need in her; they matched beyond what either of them ever expected.

She felt him smile and heard a low, delightful laugh rumble from him as she settled down to sit on his knees. Max ran his fingers through her hair, sending tingles out through her fingertips. "That," he said, his eyes bright as the starlight on the river current behind them, "was officially wonderful."

She couldn't help but laugh herself. "You are a very good dancer."

"Surprised you, did I?"

She leaned in again. "In a million ways."

Chapter Fourteen

If anyone had told Max he'd spend a Sunday night making a complete idiot out of himself with a Ping-Pong ball and a straw in front of a tableful of teenagers, he'd have laughed in their faces. The youth-group brand of fun was never his thing, even when he was the age to be in one. None of which explained how much he was enjoying himself tonight. This riotous version of "air hockey" had him laughing and puffing so hard he was starting to feel dizzy. With a conspiratorial look to Simon, Max sent the Ping-Pong ball the boy's way and Simon shot it into the makeshift goal on the opposite site of the table. Victory hoots shot up from "Team Si-Max," lording their conquest over a gangly sophomore and his uncle, the town banker.

"We advance to the finals after dinner!" Simon pumped his fists into the air. Max gave him a high five, enjoying the boy's enthusiasm. It was clear the boy felt less stress here than at school.

"I'm too old for this," complained a grandfatherly type Max recognized as George Bradens, the retired fire chief and Clark's father.

"Aw, c'mon, Chief—you used to be full of hot air," another man Max vaguely knew from the firehouse kidded George. Max had fun watching the two tease each other. His own dad was always so serious and task oriented—Max could have never invited his father to something so raucous as Friends Night. Max found it a pleasant surprise to know that, at least at Gordon Falls Community Church, "spiritual" didn't always have to mean "serious."

"Hey," Simon pointed out, "Ms. Browning is here."

Sure enough, Heather sat down at a dinner table with a gaggle of high school girls. "She didn't mention she was coming," he replied, trying to keep the warmth of her tender kiss from creeping into his voice. He hadn't seen her since that night, and the memory flashed through him as he watched her laugh at something. She was really getting to him.

"She shows up for dinner a lot. She's like an adviser or something."

During dinner, Max tried to keep up a conversation with Simon and meet his friends while at the same time he could feel Heather in the room with him. He would sense her gaze and look up from spaghetti or chocolate pudding to find her eyes across the room. It was as if the world were moving on two different levels—one with Heather and one with everyone else. He couldn't decide if the sensation was unnerving or exhilarating. Maybe even both—a whole new thrill for this consummate thrill-seeker.

He was elated when Team Si-Max took first place in the air-ball finals, winning an absurd trophy fashioned from tinfoil-covered paper cups. "Our champions!" Heather beamed, giving Simon a quick hug and Max one that lasted just a bit longer. Max was starting to find the scent in her hair downright addictive. From the flush in her cheeks as she stepped away, he was starting to have the same effect on her. "So, how are you enjoying Friends Night?"

"It's not at all what I expected," Max admitted.

Simon launched a superior look at Max. "*Told you* it'd be fun."

"You did. And you were right. Try not to lord it over me, okay?"

"I dunno." Simon's face lit up in the smirk that was quickly stealing Max's affections. "That'd be hard." He looked at Heather. "I need something to drink after all that huffing. Want anything?"

"I'm okay. I'll supervise Max while you're gone— just so you don't worry." Max had always found *sparkling* such an overdone description for a woman's eyes, but the word sure fit tonight.

"Yeah," Simon said as he headed off toward a tub of ice filled with bottles of root beer. "He can't be trusted."

"Funny." Heather sighed as Simon wheeled off to join some friends. "I told Mrs. Williams just the opposite Thursday morning."

Max's mood lost some of its joviality. "Convinced I was behind Simon's escape, was she?"

"I think she's just trying to figure out who this new Simon is and whether or not the changes she's seeing are a good thing. Don't fault her for her suspicion. I've got files of stories of teens led down wrong paths by the very adults who were supposed to be helping them."

Suddenly, it was crucial that he know. "Do *you* think I'm helping Simon?"

"I do, and that's exactly what I told her. I think the fact that Simon felt he could come to you kept him from making a far worse decision Wednesday night." She tucked her hands into her pockets, and Max knew why. The urge to reach out and touch her was so strong, but this wasn't the time or the place. Max Jones erring on the side of discretion. It was a wonder the world didn't tilt in alarm. "Yes." She sighed the word in a way that spread a cheesy but wonderful glow in Max's chest. "You are helping Simon more than probably either of us will ever know. Will you cringe if I call you an answer to a prayer?"

Max had been called a lot of things in his day, but never that. "Yeah, I will. But go ahead."

Heather could barely contain the bubbly joy she felt watching Max and Simon say good-night as the evening's victors. There was no formal reason for Heather to be there tonight. As a youth-group adviser, she was welcome at any of the Sunday night youth-group events, and she'd wanted to watch Max discover how much fun church could be. Her heart was in a dangerous place with Max: if things were going to move forward, she wanted to know faith was becoming a part of his life. The way he looked tonight—laughing and cracking jokes and meeting people—that was as much a gift as his exquisite kiss. *Am I ready to trust him with my heart? Has Max healed enough to be slow and careful with it? Or will I be hurt again?*

"Hey there."

Heather turned to find Melba Bradens. "Hi. Your father-in-law sure had a good time tonight."

Melba's sigh reminded Heather it had barely been two weeks since Mort's funeral. "It's good to be silly after all that other stuff."

"How are you feeling?" Heather touched Melba's arm. "Is it still really hard?"

"Yes." Melba blinked back a few tears. "And no." She smiled. "I wanted you to hear it from me."

"Hear what?"

Melba's hand slid to her stomach. "I'm pregnant. A little girl. In March."

Heather wrapped Melba in a huge hug. "Oh, that's wonderful. Really wonderful." She pushed the woman to arm's length. "You don't even show. I mean, you do—you look wonderful. Did—" she was almost afraid to ask "—did your father know?"

Now a tear slid down Melba's face. "We told him." She laughed and swiped the tear away. "Actually, I think we had to tell him about twelve times, but I'm positive it sunk in."

"That's so sweet. What did he say?"

"He asked if we could call her Maria after my mom. He actually laughed and said he was glad it was a girl because he'd feel bad asking us to give anyone a name like Mort." She sniffled. "I would have, you know? Well, okay, maybe as a middle name, but I would have."

Heather squeezed Melba's hand. "So it'll be Maria Bradens?"

Another tear escaped to slide down Melba's cheek, and Heather felt her own eyes brim over with the bittersweet balance of it all. "Clark gets to choose the middle name, and he hasn't done that yet, but yes." She managed a damp laugh. "He made a joke about Morticia the other day, though, so I know he's working on it."

Heather leaned in. "So, how many pairs of baby booties have you knit?"

Melba winced. "Six. It was the only thing I could do until I could tell everyone. I've knit dozens of baby booties before, but in a way I feel like I've been waiting my whole life to knit *my* baby's booties. That's kind of sick when you think about it, isn't it?"

"Not at all. Congratulations. I'm so happy for you and Clark." One of the reasons Heather wanted to learn to knit from Melba was so that someday she would be able to do exactly what Melba was doing. It had always stung her that she'd never found the time to let Grannie Annie teach her to knit before the wonderful old woman had passed on. How many pairs of socks had Grannie Annie knit for her as her leg was healing? Families were where healing was born. How life went on. Heather hoped that when God gave her a family of her own, she'd glow just as much as the woman smiling in front of her.

"So what about you and Max Jones? Don't think I didn't notice the way he looks at you. And let's just say your dinner at The Black Swan didn't go unnoticed."

Some days it seemed as if nothing in Gordon Falls was ever private. Not to mention how impossible it was to blend in beside Max. Heather wasn't quite sure she was ready to be that public about Max, even to a friend like Melba. "He's doing wonderfully with Simon."

Melba leaned back against the wall and crossed her arms over her chest. "That's not what I asked."

Heather felt her face heat up. "Well, maybe there's something there, but…"

"Oh, there's something there all right." Melba's eyes were kind behind the teasing.

Heather simply pushed out a breath and shrugged her shoulders. "I don't really know yet. Parts of him are so amazing. But he's wild and loud."

"Well, you know what they say about opposites." Melba cocked her head to one side, offering a smile. "Maybe you'll be perfect for each other." She looked into the room, where Max was telling some rousing and evidently funny tale to an audience of teens. "The kids love him. That's always a good sign, right?"

"Not if it's because he's just a great big kid himself." Mr. Williams had said something to that effect after lambasting Max for aiding and abetting Simon's escape.

Melba gave a small hum. "Maybe you should get your eyes checked, because that is most certainly a man. A handsome man who can't seem to stop staring at you."

"I just need to be more…sure…than I am now. It's going to take time, and Max doesn't strike me as the patient type."

"So give it some time. I have a feeling Mr. Hot Wheels might just surprise you."

Heather nodded. She was certain Max would surprise her. She just couldn't be sure if the surprise would be a happy one.

Chapter Fifteen

Two days later, Max found himself in an Iowa college library. Such academic surroundings were not his home territory. An internet search was about the furthest he'd go in the name of research, but he'd uncovered a story of a World War II wounded aristocrat funding a nature-path renovation that would accommodate a wheelchair, and he thought it would make a nice bit of info to add to an event AA was planning in another Iowa city. The scarcity of available materials meant actually going to a library to do it old-school—microfiche readers and old files of yellowing newspapers. At first it seemed like a pain, but it was getting too cold to go out in the *Sea Legs* and Max had decided he needed the three-hour drive to think over everything that had happened lately.

"May I help you?" the librarian asked.

"I need newspaper files from 1980 to 1984 on the Baker trail-system renovation. Your website said those aren't electronic yet, right?"

"No…sir, they're still on microfiche. Our electronic archives only start in 2000." Max found it amusing that she seemed to have to think about whether to call someone dressed like him "sir."

"Can I get to the readers and the files in my chair?" Max pictured a musty file room down several flights of stairs.

"You can access the readers fine, but I'll have to bring the hard-copy files up to you one year at a time."

It sounded as if he was going to be there for a couple of hours. "That'll work for me. Lead on."

The librarian removed the chair from in front of one of the ancient-looking microfiche reading machines, gave him a few slips to fill out and within fifteen minutes Max was trudging his way through endless images, feeling like one of Heather's high school students working on a boring research paper. Academic research was definitely not how he liked to spend his time.

By the third reel, Max needed a break. He wheeled up to the reference desk and put in an order for the files of hard-copy issues he'd managed to identify as likely sources for the information he needed, then asked for directions to the nearest decent cup of coffee.

The diner half a block down was not only accessible, it had free internet access. Max flipped open his laptop for a little twenty-first-century coffee break, deciding that not all small Iowa towns were boring and backward.

Come to think of it, Heather had said she was from Iowa, hadn't she? Would an internet search bring up any high school pictures of her? Had the town made a big deal when she'd graduated despite such a traumatic injury? Normally, Max wasn't in the habit of cyber-sleuthing women of interest, but the query seemed the perfect way to recharge his history-numbed brain cells. Counting backward, he guessed her high school graduation at somewhere around 2004, typed that and her name into his search engine, and started in on his very good coffee.

He found four photos of the small graduating class—there couldn't have been more than fifty students—and a pair of articles on "inspiring seniors." Heather looked young and fresh-faced, a cheerful but wobbly smile under her mortarboard cap. She had the beginnings of the beautiful woman she was now, but a shy and cautious nature came roaring through in the way she posed for pictures. In fact, he saw more of Simon in those photographs than the Heather he'd come to know.

The Heather he'd come to care about. A lot.

He clicked a few associated links, ending up at two articles covering her accident and the resulting burns. Another article covered the driver's charges—the ones that had so angered Heather's father. Max could see where Heather's father's fury came from: the article was clearly written to cast the boy as a victim of his youthful indiscretion. There wasn't a single mention in that article of Heather's injuries and the resulting medical consequences.

It was the next set of links that dropped his jaw. They were from a few years later—her senior year in college, as far as he could tell. They were engagement announcements. Heather had been engaged.

She'd never mentioned it, and he'd have thought something that significant would have come up in the conversation by now. Who was this Mike Pembrose, this all-American farmboy-looking guy who had captured Heather's heart in college? And, more importantly, what had broken them up? He began clicking on links about Pembrose, curious and surprised at the jealousy rising in his gut.

Pembrose was a medical student. "Dedicated," one hometown paper announcement declared, "to the treatment of the diabetes that has afflicted him since childhood." That felt significant, although Max couldn't say why.

Two more links led to bits of information: one was an announcement of Pembrose joining a medical practice last year in Des Moines, his name mentioned on a fund-raising committee. The second, a post in a forum for diabetics, gave him the most telling detail of all. The comment thread was about when a man should tell his girlfriend he was diabetic. Pembrose—at least it sure looked as if it was Pembrose—wrote a long post about how challenging the issue was for some couples. "As involved as my disease was, my girlfriend knew about it, but we never really discussed it. I never tested in front of her. I kept my insulin out of sight. I never talked about the complications. That was a dumb thing to do, but I think I knew somewhere inside that she couldn't handle it. I learned I was right. She ended up breaking off the engagement—my future marriage yet another victim of the Big D."

That didn't sound like Heather. Then again, did he really know her that well? It was a few years ago, but could someone's basic nature really change? And given the nature of their conversations, why hadn't this come up? Why hide that she'd been engaged before?

Granted, this was Pembrose's side of the story—and at least the guy had the decency not to call the lady out by name—but could it be anyone other than Heather? Luke Sullivan's words about women came back to him:

They only think they can handle it. Then everyone finds out how ugly it can get.

She's different, his heart argued with a force Max hadn't expected. *No, she's not different,* his head countered. *When you let her in far enough to see all of what it's like, it'll be over. Sullivan said it. Pembrose said it.* Could he even hope to have enough of a sense of things to call them wrong?

Talk to her about it. Alex had taught him the virtues of going straight to the source when a problem arose. Only he knew what would happen if he did. She'd swear by her loyalty now. She'd say all those sweet and hopeful things that turned his jaded defenses inside out. She'd convince him. He'd believe it because she'd believe it. And then, like Mike Pembrose, he'd be too far in when the bottom fell out. Reality never had to play fair—wasn't he walking...*rolling* proof of that?

Max slammed his laptop shut and stared out the diner window at the charming little town. It looked like someplace Heather would have grown up, all quaint and friendly and rural. Then the corner of his eye caught the three people from the counter staring at him. They averted their eyes the minute he met their gazes—no smiles, no friendly hellos, just the embarrassment of having been caught gawking. For a handful of moments Max considered getting in his car and heading west instead of back east, of just ditching the whole "have a real life" dream and embracing his life as an oddity drawing stares.

You can't do this alone. The infuriating truth was that Max needed other people to survive: doctors, aides, money, an accessible place to live. He couldn't pretend not to need JJ; for all his bravado, he wasn't ready to be all alone.

Max stared at his now-cold coffee. *I don't know what to do.* He was surprised to find the thought feeling closer to a prayer. Alex always said he went to God with his problems—and Alex was the best, most creative problem solver Max knew. Heather, JJ and many of the other nice people at Gordon Falls Community Church had said the same. None of that made him feel better. *I don't know who to believe,* he admitted, still staring into the fragrant brown liquid. *I can't believe God, Heather, Sullivan, Pembrose and Alex all at the same time. I'll have to choose.*

"Oh, no!" Heather dropped the file she was holding as Simon Williams rolled into the administrative suite with blood all down one side of his face. "Simon, what on earth happened?"

"Three guesses," Simon said with a sneer, his voice dark and sharp. He spun his chair toward the nurse's office as the door behind him filled with the algebra teacher, a hefty man who was currently wrestling a fuming Jason Kikowitz into the office by one elbow.

"No," Heather said in disgust more to herself than to anyone else. "I'd hoped we were past this." She shot up a quick, silent prayer for wisdom, squelching her own rising temper.

"Mr. Kikowitz" came Margot's equally displeased voice. "What a disappointment to find you in my office again."

Heather stood up, momentarily stumped as to whether to head left toward the nurse's office or right toward the principal's. Simon won, and she walked to the left. "Simon, are you all right?"

"Fine!" Simon barked, slamming the nurse's office door shut behind him. Clearly, he didn't want questions right now. At least not from her.

"I don't know what Jason said to him in Study Hall," the teacher said, wiping his hands off with a tissue from the secretary's counter, "but suddenly there was a whole herd of them shouting. When Jason tried to tip Simon's chair over, Simon turned on him and rammed him so hard Jason fell over. It went downhill from there."

"Stupid baby raked my shin open with his baby carriage, that's what!" Jason pointed to his bloody shin. "I've got a game on Friday and this hurts like—"

"Enough!" Margot cut in before Jason's language went south. "What did you say to Simon to start this?"

"Candace Norden told me she got hired to be Simon's babysitter."

Heather slumped against the wall, her eyes closed in a wave of regret.

Jason went on. "Little twerp made fun of my algebra grade—"

"Your *failing* algebra grade," the teacher cut in, earning a "don't make this worse" look from Margot.

"So I called him a baby who needs a babysitter. Then he called me a thug."

Heather winced. "Thug" had been Max's term of choice for Jason.

"You can imagine how things went from there," the teacher concluded.

Margot steepled her fingers. "Jason, this isn't the first time. This isn't even the first time with Simon."

"He hit me!" Kikowitz actually sounded surprised.

"And not just with his chair—the little nerd actually tried to punch me."

Heather's stomach began to tie in knots. This was not the kind of confidence she was looking to foster in Simon. *Please, Lord, do something!*

"I'll find out soon enough if that's true, but let's keep this conversation about you. I warned you if there was another incident, I'd have to suspend you. I don't make empty threats, Mr. Kikowitz. You're suspended for two days beginning immediately. And that includes Friday's game."

"But we're playing Bradleton on Friday!"

"It might have been helpful to remember that before you baited Simon Williams into a fight. Straighten up, Jason. Any more suspensions and you risk your graduation." As Kikowitz took a breath to launch an argument, Margot stood up and called out past Heather to the school secretary, "Please call Mrs. Kikowitz and inform her Jason is to leave immediately and why." She pulled some forms out of her desk and handed them to Jason. "I know you drive to school, so I suggest you go straight home. These must be signed by both your parents before you can return on Monday. What you do next could decide your whole year, Jason. I'd take some time to think about that if I were you."

Jason stood and kicked back his chair. He stared daggers into Heather's eyes as he stomped past. "Gonna defend your little handicap project, are you?"

"No," Heather said, her voice a lot calmer than she felt. "I think he did that all on his own, thanks." She'd never wanted to call a student the slew of names that flew through her head right now. How did someone so young get so mean? For all his saber rattling,

Jason wouldn't last two weeks facing all the challenges Simon or Max endured. Someone needed to take that boy down a peg before his arrogance ruined his future.

And Candace. How could Candace go and betray Simon after promising Max she wouldn't? Max's brilliant solution was falling apart right in front of her and there didn't seem to be anything she could do to stop it. There were only three periods left in the day, but that was more than enough time for word to spread about Simon's "babysitter." This was a disaster.

The nurse's office door opened, and Simon emerged, a series of bandages on one cheek and a few more on his right hand. His shirt had a rip in one shoulder and blood on the collar. He looked as dark and angry as Heather had ever seen him.

"Simon." Margot's tone held the cool, soft edge of a principal about to do something she hated. "In my office, please."

Heather made to follow him, but Margot put her hand out. "No. I think you'd better sit this one out."

Heather left the office, walked calmly to the faculty washroom, locked herself in the last stall and cried.

Chapter Sixteen

Max wasn't in the mood to go home after his discovery at the library, so he stopped off at the Adventure Access offices. He'd banged around for an hour, pretending to work, but was just about to call it a day when he looked up to see Heather coming in the office door. Headquarters was at least twenty minutes west of Gordon Falls and, from the looks of it, she had fought tears the entire drive. All his agitation over what he'd learned pushed itself aside as he grabbed the box of tissues off a credenza and met her as she sank onto the couch that served as AA's meager waiting room.

Alex and AA's equipment guy, Doc, were out setting up a trade show, so this afternoon the office was staffed by just Max and Brenda, a bright young amputee with wide eyes and outstanding computer skills who handled the phones and the other administrative tasks. At four employees, AA wasn't big enough to have individual offices, placing workplace privacy at a premium.

Brenda grabbed her crutches while she sent Max a look of understanding. "Hey, I was just craving a latte, so I'm going to the corner, okay?" Max shot her a grateful smile before returning his attention to Heather.

"What's happened? Why'd you come all the way out here?" He nodded toward Brenda's desk. "We've got phones."

His attempt at humor fell far short of the mark. She almost didn't need to ask "Has Simon called you?"

"No." He checked his watch, the early hour doubling his worry. "School's still in session and he's not supposed to call then, which makes me wonder why you're here. Heather, what's happened?"

Her eyes turned as hard as he'd ever seen them. "Jason Kikowitz is what happened." She pulled a tissue from the box Max held out to her. "Well, he and Candace."

Max felt bile climb the back of his throat. "She didn't."

"That or Jason got it out of her somehow. Does it matter? Kikowitz let the whole story loose in Study Hall, and it escalated into name-calling and punch-throwing. On both sides."

Max wanted to hit something. Or someone. Hard. "That overgrown creep of a... Wait, did you say both sides?"

"Yes. Simon and Kikowitz got in a fight. Simon deliberately rammed him with his chair and then threw punches at Kikowitz. You can imagine what result that got."

"Simon fought back?" Max shook his head. "Good for him."

"No," Heather nearly shouted. "Not good—it's bad. Simon can't hope to match a brute like Kikowitz in a fight. Besides, it's not the way to solve something like this. All it got Simon was a week of detentions and a split lip." She glared at Max. "I can't believe you'd think Simon fighting is good." Her eyes narrowed. "And maybe that's half the problem right there."

Max ran his hands down his face. "You'd rather Simon just lie there and take the kind of grief Jason Kikowitz dishes out?" Heather's resulting expression told him she expected just that. "I thought the whole point here was to give Simon the confidence any other kid his age would have. Any other kid his age would have fought back. Or at least tried to. Sure, I would have loved it if the whole business with Candace never came out, but I knew there was a chance it would fall apart. And I knew that if it did, it would be up to Simon to decide how to handle it. Didn't you?"

She pushed up off the couch, pacing the room. "No. I had more faith in you than to coach Simon to stand up for himself like that."

Max swiveled to face her. "Whoa, there—listen to what you just said. It's not bad that Simon stood up for himself and it's not on *me* that he did. I did not coach him to pick fights with Kikowitz. I'm the guy who persuaded Candace to keep it quiet, remember?"

"It didn't work, did it?"

"It was a long shot and I always knew it. You want someone to blame? Blame Simon's parents for hiring a sitter in the first place." Max threw his hands up in disgust. "They're behaving like he's five years old. Even you have to see there's no medical reason he can't be on his own for a few hours."

She knew he was right about that; he could see it in her eyes. "It's not my job to tell someone how to parent their child."

That sounded like too convenient an out, and he was already mad at Heather. "You're supposed to have Simon's well-being in mind, his growth into a—" Max searched for a sufficiently clinical term "—successful young adult. I'm telling you his parents are standing in the way of that. Brian Williams handed Simon to Kikowitz on a silver platter the way I see it. For Simon to lie there and take the ridicule and abuse without defending himself would have made it ten times worse."

Heather stood there, hands on her hips. It burned him that she willfully stood over him—she'd never pulled that kind of tactic before. "That is way out of line, Max, even for you."

"How can you stand there and tell me Simon is at fault?" He pushed back away from her, needing distance and finding it infuriating to have to crane up to look her in the eye. "I don't see how you can think it's okay to give him detention when Kikowitz was picking fights with him. It's like there's no self-defense clause in high school."

She followed him. "There *is* no self-defense clause in high school. Zero tolerance means exactly that. Hitting back is the same as hitting. I don't know how your world works, but I don't have the luxury of shades of gray. Simon's just as guilty of fighting in school as Kikowitz."

"So the guy can wind up and do it again tomorrow and Simon's supposed to just duck?" Whether it was a logical conclusion or not, Max's gut was boiling as if Simon were being thrown to the wolves. And he was coming to care too much for the little guy to just stand by and watch him get eaten. "How fair is that?"

"Jason Kikowitz is expelled for two days and barred

from playing football this weekend—but only because it's his third offense." Heather threw away the first tissue and grabbed a second, now pacing around the greeting area. "I don't know what the punishment is for Simon because Principal Thomas *excluded* me from the meeting."

Ouch. That began to explain why Heather was here instead of at work. He'd have stomped out of the office at a shutout like that, too. Even though it was a dangerous question, he ventured a "Why?"

She turned to bore into him with fierce eyes. "Seems I may have lost my professional distance on this one."

The hurt in her eyes dug sharply into his chest. The size of her heart was what made Heather so wonderful and so impossible—she couldn't invest halfway. She couldn't be careful with her affections. Only she had done just that with Pembrose, hadn't she? He wanted to grill her about it but knew this was far from the time for that conversation. When had the stakes in all this become so personal? What was he supposed to do now? He tried to form a response but came up empty.

His silence seemed to deflate her. She sank back onto the couch. "I've failed Simon in the worst possible way. My job was to help him avoid things like this and now look." Her words were soft and wounded.

Heather's despair cut through his anger. As hard as she was being on him, she was clearly blaming herself, too. "I don't see it that way."

She narrowed her eyes. "And how do you see it?"

"You think this could have been avoided, but it couldn't. Simon's gonna get picked on no matter what you do." The office phone rang, and he let it go to voice mail. "If you think that by some marvel of programming or counseling you can protect Simon from jerks, you're dreaming. The jerks are out there. They always have been and that won't change anytime soon." He wanted to move closer, drawn by the failure that seemed to drag her shoulders down so hard, but his own hurt demanded he keep a distance. "Thinking Simon can be protected from them makes you just like Mr. and Mrs. Williams, trying to keep Simon under glass." He knew that brand of suffocation and was happy to help Simon push back against it. "Look, I am sorry Simon got punished, but I can't see my way to being sorry he stood up for himself the way he did."

Her hands fell open on her lap. "How can you say that?"

"Even you have to know how guys like Kikowitz work. He's trolling for weakness. As soon as Simon shows even a bit of strength, he'll go looking elsewhere. It's not a perfect solution, I agree, but I don't think this is the full-out failure that you're making it."

"Oh, and his right hook to Jason Kikowitz is proof of my effectiveness?" She cocked her head at him, puzzled hurt all over her face. "I can't believe you're okay with this."

Max swallowed. She'd been deeply hurt and she'd driven twenty minutes to him for comfort. Even he wasn't too much of a jerk to not realize that ought to count for something. "I'm not okay with it. I hate that it happened. You're upset. Simon disappointed you." Feeling Mike Pembrose's comments banging against the back of his brain, he forced himself to add, "He's lucky you care so much about him."

"I do care about Simon. Margot's right—I have lost professional distance. I just can't shut it off, you know?

He's so special." She looked right into his eyes and Max felt as if she could see far too much there. "He's got all these special people in his life now."

How was it this could be the same Heather who hadn't been strong enough to stand by her fiancé? Had the war zone of working in a high school strengthened her? Could he risk his heart on that? *My world would eat you alive,* he thought. If she could get so worked up about Simon, if she could walk away from Mike Pembrose just because he was a diabetic, how could he ever think she could handle what life slung at him every day? She needed to be made of much tougher stuff if they were ever going to make it, and she just wasn't the tough-stuff kind.

If Brenda hadn't appeared in the door, he might have dared to ask her about that history. As it was, Heather said a flustered goodbye and hurried out. Max couldn't decide if he wanted to thank Brenda or curse her.

He settled for texting Simon.

Heather didn't go home. She couldn't face the walls of her empty apartment, not with the way her feelings were in their current state of jumbled mess. *Did I fail Simon, Lord? Is there something I need to learn from this?* She drove to the riverbank, wanting the solace of the water and knowing Max wasn't there right now. The little dock off Max's cabins seemed a good place to sort things out.

October was such a beautiful time in Gordon Falls. The trees were spectacular, God's exquisite palette splashed across a clear blue sky. The air was just nippy enough to feel clean and crisp, not yet cold enough to bite. Now, looking out over the flowing river, it was easy to think the world was moving along as God intended—not as humans had hopelessly muddied it up.

"It's my favorite place to think, too." Heather turned to see JJ, a bucket of cleaning supplies in her arms and a curious smile on her face. "Shouldn't you be in school, young lady?"

Heather moved over on the bench, patting the space next to her. "I got asked to leave. Actually, no, that's not true. I got shut out of a meeting and I stomped off. Not exactly exemplary behavior."

"Not like you at all, either." JJ sat down. "What on earth happened?"

Heather slumped lower on the bench. "A fight broke out at school. Simon—Brian Williams's son, the one Max is helping—and Jason Kikowitz."

"Kikowitz beat up on Simon?" JJ cringed. "Didn't he try something earlier this year? He laid into Simon again?" She shook her head, her long blond ponytail swinging as she sighed. "Why some kids can be so mean…" She met Heather's eyes. "Is Simon okay?"

Heather ran her hands through her hair. "It depends on who you ask. I think it's terrible that Simon tried to fight back, but your brother thinks it's a good thing Simon is standing up for himself."

"Sounds like my Max all right." JJ pulled her knees up and hugged them. "Bullies like Kikowitz make me so angry. Max did his share of terrorizing in high school—he ought to know better."

The memory of Simon's wounded eyes brought the lump back to Heather's throat. "I was so sure Max's idea was going to work."

"What idea?"

Heather related Simon's escapade, Max's solution,

Candace's promise and the subsequent betrayal. She left out the part about Max's heartbreaking admission and the kiss that still took her breath away. She was falling for Max, hard. "He's doing amazing things for Simon, JJ. He has such a heart, if only…"

"If only he'd stop shouting so loud?" JJ finished for her, a wistful smile on her face. "I know." She looked out over the water. "You know, I'd have never said this at first, but Max is a better man on wheels than he was when he could walk. It's changed him. I think he'll continue changing." She returned her gaze to Heather. "With the right person beside him. Has he figured out how much the two of you have fallen for each other yet? Or do you think you'll have to hit him over the head?"

Heather felt her jaw go slack. "You know?"

JJ laughed softly. "I'm his big sister. And your eyes light up when you talk about him." She nudged Heather. "Even when you're complaining about him. That's a contradiction I'm very familiar with."

"At first, I was so sure he and Simon would end up a disaster—no offense." Heather put her hands to her cheeks, certain she was blushing like a teenager. "And then I thought he was exactly what Simon needed. And now…I have no idea."

"Well, he's not done yet. Mr. Hot Wheels is a bumpy ride—I don't have to tell you that. But his heart is in the right place on this one, and I think Simon has a few things to teach Max."

"I think so, too." Heather recalled the energy in Max's eyes when he talked about Simon—the boy brought out something extraordinary in Max. It was close to the unforgettable glow she'd seen in his eyes when he'd looked at her that night on his porch. There

was so much tenderness in that man that the world
never saw. Could she bring out something extraordinary in Max? She knew he was bringing new and marvelous things out in her.

"I think you're really good for him, Heather. I admit,
I was nervous at first—Max was a veteran heartbreaker
before the accident—but I think God's up to something here."

"Oh, I…"

"He was really touched by the knitting ladies, you
know. I'm sure he never admitted it, but he talked about
them for half an hour when I saw him the other day.
Alex and I have been trying to drag him to church again
since the funeral, but *you* made it happen." JJ pulled in
a deep breath. "Can you imagine what God could do
with a guy like Max? The people he could reach? The
lives he could change?"

She'd had the same thought herself. Max never did
anything halfway—if his faith ignited, it would be
spectacular. "He told me he's still angry at God for
dropping him."

A sister's heartbreak filled JJ's eyes. "I know. What
did you say when he told you that?"

"I told him I believed God caught him just in time."

Affection replaced the heartbreak in JJ's features.
"What did my little brother say to that?"

Heather took a deep breath. "He kissed me. Actually,
I think I may have even kissed him first."

JJ blinked back tears, something Heather hadn't seen
this tough warrior of a woman do very often. "I was
wrong, Heather. I think you're good for Max. Really
good. Don't give up on him when he makes a mess of
things, okay? He needs you."

I think I need him, Heather thought. *But he needs You most of all, Lord. You'll have to shout loud to get through to Max Jones.*

Chapter Seventeen

Max's wheels skidded on the firehouse floor as he zoomed in one of the open bay doors. The older guy everyone called Yorky looked up from the supplies he was shelving. "Hi, Max. JJ's in the kitchen."

Max knew the way, but his path ended up being blocked by the tightly packed tables in the dining room. After a conversation with Simon an hour ago, Max was angry enough to knock over every table in the county, but that wouldn't solve anything. Frustrated and stalled, he resorted to yelling "JJ" until her head popped out of the pass-through window from the firehouse kitchen.

She'd either talked to Heather or Brian, because she already knew. Her expression said that loud and clear. Fine. He wasn't in the mood to recount the gruesome facts anyhow. She took her time coming out of the kitchen, wiping her hands instead of looking him in the eye. Without a word, she moved a series of chairs so they could sit at the farthest dining room table. "You want a soda?"

As if that would help. "No," he snapped. "I do not want a root beer to make it all better." He liked the stuff, and the firehouse was always in full supply of Gordon Falls's official beverage, but he wasn't even remotely in the mood.

"I'm sorry about what happened to Simon." After a second, she added, "Aren't you supposed to be in Iowa today?"

"I was." He didn't want to offer any further explanation than that.

JJ frowned. "I know you've invested a lot in that kid. I'm really sorry he got a week of detentions. Doesn't seem fair, does it?"

Max ran his hands down his face. "According to Heather, it's all equal as far as the school's concerned. Kikowitz's mean left hook is just as punishable as Simon's weak attempt to fight back." He looked up at JJ. "Am I wrong for being glad Simon tried to stand up for himself? If it was me, I'd have slugged the guy, too."

JJ offered a melancholy smile. "You did, back in school. Twice, if I remember right."

Max laughed darkly. "I beat up Noah Morton for leaving you at the homecoming dance, didn't I?"

"Not your best moment, but you meant well."

"He's going to keep baiting Simon—I know he is. The kid's a predator, and he's picked out Simon as the weakest of the herd. Someone needs to teach that bully a lesson."

"That someone is *not you*. The last thing Simon needs is you deciding to show Jason that a guy in a chair can throw a decent punch."

"Do you know how much I want to?" Max planted his elbows on the table, hands fisting at the thought of what Jason had done to Simon for no reason other than pure meanness. "If I saw him across the street right now, I could—"

JJ put her hand on Max's arm. "But you won't. Max, Simon looks up to you. What you do now is going to teach Simon how to deal with the world. Look, you've made some progress with Brian—he told me so just yesterday. You're helping Simon. Don't blow it all to pieces over someone like Jason Kikowitz."

Max rested his forehead on his upright fists. "I'm just so...mad. We work so hard to give people an equal shot and guys like Kikowitz can wipe it all away in ten minutes." He'd always wondered when his passion for Adventure Access would rise to the level of Alex Cushman's, but he hadn't counted on it happening out of sheer vengeance. He doubted this was the kind of motivation Alex would condone.

"Go take the boat out, go shoot hoops with the guys here until you've burned it off, but *burn it off.* Don't show Simon the wrong way to handle this."

Max simply groaned. He really wasn't in the mood for a big-sister lecture.

"We just had a training session, so there's a bunch of the younger guys out back. Go shoot hoops." As if to drive the big-sister thing home, she stood up and planted a kiss on the top of his head. "It'll feel good."

He knew what would feel *terrific* right now, and it wasn't the condoned plan of behavior, that was for sure. Anger boiled up in him like a furnace fire, heating his thoughts and shredding his patience. This thing with Simon and Kikowitz touched on so many parts of his life, he couldn't seem to escape it. He couldn't outthink it, couldn't solve it, couldn't appease it; he could only endure it. While he had a lot of physical endurance, his emotional endurance had pretty much run dry in the months since he'd fallen off that cliff.

"Hot Wheels!" Jesse Sykes waved to him from under the basketball hoop that stood at the little concrete yard in the back of the firehouse. "Good. I need somebody I can beat." He bounced the basketball straight at Max.

Max caught it in one hand, aimed and sent it through the hoop. "You mean you need a beating to take you down a notch." The sound of the ball clanging through the chain net was satisfying. They started a rousing game of one-on-one, which eventually became two-on-two as some of the other guys came out to join. Without making a big deal out of it, these guys always found a way to make Max feel as if he fit in. It just made him ache harder for Simon to have the same experience.

He missed two shots in a row because his thoughts were tangled around Simon's plight, losing the game for his team. Jesse reached into a bin and tossed Max a towel. "What's up with you?" Jesse asked, wiping the sweat from his own brow.

At first Max hesitated—talking about it would just make it all surge back up. Only these guys knew Brian Williams as one of them. They knew Simon, and many of them had taken a shine to him like Max had. Maybe they could help the boy feel as if he wasn't so alone. "It's the thing with Simon Williams."

"Oh, man," said Wally Foreman, collapsing on a bench that sat at the edge of the concrete. "Heard about that."

"I had Kikowitz's older brother in my class when I was in high school," another guy shared with a grimace. "Big and mean runs in the family, if you know what I mean."

"I've never seen Williams so mad," Jesse said. "That kid means everything to him."

"I feel for Simon," Wally offered. "Hard to live something like that down, you know? Kid's gonna hear *babysitter* called after him in the hallways for years." A little geeky himself, Wally's eyes went hard and narrow. "I hated high school."

Jesse leaned in. "I hate to say it, and I'd never tell Brian how to parent his son, but I was glad to hear that Simon stood up for himself this time. That kid needs to strike back and strike hard if he's ever going to be able to hold his head up at that school. Guys like Kikowitz feed on this stuff unless you shut them up."

The churning in Max's gut was growing by the minute. "I can't tell you how much I want to string that kid up by his expensive sneakers and show him he's not as tough as he thinks he is."

Wally raised one eyebrow. "So why don't we?"

Jesse stilled. "What are you saying?"

"I'm saying we should show Kikowitz that the Gordon Falls Volunteer Fire Department looks after its own. You mess with Williams's kid, you mess with us. I'm not saying we should hurt the guy, just give him reason to think twice before he gets into it with Simon again."

"Let Simon know we've got his back." Jesse nodded.

Stop this, a little voice in the back of Max's mind whispered. It was far too easy to ignore it. "I don't think Brian would go for it." Some part of him knew the weakness of that objection.

"Who says Brian has to know?" Wally grinned. "Probably better if he doesn't, actually."

"I'm in," Jesse said. "I'd happily put Kikowitz in his place. A little community service, if you ask me."

This is wrong, the little voice began to shout. It sounded way too much like Heather. Well, all Heather's ideas and spiffy activities hadn't helped Simon one bit, had they? Bullies only spoke one language, and Max had been fluent at his age. He'd know just how to pick on Kikowitz's weak spots. He'd tell the guys how best to frighten Kikowitz but stop them before they went too far. Simon would know there were more people on his side. "Appealing as it sounds, we can't hurt him. This has to be a warning, not a payback. And I can't really be involved."

The three other guys looked at him.

"But I can drive."

Heather rested her head in her hands the next morning and tried not to cry. The only grace was that Jason Kikowitz's father had railed at her on the phone rather than coming in to personally convey his outrage at what had happened last night.

"I agree this is an awful development, Mr. Kikowitz, but as it didn't take place on school property, I'm not sure what I can do." A group of three young men—and there was little doubt in her mind who at least one of them was, even though she couldn't quite yet figure out how, since no one had yet mentioned a wheelchair—had cornered Jason in the parking lot of Dellio's diner last night and pushed him around, shouting threats should he try anything else against Simon Williams.

"Jason tells me the hoodlums that roughed him up got into a dark car with flames painted on the sides,"

Mr. Kikowitz growled into the phone. "He said you'd know who owned that car, Ms. Browning. Do you?"

The "yes" of her reply felt like thorns in her throat, sharp and wounding.

"What are you going to do? I demand you do something about this!"

That was just it—this problem was so enormous and so painful she couldn't even think of how to respond. It was as if Max had handpicked the worst way to betray her trust, the most painful act to shred everything that had grown between them since that night on the porch where she'd told him he wasn't broken. She was wrong. Max was broken, and he'd now broken everything else within reach.

"Are you listening to me?" Mr. Kikowitz yelled. "Do I have to take my son's victimization up with the police?"

Victimization. While what happened to Jason was wrong in every way, did his father really see his son as a victim? Did he have no sense of how Jason had begun the chain of events that had brought everyone to this awful place?

"No, Mr. Kikowitz, I hope that won't be necessary. I'm glad Jason wasn't hurt. Where is he now?"

"He's at home of course—he's been suspended for the rest of the week, remember? Besides, why on earth would I let him back into school after a thing like this?"

"Believe it or not, I think school may be the best place for him right now. I might be able to arrange an in-school suspension given the circumstances. It would give me a chance to talk to him about all this."

Mr. Kikowitz snorted angrily. "I'm not about to send him."

"I understand. Please think it over and let me know if you change your mind." Some petty part of her wanted to remind Mr. Kikowitz that his son had been suspended for doing what had just been done to him—in all honesty, for doing even worse, since Jason had drawn blood.

It didn't have much effect. "I lay this at your doorstep, Ms. Browning. I expect some solution from you before the end of the day. That's the only consideration that will change my mind." His voice held no hint of cooperation or concern, just pure demand. She wondered if he barked orders like that to Jason every day. How fathers and sons could tangle each other into knots. Fathers and daughters, too.

The world was one giant ball of hurt and it wasn't even 9:00 a.m. Heather picked up her keys and headed to the last place on earth she wanted to go: Max's cabin.

Chapter Eighteen

Max was just finishing his morning coffee when he heard a car pulling into the cabin parking lot. Seconds later his door banged open and JJ stalked into the kitchen.

"What is wrong with you? How could you possibly think that was a good idea?" Her eyes flashed in anger.

He didn't bother denying it. He hadn't even made any attempt to hide what they'd been doing last night, so he simply didn't say anything.

JJ sat down carefully, as if moving too fast would let her temper loose. "I've just come from a twenty-minute meeting—no, a twenty-minute department-wide *dressing down*—from Chief Bradens about a certain group of firefighters who roughed up Jason Kikowitz last night. Brian Williams came storming into the department this morning furious, and I don't blame him." She dropped her forehead into her hands.

"What are you doing? Reliving your glory days back in high school, shoving kids into lockers? This is beyond stupid, Max. *Irresponsible* doesn't even cover it.

I'm—" she looked up at Max with sharp, angry eyes "—I'm ashamed to be your sister this morning."

He paused, making sure she was finished. "Not your brand of tactics—I get that." He didn't mind taking the heat for this. Not if it called dogs like Kikowitz off Simon. If having that kid's back knocked him off the "inspirational survivor" pedestal JJ and Alex kept shoving him on, then he'd gladly take the hit.

"What you don't get is how much damage you've done. To hear him talk, Simon Williams will be lucky Brian ever lets him out the door to pick up the mail now. Why didn't you just paint a bull's-eye on the back of his wheelchair, Max? Brian is convinced Simon is a walking target now, and I don't think he's wrong."

"Simon *isn't* walking. That's the whole point here."

She slammed her hands on the table. "Stop that!"

"Stop what?"

"Stop making everything about being in that chair. This has nothing to do with your injuries and everything to do with the kind of person I thought you were. *Were.* Because obviously I was wrong."

"You would have preferred I go over and have a deep, meaningful conversation with Jason Kikowitz?"

JJ stood up, bristling. "I would have preferred you act like an adult. I would have preferred you show Simon what it means to be a man instead of just another bully."

"Didn't the army teach you never to take a knife to a gunfight? The only way to deal with Kikowitz is to back him down, JJ. Simon couldn't do it, so I did it for him. Well, with a little help from some guys who were *all too happy* to give Kikowitz what he deserved. It's not like we beat the guy up or anything."

"Threats. You think threats were the way to go on this one?" She blinked at Max. "You think you stepped in on Simon's behalf. You don't even know how wrong you are on this, do you?"

Actually, he had known it on some level all along. It wasn't hard to go back to being the bad guy when he was so practiced at it. It took way too much energy to be a good guy with everyone staring at him. Luke Sullivan's "stop caring" attitude was gaining traction ever since he'd seen Mike Pembrose's post. The whole pipe dream of a future with Heather was a bubble that was bound to pop soon; he could see that now. Life only afforded guys like him certain benefits, and being upstanding didn't have to be one of them.

"Alex is on a plane right now or I'd tell him to come over here and fire you this minute. You're an idiot, Max, throwing away every good thing you've been given."

A sickening pity filled her eyes, and he hated that more than anything else she could say. "Oh, yeah, look at me, swimming in blessings."

He heard his front door open. "You *are*," JJ said. "That's the worst part of it. If you'd only—"

She stopped talking as Heather walked silently into his kitchen.

"I think I'd better go now," JJ said quietly. "We're shorthanded at the station, since three guys just got suspended from duty for a week." She looked at Max. "Dishonorable conduct." She said the words as if pronouncing sentence on him.

Heather stood eerily still, her mouth drawn tight and her eyes cold. He wouldn't meet her glare, instead staring into his coffee and stirring it with a false indifference.

"Why?" It was more of a whisper, a moan, than a question.

"Because it had to be done."

"I can't think you believe that."

He leaned back in his chair. "Know me that well, do you?"

"I thought I did. Today, I'm not so sure."

Max didn't answer.

She took a step into the kitchen, and Max got a whiff of whatever it was that made her hair smell so good. A tiny knife twisted in his gut. "Do you remember how I told Mrs. Williams I trusted you to do right by Simon?" She looked up and breathed in, doing that thing women did when they tried not to cry. The knife twisted harder. "I told her I believed in you. Do you know what it felt like to face her this morning? For me to agree with her that Simon should never spend time with you ever again?"

"Simon will be fine from here on in. Kikowitz will leave him alone. He doesn't need me."

"You think he'll be fine? You are so wrong. Simon's parents asked me about homeschooling him. They've decided the public school system can't meet his needs. That glass you think Simon is trapped under? It just came down hard and fast and airtight around him. I hope you're happy."

The anger—and yes, the regret—Max had been swallowing all morning roared up with a force too strong to stop.

He fought back with the only weapon he had. "As happy as you would have been with Mike Pembrose?"

Heather felt as if she'd been struck by lightning. Mike Pembrose? How had Mike been dragged into this?

The shock of Max's question was instantly swallowed by a wave of regret. How could she think that what had happened with Mike would not follow her to Gordon Falls eventually? Wanting to put that sad chapter behind her was never the same thing as being able to escape it. She'd not made peace with that episode, and now she was paying the price.

"How do you know about Mike?" She hated how pain laced her words.

"I think the question is, why didn't you tell me about Mike?"

There wasn't a simple answer to that question. "He isn't part of my life anymore."

Max scrubbed a hand across his chin. "Yeah, you saw to that, didn't you?" He hadn't yet shaved, and the scruff gave him a regrettably rugged handsomeness she didn't want to notice. She'd come to Max's doorstep thinking life couldn't have tangled any further, and he'd proved her wrong.

She leaned against the counter, feeling slightly ill. A stronger woman would have been able to push back against this clear diversion, but this morning she wasn't that woman. "Tell me what you know."

Draining his coffee cup, Max gave her a hollow look. "Not much of a story. According to Mr. Pembrose, you found out he had diabetes and couldn't hack it. Did you give him the real reason you broke off the engagement? Or did you make up an excuse?"

It was so much more than that, but Heather wasn't sure she was capable of explaining it to Max. Not in the middle of all this. The words wouldn't come.

"You can see how I might find this crucial information." Max's bitter tone sliced the air between them. "Since we're on the whole trust issue, as you say."

She shut her eyes. One black moment piling onto another—it seemed beyond unfair. "I can't discuss this now. Now has to be about Simon. Can you see that?"

"I'll talk to Simon. I'll explain why we did what we did, why Kikowitz will likely leave him alone now. His dad will come around."

"No." The one clear point in all this was that it had to stop. Here. Now. Before any more harm was done to anyone—including her. "You will not talk to Simon. Your relationship as his mentor is over. Your relationship—" she took a breath to steady her voice, feeling as if her throat were tying itself into knots "—with me is over. You are not to come to school." *To see me or Simon,* her broken heart added. "Simon's parents have forbidden you to contact him, so don't call or text him or go by the house."

"Well, I was getting too busy for all this anyhow." The worst thing of all was that Heather could see right through Max's act: he was applying that hard shell, pretending as if this were no big deal. His cavalier words couldn't mask the regret she saw pinching his features. The way his lips thinned and he swallowed harder. "I don't think he'll need my protection now anyways."

He needs your affection. She wanted to hate what Max had done. It was wrong in dozens of ways, and she had every right to be furious. But even all that couldn't wipe away the fact that Max had done it because he cared about Simon. It had come out in the worst possible way, but hadn't JJ said something about Max's spectacular gift for messing up? Hadn't she been warned?

"You won't lose your job or anything, right?" His

voice pitched up just the slightest bit. "You had nothing to do with this."

"I don't know. I don't think so." She said the next words with more bitterness than she would have liked. "You're a grown man. No one expects me to control what you do on your own time off school property." After a second she felt compelled to add, "No, I think the big loser here will be Simon. You've managed to snatch back everything you gave him. I hope you can live with that."

Max pushed away from the table, spinning away from her under the pretense of putting the coffee creamer back in the refrigerator. He kept his hand on the handle for a long moment after he shut the door, knuckles whitening from how tightly he gripped.

Heather was nearly certain this would be the last time they spoke. She'd see him around town, of course, but there would be no more dances, no more dinners at The Black Swan or pie at Karl's. The knowledge gave her enough courage to speak her mind.

"Do you want to know why I broke it off with Mike?"

Max neither answered nor turned around, although he took his hand off the refrigerator handle and let it fall to his lap.

"Yes, I was scared when he shared his diabetes with me. I had spent so much time being the sick one that I was afraid I couldn't help anyone else through something so big for a whole life. So I admit that was part of it." Max's shoulders fell a bit, an "I knew it" gesture.

"But it wasn't all of it. Mike *became* his condition once he stopped hiding it from me. He let it rule him, let diabetes drive every aspect of his life for every minute.

He complained constantly. He made me watch him take his insulin injections, moaned about what he couldn't eat, kept a list of side effects and complications in his wallet. There were conversations where he told people he was a diabetic before he introduced me as his fiancée. He lived in fear. He refused to have a family, afraid to pass along what he called 'the curse of his body' to our children. Mike chose to make himself a victim, and I knew I wasn't strong enough to marry a victim."

She almost didn't say it. But if this was going to be her only chance, she didn't want to regret leaving it unsaid. "You are not a victim. That's what I'd hoped you would teach Simon. You were the strong one—you are determined to have all the life you can despite what's happened. I soaked that in, being close to you. I was starting to believe…" She let her voice trail off, and everything inside her wanted to crumple up into a ball of disappointment. Heather took a breath and made herself finish. "You're not a victim. Instead, you made Jason Kikowitz into a victim. And Simon. And me. So if you think that I'm walking away from you for the same reason I walked away from Mike, you couldn't be more wrong."

Chapter Nineteen

The door shut behind Heather, and Max's cabin felt bombed out, hollowed out, whatever was twelve times beyond empty. Times like these he most hated the limitations of his body. The urge to kick, to explode in a running, throwing rage couldn't be contained in arms and fists. He drew in angry, rumbling breaths, wanting to roar at something but having no target. This anger, this ticking time bomb of pent-up frustration was about to go off—had already gone off, if he really thought about it—and it needed speed and force to defuse. Speed and force—the very things he lacked.

He'd done the right thing. He alone knew Kikowitz needed a good scare, and he'd seen to it. That had to be true. The creeping doubt, the black regret that started in his stomach and seemed to feed on the looks in JJ's and Heather's eyes, that was sentimental nonsense. After all, no one was breaking down doors and shouting lectures at the other three from GFVFD.

Well, no one except Chief Bradens. Yeah, well, what did an upstanding do-gooder like Clark Bradens know about guys like Kikowitz? Thugs like he'd once been?

People like Bradens, like Heather, they wouldn't last a day in his world. He was kidding himself if he thought he was anything but alone.

Alone. The word set fire to the exploding feeling again. Needing to smash something, Max took the empty coffee cup and hurled it to the floor. He wanted it to break into a thousand furious pieces, but the sturdy stoneware only bounced off the Formica, sending off one pathetic chip. He couldn't even reach down to pick it up and hurl it against something else.

It was good that Heather had ended it, no matter what she said. It hurt so much to watch her walk out that door now, it would have killed him if he'd gone ahead and fallen in love with her. He felt as if his heart was bound in barbed wire as it was. For the first time since the accident, Max wished he felt less instead of yearning to feel more.

There was one person who would understand what he was going through right now. Max scrolled though the contacts list on his cell until he found Luke Sullivan's number.

A woman's voice answered. "Hello?"

"Is Luke there?"

"Um…who is this please?" Whoever it was Luke had chosen as his companion for the night, she sounded decidedly unhappy.

"This is Max Jones. We're—" he groped for the right word "—business associates."

"Then you know Luke isn't in a position to talk right now." At Max's pause, she added, "I mean, you do know, right?"

"I'm not sure I follow you, Ms. …."

"Sullivan. Terri Sullivan. I'm Luke's sister." He

heard her let out a big breath. "Oh, man, you don't know, do you?"

"Know what?"

"Luke rolled his car Monday night. He was out drinking with some race buddies and he...well, he..." Her voice broke. "He's in a coma, okay? So it's not like he has time for business associates right now."

"I'm sorry." What else was there to say?

"Look, I gotta go. I... Well, I gotta go. I was supposed to be at the hospital ten minutes ago."

Max stared at the phone for a whole minute after the call ended. Sullivan's original injury had come from a drunk-driving accident. And now this. Some hero. Some champion. What a waste of a life.

Suddenly, the tiny cabin couldn't contain him. He needed space and speed, and there was only one place to really get it. In two minutes he'd grabbed a sweatshirt and was out the door, rolling down toward the docks and the *Sea Legs*. Who cared that it wasn't sailing weather? It was cold, but it was windy, and wind meant speed, wind meant power, and right now he needed as much of both as he could grab.

Max worked so fast to get himself into the boat, he nearly slipped twice in the process. Everything took so long in a chair! He slammed his seat into place with such force the whole boat shook; he yanked the dock lines fast enough to send them humming along the cleats, leaving friction burns on his palms. The pain felt good. Pain meant he was alive, meant that he was feeling something other than the anger.

The chilly late September wind sent the *Sea Legs* hurling through the river and whipped Max's hair hard against his face. Max pulled the sails in tighter, wrestling every bit of speed he could from the wind. The current put up a battle, but he welcomed it. He was itching for a fight. The craft sped across the water, up daringly on one keel, fast and feisty and satisfying.

His tension unraveled a notch with every mile, the speed and movement releasing the bristling ball of anger trapped in his chest. He took in a breath and yelled across the water, listening to the sound echo in the wide-open space. Gordon Falls and all its expectations faded behind him; the gray blustery sky ahead matched his thoughts. He bellowed again, just because it felt so good.

No matter how hard he tried, Max could not stop his thoughts from turning to Simon. Simon would never be allowed escapes like this. Stranded at home, surrounded by fear disguised as care, the kid would slowly and surely rot. He'd never know that life—even life in a chair—outlived high school, opening up beyond that tiny, petty world into a place where sports, camping, travel, jobs and all kinds of things awaited him. He'd probably never kiss a girl.

Kissing a girl was the most amazing thing. Kissing Heather had been like swallowing light, like drinking brilliance. Even now his neck remembered the feel of her hands. Even though relationships were off the table, Simon ought to know the exquisite sensation of a woman's hand slipping around his neck.

And you shoved her away.

The thought stabbed hard.

His retaliation to Kikowitz had nothing to do with Heather. He'd done it to protect Simon, not in some kind of psychobabble lash-out against intimacy. He hadn't sabotaged his relationship with Heather—it would have crashed on its own given time. Sure, this felt beyond lousy right now, but numbness was his gift in the world, wasn't it? What had Sullivan said? The first letdown feels like being dropped a mile?

A mile? Try ten miles. Try a thousand.

And now where was Sullivan? Lying in a hospital bed trying to stay alive. Again.

The boat shuddered and lurched, yanking Max from his thoughts to realize he'd come too close to shore and nearly beached the *Sea Legs* up on the muddy riverbank. He shook his head, pulled up the rudder a bit and luffed the sail enough to let the boat skid back into the deeper water. *Pay attention, Jones. Don't add stupid to stupid.*

You shoved her away. The convicting thought wouldn't go away. Max brought the boat about, returning it to its smooth speed through the river. He wanted to stop thinking, to outrun his thoughts and burn off his anger. Only he wasn't angry anymore. The wind and water had done their trick and tamped down the storm inside him. He just didn't like what was left.

You looked for reasons to leave her. You handed her a reason to leave you. Worse yet, you used Simon as your excuse to do it.

He could run this river all the way up to its source, and he wouldn't escape that conviction. On some level—maybe not then but certainly now—Max knew he'd helped orchestrate the revenge on Kikowitz because it would prove to Heather that he wasn't worth her affections. And that was so much easier that trying to live up to them, because that meant risking an eventual heartbreak.

The thought made him laugh. Max Jones, consummate risk taker, was running from risk. He pointed a finger at the blue heron standing gracefully in the shallows to his left. "That's right," he lectured the bird. "You know what those therapists say—pain is the mother of stupid. Fear is the father of stupid. And me, I've just been the prince of stupid, haven't I?" The bird only blinked and turned away as Max turned the boat back toward Gordon Falls.

He thought some sort of solution would come to him as he guided the boat back home. It didn't. He only knew he didn't want to be like Luke Sullivan, didn't want to keep everyone at a distance when that distance would eventually strangle him. Because while the world thought Luke had everything, it turned out Luke had nothing.

Now what? Max was pretty sure some whopping apologies were involved, only he didn't know quite how to make that happen. Truth was, he still wasn't sorry for getting to Kikowitz, just sorry for the fallout. And he was still terrified of getting in too deep with Heather only to learn she couldn't handle life with a paraplegic. Only he was also just as terrified of losing her, which he was pretty sure he'd just done.

How fair was it that Alex, the master problem solver and the guy who said he was on Max's side, was in San Francisco for the week? This was not the kind of thing to handle in text messages and continually dropped cell-phone calls. *Great.* He scowled to himself. *Now where do I go?*

Max nearly groaned aloud when he turned the boat about to see the gleaming white steeple of Gordon Falls Community Church poking above the fall foliage like some kind of sign someone had put there. "Aw, come on, really? That's a bit Hollywood, isn't it?" Max asked the sky.

He knew what JJ would say. He knew what Alex would say. For that matter, he was pretty sure what Heather would say.

The words of one of his therapists rang in his head. *If you think you're going to fall, grab on to the nearest sturdy thing.*

Well, okay, Lord, Max tentatively informed God as he tied the boat up. *This is me grabbing.*

Thursday morning, Heather stared at the vicious orange letters spray painted onto the sidewalk in front of Simon Williams's house. Graffiti of any kind—much less the hateful outburst this displayed—seemed so out of place in quaint Gordon Falls. It shouted at her from the sidewalk. It poked at her from the fingers of the neighbors who pointed and stared. It pummeled her from the wounded look in Simon's mother's eyes as she peered out their living room window.

Someone—and it didn't take a genius to figure out who—had painted *gimp* on the sidewalk. She wondered if Jason Kikowitz had known the slur was viewed among the worst in the disability community—something so cruel it could barely be said by one person with a disability to another and could never be used by an able-bodied person. Had he known and wielded that? Or had it been a terrible happenstance?

Oh, Lord, how could You allow this to go so far? Her mother often employed the term *heartsick.* She told Heather she was "heartsick" over how things had deteriorated after the driver of her accident seemed to go unpunished. She'd been "heartsick" at how Dad let the injustice of it consume him. Heather was heartsick now. Unbearably heartsick at how a situation that had once been so filled with promise now compounded sorrow upon regret upon destruction. *It's all gone so horribly wrong, Lord. You're going to have to show me what to do because I truly don't know.*

The fire chief's red truck pulled up the street, and Chief Bradens's eyes looked as bad as she felt. Three other men got out of the truck and began pulling equipment out of the back. "The boys are here to power-wash that off the sidewalk. I've already talked to the police because I think these three ought to be the ones to scrub it off."

Heather thought she knew why, but she asked anyway. "Those three?"

"I'm sorry to say those three louts were the ones to rattle Jason Kikowitz's cage the other night. Well, them and someone JJ is probably yelling at again right about now. If you'll excuse me."

Chief Bradens walked his men up to the front door. She saw Brian wave his arms angrily, pointing at the three young men who had the good sense to look ashamed of themselves. The door slammed shut. Chief Bradens shook his head with the same disappointed frustration she'd been feeling and ordered the crew to get to work.

She looked up to offer Simon a friendly wave—just the smallest show of support—but the shades had been drawn. Sighing, Heather walked up to the door and rang the bell. It might do more harm than good, but she couldn't just stand there and not at least try to reach out to Simon.

Mrs. Williams was slow to come to the door, opening it only far enough to show her face. "Morning."

"I was wondering if maybe Simon would like to talk."

She didn't look too keen on the idea.

"Or," Heather tried, "at least I'd like the opportunity to tell him how sorry I am about all that's happened. Please."

"Let her in, Mom," Simon called from somewhere behind the door.

Mrs. Williams reluctantly opened the door wider and gestured Heather inside. Simon was in the living room of the tidy home, slumped on a recliner while his chair stood empty in a corner of the room. He looked like every other fifteen-year-old boy in the world sprawled on the chair like that, boasting a T-shirt and jeans and playing with some electronic device he had on his lap.

Heather sat down in the chair nearest him. Mrs. Williams stood in the archway to the room, arms crossed, watching.

"Mom…" Simon whined, glaring at his mom. "You mind?"

To Heather's surprise, Mrs. Williams unfolded her hands. "I'll be in the kitchen getting lunch started if you need me." She gave Heather an "I'm watching you" glare before she left the room.

Simon switched off the game and tossed it on the coffee table. "They're beyond mad, you know. I've never seen Dad so worked up."

Heather couldn't believe Simon's tone of voice. "They have every right to be. What happened was horrible. I'm really, really sorry."

"Yeah, well, that's high school. One rotten day after

another. Mom grounded me for getting detentions, which is pretty funny, since she never lets me go anywhere anyway. Kinda dumb."

"I wish you were coming back." It was true. Even though she could understand the Williamses' decision, she felt as if high school had so much to offer Simon. She believed things could get better, even though she had no idea how.

Simon shot a look toward the kitchen. "You and me both. Homeschool? Puh-lease."

Heather didn't know what to say. She'd expected Simon to want to stay home, not return to the scene of his torment. "You want to come back?"

Simon waved his hands around the room. "Would you want to spend all day in here? With them?"

The home was lovely, and his parents spared no effort on his behalf. How very like a teenager to find such an environment intolerable. "What about Kikowitz?"

"He's a jerk. I hate him." Evidently Simon didn't see what that had to do with it. He held up his phone. "I got a text from Candace. She told me she felt bad about letting it slip to Jason, that he'd sort of pulled it out of her when she hadn't meant to say anything. She said she'd understand if I didn't want to help her with her algebra anymore, but that she'd be really glad if I still could." He shot Heather a knowing glance. "She got another D. Really, it's not that hard—the girls in my class seem to get it okay."

"Simon." Heather tried to hide her astonishment. "Aren't you upset by what's happened?"

"Sure I am. It rots. Kikowitz is a jerk." He leaned in. "And I gotta say, Max is kind of a jerk, too. I mean, it's nice that the guys tried to help me out and all, but even

I could have told him something like this was gonna happen. Aren't adults supposed to know better? My parents will never let me play hockey now."

"Yes." Heather could not help but laugh. "Adults are supposed to know better." In many ways Simon was already so much wiser than his years. "I'm glad to know you see Max's response wasn't the right one."

"It was kinda cool but sorta stupid. How many other freshmen have henchmen?"

Maybe Simon wasn't as wise as she thought. "Henchmen?"

"That's what Dad called them. Well—" the boy smirked "—Dad called them lots of things, but he said they were no better than some villain's henchmen, getting revenge on the bad guy by being bad themselves."

"Your father is right, but I think *henchmen* is going a bit far." *That's Max Jones,* she thought. *Always going a bit too far and luring others to do the same.*

"I see it like this. When a mean kid trips and falls in the lunchroom, you know you shouldn't enjoy it, but you do. You know what I mean?"

"Simon, revenge is a really slippery business." She thought of her father and how the pursuit of justice had slid so easily into the craving for revenge. She'd found and read some of Max's earliest press statements from his accident, and she'd seen the same dangerous hunger in his words. She thought Max had grown beyond it; she knew her father had buried himself in it and now she wondered if her role here was to ensure Simon never went there at all. She scooted her chair closer. "I know you go to church, so I know you understand that God needs to play a part in how you handle all this. Your response to all this has to come from who you are, not who Jason is. Or who Max is. Or even who your parents are."

Simon shrugged his shoulders. "Pastor Allen was here this morning—Mom and Dad called him right after they called the police and school. He said pretty much the same thing. About me, that is—he left out the part about Mom, Dad and Max."

"Well, Simon, what do you want to do about all this?"

Simon slumped back against the chair cushions. "I want it all to go away. I just want to go to chemistry and Ping-Pong Club and have it all go away."

Heather slumped back against her own chair. "I hear you on that one."

Simon raised an eyebrow at her. "You're really ticked at him, aren't you?"

"Who? Jason? You bet I am."

"No, Max. I heard my mom telling my dad how you told her she could trust Max to be a good influence and all. Sorta botched that one, didn't he?"

Heather remembered thinking once that Simon might have a good deal to teach Max. "Yes, he missed it by a mile."

"He's still figuring it out, I guess. He's been in his chair, what, a year? I've been in mine my whole life. We've gotta give him time."

Heather smiled. "How old are you again, Simon?"

He grinned. "Sixteen in December."

She gave his hand a squeeze, and he groaned and flinched like every other teenage boy she'd ever known. "No, you're not. You're much, much older than that." She stood up, a silent prayer of thanks that God had made her path clear. "Do you really want to come back to school?"

"Better than being cooped up at home, even with Kikowitz."

"Okay, then. I'll see what I can do."

Chapter Twenty

"**M**om?" Heather gripped the phone tightly.

"Heather? It's Thursday. Aren't you in school?"

She sank into the couch. "I'm not going in today."

"Honey? Are you all right?"

"No." What was the point of hiding it? "I mean I'm fine—physically—but I need some advice."

Heather could hear her mother settle into her chair. "All right, then, what about?"

"Did you ever get to the point where you could forgive Dad for the way he behaved after I got hurt? I mean, did it ever get better with him, or between you?"

She heard Mom suck in a breath. "That's a big question. Maybe it would help if you tell me why you're asking."

Heather spilled out the whole story. In between fits of crying and anger, she chronicled the stormy progression from choosing Max as Simon's mentor to the horrors of what had been scrubbed from Simon's sidewalk. "I'm hurt. Simon's hurt. The fire department is hurt. I think even Jason Kikowitz is hurt. Mom, this went from bad to amazing to worse so fast I can't figure out what to do."

"Oh, honey, I'm so sorry you've been tangled up in such a mess. It hardly seems fair. You've had more than your share of this kind of thing already between Mike and your dad. I had no idea things had gotten so...personal...between you and this Max fellow."

Heather sank farther into the couch cushions, suddenly exhausted. "It sort of crept up on me. How can someone be so wonderful and then so horrible?"

Her mother's sigh held so much regret. "I asked that about your father so many times. He loved you so much. He would do anything for you. But your accident seemed to bring out something...I don't know...raw and angry inside him. Something that became bigger than him, something that swallowed up all the love inside him even though I think it was born out of his love for you." She paused before adding, "Yes, I forgave him, but it was a long time before I could."

Heather was hoping for something that would feel more like a solution. Instead, her mother's words made her feel as though she were living in a continual cycle of the same problem. As if injury, disease and their aftermath would haunt her the rest of her life.

"Why do you think Max did what he did? Did he tell you?"

"He thought he was standing up for Simon. Letting the bully kid know that there were bigger, stronger bullies who would defend Simon. He said he thought it had to be done, and he'd take the heat for it so that Simon wouldn't be a target again. Only he's just made Simon a bigger target—and let all of us down in the bargain. How can he claim to care about me and do something like this when he knew I was trusting him with Simon?" She grabbed a tissue off the coffee table as the tears started up again. "How, Mom?"

"He went about it all wrong, absolutely. But even I know that people lash out when something precious to them is threatened. I'm not making excuses, but it may be that Max wasn't quite ready for how much he'd come to care about you and Simon."

"He picked the worst way to show it."

"Oh, I agree. But even your father's vengeance began with his deep love for you. Your father just kept on going down the sinkhole, getting darker and darker. Seems to me Max will either wake up to what he's done and try to set it right, or he'll head down a sinkhole of his own."

"What do I do?" Her words sounded like a little girl's whine.

"I don't know that there's much you *can* do right now. Try to be there for Simon—do what's best for him. Pray. If Max is the man you think he might be, he'll own up to how he's hurt you. Your heart will tell you what to do then."

"What if it tells me to walk away? Like I did to Mike?"

"You know why you left Mike. Don't start doubting that decision just because it's come on you again. You are a survivor, Heather. You've healed from more than most people your age. God would not want you with someone who will hurt you. I'm certain what Max does next will tell you what you need to know. But I'll still pray." Her mom's voice took on the edge of tears now, too. "I've never stopped praying. I'm so proud of you. You know that?"

"I do, Mom. Thanks."

Heather set down the phone and echoed her Mom's advice. "Okay, Max Jones. The ball's in your court." She remembered the way Max had flung himself out of his chair to make Simon feel better that afternoon they had played Ping-Pong, and her heart twisted. *Get through to him, Lord. He could be so wonderful.*

"Will you tell him to give me a call or stop by the cabins?" Max handed the church secretary a card, feeling naive for expecting Pastor Allen to be free and available whenever a sorry soul came waltzing into church in need. God probably only worked like that in the movies. Then again, when that steeple had appeared in his sights, all lit in sunshine like a neon arrow pointing "Go here"...

A thought struck him. "Hey, what's the name of that older lady from the knitting group, the short one, kinda feisty? Her name starts with a *V,* I think..."

"Violet Sharpton?"

"Yes, her. Are you allowed to give me her phone number?"

"I won't need to. She's just down the hall in the church library. You can go talk to her yourself."

Max found himself not entirely ready to put this particular plan into action. Still, he'd heard the knitting ladies talk about how shawls were best for times when words wouldn't do, and he knew he didn't have the words to apologize to Heather. He'd hoped that talking with the pastor would help him find the words...but maybe he could show his remorse in another way. Max wheeled himself out of the office in the direction the secretary had pointed, trying not to think that maybe

Pastor Allen wasn't available just so Violet Sharpton could hear his outrageous request. *I'm not ready to be one of JJ's "God appointments."*

When he turned into the library, Mrs. Sharpton was standing at a table stacked high with children's books.

"Hot Wheels! You're the last person I expected to see today. How are you, Max?"

How to answer that? "I'm in a bit of hot water, Mrs. Sharpton, and I think I might need your help."

She whipped off her glasses and came around to his side of the table. "Well, now, that's a mighty intriguing answer. Let me sit down and you can tell me what's up."

At first he yearned to spill out the whole story, but he decided some of the details weren't quite public and perhaps it was time to show a little discretion for a change. "I've done something that's hurt Heather Browning, and I'd like to ask you to make a special prayer shawl as my way of apologizing."

The older woman folded her hands. "Oh, my. That sounds serious."

"I suppose it is." Max cast his eyes around the room, suddenly self-conscious. This was a silly, mushy idea and he shouldn't be here. And yet it also seemed like the perfect gesture. "It's…it's not something I can easily fix. As a matter of fact, it might not be something I can fix at all, which is why I think the shawl might be a good idea."

"Means that much to you, does she?"

The older woman was making grand assumptions, but her eyes were so amused he found he couldn't get angry. "Well, I don't really know yet, Mrs. Sharpton."

She waved his denial away with a *tsk*. "Call me Vi. And of course you know. You wouldn't be here with your face so red if you didn't." She gave him a "fess up" look that would have had him sinking guiltily into a chair if he wasn't already in one. "What did you do, son?"

He really didn't want to go into it. Then again, if Gordon Falls worked the way everyone said it did, everyone would know before the end of the day anyhow. He told her the shortest version of recent events he could manage.

"Well, now, I don't know what to say." She planted her thin little hands on her hips. "Half of me wants to clap you on the back for giving that hooligan a what for, and the other half wants to knock you upside the head for showing such a poor example. What ever made you think that was a smart idea?"

Before he realized it, Max had spilled the whole business about Mike Pembrose and the speech Luke Sullivan had given him. He hadn't even told most of that to JJ, so he had no idea why it all came out to this little gray-haired spitfire of a woman who somehow seemed kind and chastising at the same time. "I think we're pretty much a lost cause, Heather and I, and that's for the best. Still, I feel like I have to do something and not leave it like this."

Vi sat back in her chair, folding her arms across her chest. "So, you've decided it's a lost cause, have you? Better to not give Heather a chance to let you down than to risk taking it any further. That Luke Sullivan was right all along, you think."

Well, when you put it that way... Max shrugged, at a loss for an answer.

Violet Sharpton reached out and whacked him on

the head. "Luke Sullivan is dead wrong, young man! And where he is right now ought to prove it to you!"

"Ouch!" Max couldn't quite believe the woman had such a left hook.

"I'm glad that hurt. You need to wake up. You're not afraid she'll leave you—you're afraid she *won't!*" She addressed the ceiling—or God, Max wasn't quite sure which. "What's the matter with young people today, wanting life all tied up in pretty bows with all the problems solved?"

"I hardly think my life is all tied up in—"

"Don't interrupt me, Hot Wheels. I'm just getting started. You got hurt bad—I get that. Lots of men I know wouldn't be able to pull themselves out of a hole like that, much less with your admirable sense of panache. You've got a right to be angry—but only for a while and not at the whole world. Heather Browning could be the best thing that's ever happened to you. Only I think you already know that. So step up to the plate, son—or wheel up to it, in your case—and grab at a chance with her. You will not regret it even if she does break your heart in the end because *you will have given it a shot.*" She grabbed his hand, shaking it with each word. "And that's what matters." Her eyes teared up a bit, making Max wonder what in life had given her all that fire.

"I'll bet Mr. Sharpton is an awesome guy."

Her expression gave Max the answer. "He was, honey. He truly was."

Had his parents ever loved each other like that? Fierce and full of life? He'd never heard Mom talk about Dad that way. Alex and JJ had that maybe, but it was still so new for them. At the end of it all, he wanted what Vi had had. Anything else wouldn't feel like enough. "I'm sorry for your loss."

She sniffed. "Don't be sorry. Be telling me what color yarn to buy."

"Do you think you could pull off pink with flamingos?"

Her smile sparkled, even with the tears still brimming in her eyes. "After your flamethrower, I can do *anything*."

Max rolled past the church office ten minutes later. "You can tell Pastor Allen he doesn't need to call me back."

The secretary looked up, baffled. "Are you sure?"

"Yep. Violet Sharpton just took me to church."

Chapter Twenty-One

Margot stood in Heather's office doorway Friday morning. "Mrs. Williams just sent me an email formally requesting Simon's withdrawal from school." Margot never sugarcoated bad news. While Heather knew that—and often liked that about her—she wished for a softer blow this morning.

"After all that conversation yesterday? All Simon's pleading?" She'd spent several hours after school yesterday helping Simon tell his parents he didn't want to stay home. She felt the failure settle around her like a lead wrapping. Margot was right—this had become a deeply personal battle for her.

"They are his parents. It's their decision."

Heather pushed away her keyboard and sunk her chin into her hands. "What do you think?"

Margot leaned against the doorway and sighed. "I think Simon is becoming his own person, and that's good. But that person is still only fifteen and may not know what's best right now. There's always next year. Or even next semester."

"That doesn't help. I hate it that Kikowitz wins. Why

does he get to come back to school and rule the lunch-room while Simon sits at home?"

"Coach Mullen suspended him from the play-offs, if that makes you feel any better."

Heather raised a doubtful eyebrow. "It should, but it doesn't."

Margot folded her hands in front of her in an "it is what it is" gesture. "Well, we've still got curriculum night to get through and I—" She caught sight of some-thing in the hallway that stopped her midsentence. "I'm going to leave you to your visitor."

"My visitor?"

Max wheeled into the administrative offices, a seri-ous look seeming foreign on his usually cavalier fea-tures.

Margot caught Heather's eye. "Unless you need me to stay?"

"No," Heather said quietly. Even after everything that had happened, how could she still be so drawn in by Max's presence? "I'm okay."

"You're sure?"

She nodded. Max, who still had not said a word, wheeled silently into her office. She let him nudge the guest chair aside, needing to keep her desk between them. "I asked you not to come to school."

"I know you did. But I can't get up the stairs to your apartment and I wasn't sure you'd come down to meet me if I called."

He was right; she probably wouldn't have. He still tugged at her heart in ways she wasn't strong enough to resist. How fair was it that he seemed twice as com-pelling now as he had when he was all boastful and defiant?

"This is for you." He placed a small package on her desk rather than handing it directly to her. She was glad of that—she didn't want to risk any touch from him right now. "Well, sort of. It's not really a gift, more of an…offering."

Intrigued, she picked up the package and pulled open the brown paper wrapping. Inside was the Never Apologize shirt she'd seen him wear multiple times. *Really?* That was his idea of an offering? As far as she was concerned, Max owed her a handful of apologies.

"I can't wear it anymore. Mostly because you're about to become the first person I've apologized to in years. I hurt you. I betrayed your trust in me, and I hurt Simon." He waited until she looked up at him before adding, "I'm sorry. I know it probably doesn't change anything, but I am sorry."

He was right; it didn't change anything. Part of her was glad he didn't go so far as to ask for her forgiveness, because she wasn't ready to give it. "Simon wants to come back to school but his parents just requested he be withdrawn for homeschooling. I tried to change their minds, but I failed."

"He wants to come back, after all that, but they won't let him?" The old defiant Max appeared in the narrowing of his eyes.

She parroted Margot's words. "It's their decision. He's their son." After a moment, she added, "And we haven't given them a lot of reasons to place their confidence in us to keep him safe." Some wounded part of her wanted to snap, *Thanks to you,* but she didn't. Max was the catalyst, surely, but he wasn't the whole problem. "Even if Kikowitz is expelled, I couldn't hope to assure them some other bully wouldn't pick up where he left off."

"That's not a reason. Life is full of Kikowitzes."

"Maybe it *is* best. Simon is so bright—he'll probably be ready for college courses by his sophomore year if he homeschools. The state college would be so much more welcoming to him than we could ever be."

He frowned at her. "You don't believe that."

She was trying to, if only to soften the sting of failing Simon. "It's not my choice."

Max ran his hands down his face. "So now what?"

"There isn't anything to do, Max." All that was left now was to slosh her way through the aftermath and pray that some good came out of the month Simon had been at school. She couldn't bear the thought that all this had come to nothing at all.

"*I* don't believe *that*."

She held up the shirt. "Then, if you want something to do, I think you should go apologize to Simon and his parents. If there's one thing you can still teach Simon, it's how a man behaves when he's wrong." She stunned herself with the force of her words.

"I doubt they'll let me."

She stood up. "Then simply let Simon see you try."

She expected Max to huff *Fine!* and wheel from the room. Instead he looked up at her with something she'd never seen in his eyes before and asked, "Will you come with me?"

It was a long, unsteady moment before she replied. "Yes."

Max had flung himself off a cliff at night in the rain and not been as anxious as he was now. Of course, he had been a different man before that night, caring about different things and not caring about a lot of things.

Somehow—and Max still wasn't quite sure how—this whole business with Simon and Heather had become a tipping point. As he wheeled past the faint orange lettering still visible on the sidewalk in front of the Williamses' house, Max knew big things were riding on the outcome of today.

"Hello." Brian Williams's eyes were as icy as his tone when he pulled open the front door. While the ramp built for Simon made it logistically easy to go inside, the invisible obstacles felt like Mount Everest. Max couldn't be certain if he'd be allowed to stay ten seconds after offering his apology, but he was going to try.

"Good afternoon, Mr. Williams." Max held out a hand, but Mr. Williams declined to shake it. It was a painful reminder of the time just after his accident when Alex Cushman had extended a hand to him, and he'd been the one to refuse the courtesy. That vengeful first meeting with Alex had eventually led to a business partnership—and a family connection now that Alex was JJ's husband. Max let that truth carry him past Brian's cold greeting and keep his optimism. *Time,* as Alex was fond of saying, *for God to show how big He is.*

"Hi, Simon. Hello, Mr. and Mrs. Williams." Heather managed to keep her tone light and cheerful even though Max knew she'd caught the father's gesture.

Max moved his attention to Simon's mother, who perched nervously on the living room couch. "I want to thank you for letting me come, Mrs. Williams. I know this wasn't easy."

She simply nodded, worrying the end of her sweater between her fingers.

"Hey, kid." Max bumped his fist against Simon's.

The gesture lacked Simon's usual enthusiasm, but Simon also didn't share his parents' frowns, so that was something. "I hope it's okay that I brought you a present." The gift had been Alex's idea, and since his boss was an acknowledged master of communication, Max had taken the advice.

The package produced a small smile from Simon. "Whoa! These are sick." He extracted a set of fingerless leather gloves—the kind preferred by wheelchair athletes. The flame motif was just an added bonus.

Heather leaned toward Mrs. Williams. "'Sick' is good, just in case you were wondering." Max was sure that would get a laugh, but it didn't.

"Try them on. I think I got the size right." He wheeled closer to Simon and helped the boy wiggle his hands into the fierce-looking gloves. "The grip is outstanding. I got these from a wheelchair rugby team, and those guys are very picky about their gloves. They should let you crush your opponents at the Ping-Pong table." He regretted that last remark. Simon wasn't likely to play Ping-Pong if he didn't go back to school. Maybe he'd ask Alex to help him find a way to get a table donated to the church youth group.

"Thanks." Simon flexed his fingers and then wobbled in his usual slow, precarious gait over to the chair in the corner of the room. The fact he could walk even short distances was going to make life so much easier for Simon. So many more things were possible for him—it doubled Max's conviction to keep him out in the world. When Simon slipped into the chair and popped enough of a wheelie to make his mother groan, Max could only smile.

Heather caught Max's eye, nodding. It was time to do what he came to do.

"Mr. and Mrs. Williams, I'd like to offer you an apology for my role in what happened. I had the chance to stop the business with Jason Kikowitz, and instead I let how much I like Simon cloud my better judgment." He directed his next words to Simon. "I wanted to protect you, and I went about it in exactly the wrong way. And you paid for it." He looked back at Simon's parents. "You all paid for it. I was supposed to be showing Simon the right way to act, and I did the furthest thing from it." The next part was hardest of all. "I'm sorry— really sorry—and I hope you'll find your way to forgiving me someday." Apologizing went against Max's nature, but asking for forgiveness felt like ripping his skin off and sitting there like an open wound. The resulting silence in the room made Max want to squirm.

"You were hugely stupid to do that."

"Simon!" Mrs. Williams chided her son's pronouncement.

"No, he's right." Max looked at Simon, newly amazed by this kid. "It *was* a supremely stupid thing to do, and I'm glad you see it that way. I wanted Kikowitz to know the guys and I had your back and that he couldn't rough you up without consequences. Only 'thugging' him wasn't the right way to do it. I let you down, I behaved like a two-year-old, and I'm sorry. But we do have your back, Simon. Know that."

"Thank goodness you don't have to go back there." Mr. Williams spoke for the first time. Simon's whole body reacted to the statement. It didn't take a counseling degree to read the body language in the room: Mr. Williams was set on Simon's withdrawal, Simon was against it and Mrs. Williams was caught somewhere in the middle.

"I want to go back there, Dad." Simon popped another small wheelie with a little rock back and forth at the top. Max was proud Simon had mastered the trick, but found this a counterproductive moment for hotdogging.

"How on earth can you want to go back there?" Mrs. Williams's tone was filled with a mother's worry.

"It's high school. Okay, it's not perfect, but there's lots of stuff I like. Things I can do. Friends I can spend time with."

Girls, Max added silently.

"You have friends at youth group. And no one's going to start fights with you there."

"I was hoping," Heather offered in a careful tone, "that we might find some sort of compromise."

"With all due respect, Ms. Browning, we've already seen how little you can do to protect my son. I think it's best we call this experiment to an end and count our blessings there was no real harm done."

"The real harm is that I get stuck at home when I could be at school." Simon sounded as put out as any teen Max had ever heard. With an insolent glare straight at his dad, he added, "Like *normal* kids."

"Simon, I'm thirsty." Heather stood up. "Can you show me where to get a glass of water in your kitchen?" Max guessed she was trying to salvage the conversation before Simon goaded his parents into an all-out battle. Max saw more of his own personality in Simon than he'd ever expected that first day the boy had wheeled meekly into the gym.

The air grew thick as Heather and Simon left the

room. This kind of diplomacy was so far out of Max's skill set that he found himself throwing up a panicked *Help!* to heaven. He tried to meet Mrs. Williams's eyes, but she looked down at her hands.

Mr. Williams simply glared at him. "Simon has changed." It was crystal clear where he placed that blame.

"Simon is growing up. He's trying to figure out who he is, and that means who he is apart from you. I was the same—actually, I was ten times worse—in high school." When that met with no reception, Max plowed on. "I think the world of your son. He's smart and so much tougher than he looks. There are so many things he could do, so much stuff out there for him to try and explore."

"It's our job to protect Simon. Surely you can see that." Mrs. Williams folded her hands in her lap.

"I get that. I know I'm not a parent, and I'm not even two years out from my injury, but I do understand." Max ran his hands down his face, straining for the right words. "But what I hope you understand is that life is filled with Kikowitzes. Guys who will single Simon— or even me—out as the weak target and pounce. Don't you want Simon to know how to handle it? Don't you want him to be able to go out into the world, go to college, have a job, travel, all that stuff?"

"Of course we want Simon to have a rich and full life."

"Then maybe the best time and place for him to learn how to handle guys like Kikowitz is now, in school, where he's got loads of support and guidance." Max leaned in, determined to put every ounce of persuasion he had into the moment. "He's so, so smart. He'll get knocked down—I know that—but Simon will get back up. Come on—he already has. He told you he wants to go back. You've gotta let him."

"You have a lot of nerve telling us what we have to do after the way you've acted." Mr. Williams crossed his arms over his chest.

The old Max would have pounced on that. Today, Max knew Brian Williams was absolutely correct. "You're right. I've got no say in this. Except that the last months I've spent out in the real world, away from the nice supportive cocoon of rehab, have taught me how tough it is to get by. It's hard. Some days it's really hard." Max shifted his gaze to Mrs. Williams, hoping the soft spot he had for Simon would come through in his words. "But I look at Simon and I see a kid who has what it's going to take. He's got so much more confidence than he did even a month ago. He's got parents who would do anything for him. He's got enough wit to defuse a situation when someone is a jerk, and soon enough he'll have the experience to know how and when to use that wit instead of a right hook or a well-rammed footrest. Please don't let my lack of good sense keep Simon from staying out there in the world."

"Your son stood up to a bully." Heather's voice came from the entryway. "That takes strength. I know he didn't do it the way we all would have liked—"

"You've all made *that* clear!" Simon shouted from the kitchen, proving the walls had ears.

"But he stood up for himself nonetheless. He's also bearing the consequences with a fair amount of maturity—"

"I'm grounded for life—did you know that?" Simon's dramatic declaration bellowed from the kitchen.

Max tried not to grin. He'd been grounded any number of lifetimes.

"With as much maturity as you can expect at fifteen." Heather finally finished her thought. "I can't say that about too many students these days."

"We'll think about what you've said," Mrs. Williams offered.

"I think we're finished here." Mr. Williams declared the visit over.

Max headed toward the door, shooting Simon a wave as he went by the kitchen. "See you around?"

Simon shrugged. "Um, 'grounded for life,' remember?"

Max mimed texting on a cell phone, raising one eyebrow. "They take away your phone?"

Simon shook his head. "Nobody's that cruel."

Max gave Simon a thumbs-up and rolled out the door, hoping that wasn't the last time he'd see Simon Williams.

Chapter Twenty-Two

Max sat at his desk Monday, completely unable to work, willing his cell phone to ring. It had been two whole days since he'd laid his conscience bare in front of the Williams family, and the lack of response was eating him alive. Simon's future had become deeply, personally important to him, and his passion for the boy's opportunities lay foreign and unsettling in his stomach.

"I'd always expected I'd catch your passion for the whole world—the 'getting guys with disabilities out into experiences' thing—but not in terms of one scrawny, brilliant kid." Max was glad Alex was in the office today, because he needed to talk this out with someone or he'd explode. "The need to make this right is driving me nuts."

As soon as the words left his mouth, Max realized how close to home that urge must feel to Alex. His boss and brother-in-law had talked many times about his old company's role in making the climbing line Max had been using when he fell. Max was here and had the amazing job he did because of Alex's persistent need to "put things right." Okay, falling for JJ may have amplified that a bit, but Max's tumult was tangled up with Heather, too.

"Who'd have guessed we'd end up with so much in common?" Alex said with a quiet smile, then pointed up and added, "Well, except for you know who." He walked over and perched on the corner of Max's desk, picking up the drawings of new "Maxed Out" lightning-bolt wheel panels that would be in the company's next catalog. "I boast I know how to think outside the box, but the Good Lord blew me out of the water on this one."

"Yeah."

Alex raised an eyebrow. "Yeah?"

Usually Max dismissed any of Alex's continual comments about how God had paved the way for this whole venture, but he knew too much now to ignore how God had intervened in his life. If anyone understood what he was going through, it was Alex. Alex, who at one point was his enemy, the man he'd set out to crush. If that wasn't evidence of God and grace in his life, what was?

"Heather said something to me one night. It's stuck with me, working on me until I could actually, well, believe it." He ran his hands through his hair, trying to put that moment into words.

Alex set the drawings down. "What?"

"The night that whole thing blew up with Simon and his parents—the first time, I mean—I got frustrated enough to spit out to Heather that I was furious at God for letting me fall." These words were hard to say to Alex, but they'd long had to learn to be honest with each other. "For dropping me."

He could see the impact of the words in Alex's eyes.

There were people who insisted it was Alex's company's climbing line that had failed Max. Max no longer felt that to be true. Lots of things were to blame for what had happened that night, but none more than Max's own arrogance. Alex's silence spoke of the whole hard journey the past year and a half had been for everyone.

"Heather said the most amazing thing when I blurted that out." Max made a point to look straight at Alex, wanting him to see that it had gone beyond hurt and blame, wanting him to believe the healing Max knew was taking place. "She said…" Max remembered the unbelievable tenderness in Heather's tone and the words suddenly caught in his throat. "She said she believed God caught me just in time."

Alex's eyes closed for a moment, and Max knew the words were just as powerful for him. "You hang on to that woman, Max Jones. She's a keeper."

Max was planning to tell Heather just what she'd done that night when he got the chance to give her the prayer shawl Violet Sharpton had made. "I'm trying, Alex. There's a mile of hurt between us right now—and I put most of it there—but I'm fighting it with everything I've got. She came with me to talk to Simon and his parents, so that's something." He sunk his head onto his hands. "This is so hard."

Alex rested a hand on his shoulder. "You've done a million near-impossible things since I've met you, Max. I'm pretty sure you can pull this off." He spun his wedding ring with his thumb. "Some things are worth fighting for with all you've got. I'm pretty sure Heather's one of them." He gave Max's shoulder a squeeze before letting go. "Although I wouldn't mind if you at least *tried* to do battle with next year's sponsorship schedule."

Max despised paperwork. Alex could whip up plans and spreadsheets and timetables with his eyes closed, but that kind of forethought was like a foreign language to Max. "It's late—I know." He groaned. "If just one of them—Simon or Heather or even Brian Williams— would call me I'd be able to think straight, you know?"

"Yeah," Alex commiserated. "I do know. But try anyway."

Max wrestled with the spreadsheet for over an hour, and even the addition of an extra-strong coffee from down the street hadn't bolstered his success. He was just about to slam something hard into his computer monitor when his cell phone rang. With a wide smile he saw Heather's name on the screen.

"Are you sitting down?"

Some part of him was overjoyed that she could make such a joke. The caution and careful nature of their conversations lately jangled his nerves. "As a matter of fact, I am. Good guess."

"I had two visitors this morning."

Please, Lord, let one of them be Simon. Please. The prayer slipped out of Max with unexpected ease. "You did?"

"Linda Williams came in this morning. She wanted to know if we could hold a place for Simon for the second semester."

Max felt the illogical sensation of his heart both leaping and falling at the same time. "You mean in January? Not now?" It didn't feel like enough of a victory.

His words must have echoed his frustration. "I

think it's a good compromise, Max. It gives everyone a chance to catch their breath and keeps the door open for Simon to come back. And it wouldn't be happening at all if it weren't for you." The tone of her voice changed completely, now soft and low. "Thank you. You did an amazing thing back there at Simon's. I wish you could have seen Simon's face as he heard you talking about him. He looks up to you so much, even after all that's happened. Maybe especially because of all that's happened."

"Then why on earth hasn't the guy called me? Texted? Anything."

Heather's laugh was sweet to hear. "They grounded him from his cell phone and computer outside of classwork until the end of the month."

"Ouch. He said they wouldn't be that cruel."

"I had another visitor this morning, too. What exactly did you say to Candace Norden?"

Max had hoped his role in that one wouldn't ever get back to Heather. She might consider it meddling if not outright manipulation. "Um…about what?"

"She came in asking for the form needed to take a non-student to the homecoming dance. Something about a bargain of a date for an A in algebra? And the chance to put something right?"

Max laughed and slapped his hands over his eyes. "I didn't really think she'd do it." That wasn't exactly true—he'd carefully couched it as an offhand comment, then prayed like crazy that that the notion would stick.

"So you *did* give her the idea to take Simon to homecoming?"

Max winced. He still couldn't read from her tone

whether Heather approved or disapproved of his plan, and things were precarious enough between them as it was. "Maybe."

"You convinced a junior on the cheerleading squad to take a freshman in a wheelchair to the homecoming dance?" Was that awe or annoyance?

"Well, okay, there may have been a little incentive thrown in about my paying for dinner at The Black Swan. They need another chance to get the ramp right, you know."

There was an exasperating silence on the other end of the phone before she replied, "You're amazing."

"Is that amazing great or amazing bad?"

He wouldn't have thought he could hear a smile over the phone, but she sighed in a way that made his heart gallop in his chest. "That's amazing amazing." Her tone required no other qualifier. Max felt his eyes shut and his shoulders unwind. He hadn't lost her. At least not completely. And she didn't know what was coming.

I've gotta win her back, Lord. You know that. I can't lose her. Not yet. Max thought about the package in the back of his van, newly fetched from Violet Sharpton, who was "amazing amazing" in her own right. He checked his watch. Ten after three meant school was done for the day. "Can you meet me at the wheel bridge in half an hour?"

"The wheel bridge?"

"Well, for you it's the footbridge, but you know what I mean." It felt delightful to be able to tease her again. Her laugh untied the knots that had been twisting in his gut for days.

"Do you ever stop, Max?"

Max looked up to see Alex holding up a note in the palm of his hand that read, "Leave now and go get her!"

"Only when there's a staircase, and maybe not even then," he told Heather.

Heather couldn't wipe the smile off her face as she drove past The Black Swan. She'd avoided the place since that night, unable to bear the reminder of how things had unraveled since then. Inside that restaurant, even despite the challenges of making that evening work, Heather had begun to believe she could build a life with Max Jones. It had been an unsteady, fragile belief, but Max's eyes, his passion for life right down to the spontaneous pirouette under the balcony, and his heart-stopping kiss had all bloomed a strength within her.

His actions afterward had put that strength to the test. She knew Max could be bitter and resentful; she'd seen his impulsive side run off with his good sense. Heather didn't want to be caught in the crosshairs of that kind of life, battling someone always on the defensive, always with something to prove. That kind of man had soured her parents' marriage, had tainted her engagement with a man who insisted that God had wronged him.

What she'd heard from Simon's kitchen was a different man. A man who could endure what life—what God—had asked of him. She had always suspected the Max on wheels had become a better man than the Max who walked. The words she'd heard at Simon's house had proven that to be true. As Heather pulled up to the parking lot that sat next to the Gordon River, she knew she was almost ready to give her heart to Max Jones.

Almost. She prayed that when she looked into his eyes today, God would grant her whatever last piece she needed to get past "almost."

He sat at the near end of the charming footbridge that was the unofficial symbol of Gordon Falls, a spectacular smile lighting up his face. That grin was accompanied by a twinkle in his eye that couldn't be classified as anything short of mischievous. Max was up to something.

Max was *always* up to something. It was one of the best and scariest things about that man.

"Hi there." The way he looked at her made her feel, well, beautiful. Not glamorous beautiful, but the inner, lasting kind of beautiful. A woman no longer afraid to be noticed. A woman capable of making a difference in someone's life—and not just Simon's and Max's.

"Hello."

She noticed a package in his lap. He caught her gaze and winked. "I'm hoping we have a lot to celebrate today."

Me, too, Heather thought as they moved toward the set of benches that sat at the very center of the bridge, one of the prettiest spots in town. "I'm so glad about Simon."

"That kid's gotten to me. I want him to succeed so bad I can taste it." He gestured for her to sit down. He was uncharacteristically fidgety, a departure from the ever-cool guy who had rolled up to school back in August. He seemed to know, as she did, that today would be a turning point for them.

"I know you do. I think it's wonderful. And he'll make it. I just know he will."

Max reached out his hand, palm up, asking for

Heather's to slip inside his grasp. "I want us to make it, too. I hope you know that. I'm scared to death we don't know how, but if God caught me when I was falling then, I figure he'll catch me when I'm falling now." He wrapped his hand around hers. "I've fallen for you." He suddenly slumped forward, a wincing sort of laugh echoing from up under his shaggy hair. "Oh, man," he moaned, still gripping her hand. "That sounded *so much less stupid* in my head." He looked up at her, cringing and smiling at the same time.

Heather could feel a smile bursting across her face. Max's awkward, imperfect declaration charmed her more than any sonnet or grand gesture. Laugher bubbled up from a joyful place inside her, a place she hadn't felt for a long, long time. "It was…was…" She groped for the right words, settling on, "Wonderfully cheesy."

She pulled his hand to her lips and kissed it. "I fell, too. And I want us to make it, too." She held his callused fingers to her cheek, reveling in the strength of them. "I'm ready, I think. I'm not going to walk away, Max. You need to know that. I don't think I can anymore. I need you too much. I think we need each other." She took a deep breath, daring herself to say what she'd already realized she came there to say. "I'm in love with you. Warts and all, wheels and all, wild and all." Some part of her was so proud to say it first. It was such an enormous leap toward the woman she wanted to be. The woman Max could help her become.

Max reached out to cradle her face in both of his hands. "I am head over wheels in love with you, Heather Browning." With that he kissed her so grandly she nearly fell off the bench, sending them into peals of splendid, happy laughter. "Oh!" he cried, smiling wider than she'd ever seen him. "I can't believe I forgot this. I was going to give this to you before my little speech…." He put his hand to his forehead and moaned, "That horrible little speech. I should have had Alex write me something."

"No," she refuted. "It was perfect. I wouldn't change a word."

Max gave her an I-doubt-that look, but he handed her the package.

Heather saw fringe first. A band of long green fringe, interspersed with a few shots of black. As she began to unfold the soft fluffy fabric, she recognized it as knitting. Only it didn't look like any of the prayer shawls she'd seen before. Opening it more, Heather uncovered an amazing design of the palest pink background with a flock of flamboyant pink flamingos standing on each end. The pattern was such that the fringe looked like sea grass and the black flamingo legs extended down to become the black bits of fringe so that the whole piece looked like two flocks of flamingos standing in the tropics. "Oh, Max! It's incredible!" And it was. It was playful and soft and just a little bit outrageous. The absolute perfect prayer shawl for her. "How?"

"Violet Sharpton. Evidently she enjoys a challenge."

Heather held it up, laughing at the soft and silly flock of her very own. She pulled it around her shoulders, feeling every bit of the affection she knew was behind the gift. "I love it." She leaned over so that the ends found their way around Max's shoulders. "I love you."

Max pulled her down onto his chair. "I was hoping you'd say that." He kissed her again, and they sat there, wrapped up in flamingos and pure joy, looking out at the fall spectacle that was the Gordon River in October.

It was as close to a perfect moment as Heather could ever hope to come. "So I guess we do have a lot to celebrate today," she whispered into Max's hair.

"We could have a whole pie each and not come close to hitting the mark." Max laughed and planted a kiss on her shoulder.

"I think a slice will do. Karl's?"

He spun the chair in the direction of the riverbank. "Hang on, darlin'—it's all downhill from here."

Heather held up the shawl, letting the fringe flutter in the breeze as they rolled toward town.

Chapter Twenty-Three

Heather still hadn't stopped grinning as she watched Karl push open the back door to let them into the coffee shop. The old man's eyes held a knowing sparkle, making Heather wonder if she and Max looked as obvious as some of the high school's more love-struck couples.

She was not prepared for the waves of applause that broke out as they rolled to the front. She'd forgotten that Karl's gave an unobstructed view of the footbridge. When she saw Violet Sharpton rise from the booth with the best view, she suspected it wasn't a coincidence.

Violet winked and gave Max's shoulder a nudge. "I guess it did the trick?"

Max puffed up his chest. "Well, now, I'd like to think I had the lady's heart before I pulled out the knitting—but it sure helped seal the deal."

Heather gave Violet a hug. "It's wonderful. I can't believe you came up with this design. I love it."

"It was a pleasure to make one for a happy occasion. Or one to *make* a happy occasion. When Max called and asked if it was ready, I knew it was time to get the Tuesday women's prayer chain fired up to help untangle this whole mess. Marge was here having coffee when she caught sight of you two out on the bridge, so she called me." The older woman's eyes sparkled. "Happiest stakeout I've done in a long, long time."

"Thank you, Violet." Max grasped her hand. "Really."

Violet pinched Max's cheek as if he'd just become her eleventh grandchild. "My pleasure, Hot Wheels."

"I may just have to learn to knit this summer when school's out," Heather offered.

"Why wait? Melba's a great teacher, and we could use a few more of your age anyhow." Violet raised an eyebrow at Max. "What about you? You could give knitting a whole new kind of style."

Heather pictured Max with yarn and needles and burst out laughing just as Max vigorously shook his head. "I'll pass," he said. "I'm not ready for that kind of adventure." He took Heather's hand. "If you don't mind, I've got some celebratory pie to eat. And thanks again. You're one awesome grandma."

Violet preened. "One awesome grandma. Maybe I can figure out a way to get that on my license plate like you do. Go on, hon. Go eat pie with your sweetheart."

Heather felt as if her cheeks were burning as she sat at the table Karl had already cleared for Max. The whole restaurant was watching them. Max would always draw attention wherever he went. Was she ready for that? Could she ever grow accustomed to standing out like this with him? He took her hand across the table, his expression warm and encouraging as if he could read her worries. He nodded toward their audience, who were peering over menus or casting glances over coffee mugs or even flat-out staring. "Maybe I could learn not to stand out quite so much, huh?"

She shook her head. "You?"

He gave her a heart-melting look. "I'd do it. For you."

Goodness, but the man could ooze charm. "Don't change. Don't you dare fade into the background."

A little boy walked up to the table and pointed to Max's wheels. "Are you a Transformer? Like on TV?"

His mom immediately planted her hands over the boy's mouth. "I'm so sorry."

"Nah," Max said, smiling. "It's okay, really." He angled out from under the table. "I'm just a guy like you, only my legs don't work as well as yours, so they need a little help. But I can do a few neat tricks." Max shifted his feet to make room on the footrest, the same as he had done for Heather that night. "Here—hop on for a second and I'll show you."

The boy looked up at his mom, who gave a cautious nod. "It'll be fine," Heather added, seeing the mom's worry. "I've done it."

Max told the boy where to hold on, then wheeled out into the aisle and did a series of spins that sent the little guy into a torrent of happy giggles. *He has such a gift for this,* Heather thought. How good it was to admire Max as much as she loved him.

"I can ride bikes like you." Max's voice held a tenderness she hadn't seen in him before. She remembered the hurt in his eyes when the little girl had stared the last time they were in Karl's. That edge was gone. "I like ice cream the same as you, and I have favorite TV shows just like you. We're the same in more ways than we're different. Don't you think?"

"'Cept you gots a girlfriend. I'm too young for that."

Max stared at Heather, holding her gaze with nothing short of a smolder as he spun the boy one last time. "I sure do. And don't worry, I'm sure you'll get your chance one day with a smile like you've got. Hey, what's your name, sport?"

"Theo."

"You go to school here, Theo?"

Theo nodded. "Yep."

"Well, maybe I can come to your class one of these days and show you all my cool wheel toys. Would you like that?"

Heather's heart swelled when Theo's eyes lit up. "Sure!"

"I've got another friend named Simon who is in a wheelchair, too. Okay if he comes along?"

The vision of Max and Simon visiting a kindergarten classroom practically reduced Heather to tears. She grabbed Max's hand as he returned to the table. "Don't you dare change. Don't you dare tone it down, ever." She swiped a tear from her burning cheek. "It's one of the things I love about you."

Max laced his fingers through hers. "*Things?* Plural? Good. Let's get some pie and you can tell me all of them."

Epilogue

"Why are we stopping at the firehouse?" Heather asked as JJ pulled into the station driveway after they'd had lunch after church one Sunday afternoon.

JJ undid her seat belt. "Max texted and I told him I'd swing by and drop you off."

The February day was unseasonably warm, and Max had made plans to shoot hoops with some of the firemen off shift. The game they played wasn't quite basketball, but some sort of game they'd dreamed up to accommodate Max's sitting versus their standing. He'd explained it to her twice and she'd even sat and watched the day Simon joined in, but she still didn't get it. It didn't really matter—it was fun and Max had developed deeper friendships with several of the GFVFD force. Max's Element in the corner of the drive now boasted an I Support GFVFD sticker on his back window like nearly every other car in town.

She knew the basketball hoop was out back, but that didn't explain why the bay was empty. Usually there was always someone cleaning trucks or washing equipment, but no one could be seen.

"They're probably in there somewhere. Let's go find them."

Heather and JJ pushed through the station doors, Heather wondering if they always kept the lights off like this. Wasn't there supposed to be someone on-site all the time? "Max?" Heather called. "Are you in here?"

"Back here." Max's voice came from the dining room, but she still saw no lights on from over that way.

JJ began flicking light switches as they went until she finally reached the doorway and threw the switch that bathed the dining hall in light.

Revealing Max amid a dozen or so firefighters standing at attention in full dress uniforms behind him.

"Down!" came Chief Bradens's command as he stood directly behind Max.

In perfect unison, the entire department removed their hats and got down on one knee. Heather grabbed the chair next to her for support.

"Since I lack the ability to do this the traditional way, I thought I'd make do with a few extra resources."

He moved toward Heather just as JJ removed Heather's hand from the chair and guided her down to sit in it.

"Max…"

"Hang on," Max interrupted, his smile a mile wide and a bit nervous at the same time. "You'll get your turn in a minute." He reached behind him on the chair and produced a small black velvet box.

Heather tried to remember how breathing worked and Max moved up right next to her, picking up her left hand and smiling at the fact that she was shaking like a leaf.

"Heather Browning, I'd like very much to spend my life with you. Will you marry me?"

Her powers of speech left the building. She nodded once, then several times, finally choking out a "Yes!" that sent the firemen into thunderous applause and hoots of victory.

Suddenly, more faces appeared from out of the kitchen. Alex smiled and whooped as loud as the firemen. Melba—now fully showing with baby Maria—ran over to give Heather a hug. Heather's mom came out of the kitchen already in full cry mode. Max's mother kissed her son and then kissed Heather, too. Within seconds the room was filled with people she knew and loved—half of Gordon Falls had been in on this, it seemed. Simon—entering his second month back at school—was there, as were his parents. Margot, Violet, Pastor Allen and even Karl.

Tonight, she didn't find she minded being the center of attention at all. Not with Max at her side, not even when Jesse Sykes began crooning the Motown song "Me and Mrs. Jones," earning him a cuff from JJ.

"We've gotta get that boy a girl," Clark Bradens moaned.

"I'm working on it," Melba replied. "He's a bit...outlandish, you know?"

"Sometimes," Heather offered, "those are the very best men of all."

* * * * *

SAVED BY THE FIREMAN

Unless the Lord builds the house, the builders labor in vain. Unless the Lord watches over the city, the guards stand watch in vain.

—*Psalms* 127:1

To Abbie

In faith that she'll discover
many wonderful directions.

Chapter One

Charlotte Taylor sat in her boss's office Friday morning and wondered where all the oxygen in Chicago had just gone.

"I'm sorry to let you go, Charlotte, I really am." Alice Warren, Charlotte's superior at Monarch Textiles, looked genuinely upset at having to deliver such news. "I know you just lost your grandmother, so I tried to put this off as long as I could."

A layoff? Her? Charlotte felt the shock give way to a sickening recognition. She'd seen the financial statements; she'd written several of the sales reports. Sure, she was no analyst wiz, but she was smart enough to know Monarch wasn't in great financial shape and a downsize was likely. She was also emotionally tied enough to Monarch and torn enough over losing Mima that she'd successfully denied the company's fiscal health for months. As she watched her grandmother's decline, Charlotte told herself she was finally settled into a good life. She'd boasted to a failing Mima—not entirely truthfully, she knew even then on some level—about feeling "established."

She'd patted Mima's weakening hands, those hands that had first taught her to knit and launched the textile career she had enjoyed until five minutes ago, and she'd assured her grandmother that there was no reason to worry about her. She was at a place in life where she could do things, buy things, experience things and get all the joy out of life just as Mima taught her. How hollow all that crowing she had done about becoming "successful" and "indispensable" at Monarch now rang. Who was she fooling? In this economy, did anyone really have the luxury of being indispensable?

Except maybe Mima. Mima could never be replaced. Charlotte and her mother were just barely figuring out how to carry on without the vivacious, adventurous old woman who'd now left such a gaping hole in their lives. It had been hard enough when Grandpa had lost his battle to Alzheimer's—the end of that long, hard decline could almost be counted as a blessing. Mima's all-too-quick exit had left Charlotte reeling, fabricating stability and extravagance that were never really there. Hadn't today just proved that?

Charlotte grappled for a response to her boss's pained eyes. "It's not your fault, I suppose." She was Monarch's problem solver, the go-to girl who never got rattled. She should say something mature and wise, something unsinkably optimistic, something Mima would say. Nothing came but a silent, slack jaw that broadcast to Alice how the news had knocked the wind out of her.

Alice sighed. "You know it's not your performance. It's just budgetary. I'm so sorry."

"The online sales haven't been growing as fast as we projected. I'd guessed the layoffs were coming eventually. I just didn't think it'd be—" she forced back the lump in her throat "—me, you know?"

Alice pulled two tissues from the box on her desk, handing one to Charlotte. "It's not just you." She sniffed. "You're the first of four." She pushed an envelope across the desk to Charlotte. "I fought for a severance package, but it's not much."

A severance package. Charlotte didn't even want to open it. Whatever it included, the look on Alice's face told Charlotte it wasn't going to make much of a difference. *Mima, did you see this coming?* Of course that couldn't be possible, but Charlotte felt her grandmother's eyes on her anyway, watching her from the all-knowing viewpoint of eternity. It wasn't that much of a stretch, if one believed in premonitions. Or the Holy Spirit, which Mima claimed to listen to carefully.

In true Mima style, Charlotte's grandmother had left both her and her mother a sizable sum of money and with instructions to "do something really worth doing." A world traveler after Grandpa died, Mima squeezed every joy out of life and was always encouraging others to do the same. Mima bought herself beautiful jewelry but never cried when a piece got lost. Mima owned a ten-year-old car but had visited five continents. She bought art—real art—but had creaky old furniture. Her apartment was small but stuffed with fabulous souvenirs and wonderful crafts. Mima truly knew what money was for and what really mattered in life.

That was how Charlotte knew the funds she'd inherited weren't intended for living—rent and groceries and such—they were for dreams and art and *life*. Having to use Mima's money to survive a layoff would feel like an insult to her grandmother's memory.

Alice sniffled, bringing Charlotte back to the horrible conversation at hand. Alice was so distressed she seemed to fold in on herself. "I wasn't allowed to tip anyone off. I'm so sorry."

She was sorry—even Charlotte could see that—but it changed nothing. Charlotte was leaving Monarch. She'd been laid off from the job she'd expected to solidify her career. It felt as if she'd spent her four years at Monarch knitting up some complicated, beautiful pattern and someone had come and ripped all the stitches out and told her to start over.

Over? How does a person start over when they suddenly doubt they ever really started at all?

Charlotte picked up the envelope but set it in her lap unopened.

"You've got two weeks of salaried work still to go." Alice was trying—unsuccessfully—to brighten her voice. "But you've also got six days of vacation accrued so…you don't have to stay the whole two weeks if you don't want to." The woman actually winced. Was this Alice's kinder, gentler version of "clean out your desk"?

The compulsion to flee roared up from some dark corner of her stomach Charlotte didn't even know she had. She didn't want to stay another minute. The fierce response surprised her—Monarch had been so much of a daily home to her she often didn't think of it as work. "And what about sick days?"

It bothered Charlotte that Alice had evidently anticipated that question; she didn't even have to look it up. "Two."

She was better than this. She couldn't control that she was leaving, but she could control when she left. And that was going to be now. "I don't think I'm feeling so well all of a sudden." Sure, it was a tad unreasonable, but so was having your job yanked out from underneath you. She had eight covered days out of her two-week notice. What was the point of staying two more days? Two more hours? Her files were meticulous, her sales contact software completely up to date, and next season's catalogue was ahead of schedule. There wasn't a single thing keeping her here except the time it would take to sweep all the personal decorations from her desk.

Alice nodded. "I'll write you a glowing recommendation."

It felt like such a weak compensation. Charlotte stood up, needing to get out of this office where she'd been told so many times—and believed—she was a gifted marketing coordinator and a key employee. "Thanks." She couldn't even look Alice in the eye, waving goodbye with the offending manila envelope as she walked out the door.

Monarch only had two dozen or so employees, and every eye in the small office now stared at her as she packed up her desk. Charlotte was grateful each item she stuffed into one of the popular Monarch tote bags— and oh, the irony of that—transformed the damp surge of impending tears into a churning burst of anger. Suddenly the sweet fresh-out-of-college intern she'd been training looked like the enemy. Inexperience meant lower salaries, so it wouldn't surprise Charlotte at all if adorable little Mackenzie got to keep her job. She probably still lived at home with her parents and didn't even need money for rent, Charlotte thought bitterly.

She reached into her file drawer for personal papers, her hand stilling on the thick file labeled "Cottage." The file was years old, a collection of photos and swatches and magazine articles for a dream house. Apartment living had its charms, but with Charlotte's craft-filled background, she longed to have a real house, with a yard and a front porch and windows with real panes. One that she could decorate exactly the way she wanted.

Just last week, Charlotte had nearly settled on using Mima's funds to buy a cottage in nearby Gordon Falls. It would be too far for a daily commute, but she could use it on weekends and holidays. She knew so many people there. Her best friend, Melba, had moved there. Her cousins JJ and Max had moved there. Melba's new baby, Maria, was now Charlotte's goddaughter. She'd come to love the tiny little resort town three hours away on the Gordon River, and there was a run-down cottage she'd driven past dozens of times that Charlotte could never quite get out of her mind. Mima would approve of her using the money to fund an absolutely perfect renovation in a town where everyone seemed to find happiness.

Well, not now, Charlotte thought as she stuffed the file into the bag. In light of the past five minutes, a weekend place had gone from exciting to exorbitant. *Get out of here before you can't hold it in,* she told herself as she stuffed three framed photos—one of Mom, one of Mima and one of baby Maria—in beside the thick file. She zipped the tote bag shut with a vengeance, yanked the employee identification/security badge from around her neck and set it squarely in the middle of the desk. Just last week she'd bought a beautifully beaded lariat to hold the badge, but now the necklace felt as if it was choking her. She left it along with the badge, never wanting to see it again.

With one declarative "I may be down but I'm not

out" glare around the office, Charlotte left, not even bothering to shut the door behind her.

Jesse Sykes flipped the steak and listened to the sizzle that filled one end of his parents' patio. He'd built this outdoor kitchen two years ago, and this grill was a masterpiece—the perfect place to spend a Saturday afternoon. He planned to use a photo of the fire pit on his business brochures once they got printed. That, and the portico his mother loved. Filled with grapevines that turned a riot of gorgeous colors in the fall, it made for a stunning graphic. Only two more months, and he'd have enough funds to quit his job at Mondale Construction, buy that little cottage on the corner of Post and Tyler, fix it up and flip it to some city weekender for a tidy profit. With that money, he'd start his own business at last.

Move-in properties were plucked up quickly in Gordon Falls, so finding the perfect fixer-upper was crucial. He'd already lost out on two other houses last fall because he didn't quite have the down payment stashed away, but the cottage he'd settled on now was perfect. It was June, and he'd planned to buy the place in March, but that was life. He'd needed a new truck and Dad sure wasn't going to offer any help in that department. A few months' delay shouldn't make a difference, though— the cottage had been on the market for ages. It needed too much renovation for most people to want to bother.

"I'm pretty sure I'll have Sykes Homes Incorporated up and running by the fall. I can still snag the fall colors season if I can buy that cottage."

Dad sat back in his lawn chair, eyes squinting in that annoying way Jesse knew heralded his father's judgment. "Fall? Spring is when they buy. Timing is everything, son. You've got to act fast or you lose out on the best opportunities, and those won't be around in September."

Jesse flipped the next steak. "I'm moving as fast as I can, Dad." As if he didn't know he'd missed the spring season. As if it hadn't already kept him up nights even more than the Gordon Falls Volunteer Fire Department alarms.

"It might not be fast enough."

Jesse straightened his stance before turning to his father. "True, but learning to adapt is a good lesson, too. This won't be the first time I've had to retool a plan because I've hit a hitch."

Dad stood up and clamped a hand on Jesse's shoulder. "Son, all you've hit is hitches so far." This time he didn't even bother to add the false smile of encouragement he sometimes tacked on to a slam like that. Jesse thrust his tines into the third steak and clamped his teeth together.

"Is it that older cottage on Post Avenue?" his mother asked. "The one by the corner with the wrought-iron window boxes?"

The wrought-iron window boxes currently rusting out of their brackets and splitting the sills, yes. "That's it."

He caught the "leave him be" look Mom gave Dad as she came over and refilled Jesse's tall glass of iced tea. "Oh, I like that one. So much charm. I've been surprised no one's snatched it up since Lucinda Hyatt died. You'll do a lovely job with that."

"In two more months I'll be ready to make an offer."

"You could have had the money for it by now if it

weren't for the firehouse taking up all your time. You have no salary to show for it and it keeps you away from paying work. You'd better watch out or this place will be sold out from underneath you like the last one, and you'll be working for Art Mondale for another five years." Dad's voice held just enough of a patronizing tone to be polite but still drive the point home.

"Mike, don't let's get into that again."

Dad just grunted. Jesse's place in the volunteer fire department had been a never-ending battle with his father. Jesse loved his work there, loved helping people. And by this point, he felt as if the firefighters were a second family who understood him better than his real one. Chief Bradens was a good friend and a great mentor, teaching Jesse a lot about leadership and life. Fire Inspector Chad Owens had begun to teach him the ins and outs of construction, zoning and permits, too. It was the furthest thing he could imagine from the waste of time and energy his father obviously thought it to be.

Mom touched Jesse's shoulder. "You're adaptable. You can plot your way around any obstacle. That's what makes you so good at the firehouse."

Jesse hoisted the steaks onto a platter his mother held out. "That, and my world-class cooking." Then, because it was better to get all the ugliness out before they started eating, Jesse made himself ask, "How come Randy isn't here?"

Dad's smirk was hard to ignore. "Your brother's at a financial conference in San Diego this week. He said it could lead to some very profitable opportunities." Jesse's younger brother, Randall, would be retiring in his forties if he kept up his current run of financial success. Randy seemed to be making money hand over fist, boasting a fancy condo in the Quad Cities, a travel schedule that read more like a tourist brochure, and a host of snazzy executive trappings. It didn't take a genius to see Jesse fell far short of his brother in Dad's eyes. A month ago, when Jesse had pulled up to the house in a brand-new truck, Jesse couldn't help but notice the way his father frowned at it, parked next to Randy's shiny silver roadster.

"He's up for another promotion," Mom boasted.

"Good for him, he deserves it." Jesse forced enthusiasm into his voice. Somehow, it was always okay when Randy missed family functions because of work. It was never okay when Jesse had to skip one because he was at the firehouse.

"Someday, that brother of yours is going to rule the world." Dad had said it a million times, but it never got easier to swallow. Every step Randy took up the ladder seemed to push Jesse farther down it from Dad's point of view. While Dad never came out and said it, it was clear Jesse's father felt that a man who worked with his hands only did so because his brain wasn't up to higher tasks.

"I don't doubt it, Dad," Jesse admitted wearily. "I'll just settle for being King of the Grill."

Mom looked eagerly at the petite fillet he'd marinated just the way she liked it. "That is just fine by me. Jesse, honey, this smells fantastic. You will make some lucky lady very happy one of these days." Her eyes held just a tint of sadness, reminding Jesse that the ink was barely dry on Randy's divorce papers. His brother's raging career successes had inflicted a few casualties of late, and Mom had been disappointed to watch her grandma prospects walk out the door behind Randy's neglected wife. This past winter had been hard on the Sykes family, that was for sure. Was Dad clueless to all those wounds? Or did he just choose to ignore what he couldn't solve?

They were in love…once…his mom and dad. Now they just sort of existed in the same life, side by side but not close. Randy had married because he was "supposed to." As if he needed to check off some box in his life plan. Jesse didn't want to just make some appropriate lady "very happy." When he fell, it would be deep and strong and he would sweep that love of his life clean off her feet.

It just wasn't looking as though that would be anytime soon.

Chapter Two

"Done." Charlotte Taylor finished signing her name at the bottom of the long sales document. She put her pen—the beautiful new fountain pen she'd bought especially for this occasion—down on the conference table as if she were planting a flag. She was, in a way. The knot in her stomach already knew this was a big deal. A good big deal. The way to get her life back on track and prove Monarch was only a bump in the road, not the end of the line. She looked up and gave her companions a victorious smile. "The cottage is officially mine."

"I still can't believe you're going through with this." Charlotte's best friend, Melba, sat with her baby on her lap, trying to look supportive but appearing more worried than pleased. "I mean, I'm happy for you and all, but you're sure?"

Charlotte had done nothing but mull the matter over in the week since the layoff, and while the timing might look wrong on the outside, she'd come to the conclusion that it was actually perfect. She needed this, needed a project to balance the stress of a job search. When she'd gone to see the cottage again and the seller had been willing to knock down the price for a cash offer, Charlotte felt as if Mima was showing her it was time to act. "I am. If I do it now, I'll have the time to do it right. And you know me—I'll have a new job before long. This is exactly the kind of thing Mima would have wanted me to do with my inheritance."

"It's nice to see someone your age so excited to put down roots." The broker—a plump, older woman named Helen Bearson, who looked more suited to baking pies than hawking vacation properties—smiled back as she handed Charlotte the keys. The large, old keys tumbled heavy and serious into Charlotte's hand. "I'm sure you'll be very happy after the renovations. Gordon Falls is a lovely place to get away to—but you already knew that."

Melba gently poked the baby Maria's sweet button nose and cooed, "Aunt Charlotte always did know exactly what she wanted, Maria. Now you'll get to see her much more often."

Charlotte couldn't really fault Melba's singsong, oh-so-sweet voice; new moms were supposed to adore their babies like that. It was charming. She'd probably be even more sugary when her time as a new mom came— if it ever came—and Maria was adorable. She'd been baby-perfect, happy and quiet for the entire long real estate transaction, and Charlotte had been grateful for the company at such an important event, even if it did take over an hour. Charlotte herself felt as if her hand would never uncramp from signing her name so many times.

Funny how even happy milestones could be so exhausting. Squeezing the new keys tight—well, new to her at least, for they looked giant and cumbersome next to her slick apartment and car keys—she exhaled. This wasn't an indulgence; this was a lifeline. Just for fun,

Charlotte rattled the keys playfully over the baby's head. Maria's little gray eyes lit up at the tinkling sound, her chubby hands reaching up in a way that had all three women saying "Aww."

Awe, actually. She'd done it. The keys she held belonged to a cottage Charlotte now owned. It was an exhilarating, thrilling kind of fear, this huge leap. The cottage had become a tangible promise to herself, a symbol that future success was still ahead of her and she could still be in command of the blessings God had given her. No matter what her new job would be, no matter where her rented city apartment might shift, this cottage would be the fixed point, the home ready to welcome her on weekends and vacations. She'd boasted of feeling established in her job at Monarch, but the truth was today was what really made her feel like an adult. She'd never owned anything more permanent than a car before this. Her chest pinched in a happy, frantic kind of excitement.

"Thanks, Mima." She liked to think Mima was as pleased as she was, sending down her blessing from heaven as surely as if a rainbow appeared in the bank conference room. Once she'd prayed and made the decision, it felt as if Mima had orchestrated the whole thing—in cahoots with God to line the details up so perfectly that the purchase had been swift and nearly effortless. Yes, she was in command of the blessings God had given her—and that was what she'd sought: a firm defense against the uncertainties of a woman "between jobs."

Sure, Melba had made the same noise about practicality that Mom had made. Charlotte knew it might have been more sensible to buy a Chicago apartment and stay in the area to job-hunt, but Mima hadn't left her the money to be sensible. Mima was all about leaps of the heart, and right now Charlotte didn't know where her next job would take her, but she knew her heart kept pulling her toward Gordon Falls as her spot to get away. She'd spent so many weekends here, the guest bed at Melba's house had a Charlotte-shaped dent in it. The hustle and sparkle of Chicago would always be wonderful, but Mima's bequest meant she could own this cottage and rent a nice place in Chicago near her next job for the weekdays. That felt like a smart plan, and everyone knew smart wasn't always practical. Who knew? The way telecommuting was taking off these days, she might work full-time out of Gordon Falls someday in the future.

"Congratulations," Melba said, trying again to be supportive.

Poor Melba. She'd always be too cautious to ever launch an adventure like this. Melba had too many people needing her—a husband, until recently her late father, and now Maria—to ever throw caution to the wind. Charlotte would have to show her how exhilarating it could be. "I own a cottage. I'm landed gentry."

Melba winced as she untangled a lock of her hair from Maria's exploring fingers. "That might be over-stating things, but I am glad you'll be here. Gordon Falls could use a few more of us young whippersnappers."

"I couldn't agree more," Mrs. Bearson confirmed as she slid the files into the needlepoint tote bag that served as her briefcase. "I'm delighted to see so many of you younger people coming into town and settling down."

Settling down. The words fit, but the sensation was

just the opposite; more of a leaping forward. It was the most alive she'd felt since that harrowing exit from the Monarch offices. Renovating this cottage was going to be about doing life on purpose instead of having it done to you by accident. Today declared Charlotte her own person, with her own roots to plant.

The older woman extended a hand. "Welcome to Gordon Falls, Charlotte Taylor. You'll love it here."

Charlotte shook her hand. "I know I will. Thanks for everything."

"My pleasure. Tootle-loo!" With a waggle of her fingers, she bustled from the conference room to the bank's lobby, where she headed over to say hello to several people.

Melba caught Charlotte's eye. "Tootle-loo?"

Charlotte winced. "She's said that every time we've met. Odd, but cute." She stared at the keys in her hand, cool at first but now warm and friendly to her touch. "I own a cottage."

"You do."

She'd been there three times in the past two days, but the need to see it again, to turn the key in the lock with her own hand as the owner, pressed against her heart. "Let's go see my cottage. My cottage. I want to make myself a cup of tea in my cottage. I brought some tea leaves and a kettle with me and everything."

Baby Maria's response to the invitation was to scrunch up her face and erupt in a tiny little rage. She'd been darling up until now, but it was clear that her patience was coming to an end. "I think Miss Maria needs to nurse and to nap. Much as I'd like to be there, I think we had better head home." Melba put a hand on Charlotte's arm. "Will you be okay on your own?"

"Just fine." That was the whole point of the cottage, wasn't it? When she thought about it, it was fitting that the first hours Charlotte spent in the cottage as its owner were on her own. "I'll be back for dinner, okay?" The cottage wasn't in any shape to call home just yet, so she'd opted to stay a few days at Melba's while she got things set up right.

"See you later, Miss Taylor of the landed gentry," Melba called above Maria's escalating cries. "Enjoy your new castle."

Jesse wrenched open another of the cottage's stuck windows and waved the smoke away from his face. The air was as sour as his stomach. He could barely believe he was standing in his cottage—only it wasn't his anymore now—talking to the new owner. Talk about a kick to the gut. "Exactly when did the stove catch on fire?"

The panicked blonde next to him pushed a lock of hair back off her forehead. "About five minutes after I turned it on." She pointed to a charred kettle now hissing steam in the stained porcelain sink. "Tea. I was just trying to make tea." Her eyes wandered to the fire truck now idling in her driveway, dwarfing her tiny blue hatchback. "I'm sorry. I probably overreacted by calling you all in for such a little fire. I was too panicked to think straight. I just bought the place today and I didn't know what else to do."

She was so apologetic and rattled, it was hard to stay annoyed at her. People were always apologizing for calling the fire department. Jesse never got that. It's not like anyone ever apologized for seeing their doctor or calling a plumber. She had no reason to be upset for calling the fire department, even for a little fire. Kitchen fires could be dangerous. One look at the dilapidated 1960s electric range told him any number of problems could have escalated from an open flame there. Sure it was a quaint-looking appliance, but he of all people knew suppliers who made stoves with just as much of that trendy vintage charm but with modern safety features. "Even a small fire isn't anything to mess with. Small fires can get very big very fast."

Of course, if *he* had been the new owner, he'd have had the sense to make sure the stove was safe before turning it on and starting the fire in the first place. The sting of his current situation surged up again. Why did he have to be on duty when this particular call came in? Why did he have to find out the cottage he'd intended to buy had been sold this way? He picked up his helmet from the chipped Formica counter, forcing kindness into his tone. "Look, don't be worried. You did the right thing, Ms.…"

"Taylor. Charlotte Taylor." So that was the name of his pretty little adversary.

"Don't ever hesitate to call on us, Charlotte. Especially if you're on your own. It's why we're here, okay?"

Her eyes scanned the smoke still hovering close to the kitchen's tin ceiling. Jesse had always thought the ceiling was this kitchen's best feature. Stuff like that was hard to find these days. Would she appreciate that or tear it down and put in a boring ceiling with sterile track lighting? "Okay." She mostly mumbled the word, her face pale and drawn tight.

She didn't look anything close to okay. Her nerves were so obviously jangled they practically echoed around the empty kitchen. "If you don't mind me asking… why the sudden need for tea? You're not even moved in, from the looks of it." Her reply might let him know what her plans were for the place. If she was plotting a teardown and wasn't planning to move in at all, he could skip the preliminaries and get right down to hating her this minute.

She flushed. "It was a celebration thing. I just signed the papers on the place today. I told Melba I just wanted to have a cup of tea on my new deck."

How had he missed this? The facts wove together in his brain, making everything worse. "You're Melba's friend?"

Chief Bradens had mentioned his wife's friend was buying a weekend cottage in town. Never in a million years did Jesse consider it might be *this* cottage. Now, annoyed as he was, he'd have to be nice. A friend of the fire chief's wife demanded special care. "No harm done that I can see." He put his helmet back down on the counter as he swallowed his sore pride. "I should check the rest of the place. Just to be safe," he said over his shoulder as he began banging open the two remaining kitchen windows when they refused to budge.

She shrugged. "Probably a good idea."

He knew the rooms of this house. A visual inspection wasn't really necessary, but it might give him a last look at the place before she stripped it of all its charm. Charlotte followed him around the empty rooms while he peered at light switches, tested the knobs on heating registers and tried the fuses in the antiquated fuse box. Did she know what she was getting into here? This was no starter project for a hobby house flipper. "You can still keep lots of the place's charm, but you're gonna need some serious updating." He raised his eyebrows at her resulting frown. "You knew that going in, didn't you?"

"I did."

She did not. Now that was just dirty pool, letting someone like her beat him to a place like this.

Some jilted part of him wanted to tell her the house was chock-full of danger, but it wasn't true. Nothing looked dangerous to his contractor's eye, just old and likely finicky. The greatest danger she faced was blowing a fuse if she plugged her hair dryer in while the dishwasher was running. Charlotte had nice hair. Platinum blond in a city-sleek rather than elegant cut. She looked relatively smart, but what did he know? Do smart people set their teakettles on fire?

He avoided looking at her by inspecting the stove knobs. "Nothing about wiring came up in the home inspection?" He almost hated to add, "You did *have* a home inspection, didn't you?" It was killing him—she looked as if she didn't even own a hammer, much less the belt sander it would take to bring those hardwood floors in the dining room up to snuff. Still, she had a certain spunk about her. It hadn't been there when he and the other guys first barged in the door, but he could see it now returning to her eyes. If she made the right choices, she might do okay. Not that he wanted her to succeed.

"Of course I did. Only now I'm thinking maybe it wasn't so thorough." She crossed her arms over her chest and her eyebrows furrowed together. "Honestly, the guy looked like he did inspections for laughs in between fishing trips. Mrs. Bearson said he was reliable, but…"

Helen Bearson. He could have guessed she'd made

the sale. Helen was a sweet lady, but the kind Jesse referred to as a "hobby broker." Dollars to donuts the inspector was her brother. "Larry Barker?" Even someone he resented as much as Charlotte Taylor deserved better than that guy—Jesse wouldn't pay him to inspect a shoe box.

Charlotte raised an eyebrow. "A mistake, huh?"

He couldn't just sit there and let her make choices from what was likely bad information. Well, he *could,* but he wasn't the kind of guy who would—even under these circumstances. Jesse shucked off his heavy firefighter's coat and squatted down in front of the appliance, opening the oven door and peering inside. "Let's just say he wouldn't be my first choice," he said, giving Barker more benefit of the doubt than he deserved. "I haven't seen anything that should have stopped your sale." In fact, he knew there were no massive problems because he'd given the house a thorough once-over himself, far beyond his ten-minute walkthrough just now. Still, the word *sale* stuck in his throat. "This could really be just an old stove, not faulty wiring or anything." He stared at a layer of grime so thick he could sign his name in it with a fingernail. "I don't think this has been used in a couple of years. You'll want to replace it."

She groaned. "But I love the way this one looks. Does it cost a fortune to rehab a stove?"

Dark brown eyes and blond hair—the effect was striking, even with a frown on her face. "You can't really rehab a stove. Still there are ones that look old-fashioned but function like new. They're pricey, but you had to have known you were going to put some money into the place."

"Well of course I did, but I was hoping to wait longer than two hours before the first repair."

Despite his irritation, Jesse liked her sense of humor. He glanced out the window to where the three other firemen were putting gear back into the truck. Normally he didn't fish for contractor work while on firefighting duty—especially given this particular circumstance—but she was pretty and clearly on her own and, well, seemed at a loss. Sure he'd regret it but unable to stop himself, Jesse swallowed the last of his pride and pulled a business card from his pants pocket. "I'm a licensed contractor over at Mondale Construction. If you like, give me a call tomorrow and I'll walk through the house with you over the weekend. I can go over what Larry said and either confirm it or tell you differently. I'll help you figure out what really needs work right away and what can wait until you've gotten over the sticker shock." If he couldn't have the house, maybe he could at least get the work, much as it would dent his ego.

She narrowed her eyes. "Why would you do that?"

He hated when people gave him "the contractor out to take you to the cleaners" look. "Because you're a friend of the chief's. Because I'm a nice guy." *Because I'm an idiot and am trying not to be a sore loser.* "And because I can make sure Mondale gives you a good price for work I could do and recommend a couple of guys for the other stuff—guys who will do it right and not empty your checkbook for the sport of it."

She took the card but still eyed him. Good. She shouldn't be trusting everyone who walked in here offering to help her, even him. She looked smarter than that, and he could bring himself to be glad she was acting like it. "So maybe you really are a nice guy," she said, still sounding a bit doubtful.

"Don't take my word for it. Look, you ought to know I don't normally pitch work on duty. Only I think Chief and Melba might ride me if I didn't offer my help, given the—" he waved at the smoke now almost completely gone from the kitchen "—circumstances. It's the least I can do."

She looked unconvinced, and a part of him was ready to be rid of the obligation. He'd tried, wasn't that enough? He gave it one last shot of total honesty. "Frankly, this place is a contractor's dream—good bones but needing loads of work. And I could use the work." After a second, he looked out the window and added, "Why don't you think about it? I've got to get back to the truck anyway—the guys are waiting for me."

She planted her hands on her hips. "No, I don't need to think about it. Can you come by after church Sunday?"

She went to church. Of course she went to church; she was a friend of Chief Bradens and his wife. Not wanting to look like the stranger to services that he was, he hazarded a guess based on when he usually saw his friends out and about on Sundays. "Eleven-thirty?"

"Perfect." She smiled—an "I'm rattled but I'll make it" lopsided grin that told him she'd do okay even if this wasn't the last disaster of her new home. Her new home. Life was cruel some days.

Jesse nodded at the kitchen's vintage molding and bay widows. "This will make a nice weekend place. You'll do just fine."

She made a face. "That's just what I was telling myself when the stove caught on fire."

"Everything looks okay, but I'd hold off on teatime until we check out all the appliances if I were you." His radio beeped, letting him know the rest of the crew outside was getting impatient. "Once you get the rest of your utilities up and running, turn on the fridge so we can check how cold it gets."

She perked up. "Did that already. Turned it on, I mean." To prove her point, she opened the ancient-looking refrigerator and made a show of peering inside. "Chilling down, nothing scary inside." Her head popped back out and she shut the door. "The dishwasher, I'm not so sure. It looks older than I am."

For an intriguing second, Jesse wondered just how old that was. She looked about his age, but he'd never been good at guessing those things. "Yeah, I'd hold off." He gestured to the single mug sitting beside a box of fancy-looking tea on the otherwise bare 1950s-era Formica countertop. "Not like you've got a load of dishes to do anyhow."

That lit a spark in her eyes. "Oh, I own tons of dishes. I collect vintage china. I've got enough to fill all the shelves in this house and my apartment back in Chicago twice over. Not that I'd put any of them in this old dinosaur, anyway." She shrugged. "Well, thanks, Officer—" she squinted down at the card "—Sykes." She held out her hand.

He shook it. "I'm not an officer, I'm just part of the volunteer brigade. So Jesse will do. I'll see you Sunday at eleven-thirty. And as for your new house celebration, go on down to Karl's Koffee and tell him what happened. If I know Karl, he'll give you a free cup of tea and maybe some pie to smooth things over. You deserve a better welcome to Gordon Falls than one from us." Jesse decided he'd call from the truck and ask Karl to do just that. Only, knowing Karl, he'd have done it with no nudging at all.

He felt a tiny bit better for pulling that sweet smile from her. "Maybe I'll do just that. Thanks."

Jesse tried to ignore the teasing looks that greeted him as he climbed into the truck. "Isn't she the prettiest run of the day." Yorky, an older member of the department who could never be counted on for subtlety, bumped Jesse on the shoulder.

"Of the week," Wally Forman corrected, waggling an eyebrow for emphasis. "Only it's not so fun for you given the circumstances, is it, Jesse?"

"Could have fooled me," Yorky snickered.

Jesse merely grunted and settled farther down in his seat. Maybe Wally would let it go.

Wally stared at him. "It is, isn't it? That's the one?"

Narrowing his eyes in the strongest "not now" glare he could manage, Jesse didn't answer.

Wally leaned back in his seat and pointed at Jesse. "It is. I knew it. Oh, man, tough break."

Yorky looked at Jesse, then at Wally, then back at Jesse again. "What? What am I missing?"

Jesse cocked his head to one side in an "I'm warning you" scowl aimed straight at Wally.

Not that it did any good. "That's the house. The one Jesse talked about buying. Sweetie-Pie up there just bought it right out from underneath him. How many more months before you would have saved up enough for the down payment, Sykes? It had to be soon."

Was Wally going out of his way to drive the sore point home? "Two." Up until this moment Jesse had managed to let Little Miss China Cabinet's sweet smile tamp down his irritation at being beat to the purchase table.

Yorky hissed. "Ouch!"

"Yeah," Jesse repeated, craning his neck back to look at the tidy little cottage. "Ouch."

Chapter Three

"Melba, I'm not the first person in the world to lose my job," Charlotte told her dear friend as they sat at her table after dinner that night. Charlotte had managed to avoid the topic of conversation with Melba for days, but tonight Clark was down at the firehouse for the evening and her friend had cornered her in the kitchen. "I wasn't even the last at Monarch—there were three other envelopes on Alice's desk."

Melba had Maria settled in the crook of her arm. "I'm just worried about you. Are you okay? You seem to be taking it well, but…"

Charlotte kept telling herself that she was handling it as well as could be expected, but she also spent too many moments stuffing down a deep panic. "Do I have a choice?"

"Not you. You'd never go to pieces, even at something like this." She caught Charlotte's eye. "But you could. I mean, don't feel like you have to put on any kind of front with me. I've gone to pieces enough times in front of you."

While Charlotte was sure Melba meant what she said,

the idea of giving in to the fear—even for a moment and even with a dear friend—felt like opening the big green floodgates at the end of town. Best to keep that door firmly shut. "I'm okay. I think I'm okay. I mean, I'm scared—you're supposed to be in my situation—but I can push through this. I'm choosing to feel more like I'm waiting for whatever God's got around the corner than I've been broadsided by a job change."

Melba leaned in. "The best part is you get to wait here. I'll be so happy to have you around."

"Well, part of the time. I expect I'll need to take lots of trips back to Chicago for job-search stuff and interviews eventually. Only it'll be great to have the cottage as a distraction. All the books say to take on inspiring new projects so it doesn't become all about the job search. This is a great time to get a serious creative groove on. I need a place outside of my résumé to channel all this energy."

All that was true, but there was still a small corner of her chest that felt as if she had planted her flag at the top of a very high mountain with no idea how to climb back down. She nodded to the thick file of plans, the one she'd taken from her desk on her last day at Monarch. "I wonder if Mima had any idea the incredible gift this is going to be. To get to fix this place up exactly the way I want it? To have enough to do that after I bought it? Debt free? It's a huge blessing."

Melba gave her a cautious smile. "I know you got it at a great price, but it needs so much work." She thumbed through the file of clippings and swatches with her free hand while Maria gave a tiny sigh of baby contentment in her other arm. "Don't you think it's a big risk to take at a time like this?"

Charlotte shrugged. "Yes, it is a big risk. But it's a worthwhile risk. Just the thought of being able to do this up right gives me so much energy. I don't care if I have to buy shelving instead of shoes. Or stop eating until October."

"You're not going to fix up the whole place and decorate it all at once, are you?" Melba turned to a magazine page showing chintz kitchen curtains. "Won't that cost more than you have?"

"I *have* to do some of the fixing up as soon as possible. The stove, the heating, the upstairs bathroom— they need renovation before they'll be usable, and all that stuff has to be done if I'm going to be able to live there. Do I need the designer concrete sink right away? Well, I don't know yet. It's probably smarter to get exactly what I want now—once you start ripping stuff out, you might as well do it right the first time rather than rip stuff up again a year later."

"Charlotte…"

"I know, I know. Stop worrying—I'm not going to take my aggressions out at the home decorating store. I should probably have the home improvement channels blocked off my cable service for now. But since I don't have a job, I can't even afford cable television, so that solves that anyway, doesn't it?" She leaned back in her chair, as if the sheer weight of Melba's doubts had pushed her there. "This is going to be fine. Really. I won't let this get out of hand."

Melba pushed the file back across the table to Charlotte. "Easy to say now, but these things have a way of snowballing. Even the remodeling costs for the house I inherited from Dad sent Clark and me reeling."

When Melba's father had died last year after a long

battle with Alzheimer's, it left Clark and Melba to re-make her childhood home into the one that now housed her new family. The transition had been complicated and expensive—going beyond what it would have cost in both time and money to start fresh with a new house—but it just proved Charlotte's point: the house gave off a palpable sense of history. She'd felt some-thing like it from the cottage that first visit. The once-charming cottage seemed to beckon to her, begging to be restored. She knew it was a risky prospect, but she couldn't make herself feel as if she'd made the wrong choice. She'd chosen a challenging path, yes, but not a wrong one. "I'm going to be fine, Melba. Now let's drop the subject and let me hold that baby."

Melba stood up and handed Maria to Charlotte. As Maria snuggled in against her shoulder, Charlotte breathed in the darling scent of baby-girl curls. "You've got the best of both worlds, Maria. Your mama's curls and your daddy's red hair. You may hate it when you're five, but guys are gonna follow you like ducklings when you're seventeen."

Melba laughed as she warmed Charlotte's tea and set down a plate of cookies. "Clark's already informed me Maria will be banned from dating until she's thirty. And no firefighters."

Charlotte applied an expression of false shock. "Well, I'll back him up on the 'no firefighters' policy, but that's kind of a tough sell. He's the fire chief, isn't he?"

Sitting back down, Melba laughed again. "I think it's *because* he's chief. He's seen a little too much of the department's social life or heard a little too much in the locker room."

"They don't seem that rough around the edges to me.

As a matter of fact, Jesse Sykes seems like a stand-up guy." Charlotte could feel Maria softening against her shoulder. Melba was right—the world was always a better place with a baby drooling on your shoulder.

"He's an original, that's for sure." Melba selected a cookie and dunked it in her tea. "I don't know about stand-up, but he sure stands out. You can trust him, though. He did some of the work here on the house. Good work, if you don't mind the singing."

"The what?"

"Jesse has a habit of breaking out in Motown hits. If you haven't heard him yet, you will. Don't you remember he sang at Alex and JJ's wedding?"

"*That* was Jesse Sykes?" Charlotte recalled a rather impressive version of "My Girl" at her cousin's wedding. She tried to imagine Jesse's soulful voice echoing in the cottage living room, but she couldn't conjure up the image. "Mostly he just made wisecracks when I talked to him this time. Funny guy."

"Oh, he's a cutup, that's for sure. And a good firefighter. Clark wouldn't put up with his antics otherwise." Melba got a conniving look on her face. "You should hire him. I think he'd be good for you. An upbeat guy to have around in a tight spot."

Charlotte narrowed her eyes. "Oh, no, you don't."

"Don't what?" Melba's innocent blink hid nothing.

Charlotte whispered into Maria's ear, "Your mama's getting ideas."

"I am not."

"Oh, yes, you are. I know you too well. Look, I know we were discussing behavior, not profession, but he's a fireman, Melba. I won't get into a relationship with a first responder no matter how well behaved. We've been through this how many times? Nothing's changed. I've got way too many memories of sitting up nights with Mom at the kitchen table."

"Your dad was a policeman, I know, but—"

"But nothing. Same stress, different uniform. Melba, I've got nothing against you and Clark, and goodness knows JJ's done terrific at the firehouse, but I know what I can handle and what I can't. I've never dated someone who does that kind of work and I don't plan to start now."

A tiny war was going on in Jesse's chest—and in his pride—as he walked up the overgrown sidewalk to Charlotte's cottage Sunday morning. This was supposed to be his cottage. The place needed loads of work, and he knew he was the best man to complete it. He'd planned the rehab of this place a dozen times, imagining living in the home as he upgraded fixtures, appliances and wiring until he could turn around and sell it for a tidy profit. Or even stay there and use it as the showcase for what he could do with other properties. But that opportunity was lost now.

The only opportunity left in this situation was to be the guy hired for the renovation job. If a woman could afford a vacation cottage at Charlotte's age, she probably wouldn't haggle over the cost the place would require to be done up right. His business sense knew that made her an excellent customer even if she was a thorn in his side. The house needed loads of work, and loads of work could mean a big check for Mondale and for him. As he lay in bed last night, Jesse told himself a job this size could leave him with even more funds than he'd anticipated making over the summer. Funds to buy another house—bigger and better to soothe his wounded pride and show his father just how savvy a businessman he could be.

All this should have had him dreaming up the perfect sales pitch as he approached the door—and yet for some reason, he wasn't. He prided himself on knowing how to optimize a customer with deep pockets, only Charlotte Taylor didn't have that entitled look about her. In fact, she looked a little…lost. The way he'd looked when he'd first put on the bulky, cumbersome firefighter's gear—right at the launch of a dream, forcing an outer confidence that didn't quite cover the dazzled and doubtful person on the inside.

As he pushed the rusty doorbell button, Jesse still wasn't sure how he was going to play it for this meeting. *Just wing it,* he told himself. *You wing it all the time.* He pushed the button again, listening for the chimes inside the house once he noticed the living room window was open to his left.

No sound. Sometimes it was useful to start a customer off with a small project, but he'd planned on something larger than a broken doorbell. He knocked on the door loudly and leaned over the wrought-iron railing to yell into the window. "Charlotte!"

A second knock and another yell produced no reply. He pivoted to see her little blue car wasn't in the cottage drive. Maybe church ran long today. He could just start without her while he waited. After checking his watch, Jesse pulled out his notes.

He'd already made his own list of what the house needed, but he'd go through the process of re-creating a list to suit her taste. He just hoped it wouldn't clash with the character of the house he saw so clearly. Catering to a client's whims was one thing—ignoring his own clear ideas on this particular place was going to be quite another. Still, he'd do it to rack up enough funds to move forward. He was bone-tired of delays and detours, not to mention his father's ever-increasing digs.

Pacing the cottage's front stoop, he toed boards and pushed harder on the railing only to have it creak and pull out from its mountings. He added the doorbell and railing to his handwritten list and began scanning the front of the house for anything he'd missed.

He'd added four more items by the time Charlotte's small blue hatchback pulled into the drive behind his large brown pickup.

"Sorry!" she called, breathless and airy in a blue print dress with a lacy sweater that rippled behind her as she came up the steps. "Church went on forever. I mean, a good forever, but enough to make me late. I hope you weren't waiting long."

Jesse waited for her to say something like "I noticed you weren't in church." Or "Have you ever gone?" or the half dozen other thinly disguised recommendations he got from Melba, Clark and various other friends around town. "No, I'm fine. Hey, JJ told me you're her cousin. You were at the wedding, too, weren't you? On the boat?"

"Wedding of the year, wasn't it?"

As the only female firefighter in Gordon Falls, JJ Cushman stuck out already before her legendary wedding to Alex Cushman on a steamboat on the Gordon River. "A big shindig, that's for sure."

"And then there's my other cousin, JJ's brother, Max." She fished for her keys and wrestled the old door lock open. "And Melba's baby is my new goddaughter. I know lots of people in Gordon Falls."

They walked through the front hallway to the kitchen, where she plunked an enormous tapestry handbag—a vintage artsy-looking thing, he was glad to notice—down on the kitchen counter. "And now I know Karl. You were right. He did give me a slice of pie for my troubles." She sighed, a happy, shoulder-heaving, contented sigh. "This is a nice town."

It was, most of the time. "It has its moments."

Charlotte began digging through the massive bag. "I made a list last night of the things I think the house needs—as a jumping-off point." She pulled out a notebook with Victorian ladies dancing on the cover. "I'm no expert, though."

Jesse put a hand to his chest. "That's okay, because I am. Only there's an awkward question I really should ask first."

"Where do I want to hide the bodies?" She didn't need the pink lipstick to show off that dynamic smile; her eyes lit up with humor.

The joke made the next question easier to ask. "No, what's your budget?"

"Oh, that." He couldn't quite gauge her response.

"I mean, you don't have to tell me," he backpedaled, suddenly feeling his poor-loser wounds had run off with his diplomacy, "but it's better if I know. I can make smarter recommendations if I have a total-figure picture on the whole project."

Charlotte hoisted herself up to sit on the vacant countertop. "That's the best part—I don't have a budget. My grandma left me enough money to do this—at least I'm pretty certain she did. This place was a leap of faith."

She didn't come out and say "unlimited funds," but her eyes sure looked as though she was ready to spend. *Must be nice to have that kind of cash.* Jesse ignored the sharp curl of envy wrapped around his gut.

Instead, he focused on how she fit in the house. Houses—even half-built or long since run-down houses—always had personalities to him. He'd sensed this cottage's personality way back, and looking at her perched on the counter, he knew her personality absolutely suited the vibe of this place. Had he just finished the remodeling, he'd probably have been delighted to sell it to her. He just couldn't get there quite yet—for all her charm, Charlotte Taylor was still the agent of the delay in his achieving his dreams.

She looked around the room with wistful eyes. "Mima was amazing." The grief was still fresh, glistening in her eyes and present in the catch of her words. Whoever this grandmother was, Charlotte missed her very much.

"Did Mima leave you her china?" Jesse wasn't quite sure what made him ask.

Her eyes went wide; big velvet-brown pools of curiosity. "How did you know?"

"You said you collect." Jesse began working his way around the kitchen, pulling drawers open, checking cabinet hinges, forcing himself to see the house through her eyes than through his own loss. "It seemed a natural guess that she'd leave you hers if you were that close."

"We were." Charlotte's voice was thick with memory. "Mima was the most astounding woman. She didn't have an easy life, but she got so much out of every moment, you know?" For a second Jesse worried Charlotte was going to break into tears right there on the countertop, but she just took a deep breath and tucked her hands under her knees. "She'd love this place."

Needing to lighten the moment, Jesse raised the charred teakettle from its place in the sink. "Even the smoke-signal tea service?"

Charlotte laughed. She had a great laugh—lively and full and light. "She might have liked the drama, but Mima was a coffee drinker. 'Strong as love and black as night,' she used to say. Drank four cups a day right up until the end, even when her doctors yelled at her."

It would be so much easier to begrudge Charlotte the sale if she weren't so...sweet. Sweet? That wasn't usually the kind of word he'd use to describe a woman, but it was the one that kept coming to mind with her. Only, she was more than sweet. She had an edge about her. An energy. She was probably more like her Mima than she knew. Spunky, maybe? No, that sounded ridiculous. Vivacious—that was it.

Jesse dragged his mind back to the task at hand. "Let's walk through the house and identify what needs doing."

It didn't take long. Half the needed improvements had already been in his head, and the other half came cascading down upon him as he assumed his contractor's mind-set and considered the house with her needs in mind. Every time the bitter thought of what he would have wanted threatened to overtake him, he wrote down a dollar figure next to a project to show himself what Charlotte's business could mean for his future. By the time he left, Jesse was looking at a proposal that might get him down payments on two different investment properties, and she didn't seem too fazed by it. Things were looking up.

Chapter Four

Jesse watched Charlotte reading through his written proposal on her back porch the next afternoon. Despite how easy it was to chat with her—and how unfairly easy she was to like—the entire situation still hung off-kilter and uncomfortable inside him like a bad joke. He admired her enthusiasm, but it felt like a punch to his ribs at the same time. Had he shown that kind of energy, the singular focus she now displayed toward this house, he'd already own the cottage by now.

Even though she'd been in town only a few days, he'd heard from several people—Chief Bradens, Melba, his fellow firefighter JJ, even JJ's brother, Max—about how Charlotte had gushed over her affection for the cottage. For crying out loud, it seemed even Karl at the coffee shop had gotten a speech about what she planned to do with the place. She'd spout off her plans to anyone who would listen.

Had he shown her initiative, acting more aggressively, more single-mindedly on his plans—the way Randy always acted when it came to business deals—Helen Bearson might have tipped him off that someone else had shown interest in the property. He could have found a way to inch past those final two months and purchase the property now. But no, his claim never went further than a comment to his folks or a vague remark to the other guys on the truck when they went past the vacant house. He'd never done anything more than occasional blue-sky thinking aloud. The plans had been there: real and detailed, meticulously compiled. But he'd kept them to himself, not wanting to be made the butt of more jokes or criticism if things didn't work out. Now the spreadsheet calculating his accrued savings toward the goal felt like a misfire. No, worse: a dud.

Of course, Jesse knew better. His nobler side told him he had no right to his resentment. He had no practical claim to the cottage. This was just another example of his biggest flaw: always hatching plans and spending too long perfecting them to get around to acting on them. Dad would probably be gratified that his trademark inaction had once again come back to bite him. He'd lost the cottage, fair and square. *You snooze, you lose. You've always known that. Maybe now you know it for real.*

The only consolation—and it was slim consolation at that—was how Jesse's gut still told him she belonged in that house. She had on these old-fashioned-looking shoes that would have looked ridiculous on anyone else, but with her flowing pastel dress and the fluttery scarf she wore, she looked as though she belonged right there on the cottage steps. "Vintage chic," his mom would probably call it. All soft and frilly around the edges but definitely not stodgy, and with an artsy edge that let him know she'd have great taste. She wouldn't gut the place and modernize it, stripping away all the history and charm—she'd do it right.

She flipped over the final page of the document he'd given her. "Wow, it's a lot, isn't it?" Despite her bright optimism, he could still read hints of sadness and confusion in her eyes. Trouble was, that determination just made him like her more. This job was starting to feel as though it could become a tangled mess all too easily— and even a mess-up like him knew it was never smart to mix business with pleasure. Even when the pleasure could land him a fat paycheck.

"It's a big job, yes. The results will be fantastic, though. You'd double your money if you ever sold."

"I won't sell." No buyer's remorse from this buyer, that was certain. He got the feeling that once Charlotte Taylor set her course, she was unstoppable.

"Okay, so you want to stay. Well, we know there are some basic repairs you'll need no matter what—like the stove and the upstairs bathroom—even if you do change your mind and decide to sell...."

"Which I won't."

"Which you won't," he echoed. "We can start with those and schedule out the cosmetic fixes and upgrades later. That way you start basic, but keep your options wide open."

She leaned back against the porch stair railing. At least this railing held, not like the wobbly one at her front door. Jesse grimaced as he remembered the photo of the gorgeous wrought-iron railing sitting in his file back home. "Maybe, but first on the list has to be my new claw-footed bathtub."

She'd gushed over the style of the old tub in the up- stairs bathroom, saying she'd picked out some newfangled Jacuzzi version that still looked antique. "New is great, but you could also repair the one you already have. Old fixtures like that are hard to find and worth keeping—especially if you want to go the sensible route."

Her eyes flashed at the mention of *sensible,* and she straightened her back with an air of defiance. "Or maybe I don't compromise. Maybe I use all this free time to do the renovation *exactly* the way I want while I can."

"Free time?" Jesse couldn't help asking.

"I'm between jobs at the moment." There was a flash of hurt in her eyes as she said the words, but it faded quickly. "It's just a temporary situation. It's not like I won't find a new job. I'm very good at what I do. Lots of companies are ramping up their online commerce. Textile arts are big business these days, you know."

She didn't strike Jesse as the sensible type. More the artistic, impulsive type. Those customers were always the most fun—provided they had pockets as deep as their imaginations—which maybe still applied to Charlotte Taylor. He didn't really know many details about what her financial situation was, nor was it his place to ask. Still, he'd seen this before, watching a customer compensate for some loss in their life by going overboard on a build. A guy's divorce-driven five-car garage had bought Jesse his new truck. After all, a smart businessman gives the customer what they want, not necessarily what they need. "You could do that."

"I could do that." Her face took on the most amazing energy when she got an idea. She was going to be a fun client to work with, and certainly easy on the eyes.

Jesse suddenly found himself wondering if he could

walk the line on this. Could he encourage her, suggest the smartest choices for what she wanted? Could he balance the indulgence of her whims while warning her against something that would prove to be a foolish purchase? Viewed practically, her windfall of free time might allow him to get more work done in less time.

He nodded to the proposal. "I'm not saying you have to compromise. A job this big would be hard to do while you were working full-time. If you set your mind to it, we could be done by September. If you've got the cash now, the timing might be perfect."

She pointed at him, jangling the slew of silver bangles on her wrist. "Exactly how I see it. God's never late and He's never early."

"Huh?"

"Something Mima always said. About God's timing always being perfect, just like you mentioned. And I've always taken Mima's advice."

"You don't have to decide right this minute. You want some time to think about it?" He had to give her at least that much of an out.

She squinted up at the sky, making Jesse wonder if she was consulting her grandmother or God or both. After a long minute, she held out her hand for the pen he was holding. "Nope. I don't need any more time. This is what I want. I want it to be perfect." She signed the proposal in a swirly, artistic hand.

This was going to be fun. In the end, they'd both end up with a showpiece—his to boast about to clients, hers to call home. Win-win, right? "Then the pursuit of perfect begins tomorrow afternoon."

Charlotte 1, Cottage 0.

Charlotte congratulated herself on the tiny victory her cup of tea represented.

A few days ago, the scorecard might have looked a lot more like Kitchen 1, Charlotte 0, but a visit from the electrician Jesse had recommended and two hours of vigilant scouring this morning had put the kitchen in working order. Stopping in at the local housewares store, Charlotte had purchased an electric kettle to hold her over until a wonderfully vintage-looking but thoroughly modern stove came in on special order. At another downtown boutique, she'd found a charming bistro table with two chairs. It felt so satisfying to buy things for the house, to launch the project that was coming to mean so much to her. It made her long-overdue Owner of Cottage tea on her back deck just about perfect. Add one of Mima's teacups and her favorite teapot, and life was wonderful.

See? I'm still here, she thought, smirking at the bright green leaves of the overhead tree. *I will not be beaten by this bump in the road.* "You know what Eleanor Roosevelt says," Charlotte addressed a gray squirrel that was perched on the deck railing with a quivering tail and greedy black eyes, peering at the bag of cookies she'd just opened. "Women are like tea bags—you never know how strong they are until you get them in hot water."

"Quoting first ladies to the wildlife, are we?" Jesse came around the corner of the house lugging a clanking canvas bag and an armful of cut lumber. "Look at you, having a proper tea on your back deck and all."

Charlotte laughed. "This is not a proper tea. It's barely even an improper tea."

Jesse settled his equipment on the bottom step, leaning against the railing to look up at her. "A Mulligan, then."

"A what?"

He grinned, looking so handsome that Charlotte was suddenly aware she was probably covered in kitchen grime. "You don't golf, do you?"

"Not even mini."

"A Mulligan is a do-over. The chance to retake a shot that went wrong."

Well, that certainly fit. "Yes, I suppose this is a Mulligan tea. I'd rather think of it as a victory lap. I'm declaring myself the winner in the epic battle of Charlotte versus the Filthy Kitchen." At least that was *one* thing she felt as though she'd won in this whole mess her life had become. "With a little backup from Mike the electrician, that is."

Jesse started rummaging through the canvas bag he had set down. "Mike made sure all your other appliances are going to work safely?"

"Everything's safe. He told me to tell you he's going to come back and do the upstairs bathroom wiring once you let him know the plaster is down."

Jesse's eyes lit up. "Demolition. My favorite part."

She cringed. "Somehow I'm not fond of the idea of you going at my bathroom with a sledgehammer." *My bathroom.* Funny how little things like that made her heart go *zing* today in a way that almost made up for her lack of incoming paychecks.

"Oh, I'm not going at it today." He held Charlotte's eyes for a dizzying moment. "You are."

Charlotte nearly toppled her teacup. "Me?"

"It's a thing of mine. First swing of demo always

goes to the customer. If they're around, which you most definitely are."

"I'm sending a sledgehammer through my bathroom wall?" She'd seen such rituals on the home improvement networks, but she didn't think stuff like that actually took place on real jobs.

"Actually, it'll be more like a crowbar to the feet of your bathtub. Since you agreed to re-enamel it, I'm pulling it out today. Are you ready to start talking about color?"

Charlotte felt as if she'd been waiting a decade to pick the color of *something,* even though that was far from true. Colors—and how they went together—were a wondrous obsession for her, and part of the lure of the textile industry. Still, this choice felt new and exciting, in a way she couldn't quite define. She snatched the top issue from a pile of home decor magazines that were sitting next to the teapot. "I already have one picked out."

"Why am I not surprised?" Jesse walked up the last of the stairs. "Let's see."

She thumbed through the magazine to the dog-eared page, then held it up to Jesse to see. "That sink? The buttercream color with the brass fixtures? That's it, right there."

Jesse took the magazine. "Good choice. For a minute there I thought you were going to show me something purple or zebra striped. The guy who does the re-enameling work is good, but he's not a magician."

For a moment, Charlotte tried to imagine a zebra-striped claw-footed bathtub. Such a thing should never exist. "I have much better taste than animal prints for bathroom fixtures. He can do the sink to match, can't he?"

Jesse peered closer at the photograph. "It won't matter. You'll need a new sink no matter what—the newer fixtures won't fit on a sink like you've got. I'll bring you some catalogues with sinks that come in a color close to that tomorrow. When you pick the style and finish, Jack will make sure the bathtub matches perfectly." He looked up at her. "You're going to want one of those old-fashioned circle shower curtains, aren't you?"

"Absolutely. And in the brass finish. Not that cheap nickel finish."

"That brass finish is exactly that—not cheap. Are you sure?"

Parts of her were completely sure. Other parts— the edges of her chest that turned dark and trembling when she allowed herself to think of how her perfect life plan had been upended—balked at the extra price. Still, how many times in life did a girl get to pick out bathroom fixtures? Ones that would last for decades? A woman's bathroom was her sanctuary, her private escape from life's tensions. Hers *had* to be just right— especially when nothing else in life was. She nodded. Did he find that charming or annoying? His expression was unreadable, and she was growing a little nervous knot in her stomach. "I've even got the shower curtain and window treatment fabric picked out."

"You're going to be fun to work with, you know that?"

"I hope so." She really did. There was something so immensely satisfying about bringing the cottage back to life. As if the house had been waiting for her, holding its structural breath for her to come and pour her ideas inside. Charlotte had engineered some major achievements at Monarch, but those hadn't given her any security, had they? This cottage offered security, right down to the soul-nurturing buttercream color of her soon-to-be-reborn bathtub.

Jesse returned to his bag, making all kinds of rattling noises until he straightened back up with a crowbar, a pair of safety glasses and the daintiest pair of work gloves Charlotte had ever seen. Her astonishment must have shown all over her face, because Jesse waved the gloves and admitted, "These are from my mother. Don't ask."

She wanted to. The gloves were adorable, white canvas with a vintage-looking print of bright pink roses. They looked like garden gloves from a 1950s issue of *Better Homes and Gardens.* "I love them." Then, because she couldn't hold the curiosity in any longer, "Your mother sent these?"

He ran his hands down his face, but it didn't hide the flush she saw creep across his cheeks. "I said don't ask."

Charlotte pulled her knees up onto the chair and hugged them to her chest, utterly amused. "Do all your customers get adorable work gloves on their first day?" Jesse's mix of amusement and embarrassment was just too much fun to watch.

"Was there something about 'don't ask' that wasn't clear here? Or do you want me to take away your crowbar and just have at the bathtub on my own?"

"No!" she cried, leaping off her chair. The thought of starting, of finally getting this project underway, whizzed through her like electricity. She lunged for the gloves and the crowbar, but Jesse dodged her easily.

"Wait a minute, Ms. Taylor. If we're going to demo together, there are some rules. I can't have customers getting hurt on the job or letting their enthusiasm run away with their good sense."

Charlotte planted her hands on her hips and squared off against Jesse, even though he had a good six inches on her five-six frame. She raised her chin in defiance. "I never let my enthusiasm run away with my good sense."

The irony of that played out in Jesse's eyes the same moment her brain caught on to the idiocy of that statement made by an unemployed woman about to launch a major renovation project. He just raised one eyebrow, the corner of his mouth turning up in an unspoken, "Really?"

Charlotte used the distraction to pluck the crowbar from Jesse's hand. "Until now," she said, turning toward the door that led into what would be the dining room.

"Took the words right out of my mouth."

Chapter Five

Jesse watched Charlotte wiggle her fingers into the work gloves Mom had sent along. If they weren't so perfect for Charlotte, he'd have never agreed to something so unprofessional as a gift of fussy work gloves. Only these fit Charlotte's personality to a tee. Mom had won them in some social club raffle, and they were far too small for her arthritic hands, anyway. With a pang, Jesse wondered if Mom had been saving them for Randy's wife. Randy's ex-wife.

He'd wanted Constance and Randy to succeed, but even he could see she wasn't the sort of spouse who would continue to endure the kind of hours Randy kept. Jesse wanted his work to be a passion, surely, but not an obsession. That was part of why he loved the firehouse—it served as a constant reminder that there was more to life than a paycheck. There was a certain poetic justice in spending his work hours constructing when so much of the firefighting battled destruction.

Charlotte's wide-spread and wiggling floral fingers pulled his thoughts back to the present. He should have remembered pulling the bathtub would be a tight squeeze in this narrow bathroom—he was so close to her he could smell the flowers in whatever lotion she wore. Something sweet but with just a bit of zing, like her personality. Jesse held out the clunky safety glasses. "Time to accessorize."

He hadn't counted on her looking so adorable, standing there like an enthusiastic fish with those big brown eyes filling the gogglelike lenses. Her smile was beyond distracting, and she looked so utterly happy. He'd been grumpy for days after he "lost" the cottage—for that matter he got grumpy when he lost a basketball game at the firehouse—but she managed to keep her bounce even when losing her job, not to mention her beloved grandmother. What about her made that kind of resilience possible?

He straddled the antiquated pipes that ran up one side of the bathtub, pulling a wrench from his tool belt to detach them from the floor. Best to get to work right away before the urge to stare at her made him do something stupid. Well, stupider than presenting her with fussy gloves and a baby crowbar. "Pry up that flange while I pull from here."

"Flange?"

Yep, stupider. More every minute. "The circle thing around the bottom of the pipe. Wedge the crowbar into the waxy stuff holding it to the tile and yank it free."

She was a parade of different emotions as she got down on her knees and thrust the crowbar under the seal. Anxiety, determination, excitement, worry—they seemed to flash across her face in split-second succession. He liked that she was so emotionally invested in the place, but it bugged him how transparent her feelings seemed to him. "Go on," he encouraged, charmed by the way she bit her lip and the "ready or not" look in her wide eyes. "You can do this."

Charlotte gave the fixtures a determined glare, then got down on her knees and thrust the crowbar under the seal. The yelp of victory she gave when the suction gave way and the ring sprang up off the tile to clatter against the pipe was—and he was going to have to find a way to stop using this word—adorable. She brandished the crowbar as she sat back on her haunches and watched him go through the process of unhooking the bathtub from its plumbing. He could have done this alone more quickly—maybe even more easily—but this was too much fun. Getting this porcelain behemoth down the stairs to his truck would be the exact opposite of fun, but he'd called in a few guys from the firehouse to help with that, even though they wouldn't add to the scenery the way Charlotte's grin currently did.

She ran a hand along the lip of the deep tub. "Mima would have loved this tub. You were smart to talk me into saving it."

The expensive Jacuzzi model she'd had her eye on seemed like a ridiculous indulgence he would have talked anyone out of buying. Especially when this one could be so easily repaired. "Tell me about her." The question seemed to jump from his mouth, surprising her as much as it did him.

Her eyes lit up with affection. "Mima? She was 'a piece of work,' Grandpa always used to say. Her real name was Naomi Charlotte Dunning, but when I was little I couldn't quite say Naomi, so I just said 'Mi' at first. Then it became 'Mima' and that stuck. I'm named after her. She was a great woman. Grandpa had Alzheimer's like Melba's dad, and Mima was a hero in how she took care of him. When he died, I know she grieved and was scared to go on without him, but she found her courage. So much so that she decided to scatter some of his ashes all over the world. And I mean all over the world. She'd been on almost every continent, and left a little bit of Grandpa everywhere she went." She shrugged. "It's hopelessly romantic, isn't it?"

"I guess." He was pretty sure his parents had already purchased grave plots at the local cemetery and probably had a file somewhere with precise instructions as to what was going to go on their markers. Dad was a firm believer in advance planning, which was why he was so quick to categorize Jesse's career as "unfocused."

Charlotte sighed. "I want to be just like that when I'm her age. I'd want to be just like that now, if I could."

Jesse couldn't think of a single family member—not even Mom—he would praise like that. Family just didn't spur that kind of adoration in his world. "Did you spend a lot of time with her?"

"Tons. She took me on a few of her earlier, smaller trips. Now I get…well—" she swallowed hard "—I *used* to get postcards from her adventures."

He hardly even needed to ask. "And you kept them, didn't you?"

"I'm going to buy beautiful silver frames for all of them and fill the dining room wall."

She had plans—ambitious plans—for every room in the house. Jesse knew a thing or two about dreaming up plans. It made him wonder where he'd be right now if he had half the determination Charlotte had to put hers in play the way she did. "That will be nice."

Charlotte leaned in, pushing the safety goggles up on top of her head. "I loved her travels, but even when

Mima wasn't going anywhere, she was great. You know those teenage years, when you think your parents are the world's worst? I would hang out at Mima's house and declare my life a disaster, and she would just sit there in her rocking chair with her knitting and let me rant. That's where I learned to knit—from Mima. She'd take me to the yarn store and buy me whatever I wanted—even crazy colors or wild novelty yarns—and then we'd go home and make something amazing with it together."

Jesse yanked the first of the two water pipes free and started on the second. "My grandmother taught me her beef stew recipe, but it wasn't quite the warm, fuzzy experience you described."

She cocked her head, sending the glasses askew so that she had to catch them with her hand. "What do you mean?"

"It was less of an 'I'm passing down the family recipe' thing and more of a 'Don't you mess this up and besmirch the Sykes family name' thing. She had no granddaughters, so I think I was just a stand-in. My brother's marriage didn't last long enough to permit any recipe sharing with his wife, anyway." He pointed to the claw foot of the tub nearest his foot. "Ready to pry that up?"

"I won't break it, will I?"

"This is a two-hundred-pound hunk of coated metal. I doubt you could even chip it."

"But it's cracked already." She really had become attached to the thing. It was a bathroom fixture, for crying out loud, not a family heirloom.

"You'll be fine." Because she looked so worried he added, "Just go slow and stop when I tell you."

That foot and the next came free easily, and Jesse was able to angle the tub out of the alcove where it sat and pry up the last two feet with no trouble at all. Once he'd turned the tub away from the wall, the offending crack could be seen. Charlotte ran her finger down the rusted crack, giving a little groan as if she was dressing a wound. "This can be fixed, can't it?"

Jesse made the mistake of hunching down beside her on the narrow floor. It put them too close. "I'm almost positive. The rust isn't that bad and my guy is an artist."

She ran her hands along the top again. "You know, now I'm glad we're saving her. It'd be a shame to ditch such a beautiful old thing just for a few hotshot Jacuzzi jets, don't you think?"

He shot her a look. "You realize you're talking about a bathtub, right? You're not gonna give it a name or anything. Are you?" Boats, pets and people got names—not bathtubs—but the way Charlotte was looking, he couldn't be sure.

The corner of her mouth turned up. "I'm not the crazy lady who names her plants and has a dozen cats. Not yet, at least. I do plan to own a cat in the near future, though, so you never know."

Jesse chose not to hide his grimace. "A cat?" Maybe he could talk her into holding off until the renovation was complete. Surely he could scour the internet for home construction cat dangers and tell a few horror stories to warn her off.

Charlotte sat back against the wall and crossed her arms over her chest. "Well, if I didn't already guess you to be a dog person, I now have conclusive proof."

"I always heard cats and yarn were a bad combination." He began dismantling the hot and cold faucets from the end of the tub. "You know, jigsaw puzzle photos of kittens tangled up in yarn balls and all."

"I'll take my chances. I'm too enamored of my shoe collection to risk the damage a puppy could do." As if it had suddenly occurred to her, she asked, "How on earth are you going to get this thing down the stairs?"

Jesse checked his watch. "A few of the guys from the firehouse will be here in twenty minutes. I should have all these fixtures removed in ten minutes, and then we can start on the sink. That we can just whack apart with a sledgehammer."

Her eyes popped. "You're not really—"

"No." She really was too much fun to mess with. "Unless you want to?"

It was the most amusing thing to watch. She was frightened of taking a hammer to her bathroom walls, but there was this corner of her eyes that lit up with the idea. The way that woman could run away with his practicality was going to be very dangerous, indeed. *Keep your distance, Sykes—the last thing you need to do is mess this up.*

"And then he took the sink out onto the driveway. I took that great big hammer, hoisted it over my head and split that sink into two pieces right there." Charlotte felt the ear-to-ear grin return, just as it had every time she remembered the sensation of cracking that sink right down the middle. "I didn't know I had it in me."

"I didn't know you had it in you, either." Melba laughed. "Honestly, I can't picture it. Sounds rather unsafe."

"No, Jesse brought me safety glasses and gloves and everything." She leaned closer to the circle of wide-eyed women at the Gordon Falls Community Church knitting group. "But I think even he was a little shocked that I broke it in half on my first try. The firehouse guys, when they came to help drag the tub down the stairs and into Jesse's truck? They were impressed. Guess all that upper-body work at the gym paid off. I'm telling you, it's satisfying. Demolition therapy is seriously underutilized."

The women all looked shocked—all except for Violet Sharpton, an elderly woman with a sweet expression and a quirky personality. She looked almost envious. "What fun!"

"It made me feel a little bit powerful." In fact, it had made her feel like a momentary superhero, a great memory to pull out when the surges of panic came. "For a woman in a job search, a little confidence boost goes a long way."

"Speaking of a confidence boost," said Melba, "show them your shawl, Charlotte. I want the ladies to see how really talented you are."

Charlotte reached into her knitting bag and produced a sky-blue shawl of mohair-silk lace. Stitched from a knitting pattern and yarn Mima had brought back from Ireland, Charlotte considered this shawl a personal masterpiece.

"Wow. You weren't kidding, Melba. That's beautiful!" Tina, one of the older ladies of the group, ran her fingers across the intricate stitch work.

"I told you, she's talented," Melba boasted. "Look at that lace work."

Charlotte held up the shawl. "It looks hard, but it's really not that complicated."

Violet somehow managed a friendly frown. "Didn't

your mother ever teach you to hush up and accept a compliment? It may be easy for you, but some of us would never make it through the first inch." The older woman looked around the room to her fellow knitters. "Can you imagine how blessed someone's going to be when they get even a basic shawl knit with that kind of talent?" The purpose of the group was to make prayer shawls, hand-knitted wraps that were prayed over and given to people in need of healing or comfort. Charlotte had sent supplies from Monarch when Melba first started the group. "Thanks to Charlotte," Violet continued, "I think we've just taken things up a notch around here."

Melba looked pleased the group had taken so quickly to Charlotte. "You all remember it was Charlotte who set us up when I began to teach you all how to knit." Charlotte was pleased, too, feeling right at home in a matter of minutes. She'd always been that way with knitters—she could walk into a yarn shop anywhere in the world and feel as though she was among friends.

Her new friends all narrowed their eyes, evidently feeling the injustice of Charlotte's job loss as much as she did. "They shouldn't have let you go," Violet said. "It's a crying shame, that's what I say, even if Chicago's loss is our gain. Still, you seem a smart cookie to me. You'll land on your feet in no time."

Charlotte wondered whether she ought to admit she said something similar to herself in the bathroom mirror every morning, pep-talking herself into facing another day of unanswered queries and diminishing funds. Instead, she just quoted something Mima always said, "From your mouth to God's ears."

"That's right," another woman, Abby Reed, chimed

in. "You've got yourself one powerful posse of prayer warriors on your side now. These ladies know how to storm the gates of heaven, I tell you."

"Good thing," Charlotte admitted as she began stitching. *Stitch,* she told herself. *Don't complain or whine, just stitch. Look confident and you'll be confident.*

"I admire you." Tina turned her knitting to start a new row. "Not too many folks your age would see the value in buying a home and setting down roots while you're still single. Shows confidence, independence, common sense—all those good 'ence' words."

"You should talk to my Ben." Abby groaned. "Since he graduated he hasn't shown any of those words except *nonsense.* You'd think a job was going to land gift-wrapped in his lap the way he lollygags around the house. Frank has threatened to force him onto the fire department in another two weeks if the boy doesn't step things up."

Violet held up the navy blue shawl she was working on, a textured piece with white stripes down the side. Melba had told her Violet was one of the newer knitters, but Charlotte would have never known it by the woman's work—she was a natural. "Think we could pray some sense into this and give it to him?"

Abby laughed. "You'd be better off praying some patience into one and wrapping it over my mouth. We keep fighting over this. I was so excited to have him back home from college, but I'll tell you the novelty has worn off."

"You were saying you needed more staff at the shop," Marge Bowers suggested. "Can't he work there?" Abby ran the town gift shop, which also stocked a small selection of locally produced yarn. Charlotte had been in there numerous times—she wasn't a parent, but it didn't take a genius to know it wasn't a place most young men would ever want to work.

Jeannie Owens balked. "Can you see Ben making sales in Abby's shop? The only thing worse would be having him selling my candy—he'd eat all my profits."

"I thought about sending him over to bag at Halverson's Grocery just to get the employee discount—that boy eats enough for five people!"

Violet pointed her free needle at Abby. "You should do that. The bag boys at Halverson's don't show a lick of sense these days. Might do them good to have a college graduate in their midst."

"I just hope they motivate Ben to find a job that actually uses that expensive accounting degree." Abby looked up from her knitting. "Hey, this is sounding like a better idea every minute."

Charlotte let her gaze wander from face to friendly face. How often had she told Melba that this was what she loved about Gordon Falls? The people shared things, getting through life side by side, warts and all. These were the women who had held Melba up during the long, painful decline of her father's Alzheimer's. They'd held her friend close when he'd finally passed away, so much so that Charlotte never worried for Melba's support when she couldn't make it out to Gordon Falls. Why, then, did she resist telling them—and Melba— how frightening being jobless was to her? *End this wait, Lord,* Charlotte finished her row of stitching as she sent a silent prayer for God's favor over the dozen electronic résumés she'd sent out earlier this morning. *Send me a job.*

"Charlotte, if you could have any job in the world,

what would it be?" Jeannie, who filled a room with sunny-eyed optimism wherever she went despite a host of personal challenges, posed the question as she poured herself a second cup of coffee.

"Oh, naturally, I've always thought about opening a yarn shop. I might do it someday, but I know enough to realize how much work it is."

Jeannie and Abby, both small business owners, nodded in agreement.

"I'm still looking to work for someone, to let all the managerial headaches be on someone else's plate for a while longer," Charlotte added.

She thought about Jesse. After they wrestled the bathtub free, she'd managed to get him to open up about his plans to launch his own business. He seemed pretty autonomous as it was, despite working for Mondale Construction, but was bursting with the urge to work for himself and call his own shots. She admired his ambition, but she could also see the dark edge of it. Jesse wanted success to show the world that he could do it, to prove himself worthy. From a few side comments he'd made, she suspected his father had a lot to do with that drive—and not in a good way. She was so fortunate to have Mom and Dad, who believed in her no matter what she did. When she owned her own business, it would be for all the right reasons. For now, it was enough that she owned her own cottage.

Chapter Six

"You've made quite an impression," Charlotte's cousin JJ announced when they ran into each other a few days later at Halverson's Grocery. This was another small-town phenomenon that still startled Charlotte—a trip to the grocery store turned into a social event every time. She'd yet to fill her basket without running into six or seven people she knew—not to mention being introduced to half a dozen new "neighbors." That certainly never happened at the city convenience mart.

"Jesse's account of your powerhouse sink demolition was the talk of the firehouse," JJ went on, as the two of them wandered down the frozen-food aisle. "As if your first-day kitchen fire hadn't endeared you to the guys already."

"I think I was hoping for less fanfare tied to my entrance into Gordon Falls," Charlotte admitted. "The past few months have been a bit more dramatic than I'd like."

"Well, if you're not into drama, you've hired the wrong guy. Jesse Sykes is as Hollywood as they come. You remember him singing at our wedding, don't you?"

Just the other afternoon she was upstairs measuring windows when Jesse either forgot she was home or didn't care that she heard him. His voice echoed stunningly throughout the empty house, and she'd stopped to lean against the wall and just listen. Smooth as silk and soulful to boot. Mima would have declared Jesse to have "a set of pipes" and Charlotte had to agree. "He's amusing, and he's got a great voice, that's for sure."

JJ's voice softened. "He's a great guy. A bit of a loose cannon sometimes, but a heart of gold." She grinned. "Mostly." When Charlotte narrowed one eye at her she added, "You could do worse."

She really didn't want to get into this with JJ again. Her cousin knew her concerns about getting involved with a first responder without them arguing it out for the umpteenth time. Anyway, it felt wrong to tell one firefighter that you didn't think you could do life alongside another firefighter. "Sure, he's got personality. He's not for me, though."

Was there anyone out there for her? She liked to think so, though she was getting frustrated waiting for him to show up. In any case, now wasn't the time for a new relationship. Now should be about being her own person, stepping confidently—if not smoothly—into the future God had for her. Dating would just muck up her thinking and add to her anxiety. And really, the last thing she needed right now was the prospect of any more rejection.

"I thought you just said he was amusing." JJ selected a bag of frozen peas and placed them in her cart.

"Amusement is not the same thing as attraction." That felt dishonest, because she did feel an attraction to Jesse. She just knew better than to act on it. "I'll admit, we're having a bit of fun with this renovation project, and I could sure use a bit of fun right now, but that's all. Besides, from the little I heard, he's got all kinds of family baggage and I don't need anyone like that."

"Who's got family baggage?" Melba and Maria came up the aisle, waving hello. *Here we go again, a party in the frozen-food aisle.* It had its fun side, but Charlotte fretted her days of throwing on sweats and a baseball hat to duck into the grocery store were over.

"Sykes," JJ replied.

Melba sighed. "Everyone's got family baggage of some kind."

"Maybe, but your family baggage is adorable." JJ wiggled one of Maria's irresistible tiny pink toes, making the baby girl giggle.

"What would Mima have thought of Jesse?" JJ asked, surrendering the toe as, with the astounding flexibility of babies, Maria pulled it up to stuff it in her mouth. All three women laughed. Even though JJ and Max were Charlotte's cousins on her father's side, Mima left a big enough impression that both sides of Charlotte's relatives knew and loved the woman. Max and JJ had come to Mima's funeral, and not just because they wanted to support Charlotte and her parents.

Mima's opinion of Jesse—or what it would have been—was an interesting point to consider. Charlotte had to think for a moment, biding her time as she filled her own handbasket with a box of frozen breakfast sandwiches. "Hard to say. She'd like his sense of humor, but I doubt she'd have found him artistic enough."

"Your grandmother always was a pushover for the poetic types, judging from the way your grandfather won her over," Melba offered, gently removing the toe from Maria's drool-soaked mouth. "It's got to be too early for teething, doesn't it?"

JJ and Charlotte shrugged. Charlotte noticed a new weariness in Melba's voice and eyes.

"I still think you should publish all those love letters as a book," Melba went on. "Your grandfather was a heart slayer on the page in his day." The new mother sighed. "Nobody does that sort of romantic stuff anymore."

Charlotte leaned over and tickled Maria. "Is my darling goddaughter cutting into Mommy's love life?"

Melba's sigh turned into a yawn. "Right behind the firehouse. Between Clark's days and Maria's nights, I'm stretched to the limit. This parenting stuff is hard."

"The chief has been wound pretty tight these days, too," JJ added.

Charlotte eyed her friend. "When's the last time you and Clark had an evening to yourselves?"

Melba's only response was a sad smile. "It's worth it."

JJ put a hand on Melba's sagging shoulder. "You two deserve to be off duty. No offense, but you look exhausted. And honestly I could use a less grumpy boss."

"That's it, I'm babysitting." Charlotte pulled out her smartphone to check her calendar. There was nothing like helping others to get her mind off her own problems. And she adored Maria. *This should be a fun task.* "When is the next night Clark has free?"

Melba rolled her eyes. "Who knows?"

"Clark does," said JJ. "Text him right now and ask him."

"Right now?" Melba seemed more interested in the

choice of green beans, and that was bad news in the romance department.

Charlotte shut the freezer cabinet door in front of Melba's face. "This instant. You're outnumbered three to one."

"Three?"

"Maria agrees with me."

Two minutes and a package of ground turkey later, Melba peered at her phone and declared, "Thursday night."

"Mission accomplished. Okay, ladies, I have to get going." JJ's face took on a glow. "Alex is heading out of town again, and I promised him one home-cooked meal before he gets on another plane."

Melba gazed after the lovestruck firefighter and then pushed out a breath as she deposited a box of biscuit mix into her cart. "I'm pretty sure Clark and I looked that smitten once."

"Exactly my point," Charlotte replied. "I'm baby-sitting next Thursday night so you and Chief Bradens can have some time to rekindle your flame."

"I'm likely to fall asleep at the restaurant table," Melba admitted. "I can't remember the last time I sat down for a whole meal. They don't call 5:00 p.m. 'the fussing hour' for nothing. By the time Clark pulls in the driveway I'm ready to take a hot bath and tell the world good-night. At least until Maria wakes up again."

The strain in her friend's eyes tugged at Charlotte's heart. Melba had been through so much since moving to Gordon Falls—the long, hard struggle to care for her father, his eventual death—she'd thanked God for sending Clark to Melba a million times over the past year. And now baby Maria added more joy to their lives, but they were both clearly tired. While Melba never complained, Charlotte knew being married to the fire chief wasn't the easiest job in the world. Dad had been only a police captain, and it had taken a lot out of Mom. She touched Melba's elbow. "You need this. Let me do this for you. It's one night. Even if Maria screams the entire time, I can handle it."

Jesse set down the nozzles he was cleaning a few days later and stared at Chief Bradens. "Really?"

Chief nodded. "With your background, you never thought about taking the inspector's training?"

"Well, no." Fire inspectors were career guys. The Gordon Falls department had only two paid employees, Chief Bradens himself and the fire inspector, Chad Owens. While some volunteer guys looked to shift to a paid professional post, Jesse never counted himself among them. As his father never missed a chance to point out, this job asked enough of him on a volunteer basis. He wasn't eager to expand that. "Chad's not retiring or anything, is he?"

"Not that he's told me. It's just that I see the potential in you."

"I don't know. Sounds like a whole lot of paper pushing to me." Chad spent more time at a desk than on a truck, and Jesse knew enough of the Gordon Falls building codes to know they could tax a guy's patience. "I'm allergic to administrative tasks."

The chief leaned up against the truck that sat parked behind where Jesse was working. "I thought you wanted to own your own business someday."

"I do."

"You'll have to get over your allergic reaction to paperwork."

Jesse gave a grunt. "Mondale doesn't do paperwork."

"That's because his wife does his billing and filing. You planning to marry into an administrative family anytime soon?"

Jesse tried to scowl, but his brain went straight to Charlotte's thick, color-coded files of renovation ideas. "No."

Too late. Chief Bradens leaned in. "And what was that?"

"What was what?"

"That look."

"What look?" Jesse turned his attention to the box of nozzles, only to have the chief kick them out from under his grasp.

"Melba tells me you've been spending a lot of time at Charlotte Taylor's cottage."

Jesse knew the connection between Charlotte and the Bradens was going to tangle him up soon, but he hadn't counted on it wrapping around him quite this fast. "It's a big job. I'm glad for the work."

"Melba thinks you might be glad for the client."

How was he supposed to answer that? "She's nice."

Clark leaned down to meet Jesse's eyes. "She is. Charlotte is a great person. She's Melba's best friend and they've been through a lot together. She's Maria's godmother."

"I know she's a friend of yours. I've been trying to do right by her because of it. I told you that."

"And I appreciate it. I do. I just want to be sure you know to tread carefully here."

Jesse raised himself up from the box. "Meaning?"

"Meaning I'd want the department's most confirmed bachelor not to stomp on the heart of my wife's best friend. She's in a vulnerable spot, and subtlety isn't your strong suit."

Jesse chose his words carefully. "Is that a command to steer clear, Chief?" While Clark Bradens was a caring leader and Jesse considered him something of a mentor, he usually kept a clean line between personal and firehouse business.

Bradens's expression softened. "I can't tell you how to spend your personal time. But I know you and I know Charlotte. I'm asking you, as a friend and as chief, to be careful. Charlotte doesn't do halfway or casual—and I've never known you to do anything but. If you choose to go after her, I'd want to know you really mean it."

"Hey, no worries there. I'm not going after her." She did intrigue him, but there were lots of reasons to leave that alone for now. Like Chief said, he needed to keep his relationships halfway and casual right now. Charlotte was a client. She was a bit too artsy for his taste. And then there was the subject of Sunday mornings. "I don't think I spend enough time in church to be her type anyhow."

The chief's expression made Jesse regret his choice of reply. "You can change that if you want. The congregation talent show is soon, and we're still looking for an emcee."

That made Jesse laugh. "Me? Master of ceremonies at the GFCC talent night? Don't you think that's a bit ridiculous?"

"Have you ever seen our talent show?" Bradens smirked. "Ridiculous is nearly a requirement. It's the talent that seems to be optional."

"Why don't *you* do it?"

"I'll have to if I don't find someone else. This year providing the emcee is the firehouse's contribution. We could really use someone who has some actual theatrical tendencies."

Sure, he was a born show-off, but Jesse still shook his head. "I think I'll pass."

"Will you at least think about it? That, and the inspector's training?"

Some days Bradens just didn't know the meaning of the word *no.* "Yeah, fine, I'll give it some thought. I doubt I'll change my mind, though, so keep looking for someone else."

"You're my first choice. On both fronts. Just know that, okay?"

Both of those fronts, but not first choice for Charlotte, huh? That stung just a little, but suited him fine, anyway. "Sure, okay."

Chapter Seven

C harlotte was regretting her final "I can handle it" words to Melba. It was eight-thirty, and Maria hadn't stopped crying since Melba went out the door at six. Charlotte had fed her, changed her, rocked her and done just about every other baby-soothing thing she could think of, but still Maria wailed.

"All right, Maria, it's a nice night, so you and I are going to go for a walk. Any more of your cries bouncing off the walls in this house and I'm going to go a little bonkers. If the river doesn't soothe you, nothing will."

Charlotte found the stroller (complete with an adorable hand-knit baby blanket) on the back porch, penned a quick note and stuck it to the fridge—all one-handed because the red-faced Maria occupied the other arm— and headed out into the warm June night.

Gordon Falls was at its best on summer evenings. The town spread itself out along the Gordon River, filling the hillsides with quaint homes and dotting the town's main thoroughfare of Tyler Street with a collection of charming shops and restaurants. It was a picture-postcard small town. Charlotte had joked about the overwhelming quaintness of the place on her first visit, but she'd come to really love the community. It was as far away from the hustle and concrete of Chicago as she could get, and she could always feel her stress peeling off her soul as her car pulled through the big green floodgates that stood at the edge of Tyler Street. Even Maria simmered down to a steady whimper punctuated by a few bursts of crying.

Charlotte headed toward Tyler Street and the far end of Riverwalk, sure to be filled with people enjoying the evening but far enough from the restaurant where Clark and Melba were dining so that she wouldn't risk running into them. She already had a host of memories connected to places in town: the housewares store where she'd purchased the new kettle. The hardware store where she'd gotten her first spare set of keys made. The grocery store where she seemed to meet everyone she knew on every visit. The boutique that was sure to be her favorite place for clothes—once she spent time and energy on clothes instead of curtains. Abby Reed's craft and gift store, which held just enough yarn to make Charlotte feel as though she hadn't abandoned all artistic civilization. She hadn't been back to her Chicago apartment in almost three weeks, and she hadn't even missed it. That place was boxy, ordinary and noisy. The cottage was on its way to becoming quiet, filled with charm and a thing of beauty to help the rest of life's stress disappear.

What are You up to, Lord? Why am I so drawn to this place? Charlotte wondered to God as she pushed a fussing Maria through the town. *I've never felt a place could make me so happy before this. It's always been people that made me happy. Only now I've lost my col-*

*leagues and Mima. The things here—the things in my
house, even—are what make me happiest now. Is that
wrong? Or just different?* Charlotte looked down at
Maria's frustrated mad-at-the-world pout and thought,
Kiddo, I know how you feel.

Her Tyler Street journeys led her down by the firehouse and Karl's Koffee. It wouldn't hurt to meet a
friendlier face than Maria's frustrated red cheeks and
tiny balled fists.

Maria's wailing ensured that most people heard her
coming before they saw her. Two grandmother-types
outside of Karl's had offered some tactics, but neither
of them had worked, and Charlotte admitted to growing
a little anxious that maybe her goddaughter was suf-
fering from something more than simple fussiness. It
wasn't much of a surprise that Maria's cries caught the
ears of the firefighters on duty as Charlotte walked by.

"Hey, is that the Charlotte?" A stocky man from the
firehouse called as he rose from his lawn chair on the
driveway.

Charlotte stopped, startled that he'd called her by
name. "Um, hi."

A younger fireman—in actual red suspenders, Charlotte noted with amusement—came out from behind
one of the bright red trucks that stood ready in their
enormous garage spaces. "Yorky, you gotta stop calling Chief Bradens's kid 'the chieflette.'" He wiped his
hands on a towel that he subsequently stuffed into a
back pocket. "Chieflette's not a name. It's not even a
real word. It's just weird."

He hadn't been saying "Charlotte"—he'd been saying "chieflette." Charlotte felt a twinge of satisfaction
that the baby's firehouse nickname sounded so close to

her own. After a second she remembered Yorky from her ill-fated first day as cottage owner.

He was currently balking at the younger guy. "Everybody in here has a nickname, why not the baby?" His eyes popped in recognition. "Hey, you're the cottage lady."

"I am." She held out her hand. "Charlotte. And I think 'chieflette' is kind of cute. It's certainly original." Which kindled a fierce curiosity as to what name Jesse had been given. Smiling at Yorky, she made a mental note to discover a sneaky way to find out. Maria gave a wail of disapproval as if to counteract her godmother's endorsement.

"She's certainly cranky." Yorky peered into the stroller. "Gas?"

Charlotte sighed and picked Maria up out of the stroller to settle her against her shoulder. "I've burped her. Twice. Some lady even tried some special colic hold outside of Karl's, but nothing seems to help."

"Is she running a fever?" The younger man went to reach for Maria's head, but Yorky swatted his hand away.

"Wash your hands before you touch a baby, son—everybody knows that." When the man pulled the towel back out from his pocket, Yorky frowned. "And no, that's not enough." For a big, burly guy, Yorky was evidently a softie for babies. "Shame JJ's not on tonight—women always have a knack for that stuff."

If women always have a knack for this, why am I pushing a screaming baby down Tyler Street? Charlotte thought, suddenly fighting a wave of insecurity. She tried to give an educated touch to Maria's forehead. "No fever that I can tell."

"Go see if Pipes is still here," Yorky said to his companion, cocking his head back toward the firehouse kitchen window.

"He left an hour ago. Him and Wally are grilling out down by the river with some of the probies."

Pipes? Probies? Some days firemen seemed to speak a different language. "Is Pipes a parent?"

That brought a guffaw from Yorky. "Jesse? Now wouldn't that be a hoot. Nah, Jesse's just got silver pipes. The guy sings to kids when they're scared from the fires. Honestly, it'd be hard to keep him around if he weren't so good at it."

So Jesse's nickname was "Pipes." The singing she'd heard echoing through her house certainly validated the name. Jesse's silky voice struck her as a Frank Sinatra–Harry Connick Jr.–Michael Bublé sort of croon, but with a decidedly soulful edge. Based on the wails she'd been enduring for the past pair of hours, getting Jesse to sing Maria to sleep seemed like the best idea in the world. "I'll go find him, if you don't mind. Where on the riverwalk is he?"

"Just south of the footbridge. Go a block farther than Karl's Koffee and you should be able to smell the meat burning."

Maria gave a yowl as if she was working up to another good fit again, spurring Charlotte to settle the fussy baby back into the stroller and turn them both toward the river. She'd pledged to herself to do anything necessary to present Melba and Clark with a happy baby when they got home from dinner—those two deserved some peace and quiet. They deserved to not feel one pang of guilt for taking an evening to themselves. "Thanks, I'm sure I'll find him."

"He'll probably hear you coming," Yorky offered with an understanding smile. "But I can page him if you like."

"No, I think we can make it to the footbridge in one piece. Thanks, Yorky." She took an immediate liking to the stocky, middle-aged firefighter. He was a big bear of a man with a heart of butter—who wouldn't like a man with that smile? "And extra thanks—you know— for playing hero the other day at my cottage."

"Nothin' doing, Charlotte. That's why we're here. You just take care of the little chieflette there and we'll call it even."

Charlotte started walking toward the river. "Chief-lette, huh? You could do worse, Maria. You've got two dozen uncles looking out after you, little lady. That's good, because with those red curls and that smile— the one you haven't shown me in hours, I might add— you're gonna need 'em."

"Aw," Wally groaned as he bit into his hamburger. "Aw, Sykes, this is carnivore perfection." He wiped a smear of Sykes's Special Sauce from his chin, a look of gastronomic pleasure on his face. "What's in here?"

Jesse smiled as he passed off a burger to another firefighter in training, or "probie," as they were known around the firehouse. "Wouldn't you like to know."

To be known for an awesome burger was a small satisfaction, but Jesse liked the appreciation. The fire-house boasted only three decent cooks, so meals were a gamble most nights. If they ever went to a professional model where the firefighters lived on-site in regular shifts, it'd become a serious issue. As it was with ro-tating shifts of volunteers on call, meals were more of a perk than a requirement. Jesse liked to make sure he was around on Thursday nights when the butcher always sent over burgers. It was a crime to see good meat destroyed by bad cooks.

A sharp cry caught his ear as he slid his spatula under the final burger and handed it off to another grateful probie. There was a baby nearby, and an unhappy one at that.

Jesse put the cover back on the grill and wiped the spatula clean on a towel. He dipped a finger in the plastic bowl of Sykes's Special Sauce, licking a tangy taste before snapping the lid into place. Man, that stuff was delicious. Maybe someday he'd consider bottling it and selling it wholesale to bars and burger joints. His thoughts were interrupted as the high-pitched wail grew louder, and he turned to see the source of the drama.

It was Charlotte Taylor. Chief Bradens had mentioned she was babysitting his daughter tonight. The strained look on Charlotte's face told him it wasn't going well.

He left the bowl on the table and walked toward the noisy pair. "Somebody having a rough night?"

"She's been like this for almost two hours. I've tried everything I know and a few things complete strangers have suggested." Charlotte pushed her hair back from her face in exasperation. "In another hour I'll be ready to cry myself."

Jesse reached back to the table to pull an antiseptic wipe from a container and used it to clean the last of barbecue and Sykes's Sauce off his hands. "I'll bet."

"Smells great." Charlotte nodded toward the grill with a weak attempt at a smile. Poor thing, she really did look at the end of her rope.

"Just gave out the last one, sorry."

"No, I've eaten. I just didn't realize your skill set included cooking."

"Oh, it sure does," one young man said with a mouth full of burger. "Sure does."

"It's nice to have an appreciative audience," Jesse admitted, peering into the stroller to see a puffy red face surrounded by a halo of Bradens-red curls. "Seems Chieflette's got a temper to match her locks."

Charlotte laughed. "I heard Yorky call her that." She gave Jesse a slightly panicked look. "I also heard they don't call you Pipes for nothing and that you're great at calming down kids. Care to work some of that vocal medicine on Little Miss Fussbudget here?" She looked just short of desperate.

It was the chief's baby. It was Charlotte asking. What kind of fool would say no? "No guarantees, but I'll do my best." A surprising knot settled in Jesse's stomach. Normally he was never given to nerves—especially about singing—but for some reason the stakes felt higher at the moment. Distracting five-year-olds at the preschool fire drill was one thing. Soothing a fussy baby in front of a pack of probies and Charlotte Taylor? Well, that was quite another. "Okay," he said, infusing his voice with confidence he didn't fully feel, "hand Little Miss Crankypants over and let's see if we can calm her down."

At first, Maria didn't care at all to be handed over to a strange set of arms. As he settled her against his shoulder, she wailed, and out of the corner of his eye Jesse saw Charlotte wringing her hands. Starting down in as low a register as he could manage, Jesse launched into a slow, soft version of Ben E. King's "Stand by Me." He remembered reading somewhere that the rumble of a deep voice in a chest was soothing to babies. When that didn't have much of an effect, he modulated up a key and began to sway around the grass with her, holding her tight and patting her back the way he'd seen his grandmother do. Halfway into the second chorus, Maria gave a little hiccup and softened her wails.

A natural tenor, Jesse was more comfortable in higher keys, and the tiny bit of progress he'd made bolstered his confidence. He was "Pipes," and while he mostly used his voice for laughs, he also knew this was his gift, the particular talent he brought to firefighting. He could serenade somebody calm in the back of an ambulance, as they made their way down the ladder or as they waited for their loved ones to emerge from a smoking building. And, okay, he was a bit of a born show-off. Showing off for a good cause like helping Charlotte help Chief Bradens? Well, that ought to be a cakewalk. When Maria calmed further, Jesse took it up another key and began dancing with Maria. He caught Charlotte's eye, winked and spun Maria in a tiny turn that actually produced a sigh from the baby.

"Will you look at that?" one of the probies said with astonished eyes. "It's like he's the baby whisperer or something."

By the third chorus, Jesse had produced an actual laugh from Maria. Well, at least it sounded like a laugh. He ignored the growing wet spot on his shoulder, focusing instead on the steady small breaths coming under his hand on Maria's back. By the end of the second song, Maria was out cold, Charlotte was astonished and Jesse felt downright victorious. He'd sung victims to calm—or something at least close to reasonable— before, but he'd never actually sung a baby to sleep.

There was a startling satisfaction in the accomplishment, which fueled a warm glow under his ribs. Very, very carefully, he lowered a contented Maria back into the stroller and then looked up to catch Charlotte's wide smile.

"Better keep walking so she stays asleep," one of the probies said behind him.

Jesse turned, head cocked in annoyance. "If you know so much about babies, Carson, why wait until now to speak up?"

"Hey," Carson replied, "I'm the oldest of eight. But no way was I going to step in and miss a chance to see the Great Sykes at work. Just keep walking for another ten minutes or so and you'll be golden."

Jesse wasn't really in the mood to see Charlotte take off down the Riverwalk. Tossing the package of hamburger buns to the trainee, Jesse said, "Okay, then, we'll walk. You clowns finish up eating and take everything back to the firehouse. Don't forget to study those handouts before the next session." Turning to Charlotte, he said, "I'll go along as a precautionary measure. In case my outstanding talents only have a temporary effect. It is the chief's baby, after all."

Charlotte shrugged as if to say, "Better safe than sorry," and began rolling the stroller down the path. Jesse caught up with her, enjoying the victory of the moment. They walked along in cautious silence for a few minutes, ensuring that Maria was safely off in dreamland.

"That was amazing," Charlotte whispered after a bit.

"Actually, that was Ben E. King. 'Amazing' is a different tune." The soft laugh his joke pulled from Charlotte was even more satisfying than Maria's doz-

ing. See? He could do the casual friendship thing here.
Bradens's warnings weren't necessary. He was just
helping a client help a friend, that was all. Besides, he
always liked to make people laugh—why not Charlotte, as well?

"The guys at the firehouse said you've done that on
calls. Sing to kids, I mean. How do you manage it?"

It was like having someone ask how he breathed. "It
wasn't something I really thought about. The first time
was my second or third call on the rig—my first real
fire. I was scared. You never really lose the fear. You
just sort of make peace with it. Anyway, back in the
upper bedroom there was a little boy. We're scary looking with all our gear on, so it's always a challenge to
get kids to come to us." The memory of that little boy's
dread-filled eyes had never left Jesse. At that moment,
he would have done anything it took to gain that boy's
confidence and pull him to safety. "I saw a poster from
a television show on his wall and I just started singing
the theme song."

"And he came to you?"

"Well, it was more like he didn't run away. I just kept
singing and walking toward him. I didn't think about
whether anyone could hear me on the radio, I was so focused on doing anything to keep that kid from ducking
back under that bed. When I got close enough, I grabbed
him and just kept singing the whole way down the stairs
and out the door so he'd stay still and not struggle."

Charlotte smiled. "Jesse, the singing fireman."

Jesse shot her a look. "Please. I've heard every version of that you can think of, and I don't like a single
one of them. It works. It keeps kids—and even some

adults—calm when calm is the hardest thing to manage. Bradens does it with his eyes. I do it with my voice."

"Clark's eyes?"

"Every firefighter has a particular gift, a talent. Chief Bradens has a way of looking right into your eyes so that you believe whatever he says. You don't question stuff like that when lives are at stake." He caught Charlotte's gaze and held it. "I take my work at GFVFD very seriously. We all do. We put our lives on the line for it."

"I'm sorry." Her voice was soft, and he regretted calling her out for her teasing. "Really."

"It's okay. Just no cracks about it, all right?" He reached out and touched her hand as it rested on the stroller handle. Something not at all casual and not at all like friendship zinged through his fingers when he did. "I think I've knocked her out cold, poor thing."

Charlotte looked up at him for far longer than was necessary. "You're my hero."

If you choose to go after her, I'd want to know you really mean it.... I don't want the department's most confirmed bachelor to stomp on the heart of my wife's best friend. The chief's warning echoed sensibly in Jesse's brain. Trouble was, the rest of him was busy losing the battle to Charlotte's big brown eyes.

Chapter Eight

Jesse stood in the doorway of Chief Bradens's office Monday morning. "You wanted to see me, Chief?"

"I did. Come on in."

Jesse crossed the room to take the guest chair in front of the chief's desk. "What's up?"

"First off, it seems I owe you some thanks for serenading my daughter the other night." Clark shook his head. "Man, that sounds odd to say."

Jesse made a serious face. "I'm not taking your daughter to the prom, sir."

Clark laughed. "Not on your life, even if she was eighteen years older."

"At least twenty-two years older, boss. And not even then." That was true. If Chief were older—and Bradens was one of the youngest fire chiefs in the state—and his daughter was anything close to Jesse's age, Jesse still wouldn't touch that with a ten-foot pole.

"Okay, well, thanks are in order anyway. It was a pretty nice thing to come home to a sleeping baby. Melba was sure Maria would give Charlotte a load of trouble, and it seems you kept that from happening.

The probies were calling you 'the baby whisperer.' It's pretty funny, actually. I think they wonder if you have superpowers or something."

"Feed those boys a decent burger and they'll believe anything," Jesse joked.

"Anyway, I wanted to know if you've given any more thought to the talent-show thing or the inspector's training."

Bradens was not usually one to push on stuff like this—Jesse was beginning to feel the pinch of his predicament. Didn't singing the man's daughter to sleep gain him a "cease-fire" on the church invitations? At least he wasn't riding Jesse for spending an hour walking around the Riverwalk with Charlotte. That hadn't been such a smart idea—that woman had begun to really get under his skin. He'd spent the next hour in the firehouse weight room burning off energy and listing all the reasons to keep clear of the pretty client.

"Yeah, look, I don't know."

The chief leaned in. "I'd take it as a personal favor if you'd emcee the show for us."

Chief's attempts to drag Jesse over the GFCC threshold were getting less subtle every time. It was bad enough when Melba had joined the choir a few months ago, and Bradens went on about fun and fellowship—which Jesse found ironic, because everyone knew the chief couldn't hold a tune if it had a handle tied to it. To Jesse, choir sounded like a bunch of people who barely knew how to have fun standing up singing old songs in silly, shiny robes. Not that he could confirm his theory; the only time he'd darkened the doors of Gordon Falls Community Church had been for Melba's father's funeral a while back, and there had been only community singing in that service.

When Jesse didn't respond, Bradens played his trump card. "Charlotte was the one who came up with the idea, actually. I'm surprised she didn't mention it to you given the success of your little command performance in the park." That settled it. Charlotte could be relentless. Jesse was sure if he said no to Bradens, Charlotte would just take up the campaign and double it.

"Tell you what. I'll do the talent show if you lay off about the choir."

"Thanks. Think about what I said regarding the inspector, though. Actually, I think you could go further than that. You're a good firefighter, but your real talent is connecting with people. Catching their focus in a crisis. Those are skills I can't really teach. You may think I'm nuts for saying this, but I think if we could rein in that crazy side of yours, you have the makings of a good chief."

Jesse sure wasn't expecting that. "Me? A fire chief?"

"Well, we've got to find some way for you to harness all that charisma for good."

He'd heard some version of that speech—one slightly less complimentary of his personality—regularly from his father. Grow up, settle down, fly straight, take action; it came in a dozen sour flavors. Jesse had really hoped the launching of Sykes Homes would put a damper on that sort of talk. He knew Chief Bradens was demonstrating faith in his abilities; it was just that the topic was a raw nerve. He liked his own plans—even if they had been detoured by the loss of the cottage—and suddenly Bradens was piling new expectations on him. "Thanks for the vote of confidence," was the best answer he could give at the moment, "but like I said, I'm allergic to administration."

"I'm trying to talk the town council into finding the funds to pay for a deputy chief."

Jesse shrugged. Bradens could sweeten the deal all he wanted, but it still didn't really fit in with Jesse's plans for where life was supposed to go from here. He switched to what he hoped was a safer topic. "Speaking of administration, Charlotte will get her occupancy permit this afternoon—we're turning the water back on later today. You'll get your house back." That little benchmark still stung, but the chief had no way of knowing that—only a few of the guys on the crew knew about Jesse's thwarted plans to buy the place. "The place is still rough around the edges but livable. It'll be a beauty, though, when she's done. That woman knows how to make full-blown decorating plans, that's for sure."

"I feel better knowing she's working with you and Mondale rather than some contractor from out of town. She's in a bit of a weird place right now when it comes to that cottage."

At that moment, Jesse saw in Chief Bradens's eyes a glimmer of the niggling suspicion that had bothered him for days. The growing sense that Charlotte might not be thinking with her head right now so much as her heart. "How so?"

"Well, don't you think she's going at this with a little too much—" he searched for the word "—drive?"

Charlotte was indeed going full out on the renovation. It was keeping him busy and swelling his paycheck, but it was also making him a bit worried. "She wouldn't be the first person to take her stress out on the

Home Shopping Network, if that's what you're saying." The desire to honor her grandmother and take her mind off her job problems could easily get twisted up in a craving to do things that might not make the most financial sense. "She's taking advantage of the free time in between jobs to give the place the attention it deserves. I can spot the difference."

Could he? He'd accepted her order for premium kitchen fixtures yesterday that were three times as expensive as the ones he'd recommended. While he felt oddly protective of Charlotte, he was also becoming aware that with the right smile, she could make him agree to just about anything. Not that it was his role to rein her in, but hadn't he promised himself to do just that? Let her splurge but splurge wisely? What she'd ordered yesterday couldn't be called a wise splurge by anyone, and yet he hadn't challenged it at all. Charlotte wasn't the only one in a bit of a weird place right now.

"Melba's worried about her." The chief gave a weary sigh. "At the same time, I'd kind of like my house to contain only two females again, if you catch my drift."

"Relax, Chief. Like I said, I should have your guy-to-girl ratio back down to one-to-two by tomorrow." As for what the additional woman would do once she was living in her project and could focus on it full-time... he'd worry about that later.

Charlotte held up Violet Sharpton's latest prayer shawl Wednesday morning with genuine admiration. Karl of Karl's Koffee had fallen and hurt his hip again, and Violet had made him a brown shawl with coffee cups dotting either end, their plumes of steam rising to meet in a swirly pattern down the middle. "Honestly,

Violet, if I were still at Monarch, I might ask to put this one—and your flame shawl and the flamingo one—on the cover of a catalogue." Violet had made a fabulous one-of-a-kind prayer shawl, with a flame motif to match his thrill-seeking style, for Max Jones after he'd been hurt in a paralyzing fall. She had exceeded that effort a few months later with one for Max's fiancée, Heather, bearing her favorite birds. A Sharpton Shawl was on its way to becoming a hot Gordon Falls commodity.

"How is the job search going?" Violet asked tenderly. "Seems like there's no loyalty to hardworking people anywhere these days." She handed Charlotte a cup of tea. "I'm just glad the Good Lord sent us another tea drinker." She took back the "Shawlatte," as she'd christened it a minute ago. "It's getting hard to hold my own against the Gordon Falls caffeine junkies." The petite woman's eyes fairly sparkled at her own joke.

"It's still early," Charlotte replied, pasting a smile on her face. "But there have been lots of nibbles, so I'm sure an offer will be here soon." She knew most of the life stories of these women, and none of them had easy lives. Seeing their zest for life despite some whopping challenges gave Charlotte courage. Compared to some of the things these woman had endured—loss of spouses, fires, debilitating diseases, children gone wrong—one layoff seemed barely worthy of complaint.

She did her best to ignore Melba's disbelieving look. The truth was, things weren't going well at all. She'd expected to be choosing between offers by now, not staring into a gaping void of tepid responses to submitted résumés. So much of this loomed out of her control, and it was driving her crazy. She needed action, momentum, anything that felt like results—but the only place she could come close to any of those things was on the cottage renovations. To do that, and do it with excellence, proved such a saving grace. It made her feel successful when success seemed to be edging out of her grasp.

Marge Bowers tugged on Maria's hand as she held the baby. "I saw the sweater your godmother made you, Maria. Your aunt Charlotte knows her stuff." It felt lovely to have her knitting skills receive compliments, especially from these ladies. Maria's biological grandmothers might be gone, but she had a dozen honorary ones here. This morning Charlotte couldn't be certain a fight wasn't going to break out over who got to hold Maria first. "Between Charlotte and your mama, I doubt you'll ever be short of hats or mittens."

"Or scarves," Charlotte added. "Scarves are my favorite."

"I like dishcloths myself," Tina Matthews piped up. "Quick, practical and there are hundreds of designs to choose from."

"Tina gives six as a housewarming gift," Melba related. "I still use my set every day."

"And now I can make you a set, too," Tina said. "Do you know your kitchen color scheme yet?"

Melba started to laugh. "Are you kidding? There are four file boxes, a set of computer files and two scrapbooks on the subject. And that's only the ones I know about."

Charlotte hoped she hadn't been too fast to pull out her smartphone and display an image of the "china-blue and white with yellow accents" color scheme she'd chosen for the kitchen. The resulting *ooh*s and *ahh*s were highly gratifying. The hand-painted porcelain cabinet knobs and handles had arrived the other day, and they were worth every premium penny.

"You've got an eye, Charlotte. Now I know just what color yarn to buy."

The idea that her kitchen sink would someday be graced with both designer weathered copper fixtures *and* a set of handmade color-coordinated dishcloths settled a warm hum in Charlotte's chest. She wasn't quite sure when it had happened, but Gordon Falls was starting to feel like home. Whole days would go by where she didn't even think of Monarch or her city apartment. That made it easier to stomach how she wasn't shuttling back and forth between multiple interviews right now.

"However long you stay, we are glad to have you," Abby Reed replied. "Gordon Falls was starting to feel a little gray-haired before Melba came along."

"And JJ, Alex and Max," Melba added.

"My two cousins have done all right for themselves here," Charlotte admitted, turning her knitting to start a new row. She hadn't really meant "married off" as her version of "done all right," but the knowing looks some of the ladies passed between them meant they'd clearly made the connection.

"Clever you, meeting the town's most charming bachelor fireman your first day in the cottage," Marge teased.

Charlotte rolled her eyes. "Oh, you wouldn't think it was so clever if you saw my kitchen filled with smoke."

"It brought Jesse Sykes to your doorstep." Vi chuckled. "Handsome and handy, that one." For a widow in her seventies, Violet had more energy than anyone else in the room. And more nerve.

"Violet, you really are a piece of work," Jeannie

Owens chastised, then broke into a smile. "I hope I grow up to be just like you."

The group erupted in laughter. "Why go for home repair when you could shoot for a man who knows his way around the kitchen?" Marge said in a loud whisper. "I've seen the way Karl looks at you. He already gives you free pie. Wait until he gets that shawl—you'll be eating free for a year!"

Violet snorted her disagreement. "Nonsense. Karl comps anybody who has to move for Hot Wheels, you know that."

Charlotte's cousin Max, who had received his knitted "FlameThrow" when a climbing accident confined him to a wheelchair, could fit at only one table in Karl's Koffee. It was common knowledge that when someone had to shift seats to make way for Max "Hot Wheels" Jones, Karl gave them free coffee. "I know we all get coffee," Marge countered, wagging her finger, "but you're the only one I know who gets pie. You're special."

Violet, usually never at a loss for a good comeback, didn't reply. She scowled at Marge, but Charlotte was pretty sure the pink in her cheeks wasn't from anger. Anyone who thought Gordon Falls was a quiet, quaint little tourist town on the river where nothing ever happened would get a surprise if they met with this group. The ladies had always been pleasant acquaintances, but they were becoming fast friends. This group had scooped up Melba when she'd come to Gordon Falls in the throes of her father's progressing disease, and now it felt as if they had scooped up Charlotte, as well.

Abby, who had offered to talk retail yarn over lunch after today's knitting session, spoke up. "You know, you could do lots of your job from just about anywhere, couldn't you? You could work for a company in France right from your home."

"If I spoke French," Charlotte admitted. "I have done international work for Monarch, and for my job before that. I used to travel quite a bit, actually. Now that's not so necessary with all the digital communication."

"There was a woman in the shop the other day buying yarn for her grandchildren. She had their video up on her phone and was holding up yarn so they could pick colors right there in front of her. And they were in New Jersey!" Abby picked up Maria, who had started to fuss a bit in her carrier. "I don't really know how all that stuff works, but it was fun to watch."

"I text my grandchildren all the time," Violet said. "I know stuff that would curl their mother's hair, but I'm keeping my mouth shut. I want them to think they can come to me if they're afraid to talk to Donald and his wife."

"You really are the coolest grandmother ever," Melba said. "I hope you'll be texting Maria when she's in middle school and hates me."

Melba's mother had been gone for years, but Charlotte recognized the still-constant loss that pressed on her own heart. How many times had she picked up her phone to send a photo or text to Mima, only to realize she was gone? It felt as if the huge hole in her life still had ragged, painful edges. Until she had a family of her own, Charlotte vowed to be the kind of support to Maria that Violet was to her grandkids. *I want to trust you'll find me a job, Lord. I want the panic to go away. Until it does, thank You for this amazing circle of women.*

She felt fresh tears sting her eyes until Tina thrust a

ball of yarn into her view. "Charlotte, what on earth did I do wrong here? It looks like tumbleweeds."

Charlotte held out her hands. "Let me look at it. I'll have it straightened out in no time." Here, at least, was one thing she knew she could fix, one problem she knew she could solve.

Chapter Nine

Jesse put down his wrench and turned the knob on Charlotte's gorgeous new kitchen faucet. "Drumroll, please."

Charlotte laughed and drummed her hands on the counter. "Ready."

The pipes under the faucet made a host of disturbing noises from behind their cabinet doors. Then, after a few tentative spurts and a gurgle or two, water cascaded from the graceful copper fixture. "Hot and cold running water for Miss Charlotte Taylor, thank you very much," Jesse boasted. "You can move in."

Charlotte was thrilled. This last renovation made the house officially livable. She'd spend her first night in the cottage tonight, even though it meant sleeping on the mattress on the floor, since she hadn't taken delivery yet on the majestic four-poster bed she'd found at the local antiques store. While waiting on some of the final utilities—and a disturbingly empty e-mail inbox—Charlotte had poured over catalogues, invaded furniture stores and even scoured local flea markets in search of perfect finds. Even Jesse had remarked that the place managed to boast a surprising amount of furniture already. It was much better to focus on the decorating progress she *could* control than to ruminate on the employment process she could not. A dozen curtains came in, but the two dozen résumés she'd most recently sent out hadn't produced any response.

She poked her head into a cabinet to produce a brand-new stovetop kettle and two mugs. "Shall we celebrate? Without the smoke signals this time?"

Jesse pulled a rag from his toolbox and wiped the worst of the grime from his hands. He had a royal-blue T-shirt on today that did distracting things to his eyes. "Tea?"

"Yogurt doesn't feel very festive, and that's all I've got in the fridge right now. I was heading out for groceries this afternoon."

"Well, if it's either tea or yogurt, I'll opt for tea. As long as it's really strong." He clearly had no interest in the brew and was consenting for her benefit. Charlotte hadn't seen that level of consideration in a guy for a long time. How nice that he sensed what an important moment this was for her, how it was much more than two mugs of tea on a flea-market table—it was a declaration of resilience. Jesse held up one finger. "Go ahead and put the kettle on...I'll be right back."

Turning the brand-new faucet lever warmed her all the way out to her fingertips. The perfection of it felt like the best antidote to the sagging job search—satisfying and empowering. This house had been waiting for her. Okay, the first welcome hadn't gone well, but despite that kitchen fire she knew the house loved her.

That was silly of course; a house was incapable of loving her. Still, how many times had she felt her knitting comfort her—or mock her when things went horribly wrong? Charlotte drew strongly from her surroundings; her tactile world had always affected her deeply. The scent of her favorite tea filling this kitchen would feel like an anointing; a blessing of her life here. A promise that it would all work out in the end. Not that she could or would explain such a thing to the likes of Jesse Sykes.

The porch door slammed as she was placing the tea cozy—one she'd knitted herself—around the steeping pot, and Jesse entered the room with a small handful of flowers and a package of cookies. "What's a tea party without cookies?" He waved the package and the flowers at her. "Although they've been in the backseat of my truck for a week—we may be looking at more crumbs than cookies."

Charlotte didn't think her smile could get any wider. He'd understood her need to celebrate. And yet his gesture wasn't forced or overwhelming; it was just an honest gift of what he could scramble together. "Are those from Mrs. Hawthorne's yard?" She didn't know her new next-door neighbor well enough to judge how much of a trespass Jesse had just committed.

Jesse made a "who me?" face. "Could be. Could be I just happened to have black-eyed susans in my glove box. Or a flat of flowers in the back of my truck. You'd have no way of knowing. You're completely innocent."

The closest thing Charlotte had to a vase was a tall blue glass canning jar, which she filled with water and set in the center of the table. She grabbed a small tin tray from a box in the hallway, laid a paper towel across it and arranged the rather sad assortment of broken cookies on the towel. The tea, flowers, mugs and cookies made a comical vignette, and he couldn't help but laugh as she placed a few restaurant packets of sugar by the teapot. "One lump or two?"

"With only a brother in the house growing up, I'm not exactly up on my tea party etiquette." He pulled the chair out for Charlotte with a dramatic gesture, then made a show of easing himself into the opposite chair. He winced a little when it creaked a bit under his weight, looking like the proverbial bull in the china shop of her furnishings. "What am I supposed to do?"

Charlotte laughed. "Drink tea and eat cookies—or what's left of the cookies. This isn't a test." She poured his cup, then her own. "This is a chai tea—it's strong like coffee, so you might actually like it."

Jesse smelled the aroma wafting up from the mug, his face scrunching in suspicion. "Doubtful. Might be good for dunking, though." He caught her eye. "I am allowed to dunk, aren't I?"

"I heartily encourage the dunking of cookies. I'm a dunker myself, you know." After a second, she felt compelled to add, "Thanks."

"For putting in your sink?" His eyes told her he knew exactly why she had thanked him, and that it had nothing to do with the sink.

"No." The word slid soft and warm between them. The aroma of chai tea in her new kitchen settled around her like a consecration, with all the comfort of a fluffy shawl on a cold evening.

Jesse added two sugars before even tasting the tea, then lifted the mug to his lips. "Um—" he paused, clearly looking for the right description "—delicious?"

"You hate it." Charlotte found she wasn't offended

at all. In fact, she was more enchanted by his efforts to hide it. "No, really, it's okay."

"I'm a coffee guy," he explained, spreading his hands in admission.

"I like coffee, too," she said, then wondered why she was trying to build connections with him. "I just don't have any in the cottage right now. I'll get some this afternoon." Why had she said that? Why was she extending social invitations to a guy she'd already decided wasn't a good match, even if she was looking for someone? "So you can have coffee while you work and all."

Plausible as the excuse was, they both knew that wasn't what she'd meant. Things were tumbling in a direction Charlotte didn't really understand or endorse. Only she knew she didn't want Jesse to leave—now or even soon. She told herself it was that she wasn't ready to be in the house all alone, but that rang as false as Jesse's compliment of her chai tea.

"So your Mima wasn't a tea drinker? Even with all the china cups and all?"

Why was it that every time Charlotte talked herself into dismissing the tug she felt toward Jesse, he'd say something that pulled her to him again? She needed to talk about Mima. A lot. Charlotte didn't like how it felt as if Mima were slipping from her memory, as if she had to speak aloud to secure all those wonderful memories in her life now that Mima was gone. It was silly—she'd never even spoken that often to Mima. Their communication in the last few years was mostly fun texts or postcards or jots of short correspondence. Why the burning need to keep talking about her? Grief did funny things to a person.

Charlotte wrapped her hands around the warmth of

her mug—despite the June afternoon heat—and wished for the dozens of china plates, cups and saucers to be surrounding her here in the cottage kitchen instead of still back in Chicago. "Mima drank tea, coffee, cocoa, anything. She was always bringing exotic blends of coffee and tea home to me. And that spicy Mexican hot chocolate. She loved that, too. When I was little, she would make me tea or coffee in my own special cup that she kept at her house just for me. A real china cup, not a plastic kiddie thing. Of course, the drink was more milk than coffee or tea, and it was loaded with sugar, but I felt so grown up when I drank it." Tears clamped her throat again. "Important, you know? She was great at making me feel like I meant the world to her."

"That's nice. A rare thing." There was a shadow in Jesse's eyes as he looked at her. A dark place behind all the sympathy. After a second or two, Charlotte realized it was envy. Hunger, even. It made her wonder if Jesse had ever had anyone in his life to make him feel important. Was that where the showmanship personality and the hero-rescuer drive came from? She'd had so much affirmation in her life, it stung to see the lack of it played out so clearly in his features.

Even though she knew it might not be a safe question, she asked anyway. "Anyone like that in your life?"

Is there anyone like that in my life?

Jesse swallowed hard. Charlotte had asked the million-dollar question, and he found himself unable to dredge up one of his smart-aleck evasive answers. Not here, not when he was faced with the collection of sweet memories playing across her face. To be so loved—it must be amazing. And then again gut-wrenching to have that love taken away. She had on a peach-colored tunic, and he watched her finger the simple gold cross that sat in the V neckline of the top. He knew, without having to ask, that it had been her grandmother's. He realized he'd never seen her without it, and that she touched it whenever she talked about Mima. He could guess that she'd put it on the day the beloved old woman had died and she hadn't taken it off since.

To love someone so hard and know they loved you just as much—that hadn't ever really been the case in his family. Sure, he'd mourn his parents when they were gone, but it wouldn't be like the loss he could see in Charlotte's eyes when she talked about this amazing grandmother of hers.

"Not like that." It seemed the safest way to answer her question. His memories of his grandparents were mostly about instructions and expectations. He and Randy got along, but they'd never been particularly close. His mom loved him—in a safe, mom kind of way—but not with the fierce, lasting affection Charlotte seemed to have known. And Dad? Well, he supposed Dad thought the pushy way he treated Jesse was what parental love was supposed to look like.

"I'm sorry." Charlotte looked at him—really looked at him, as though she could see all the regrettable things going through his head. No judgment, just awareness. A sad sort of understanding that wandered a little too close to pity.

Guilt twisted Jesse's gut. "Don't get me wrong, my parents love me and all, but they don't really—" he couldn't find a word that didn't sound ungrateful and even petulant "—root for me." He pushed out a sigh and took another swig of the tolerable tea just to buy time to think. "I have a younger brother, and he does all the expected stuff. All the right, successful things moms and dads think their kids ought to do when they grow up. Great job, big house, all the trimmings. They say they don't compare, but…" He found he didn't want to finish that sentence.

"You save people." She said it with something close to awe. The wideness of her eyes pulled at him. He was wrong; it wasn't pity he saw in her features—it was "you deserve so much more." It wasn't fair what that did to him. He wasn't prepared for how she got to him without even realizing what she was doing.

"Yeah, I think that confuses them most of all. The whole volunteer firefighter thing makes no sense to them. Why risk myself for nothing? At least that's how they see it. Mom never comes out and says it like that, but Dad never minces words on the subject."

Charlotte picked up a broken cookie. "Your dad doesn't like you in the volunteer fire department?"

"He thinks of it as a waste of time. Or close to that— I don't think he's been quite that harsh. More like an unnecessary distraction that seems to be keeping me from reaching my professional potential." Jesse picked up a piece of cookie and dunked it in the mug. "He'd be happier if I were more successful."

"More like your brother?"

"If you mean my brother whose marriage just fell apart and who is working on his second ulcer, then you can see why maybe I don't share the old man's opinion." Jesse hadn't meant the words to come out with quite that much edge, but Charlotte had hit a nerve. "I have my own idea of success. I have big plans for a remodeling business." He stopped himself there, afraid that if he launched into those plans he might reveal how he'd wanted this cottage as his first project. Right now he didn't want Charlotte to know that. It would make everything weird, and it was weird enough already.

"You're different than him."

The simple words struck a completely separate nerve. The hungry nerve, the unfed craving. She managed to meet some need in him he wasn't even aware of until she'd waltzed into Gordon Falls and stymied his plans. How had she managed to articulate the one thing, the one thought, that he could never seem to get his parents to understand? "Completely." He didn't trust himself to go any further than that.

"I don't think I'd like this brother of yours very much." She'd said it casually, before either of them realized the natural progression of that thought. It unwound itself in Jesse's brain like a mathematical equation: *if C dislikes R and J is the opposite of R, therefore C must like J.* She knew it, too, for suddenly she stared too hard at her cookie instead of looking at him.

He had to find some way out of this too-close moment. "You'd hate his cooking."

"Most guys can't cook their way out of a paper bag." Charlotte was trying, as he'd done, to lighten the moment, but it wasn't working for either of them. "Well, evidently, except for chefs, and you and your burgers."

Ah, now she'd done it. Had she knowingly thrown that door open, or just by accident? He puffed up his chest. "I am an outstanding cook. I could probably cook circles around half the restaurants in Gordon Falls, and not just on firehouse fare. I'll have you know my skills extend far beyond chili and burgers."

Her eyes narrowed at his boasting. "Do they? So not only can you install ovens, but you can use one, too?"

There was just enough tease in her words to seal her fate. "I'm on duty tomorrow night, but Friday you are going to find out just how well this man can cook his way out of a paper bag. As a matter of fact, I could probably cook a paper bag and you'd think it was delicious." Before Charlotte could put in one word of protest, Jesse stood up and began opening the mostly empty cupboards and fridge, taking stock of what was here and what he'd need to bring. "You said you were going to the grocery store and back to Chicago for a load of stuff tomorrow, right?"

"Yes?" She looked as if she had just opened Pandora's box and wasn't sure if she should start regretting it.

"You're coming back Friday? You've got a saucepan?" He circled his hands to mimic a deep round pan just in case she didn't know her way around a kitchen.

"I'll be back Friday. And of course I have a saucepan." Her hands crossed over her chest.

"Frying pan?"

"Yes. Two, in fact."

He scratched his chin, the meal planning itself in his head already. "Bring both." Grabbing a receipt from off the counter, he started writing. Within five minutes he'd given her a list of items and suggested tableware. This was going to be fun. If there was anything Jesse Sykes knew how to do as well as build things, it was cook things. Delicious, incredible things. Friends cooked for friends all the time, right? It wasn't a date. Not even close.

Charlotte sat there, running her hand down the list with her mouth open. "Um, I've got everything on here but a cheese grater."

"I'll bring mine. And my spices. I don't trust the grocery store stuff most people get—no offense, but it makes all the difference. Can you be back in Gordon Falls by five-thirty?"

She shrugged. "Works for me."

Charlotte's smile held the tiny hint of "you gotta be kidding me" that touched the edges of her eyes. It kindled an insane need to put that doubt to rest and flat-out amaze her. Jesse knew—down to his boots knew—that he could. He just wasn't going to take the time to analyze why.

Chapter Ten

Charlotte pulled open her back door Friday night to the sight of Jesse holding a pair of stuffed grocery bags. A bouquet of flowers tottered on the top of one bag while a loaf of delicious-smelling bread poked out of the other. He grinned. "Hungry?"

She grabbed one of the bags and held the door open. A whiff of "clean guy"—that extraordinary mix of soap and man and a hint of whatever it was he put on his hair—wafted by as he passed, and Charlotte felt her stomach flip. Maybe she should have stayed in Chicago and said no to this little feast. That probably would have been the smart thing to do, but this didn't really feel like a date, and besides, Jesse didn't strike her as the kind of guy who took no for an answer.

Still, there was no denying the guy was seriously attractive. And toting incredible food. God must have known what He was doing when He ensured she wouldn't be hosting Jesse alone.

Just as he put the bag down on the counter, Jesse caught site of Charlotte's new housemate. His entire face changed.

"You have a cat."

Jesse said the words slowly, biting off the end of the last word with a sharp *t*. This was clearly not a welcome revelation.

"I do." She forced ignorant cheer into her voice. For the fifth time today, Charlotte wondered if Melba had known *exactly* what she was doing when she'd presented her with the furry little wonder when Charlotte got back from Chicago this afternoon. She walked over to the kitchen seat where her new companion sat staring suspiciously at her guest cook. "Jesse, meet Mo."

Mo curled up the end of his tail in something Charlotte hoped did not translate to "I was here first."

"Hello, Mo." Charlotte could practically watch Jesse's back straighten. Dinner was in danger of becoming a territorial battle, and the man had been here all of thirty seconds.

"You brought a cat into a house under renovation." Charlotte could practically hear Jesse's brain trying to link the two ideas. While he never said it, and was trying hard not to look it, the man's every pore seemed to seep "Are you out of your mind?" She watched him mentally sift through potential verbal responses before he settled on "That will make things interesting." Then he set down the bag of groceries they'd both forgotten he was holding.

Charlotte, who'd already set down the bag with the bread, walked over and stroked Mo. He arched his back up to meet her hand, keeping one yellow eye on Jesse as if to say "See? She likes me." "Melba gave him to me as an early birthday present. She has a cat she loves very much."

"I remember." They weren't happy memories, that much was clear. He chose his next words carefully. "I'm surprised Melba failed to remember that working on the house with Pinocchio didn't go especially well."

Mo apparently took offense to that, leaping in a brown, black and white streak toward what would be the dining room. Evidently he wasn't going to stand around and listen to Jesse defame his character. She imagined he'd head up to the bedroom soon, as the mattress on the floor had become his favorite spot since this afternoon. "She mentioned it might be a bit of a bumpy ride at first. But I love Pinocchio, and he was great company curled up next to me in the guest room at Melba's. Mo's been fine and settling in all day. It'll be nice to have company. You told me you were a dog person, but I didn't realize that meant you were an anti-cat person."

Jesse began taking items out of the bag. "I'm not an anti-cat guy. I just recognize that construction can stress animals out. You may be in for a bumpier ride than Melba let on." She watched him choose to get past it, pushing out a breath and turning to her with the bouquet of flowers from the grocery bag. "These are for you. Paid for, fair and square."

She didn't want to let Mo ruin the evening, either. She'd considered Mo a convenient excuse, a way to cut the evening short if things felt as if they were getting too close. Now, looking at him all spiffed up and offering a bouquet of flowers, Charlotte realized she liked Jesse. She *really* liked him. And that could still be okay; one dinner with him didn't constitute a lifetime of sirens and anxious nights. It was just a friendly dinner. She didn't have to stress over it the way she might have over a *real* date.

She took the flowers, delighted that he'd chosen a

mixture of wildflowers and sunny pastels rather than something serious like roses or ordinary like carnations. The arrangement fit the room, fit the sturdy little table that would host their meal. "Thank you. They're lovely. I brought a vase from my Chicago apartment, too. I was going to put some greenery from the backyard in it, but this is much nicer." She reached into a box on another counter, found a doily Mima had crocheted and set it on the table with the vase right in the center.

They worked together on the meal as easily as they had worked on the bathtub. Jesse was masterful in the kitchen, doling out small jobs like chopping shallots while hovering over four different pans of delectable-smelling food. It made the cottage feel like a true home. A meal with friends.

Only it didn't seem to want to stay just "a meal with friends." Jesse would catch her eye every now and then, smiling confidently as he explained why this had to boil for just a minute more, or why that ingredient had to be added just a little at a time, and her pulse would catch just a bit. He sang snippets of Sam Cooke's "You Send Me" while he worked, and his voice swirled around her as it filled the kitchen. Then he lifted the lid on one saucepan and spooned up a creamy white sauce that smelled delicious. Jesse tasted it, eyes closed in assessment, added a little more of something, then tasted again. His resulting smile beamed of victory. "Here, try this." He held out a spoon, and Charlotte couldn't have refused for all the world.

Had someone told him Alfredo sauce was her favorite? Had he run into Melba or Clark at the grocery store? Or was this just another way Jesse Sykes knew how to keep his customer happy? "Oh," she said, going beyond just a taste to lick the spoon completely clean. "Oh, my. Wow."

"My family may be Anglo, but Italian is my specialty. Douse that handmade fresh spinach fettuccine with this, add the Brussels sprouts I've got going over there, and you'll think you've died and gone to heaven."

Charlotte winced. "I'm…um…not really a fan of Brussels sprouts." Actually, she didn't know anyone who was a fan of Brussels sprouts.

"You haven't tasted mine." He said it as if resistance to his particular brand of vegetable would be impossible. The tone of his voice made her believe him. Or at least want to believe him. "Close your eyes."

She gave him a look. "A bit dramatic, don't you think?"

He gave her a look right back. "You'll eat those words right after you eat my Brussels sprouts."

Parking a hand on one hip, Charlotte countered, "You know that sounds ridiculous, don't you?"

Jesse wagged his fingers in front of her face until she rolled her eyes before squinting them shut. She heard him fiddle with the top of a saucepan, then the sound of his voice very close and soft. "Open." He sang the word more than said it, his tone smooth and coaxing. She felt him close with her eyes closed, smelled the soap on his skin now mixed with the marvelous scents of his cooking. Maybe Brussels sprouts had been given a bad rap. She felt the fork against her tongue and bit down on what he offered.

Oh.

Brussels sprouts were the epitome of gross vegetables, the thing universally turning up child and adult noses everywhere. These could not have been Brussels sprouts. They were crunchy and a bit crispy, with something savory hiding between the tiny green leaves. Half a dozen different tastes and textures mixed on her tongue. This was the chocolate cake of vegetables. It couldn't be those nasty green orbs everyone avoided in the produce aisle. He was tricking her; he had to be.

Charlotte opened her eyes wide, unprepared for the closeness of Jesse's triumphant face. There was a second piece on the fork, which she immediately ate. "Wow," she said with her mouth full. He was so close, so dauntingly handsome, and he had just fed her his cooking. At this very moment, Jesse Sykes was the most attractive man on earth. Denying it was just plain impossible. "That's a vegetable?" she whispered, just for something to say because his nearness was fogging her thinking.

"You should see what I do with butternut squash," he boasted, "but this is a personal specialty." He reached out and brushed a bit of sauce or butter or whatever that splendid concoction was off her chin. She shivered at his touch, fighting off the dizzying sensation his brown eyes kindled in the pit of her stomach.

Talk. Talk before you do something else, something you don't want to do right now. "Every Brussels sprout on earth should stand up and thank you." She hated how flustered she sounded, hated how he knew exactly how he'd wowed her and was currently reveling in it. "I hope you made a lot of those." She ducked out of the dazzle of his eyes to peer into the covered pan.

"Pace yourself. You'll want to save room for dessert."

The man had made dessert. That was just plain fighting dirty. If this man produced a cheesecake then all hopes of sensibility were lost. Charlotte puttered around the kitchen, fighting the sinking feeling that was like drowning but a whole lot sweeter.

Jesse stood still, watching her, as in control of the moment as she was out of it. "You want to slice up some lemon for the water?" The words were mundane enough, but his eyes seemed to say "So I don't kiss you right now up against the refrigerator?"

There was a journal page upstairs in Charlotte's bedroom listing all the reasons why dating a firefighter was a bad idea. Right now Charlotte couldn't remember a single one of them.

Jesse had eaten in some pretty spectacular restaurants, had even done the firehouse's entire Thanksgiving dinner last year, but no meal had ever filled him with the satisfaction of Charlotte's little table currently spread with his cooking. Even Mo—the predatory little beast—had come in from the living room to view the spectacle, perhaps hoping to leverage his cuteness into a little creamy Alfredo sauce.

Jesse gave him a "my turn" glare as he walked over to pull out Charlotte's chair for her. The urge to run a hand through the cascade of her blond hair caught him up short, and he nearly tripped on his way around to his side of the table. His plan to keep the evening light and friendly was falling prey to the look of utter delight on her face. It sank deep into his chest and settled there like a craving. She took such a rich pleasure in the world, in small things, in things he often took for granted. What gave her such a rare capacity for joy like that? Even in the face of all the obstacles life had thrown at her recently?

He settled himself in his chair and reached for the serving spoon. "Dig in."

She cocked her head at him. "No grace?"

It took him a minute to realize what she'd said.

"Grace," she repeated. "Over the food."

"Um, sure," he said, fumbling. "Why not."

Charlotte extended her hand for his. Jesse was sure a man ought not to feel the sparks her hand left in his palm while saying prayers. He told himself not to luxuriate in the softness of her hands while he closed his eyes. He'd never been the hand-holding kind of guy, but right now holding her hands felt to him like whatever he saw shoot through her eyes when she tasted his cooking.

"Thank You, Father, for this wonderful meal Jesse has set before us."

Jesse wasn't prepared for her words. He was expecting some rote little poem, some Sunday school verse said in memorized monotone. Charlotte was praying. Real, actual, as-if-she-talked-to-God-every-day conversation. Over his food. "I'm grateful for this house, for all You've made possible, for all the work that went into this delicious food. I am, quite surprisingly, thankful for Brussels sprouts, too. Who'd have thought?"

Jesse opened one eye to see her smiling, eyes closed as she carried on the easy dialogue. He'd not seen grace—or even prayer—ever look like this. It startled him, shaking something loose that felt as if it didn't belong rattling around under his ribs.

"Bless the hands that prepared this food," Charlotte tightened her grip on Jesse's hand, making his pulse gallop for a moment, "and may it nourish our bodies. In Your Son's name, Amen."

"Amen," Jesse gulped out, hoping that was the right

thing to say. He was still trying to work out what had just happened. Chief Bradens had been known to say a formal grace over meals at the firehouse, but they never sounded like that, and they never made him feel as though someone had just hit him with a thousand-watt floodlight, dazzled and blinking for focus.

"This looks incredible. I want to stuff myself silly—I've tasted all of it and I think you're about to meet my piggish side."

"Knock yourself out." He wanted to see her piggish side. He wanted to see her unrestrained enjoyment, to hear her groan with delight and lick the sauce off her fingers and ask for seconds if not thirds. He'd enjoyed lots of compliments on his food before, but those mostly fed his ego. Her pleasure in his cooking only made him want to make her happier. That wasn't the kind of self-less gratification Jesse was used to, and he didn't know how to deal with the feeling. He only knew he liked it, and he wanted more of it.

He ate with enthusiasm. He watched her eat with relish, going on about this project and that fixture between raves over the food and sighs of what could only be termed gastronomic infatuation. The combination of Charlotte gushing over his food and espousing big renovation dreams was like catnip to Jesse—to put it in Mo's terms. His insides were buzzing like live wires, sparking with every small touch, every adorable look. More than once he yearned to kiss the Alfredo sauce off her cheek, off her lips, no matter how stridently Chief Bradens and his own sense of caution had warned him off. He had found women disarmingly attractive before, but this was a whole new scale of allure.

"I think I should go ahead and get the custom ironwork for the front steps. I just don't see anything I like as much in the catalogues. I love the idea about Mima's quilt motif worked into the front railings." He could see it as clearly as she could. The price tag started not to matter. There was something about being near her, as if she gave off some kind of magnetism he was helpless to resist. "Irresistible" suddenly wasn't a clichéd description—he found Charlotte wholly, genuinely irresistible. This was becoming dangerous on any number of fronts.

By the time he made coffee and doled out French vanilla ice cream to start melting all over the berry cobbler he'd pulled out of the oven for dessert, Jesse felt his personal and professional warning system completely short-circuit. She was talking about imported glass tile backsplashes and granite countertops while she tore off a piece of bread and mopped up the last bit of sauce off her plate. He knew just the color stone that would set off her eyes, and it no longer mattered that it was the most expensive. She was Charlotte. The world would line up to do her bidding because at that moment, he would have said yes to anything she asked. Even the dumb cat. She had him hooked. What made him most nervous of all was that he could already feel the ache that would start when he walked out this door tonight and never let up until he was near her again.

It scared him to death. He knew he was on the verge of a terrifying loss of control he wouldn't have predicted and couldn't contain. Jesse knew guys who got this way about fire—it drew them, fascinated them, nearly possessed them in a way that made them fearless. *It's also what gets them hurt or killed,* he reminded himself. When emotion overpowered thought, damage happened. The very thing he'd hoped to give Charlotte in this project—an objective eye, a grounded opinion as to what was a worthwhile splurge and what was reckless spending—was about to go out the window. This was not good.

Jesse turned back from returning the ice cream to the freezer and found her already digging into the cobbler right there at the counter—she hadn't even waited for him to set them down at the table. She had a spot of purple right at the corner of her mouth, and she let out this intoxicating little hum as she found it with the tip of her tongue.

That was it. Without a thought to the consequences, without even wondering if she'd welcome the advance, because every cell in his body already told him she would, Jesse kissed her.

The taste of his cooking on her lips was enthralling. When her initial surprise melted into surrender, he lost the ability to think straight. But when Charlotte began to return his kiss? That put him over the edge. Who cared what Bradens thought? It was one night, one dinner, one kiss. One really amazing kiss.

"Jesse…" She gasped his name, falling back against the counter as if the house had shifted off its foundations. He felt the same way, as if the world was whirling around him, spiraling out from the place where her hand still lay on his chest.

He put his hand atop hers, wondering if she could feel the pounding. "I…um…" He knew he should say something smooth, something casual and clever, but he came up empty. She'd undone him with one kiss, fright-

ening as it was. He craved another kiss so much that
he feared being able to control himself if he took one.

Not good, Sykes, not good at all.

Chapter Eleven

Crash. The moment came to a loud halt when a dish clattered to the floor. Mo had, at some point, leaped up onto the countertop in an effort to get at the melted ice cream and had succeeded in knocking over the cobbler dish. The cat screeched and bolted back into the dark of the living room. They both looked down to see white cream and purple cobbler splattered all over the floor and Charlotte's light-colored pants.

Charlotte didn't know whether to thank Mo or to kick the furry, meddling feline to the curb. The moment— whatever it was—was gone, replaced with a sticky mess and the casualty of one of her favorite pairs of pants.

Jesse had already grabbed a towel from the counter and was picking the pieces of the plate off the floor, muttering unkind things about cats. She stared at him, wanting to blink and shake her head, needing to know what had just happened and whether or not she should regret it.

It had been a spectacular kiss. The kind that made her sensibilities go white like an old-fashioned flash-bulb, the kind that ought to be the first kiss between soul mates. Only now that the bubble had popped, she could name half a dozen reasons why Jesse Sykes was not the mate of her soul. And as for Jesse himself, if the kiss had affected him the way it had her, it no longer showed.

"See, not too hard to clean up." Jesse slid the broken china into the wastebasket and tossed the purple-blotched towel into the sink. "I don't think you can say the same for those pants." He turned to her, an "oh well" smile in his eyes, as if it had been a simple kitchen mishap. "There's enough dessert to start over."

"I don't think we ought to." She knew she didn't sound at all convinced. She wasn't—confused was closer to accurate.

His disappointment was so appealing. "Really? My cobbler's even better than my Brussels sprouts."

Charlotte leaned against the cabinets. "Jesse…"

He leaned up against the same cabinets, inches from her. "Hey, it's okay." He shrugged. "But it was a really nice kiss."

She shut her eyes for a moment, slipping her hand up to press it to her own lips while she launched a prayer up to heaven for the right words. "I know there's something…here." She opened her eyes again, wanting to make him understand. "The meal, the kiss— you know how to sweep a woman off her feet. It's just that…" How could she make him understand when she wasn't even sure what she wanted at the moment herself?

He put a hand to his chest as if wounded. "I feed you fettuccine Alfredo and you shoot me down? Ouch." His words were harsh but his eyes held that teasing glint she found most irresistible about him.

"I need to take it a whole lot slower than this." That much was true. She still hadn't figured out if, in the space of one meal, Jesse Sykes had truly disintegrated her conviction not to get involved with men in his line of work. Had she truly overcome that fear? Or was it just pushed aside by Jesse's...*Jesseness,* just to return later when her guard was down? "I like being with you," she admitted, "but we have a lot of ground to cover and a bunch of things we have to...I have to work out. Or through. Or something." She let her head fall back against the cabinets. "'It's complicated' sounds so stupid, but it is."

"It doesn't have to be. I don't think this has to be a big, complicated deal. I do know I don't want tonight to end here, like this."

"Maybe it's better that it does. At least for the sake of my pants." *If not my convictions.*

Jesse ran one hand through his hair. "I'll tell you what. Why don't you go upstairs and get those into water or soap—or whatever you do to get blueberry out of something—and I'll clean up here? Then we'll figure out what comes next. No sweeping off of any feet."

It seemed as good a plan as any. She needed fifteen minutes out of the pull of his eyes, away from the way he seemed to fill the room and cloud her thinking. "Okay."

Charlotte dashed upstairs, slipped into a pair of jeans and filled the bathroom sink—the beautiful bathroom sink Jesse had installed three days ago—with cold water and soap. She dunked the stained pants into the sink and scrubbed a few seconds before stopping to stare at herself in the mirror.

What do you want, Charlotte? What do you want to do about that man downstairs in your kitchen?

She knew Jesse. Knew his character and personality as if they'd spent years together instead of weeks. He probably thought she hadn't noticed his reaction to her prayer over the food, but she'd seen it. It was so strong she'd nearly felt it. Still, all that awareness wasn't the same as a man of faith, a man whose soul could match with hers. In all the time they'd spent together they'd only skittered around the topic of church and God. She knew his dreams, but not his values. And quite frankly, it wasn't hard to guess at his reputation where women were concerned.

And then there was the question of firefighting. It wasn't his whole life, as the police force had been for Dad, but it was a big part. Would it always be there, or would his volunteer duties eventually fade as his business grew to take more and more of his time? And was dating your general contractor ever a good idea? The questions seemed to rise up and swallow her clarity the same way the rising bubbles rose up to cover her hands.

Mo wandered into the bathroom, drawn out of his hiding spot in her bedroom by the lights and sounds of her spontaneous load of laundry. Charlotte pulled her hands from the suds and pointed a finger at the cat. "The jury's still out on you, mister."

Mo simply sat down on the tile and wrapped his tail around his legs, a picture of all the calm and patience she currently lacked. If he had any advice or warning, she couldn't decipher it from his eyes. Charlotte would have to work this one out on her own.

She touched the framed photo of Mima as she passed it on the hallway table at the top of the stairs. *What do*

*I do, Mima? Why is this man in my life now when you
aren't here to tell me what to do with him?*

Charlotte had enough married friends to know that
to come downstairs to a man responsible for a spotless
kitchen was a wonder indeed. He had his stuff packed
up in the grocery bags but his face told her he wasn't
the least bit ready to leave. "Talk to me," he said as he
sat down at the table she now noticed was set with two
cups of coffee. "Tell me what's whirling around in that
pretty head of yours."

She sat down. Talking about this was a good idea,
and she was glad for the table between them. She knew
he wasn't clouding her thinking on purpose, but that
didn't mean he wasn't very good at it. "I'm worried this
won't turn out to be such a good idea."

"Because I'm working on your house."

She owed him the further explanation. "That's just
part of it." She ran her hands across the thighs of her
jeans, wiping the last of the water from the upstairs
washing project. "My dad was a policeman."

His face changed, understanding darkening his features. "I didn't know that."

There was a lot he didn't know. That was the whole
point. "I've spent a lot of nights watching my mom get
eaten alive from the stress of waiting for bad news. I
made a promise to myself that I'd never let myself in
for that kind of life."

Jesse leaned back in his chair. "You've known I was
a firefighter literally from the moment you met me."

"I didn't say I couldn't be *friends* with you." That
felt like a weak defense.

"Friends don't kiss like that. But this doesn't have to

become superserious overnight, Charlotte. It's not an all-or-nothing proposition."

Charlotte's chest was filled with a mixed-up host of reactions. He'd felt it. Of course he'd felt it—how could he not feel what she felt humming between them? Only Jesse looked so much more in control of the situation than she felt. "Look, I'm kind of an impulsive person." Was she explaining her choice in backsplash tiles or how she'd kissed him back?

"Really? I hadn't noticed." Did he have to smile like that? All velvety and cavalier?

She struggled forward, telling the flutter in her stomach to behave itself. "It makes it hard to hang on to certain...challenging convictions."

Jesse gave her a look that said he rather enjoyed challenging people's convictions. Right—there was one of the problems with this whole situation. "Okay."

"My faith is really important to me. Maybe more now than it's been at any point in my life. It'd be a bad idea to get serious with someone who couldn't share that with me. I know you don't get that, but—"

"I do get that."

She hadn't expected that response. "You do?"

"I liked your grace. Never heard it done quite that way before. I'm okay with it."

"I'm glad to hear that, but it goes a bit deeper for me than table grace. There are—"

He cut her off. "Do you know I said yes to emceeing the talent show at your church tomorrow night? I figured maybe it was time I stopped ditching that stuff."

Oh, he'd managed to say the one thing that made resistance harder. "Clark didn't tell me you'd said yes."

"I told him I wanted to tell you myself. Surprise

you at the end of tonight. I've seen you, and Chief, and Melba, and even JJ when you talk about going to church. I want to know what it is you all have over there. I just don't know how to try it or if it will stick. But you came up with the perfect introduction, didn't you? Doesn't that count for something to you?"

Lord, couldn't he be a jerk or something? You know me, I'm going to go all optimistic and hopeful now and I'm having enough trouble thinking practically already. "If we're going to be..." She didn't know how to finish that sentence without revealing how very attractive she found him, and Jesse surely needed no encouragement in that department.

"Hey," he said, taking her hand. She knew she ought to pull away, but she couldn't muster up the resistance. "Who actually knows what we're going to be? I'm not so sure why you have to plot this out right now. Can't we just wait and see?"

He meant well, but Charlotte knew herself, and she had a bad habit of throwing herself headlong into relationships that ought never to have been pursued. It didn't take a rocket scientist to know there was some serious chemistry between them, and that could make it hard to pull back before it was too late. "Well, the term *playing with fire* does come to mind."

"I'm a fireman. I think we'll be safe. How about I finish my coffee and leave like the gentleman I am? I'll see you at the talent show tomorrow night, and maybe we can try a dinner Sunday. Someplace easy and friendly, like Dellio's."

Those events—she refused to call them dates, even in her head—felt safe.

"I won't even be sitting near you at the talent show.

There'll be something like sixty people between us. Then at dinner we can talk some more," he continued. "I can hear you say grace again."

If he was willing to come to church and be part of the talent show, if he was willing to let her say grace over burgers in public, there had to be an openness to faith about him. He was putting in an effort; she ought to at least meet him halfway on this. "Okay."

Jesse finished his coffee in one gulp—something she'd seen Melba's fireman husband do, so it must be a professional requirement—then stood up to leave. She stood up, as well.

He held his hand out, an oversize request for a formal handshake. "Friendly, see?"

When she offered her hand, he pulled it to his lips and left a soft kiss there. "Well, mostly." Without any further explanation than that, Jesse gathered up his things and headed out the door.

Jesse stood in his kitchen, staring at the still unemptied grocery bags, sorting through the puzzle of his feelings. Exactly what had happened tonight? He knew how to wow a lady, always had. It was an extension—however egotistical—of his urge to please people. He liked making customers happy, helping fire victims, making women feel special.

Whatever it was he felt for Charlotte, it was a whole new thing. He found himself disturbingly desperate for her—but not at all in a physical sense; it was so much more than that. This was much more consuming than a merely physical attraction. There was some gaping, empty hole he couldn't seem to hide from her. Worse, not only could she see it, she effortlessly filled it. As he paced his kitchen, Jesse had the uncomfortable sensation that his life had just cracked open to make room for her and nothing else would ever fill the space that made.

He tried to tell himself that urge to make her happy, to watch the delight spark up in her eyes, was ordinary, an ego boost, the way it was with everyone else. Only with Charlotte, it wasn't. It was the closest thing to a purely selfless urge he'd ever had, and he had no idea what to do with that. Oh, sure, lots of people thought of his work at the firehouse as selfless, but it really wasn't. It was a hero thing. He liked playing the hero—the stakes at the firehouse were just a bit higher than when he built someone the garage of their dreams.

The old Jesse would have kissed her again even when he knew better. He'd never, ever have pressed his advantage with a woman, but he would have been far bolder than he was tonight. It was as if someone had changed the rules on him without notice.

Without his consent. Chief Bradens really was right: Charlotte hadn't learned how to go in small steps—not in relationships or renovations or maybe even in life. Could he be the man to show her how to slow things down? Lighten up and have a little more fun? Learn that a few dates and kisses could be just that—a few dates and kisses? It was worth a dinner at Dellio's to find out.

And beyond that…he'd figure it out when he got there.

Chapter Twelve

Well, who would have guessed it?

Jesse stood on the stage of Gordon Falls Community Church's meeting hall, hand on the microphone, about to open the church's talent show as its guest emcee and baffled by the open welcome in all the faces he could see. He'd thought of himself as an intruder—an impostor up here on the stage, where someone well-known in the church should have been. No one else seemed to see it that way. Everyone had been nothing but warm and friendly.

"Good evening and welcome to tonight's Taste of Talent. If you haven't filled your plate from the dessert table at the back of the room, you don't know what you're missing. And hey, if any of you find yourselves overcome with the urge to bring me some of that raspberry cheesecake, by all means don't hold back." He couldn't help himself from directing that last remark right at Charlotte.

Instead of feeling awkward, the past half hour of setup had been surprisingly fun. What he'd told Charlotte was true; he'd never had anything against going to the church. So many of his friends already did. It was just that he dreaded the hurdle of that first visit. By happenstance—or design—this gig handed him the perfect opening. "We're going to start things out tonight with a touch of class, and a lot of brass. Let's listen to the Senior High bell quartet."

He looked out over the sea of friendly faces from his stool at stage left, seeing proud, smiling parents among them. Honestly, even here he felt like a bit of a celebrity—and he was a man given to enjoying attention. "Aren't they talented?" he asked the audience, as the quartet cleared their many bells from the stage. "There's more where that came from. This is one talented congregation, I'm telling you. Here's what's up next…"

And so the evening progressed, act by surprising act. Jesse's initial comments about the flood of talent were just to be nice at first, playing to the audience. Eventually, they gave way to genuine astonishment, soundly trouncing Jesse's preconceptions of hokey church festivities. Max Jones, Charlotte's cousin and no stranger to the firehouse through his sister, JJ, did a hysterical lip-synch of an Elvis tune with the high school boy he'd been mentoring for almost a year, Simon Williams. "Talk about true rocking and rolling," Jesse cracked as the pair—who both used wheelchairs—popped a dual pair of wheelies and spins as they moved offstage. Jesse felt a warm glow as he watched Simon's dad, Brian, also a firefighter, give his son a standing ovation. The kid had come a long way, and he knew that Brian credited the support of this church as much as the partnership Simon had with Max. Jesse and Max—and a few of the other younger firefighters—had made a few mistakes in their efforts to help Simon, but everyone had learned their lesson, and even Simon's mom had given Jesse a warm welcome.

And where had Fire Marshal Chad Owens hidden his surprising juggling talents? He was normally a laid-back guy, but the audience hung their mouths open when he proved a pretty talented trickster. Those open mouths served them well, for Chad's finale was to juggle a dozen of his wife, Jeannie's, beloved chocolate caramels, tossing them into the audience as his final trick. Jesse would have eaten a handful if the sticky confections wouldn't have rendered him speechless for five minutes at least. He stuck with one, making a big show of chewing with the appropriate *mmm*s. "Well now," he managed, still sounding as if he had a mouthful, "guess they really meant it when they called this Taste of Talent."

There were other acts—some silly, some heartwarming. Even the regrettable ones—someone needed to tell Nick Owens an eleven-minute drum solo was hard on the ears—brought a smile and a hearty round of applause from the audience. The trio of curly-blond-haired girls who couldn't have been more than five didn't do much more than sway and spin in their frilly pink tutus, but no one cared. Instead, everyone cheered and snapped photos like paparazzi when the ballerinas took their bows, bursting into louder applause, mixed with laughter, when one little girl rushed over and hugged Jesse's leg, leading him to take her hand and twirl her like a ballroom dancer as she left the stage.

Every time Jesse thought the evening couldn't get more enjoyable, some new moment would capture his heart. He was having such a terrific time, Jesse decided he'd have to eat his words and thank Charlotte for pulling him in to the event. Charlotte must have been thinking the same thing, for every time he caught her eyes, her smile broadcast "See, I told you this would be fun."

What really brought the house down, however, was one of the final acts. Jesse knew JJ's husband, Alex, played the ukulele and was known for his campy musical sense. As such, it wasn't a big stunner when he took the stage and began strumming "By the Light of the Silvery Moon." What no one saw coming was when Violet Sharpton and Karl Kennedy—of Karl's Koffee fame— sashayed onstage and broke into a snappy duet. No one knew either of them could sing, but they were fabulous. When they added an adorable half-limped, cane-assisted little soft-shoe dance on the final verse, Karl yelping, "Slow down, son, I can't hoof it that fast with my bad hip," to a guffawing Alex, the crowd spared no effort to urge them on. They got a standing ovation, and deserved one. Jesse himself was smiling and laughing so hard he could barely take the microphone as the curtain behind him closed.

"I don't know how we're going to follow that act, folks," Jesse proclaimed, wiping his eyes. He hid his satisfaction at the frantic scrambling behind him from the other side of the curtain. "Oh, no, wait," he said in mock surprise. "As a matter of fact, I do." Drums behind him hit the *ba-dump-ching* that was the standard musical punctuation for bad jokes, and Jesse knew his own surprise was nearly ready. He'd successfully managed to keep his contribution a secret. If a church was going to ask him to emcee a talent show, they'd better be prepared for what they got.

A hidden set of drums began a steady beat behind

him. "Ladies and gentlemen, presenting for the first time ever on this or any stage, for your listening enjoyment…" A base guitar joined in with a bluesy swagger. "I give you…Jesse Sykes and the Red Suspenders!"

The curtain parted to reveal a band composed entirely of hidden talents from the Gordon Falls Volunteer Fire Department, decked out in black shirts and those cheesy red plastic fire helmets Wally's sister had found at the local party store. And, of course, red suspenders. The applause and laughter from the audience was enough to fuel Jesse's gloat for a month.

It had started out as a joke, a wisecrack from Yorky when they found out Jesse had been cornered into serving as the evening's master of ceremonies. A "wouldn't it be funny if…" that took on more and more momentum until the idea seemed too good to pass up. When Wally shared that he played the drums and Tom Matthews offered to fish his bass guitar out of the attic, the Red Suspenders were born. Jesse reached behind him, knowing Tom held out his next props. As the lead guitar riff began, the hoots of encouragement and surprise doubled. When Jesse donned the red hat and a pair of sunglasses, the crowd went wild. Chief Bradens was laughing so hard he was alternating between wiping his eyes and hiding them.

Going to great lengths to rehearse in secret, the guys had worked out a squeaky-clean, church-worthy four-song list that dipped into gospel, soul and just enough rock to enthrall the youth group. By the second song, the audience was clapping along. By the third song, they were on their feet. When the bass guitar and drums kicked into the familiar introduction to "Stand by Me," Jesse was pretty sure he saw Charlotte go pink. This was going to be fun.

Charlotte watched Jesse up there on that stage and felt her heart run off against her wishes. She didn't want to be falling for this boisterous, all-too-charming fireman, but there didn't seem to be much she could do to stop it. Melba sat next to her and would catch her eye after this remark or that heart-slaying grin, and she tried to feel neutral about the guy. Clearly Melba could see she was failing. Of course, Melba had no qualms about pairing off with a man from the fire department, even if she was kind about Charlotte's resistance.

Charlotte had gone so far as to talk to Clark about it. Clark had grown up in a firefighting family—the son of the former chief—and he had freely shared that things had been hard on his mom. He told her he understood her hesitation and respected it. "I remember how much my mom had to endure," he said. "I understand why you'd choose to avoid it. I'll say this, though. If the right guy comes around and happens to wear a uniform, I think you'll find a way to handle it."

Charlotte was terrified the right guy was standing right in front of her. She shut her eyes for a moment, even as she felt Jesse's presence from the distance across the room. Jesse was dead wrong about a crowded room making being with him any safer. *Lord, You know the effect that man has on me. If this isn't where I should be heading, I'm going to need an escape. I'm losing perspective.*

Melba leaned over and whispered in Charlotte's ear, "He keeps looking right at you, doesn't he? I mean, it sure looks like it."

That was not helpful. Charlotte had spent the past twenty minutes trying to tell herself the sensation of Jesse singling her out in the crowd was just an emotional illusion. The trick of a good entertainer—an *amazing* entertainer, really, Charlotte admitted to herself as she watched him sing on the stage, backed up by the rest of the Red Suspenders. The combination of silly plastic fire hat and bad-boy black sunglasses was downright irresistible.

As the band began the introduction from what Charlotte knew had to be "Stand by Me," Jesse took off his sunglasses and made a show of peering into the crowd. Charlotte told herself to slump down in her chair, useless as that tactic might be. Her breath—which had momentarily stopped—let out when Jesse called, "Maria? Maria Bradens? Where are you, darlin'? I know you like this one."

Oh, please let him just play this to Maria. Don't let him realize what his voice singing this does to me.

"Home with the sitter!" Clark called back, laughing.

That was right. Maria wasn't even in the building. With a pulse that ricocheted between fear and thrill, Charlotte watched as Jesse unhitched the cordless microphone from its stand. He stared straight at Charlotte, those high-voltage eyes at full force. "Well now, I'll need someone else. Another fine young lady who might be partial to this song." His voice was silken, all confidence and charisma as he stepped down off the stage and began walking right toward her. "Any takers?"

Charlotte felt as if her cheeks were as red as his hat. She tried to hide her face behind her hands but Melba pulled them down. As the fireman behind the keyboard launched into the song, Jesse passed his hat to Clark, pulled Charlotte to her feet and began to sing the lyrics, about not being afraid even when the night was dark. It was as if he sang directly to every fear and every worry. His voice seemed to find every bit of resistance she was trying to hang on to, every memory of her mother alone and staring at the unused place setting on their kitchen table. He was pulling all the stops out, pulling her under in the process.

When he turned back toward the stage, Charlotte practically fell into the chair. She'd forgotten how to think. She'd forgotten how to breathe. When he pitched his voice up into a soulful wail for the second verse, showing a level of talent she'd never expected—nor had anyone else, from the level of applause that was roaring up from the audience—she'd have followed him anywhere.

And that, right there, was the problem. *He is irresistible.*

What he did next hit Charlotte as clearly as if someone had tossed a glass of water in her face. Two rows down, Jesse found the high school French teacher and began singing to her. The woman looked exactly as Charlotte had felt when she'd been in that position: dazzled. Jesse asked her how to say "Stand by Me" in French and began singing the chorus in French, even getting her to sing with him.

Was his attention—the attention that, a moment ago she thought was just for her—an act? She watched the woman lay her hand on her chest and sigh, realizing she'd done the exact same thing herself. When he picked a third woman out of the audience and charmed her just as effectively, a foolish, hollow feeling crept up Charlotte's chest. She had no idea if Jesse was genuine in his attention to her, genuine in his attention to each woman he'd singled out of the audience, or simply applying his talents at showmanship.

Either way, it drove home a point she'd managed to miss—or chose to miss. Hadn't Jesse made it clear after that kiss back at the cottage that he felt no pressure for them to be serious? She'd been too dazed then to recognize what he was really saying—just as she was barely clearheaded enough now to realize the truth.

He wasn't ready to *offer* her anything serious.

Jesse, who displayed so much of his charm but hid so much of his nature, who gave away his talents but locked up his dreams, who was as impressed by her drive as he was bewildered by it, didn't know how to truly, deeply commit. Not to God, not to a woman, not to his business plans that never seemed to get off the ground—not even to just one woman when it came to dedicating a special song.

Worse yet, part of her didn't even care. Even in the face of all her reservations, he enthralled her as he caught her eyes one last time before he stepped back up onto the stage. Despite everything she just saw, her breath caught as it felt as though he was singing just to her.

Charlotte was defenseless. The past few minutes had startled her into the awareness that she would fall for him far too easily—and get her heart broken when he stopped short of returning that love. On her good days, her resistance might stand up for a while. On a bad day, she'd give in instantly. Hadn't his kiss in her kitchen

proved that? Her attraction to Jesse overrode her good
sense even when she tried to stop it. With a gulp she
realized that if he had tried to kiss her right in the middle of that song, with his eyes pulling her in like that,
she very well might have let him, and returned it with
the same intensity if not more. In front of everyone.
Despite all the reasons she knew she didn't want to get
involved with him. Because she *wanted* to get involved
with him. She hadn't stopped thinking about him. She'd
always imagined herself falling that hard for the perfect guy—and Jesse Sykes was not the perfect guy. He
was a great guy, an amazing guy, but he was not the
right guy for her.

Sure, it was impulsive. It was probably even cow-
ardly and childish, but none of that stopped Charlotte
from making the quickest exit possible while the crowd
moved toward the stage to congratulate the Red Suspenders for stealing the show.

She was glad she'd walked to the church tonight,
grateful for the space and dark and calm to help sort
out her thoughts. Jesse was magnetic—in every sense
the word implied. As she worked the brand-new lock
on her front door, she recalled the unsettling realization
she'd come to the other night: her extravagant renovation plans were partially to keep Jesse around.

*Lord, I'm a mess. I'm getting all tangled up here.
Help!*

As she dropped her handbag in the hallway, her cell
phone rang. She didn't even have to look at the screen to
know it was Jesse. "Hey, where'd you go?" He sounded
so exuberant.

"I'm home."

"Home? You went home?"

"I'm sorry," she replied, leaning against the wall without even switching on the light. "Look, that was just a bit much for me."

She heard him push out a breath. "What? The song? I know you like that one. I was just having fun."

Could he have picked worse words? "Just having fun."

"Wait, what's wrong here? Did I embarrass you? I'm sorry if I did that, okay? I thought you'd like it. I like singing to you. You looked like you were having fun."

She couldn't help her reply. "Oh, they were all having fun, I'm sure. You're quite the showman."

Someone tried to grab his attention, and she heard Jesse shoo them away. "Are you upset that I sang to you in front of everyone like that?"

She wasn't, and that was part of the problem. "No. It's just... I don't know. I just wanted to get out of there, okay?"

"No, it's not okay. I'm not quite sure what I did wrong here, but I don't want to leave it like this. Talk to me. Better yet, give me ten minutes and I'll be over there."

"No, don't." She squeezed her eyes shut, knowing what a stab that might be but then wondering—with the way he was always careful to hide what he was feeling— if that would be any kind of a dent to him at all.

"I'm at a loss here, Charlotte. C'mon, talk to me."

"It's... I'm okay. Stunned, maybe. Give me time."

"I sang to lots of people. But I especially sang to you. We've got a history with that song, don't we? Wait... are you upset that I didn't sing it only to you? Is that what this is about?"

It sounded so petty, so hopelessly infatuated when he said it, that Charlotte cringed and sank against the wall. There was more to it than that, but she couldn't put it into words. She couldn't even answer him.

"Whoa. It's not like that. It was an impulse, an entertainer thing." After a moment he said, "I'm a jerk. A show-off. Let's talk about this. Dinner tomorrow, right?"

It wouldn't help. She'd just see his eyes and the whole tumbling would start all over again.

"Charlotte...don't make this into something it wasn't. If you won't let me come over there now, at least let's do dinner like we planned."

"I just need to...I don't know, sort this out somehow. Good night, Jesse, you were amazing. Really, really amazing."

She heard him fending off someone else, then come back to the phone. "Dinner. I'm not hanging up until you agree to dinner."

She didn't have the nerve to fight him off right now. "Okay. Dinner." She ended the call.

Would anything change in twenty-four hours? Was she being fair if she didn't allow Jesse a chance to explain himself? Charlotte had no idea. Half an hour of sitting still and trying to listen for God brought no clarity. Fifteen minutes of petting Mo and staring into his wise yellow eyes didn't help, either. Knitting—her usual solace of preference—lasted less than ten minutes. Finally, in desperation, Charlotte turned on her laptop to look over her e-mail.

There, at the top of her inbox, was an e-mail from Borroughs Yarn and Fabric Supply in Stowe, Vermont.

Every knitter knew Borroughs was a great company, a maker of high-quality yarns. Now they were developing an admirable reputation for inventive patterns and clever supplies for all kinds of textile arts. They'd already taken many of the steps she'd been trying to get Monarch to consider in utilizing digital media. Their blog was gaining serious traction—they were getting it right and seeing results. And they were asking her to come out for an interview after the upcoming Fourth of July holiday to discuss the possibility of heading up their new online commerce department.

I need this. Even if I don't get the job, it will put a bit of space between Jesse and I so I can think. Thank You, Lord. I knew You'd make a way.

Charlotte replied that she'd let them know as soon as her flights were booked. Now she'd have something to put some space between her and that charismatic, problematic fireman.

Chapter Thirteen

"Vermont?" Melba looked as shocked as Charlotte had expected her to be.

"Well, just part of the time. Or all of the time if I want it, and the company and I can come to an agreement." They were having a spontaneous post-church picnic on a blanket in Melba's backyard, watching Maria kick and wiggle.

"Vermont?" Melba said again. "And you're actually considering it?"

"I was laid off a month ago today. I've been putting out feelers every day since then, and all I've got to show for it is a few phone interviews that made me feel inept and a stack of carefully worded deflections." Maybe it wasn't such a smart idea to have kept how badly the job search was going from Melba all this time. "There aren't as many jobs out there as I thought there were. Monarch's not the only company feeling the pinch."

"But you're here. You want to be here." Melba scooped up Maria as if to shield her from the news. "Don't you?"

Charlotte sighed. "Of course I do. But I need a job,

and there don't seem to be any jobs for me here." It was the first time she'd spoken that truth out loud, and it let loose the growing tendril of fear in the pit of her stomach she'd been trying so hard to ignore. She'd been so sure of her path up until now. So convinced God had led her straight to Gordon Falls.

So sure she never wanted to be attached to someone like Jesse Sykes.

Melba settled Maria into her lap and furrowed her brows. "Did your mom finally get to you?"

Charlotte's mom, usually supportive, had lately begun to express concerns about Charlotte buying the cottage and sinking so much of her inheritance into the renovations. She hadn't said anything during the sale and the first days, but telling comments had started sneaking their way into conversations. A doubt here, a question there, a disapproving silence after renovation updates on the phone. The unspoken current of "and you still don't have a new job" ran constantly under every conversation. "Let's just say she hasn't been enthusiastic in her support."

Normally she didn't let her mother get to her that way, but the undeniable truth was that Charlotte was starting to worry about it herself. The gorgeous high-end kitchen faucet that cost twice as much as the standard—was that really what she needed? The armoire from the antiques store—was that really "the most darling thing she'd ever seen" or had it seemed that way because she'd gotten two rejections that day? The credit card bill had come last night, and it hadn't been pretty. Sure, she had the funds for now, but she couldn't—shouldn't—keep up the spending like this. Things were starting to come unraveled around the edges; she knew it on some level, just didn't know what to do about it.

"Don't let her get to you, Charlotte. You love that house. You belong in that house."

That was still true. Charlotte leaned back on her elbows, admiring the emerald-green of the leaves as they fluttered in the breeze overhead. It was so wonderfully green here. Everything seemed to be thriving—well, everything except her. "I didn't say I was going to sell the house. I just may not get to live here for a while."

"What are you going to do?"

"I'll still finish the renovations, but I might have to rent it out for a while."

Melba twirled a leaf over Maria's head, watching how her eyes followed the shapes and colors. "I can't imagine anyone in that house but you. You can't rent it to just anyone."

"Actually," Charlotte said carefully, keeping her voice as neutral as possible, "I was thinking of asking Jesse if he wanted to rent it. I know he just lives in an apartment now and it might make it easier to finish the renovations."

"Yes." Melba raised her eyebrows. "Let's talk about Jesse. About what's going on between you two. You could have lit half the valley on the sparks flying between you two at the talent show last night."

"He's a showman."

"Yes, he is. But while he sang to some other people, it was a whole different thing when he sang to you. And you still haven't told me about Friday's dinner in your kitchen. I want to hear it all—everything from dinner to why you disappeared after the talent show."

Bit by bit, Charlotte unfolded the entire story of dinner at the cottage. It felt useful to put the thing into words, to try and describe—if she couldn't hope to explain—what had sprung up between her and Jesse. Melba's response was an unlikely mix of surprise and "I told you so." She, of all people, could understand the pile of conflict mounting in Charlotte's heart.

"Wow," she said when Charlotte finished her tale and fell flat on her back on the blanket. "I mean, really, wow. This is a side of Jesse I don't think anyone's ever seen. He's mostly just a goofball around the firehouse, but it seems the man is an insufferable romantic."

Charlotte put her hands over her eyes, the vision of Jesse's magnetic gaze heating her cheeks all over again. "So what if he is? That doesn't mean he's capable of—or even looking for—commitment. Come on, your own husband called him 'an insufferable bachelor.' I don't want to be just another member of the Jesse Sykes fan club."

"I'm sure you can tell the difference."

"No, I can't. Not yet," Charlotte admitted, rolling onto her stomach to bury her face in the blanket. "I was defenseless when he sang to me in my kitchen, too. 'You Send Me' while he made the Alfredo sauce."

"The Sam Cooke song? I think I'd melt right into the Alfredo."

"I'm pretty sure I did. And the kiss…" She rolled back over and draped her hand over her face dramatically. "Glory, but that man can kiss. I was a goner. If it hadn't been for Mo, I'd have been in serious trouble. I *am* in serious trouble." She sat up. "That's what makes it so hard—I can't tell what's genuine. If he was just a guy on the make, I don't think he would have backed off when I asked him to in my kitchen. There's really something there. But you saw what he did to those other women in the audience. I don't know what's real. I'm not even sure he knows."

"I don't, either, but I'm pretty sure moving to Vermont isn't the answer."

"But it could be. I've lost my job and Mima. I'm not in a good place to think smart right now."

"Have you talked to him about any of this?"

"We were going to talk at dinner tonight, but he called me earlier and said he got pulled onto duty and we have to postpone. What if some time and distance is exactly what I need? The cottage will still be here in a year, and I'll be stronger."

"And Jesse? What if he's not here?"

That would be okay, wouldn't it? That would mean God had helped her shut a door she wasn't strong enough to shut on her own. That was what she'd prayed for, what she'd come to understand as the opportunity this Vermont job offer presented. Only if that were true, where was that sense of assurance, that ability to leap forward that had always been her strength? "Then I'll know it wasn't supposed to work out."

Melba gave her a doubtful stare. "You need to talk to him, Charlotte. You need to tell him in person that you're thinking about the Vermont offer. You need to ask him outright what's going on between the two of you."

"I know. I know. We'll have dinner tomorrow and I'll do it then."

Chapter Fourteen

There was a reason most firefighters hated the Fourth of July.

It was as if the world was ganging up on him to make sure he didn't have enough time to think through what was going on with Charlotte. Three false alarms, two parades, multiple firecracker-related incidents and four guys sick on the squad. As Jesse was fond of joking, "Some weeks it just didn't pay to be a volunteer firefighter." And that wasn't even counting the two construction jobs that were stymied by the holiday and back-ordered supplies.

He'd used the time away from Charlotte to go over that night at the talent show a dozen times in his head. It wasn't as if he'd planned what he was going to do when he went into the audience, but the way Charlotte looked at him had practically pulled him offstage. He loved what his voice did to her eyes, the way his touch could raise color in her cheeks. They had such a strong connection that he felt just a bit out of control when he sang to her.

That wasn't how it was supposed to happen. The leap

in his gut made him pull back, made him resort to old tricks and play up to other women in the audience. He'd known exactly what he was doing when he'd shifted his attention to the high school teacher, had even guessed how Charlotte would react. It didn't surprise him that the other women were as entertained as Charlotte was. It did stun him that he didn't enjoy their blushing smiles. He'd walked back to the stage that night not wanting to sing the final chorus to anyone but Charlotte. That was not who Jesse Sykes was. He wasn't ready to be so serious with Charlotte, or with any one woman right now.

Still, he couldn't stay away. The tone of her voice—the hurt and confusion when they'd spoken on the phone—echoed in his head no matter how hard he tried to shake it off. He told himself it was okay, maybe even a good thing, that things felt off-kilter when they'd talked. It was for the best that things had cooled off considerably when he was forced to postpone their date for Dellio's until after the Fourth. This unpredictability was part of his life, part of why he couldn't get serious with a woman. It was better that they'd have to take separate cars, because he was still wearing a beeper tonight, on call in case one of the other firefighters called in sick with whatever nasty bug was still making its way around the firehouse.

If he got called in out of their dinner, the interruption would be a sore spot for Charlotte. Still, the firehouse and its demands were part of who he was. If anything were ever to work out between them, they'd have to figure this part out. He just didn't know if that was possible. He still wanted to take this in small steps, and he just didn't know if Charlotte was capable of small steps in anything.

Even though it had been his idea, Jesse found Dellio's an annoying opposite of their first dinner. It was a local favorite; a noisy, greasy, delicious diner—one of the few places Jesse felt produced burgers nearly as good as his own. And the French fries? They were legendary—everybody loved them.

She was waiting in his favorite booth. That had to be a good sign. Despite all the complications, he still wanted tonight to go well, still wanted to move things forward and halt the backward slide they'd taken. Other women had never wandered continually into his thoughts like this—even on the job, where he used to be known for his single-minded focus.

"Glad you finally made it." She was trying to make a joke of it, to keep things light, but it was clear the long postponement had hit a nerve.

"Yeah." He surprised himself by hiding the beeper in his pocket and switching it to Vibrate so that she wouldn't see he was on call. *Cut her some slack, okay, God?* He was equally surprised to feel the tiny prayer rise up out of him, hoping the God she spoke to so easily had enough kindness not to rub salt in the wound tonight. *No calls—I'd consider it a favor.* He switched subjects. "How's Mo settling in?"

"Generous of you to ask, considering. He's doing okay. He hasn't broken or shredded anything, if that's what you mean, but there isn't a lot to shred just yet. I can't really hang curtains downstairs until the new windows get installed."

Of course she had to mention the back-ordered windows. "They'll be here in ten days, they tell me. The two new doors are supposed to come in tomorrow, along with the closet fixtures, so I can get started on those as soon as things calm down." She'd ordered top-of-the-line interior doors for the upstairs bedrooms, but the master bedroom closet was the thing that really stunned him. She'd moved one wall and taken a corner of the upstairs hallway to build out what she termed "a decent-sized closet." Jesse would have considered something half that size "decent." This was edging closer to decadent. And expensive. She'd gotten defensive when he made even the tiniest remark about the cost.

"The sink's working great, and everything in the bathroom is just perfect." She was picking at the edge of her menu with one fingernail.

"Glad to hear it. That tub looks just as good as a new one, don't you think?" *Come on, you're supposed to be patching things up with the lady and the only conversation you can manage is plumbing fixtures?*

"It was a good idea. I've got a few more ideas I want to try out on you, but let's order first."

Things eased up once the food came, but while he waited for her to bring up the subject of the talent-show night, she failed to raise the topic. Should he bring it up first? That didn't feel right—it was mostly her issue; he should follow her lead.

Instead, Charlotte said a quiet grace over the food—not as long as the prayer she'd said over their previous dinner, but it had the same effect on him. To be continually thankful like that—over something as mundane as burgers and fries—it got to him. When she added a plea for safety for Jesse and all the Gordon Falls Volunteer Fire Department, his heart did a startling twist in his chest as if the prayer had physically embedded itself there. Her voice took on a different quality, soft and lush, lively and yet peaceful at the same time. Jesse found himself easily and even gladly saying "Amen" to her blessing over the food.

The effortlessness he was so drawn to in her cottage came back to their conversation bit by bit. Maybe things had settled on their own—and that was okay, wasn't it? He didn't want to make this more complicated than it already was. That smile—the one that managed to tumble his insides in a matter of seconds—came back. Still, it was easy to see she had a lot on her mind, and at some point they were going to talk about whatever went haywire between them the other night.

"So." He decided to press the issue when they were halfway through the heart-attack-on-a-plate hamburgers and they still hadn't talked about whatever she needed to say. "What's up?"

"You mentioned your apartment lease was nearly up the other day." He'd expected a deluge of emotional questions and concerns, not that. She fiddled nervously with a French fry, drawing artistic circles in the puddle of ketchup on her plate. What was going on?

"I did," he replied slowly, cautiously.

"I don't know if you'd find this at all appealing, but if I ended up taking a job offer out of town, would you consider renting the cottage for a year?"

Where had that come from? And what did a question like that mean given everything that had gone on between them? "You're leaving?"

"No. I mean, I don't know. What if I have to? It hasn't...well, it hasn't been as easy to find a new job as I'd hoped."

If this was about how he'd behaved at the talent show, the cottage was no place to take it out on him. Rent? Why? "Well, sure it's a tough market out there, but..."

It surprised him how much the thought of her leaving stung him.

"I don't want to spend my days marketing widgets just because it's the only marketing job I can do from home. I want to work in the fiber industry. Textiles at the very least. There are only so many companies big enough to hire. I've gone a whole month with no serious prospects. Now there is one in Vermont that's starting to sound promising and…well…I may need to go where the work is."

This seemed a hundred miles from the impulsive, passionate Charlotte of just a few days ago. He reminded himself that she'd wanted to slow things down. She'd put the brakes on their relationship, and he was happy about that. Wasn't he? That didn't explain the irrational annoyance climbing up his spine. He hadn't wanted to get serious with anyone, least of all her, so he knew he shouldn't be ticked that she was considering an out-of-town offer. It made no sense. "I suppose that makes sense," he said, just because he couldn't come up with anything else to say.

"What do you think?"

Was she asking him if he'd take the lease? Or was she looking for him to ask her to stay? How was he supposed to know the right answer to a question like that—especially after the other night? He sat back in the booth. "Are you leaving?" The words made her flinch just a bit—they'd come out sharper than he would have liked.

"I just said I don't know yet. I don't want to go—" she gave the words an emphasis that made Jesse's insides tumble in eight different directions "—but what if I don't have a choice?"

"You always have a choice, Charlotte. If you really want to stay here, then you can find a way to make it happen." He looked at her. "Vermont? You don't really strike me as the rural New England type." He knew it wouldn't sit well, but he had to ask anyway. "So now you're sorry you bought the cottage?" If she were to walk away from it now, it would feel like rubbing salt on the wound she'd dealt him by buying it out from under him in the first place.

"No. I'm not sorry. I'm not saying Vermont's perfect, but it may have to do for a little while. And I don't want to sell the cottage. I'll want to come back to it. I love it and I want to keep going on the work on it. But I can't stomach the idea of just anyone living there."

So I'm a convenient stand-in? "I'm not so sure that would work." It was time she knew the full story. It was clear she needed to know. "Look, Charlotte, you should know that this hasn't exactly been a cakewalk for me seeing you in that house. I'd been plotting to buy the cottage for months before you showed up."

Surprise widened her eyes. Maybe now she'd understand why this might be an especially touchy subject.

"The reason why I have all those good ideas on what needs to be done is that I've been thinking about it all year. I just needed two more months to save up enough for the down payment. Not all of us get windfalls from loving grandmothers, you know."

Windfalls from loving grandmothers? The edge in Jesse's words cut off Charlotte's breath. Did he realize how hurtful that sounded?

"The home you were going to buy to launch your business was my cottage?" Suddenly everything that had transpired between them became suspicious, as if he'd been working some hidden agenda she wasn't clever enough to notice. Was it so hard to believe he'd played to her just as he played to other women in the audience—that she was just a customer like any other—after hearing that fact?

"Was. So you can see that renting it from you might be a bit of a touchy business for me?"

"Why didn't you say anything about this before?" It made no sense that he'd keep it from her unless there was some reason behind his silence.

He pinched the bridge of his nose. "Leave me just a little bit of pride in this, won't you? I didn't have any legal claim to the cottage—I just hadn't moved fast enough when you struck like lightning. The gracious loser thing doesn't come easily to me. I figured it'd just make things uncomfortable between us if I brought it up."

"So if you couldn't be the owner, you'd get the owner as your biggest customer, is that it?" She began to think through every decision he'd encouraged or discouraged, wondering if his charming helpfulness was ever fully genuine.

"No, that's not it." He planted his hands on the table, his eyes darkening at the accusation. "My offer to help was mostly on the level."

Well, that was a telling choice of words. "Mostly?"

"Of course I saw it as a good business opportunity. Your house represented a big job for me, and I needed a big job. I won't say I wasn't ticked at first. I was. But you clearly needed help, and I knew that I was the best guy for the job. And it wasn't long before it became more than business. You know that." He tossed his napkin on the table, and for a moment she wondered if he'd simply stand up and walk out. He didn't.

Instead, he leaned in. "I'd procrastinated on my plans too long and it came back to bite me—that's not a new lesson for me. This one just hurt a bit more than the others, and maybe that's good." His eyes took on that intense quality that always pulled her in, always made her heart skip. "Charlotte, you belong in that house. Every time I said that I meant it. You belong there. Why on earth are you leaving it? Leaving here?"

At that moment, it struck her that she was waiting to hear "Why are you leaving *me?*" Only that was not what he said, and that omission said everything. "I don't know that I'm leaving. I don't want to leave. But if I can't find a job here, I may not have a choice. I'm just trying to find a good solution for the property if I have to go." She paused, struck again by the enormity of his omission. How could he spend so much time with her in that place and keep his original intentions from her? It felt so manipulative. All the intensity of his persuasion at dinner, his attentions at the talent show, they all felt fabricated now.

"So that's what I am? A useful solution?"

She was not using him. She'd made the suggestion to be helpful. Yes, to both of them, but she hadn't used him the way he'd used her. "That's not fair. I didn't know you wanted the cottage. And the reason I didn't know was because you hid it from me."

"What, exactly, would have been the point of telling you? The only thing it would have done was made things awkward. As it was, things were pretty great." He ran one hand down his face. "Well, to tell the truth, I don't know what things are right now." His phone vibrated loudly in his pocket. "I thought we had something going on at dinner the other night, and I thought we had fun at the talent show, but how it got all serious and complicated all of a sudden is beyond me." His phone continued to go off and he grumbled while he fished it out.

This whole thing was a mess. "Jesse..."

Jesse practically threw the device on the table as the firehouse sirens began to wail through the night air. Charlotte realized it wasn't his phone at all, but the firehouse beeper. "You're on duty?"

"I'm on call," he growled. "And now I have to go in." He muttered a few unkind words under his breath as he slid out of the booth and tossed a pair of twenty-dollar bills on the table. "We're going to have to finish this—whatever this is—another time."

Charlotte stared at her food, the delectable burger having lost all its appeal. Jesse couldn't have picked a worse moment to be called into the firehouse. She tried to summon a prayer of sympathy for whoever's home or business was facing the threat of fire, but self-pity overpowered her better nature. Right now, she selfishly despised the siren.

Here, in a single moment, was every reason why she and Jesse wouldn't work. They didn't consider the same things important. He should have told her the minute they'd sat down that he was on call. He should have told her he'd been eyeing the cottage before she bought it.

He should have told her he wanted her to stay in Gordon Falls.

I got it all wrong, Mima. This isn't what you would have wanted. You were looking to give me adventure and I turned it into foolishness. If I had only waited,

*thought some more about what I was doing, I wouldn't
be in this mess.*

She fought the urge to do something, to move or
talk or do anything to stem the discomfort now crawl-
ing under her skin as if her emotional state had taken
on physical symptoms. *Sit and think, don't react,* she
told herself, but it didn't help. She was a whole ball of
reaction.

Charlotte ate two more bites of her burger before giving up. She flagged the server and asked to have both
meals boxed up, grateful most of the Dellio's staff was
familiar with the firehouse and used to people dashing
out midmeal. She added a few more bills to cover the
tip and left the restaurant, knowing she'd hold the sight
of that half-empty booth with two meals in her head for
a long, long time. One person with two plates of food—
how she knew and detested that view.

She made sure her route home didn't take her past the
firehouse. When she pulled into her driveway, the glow
through the curtainless front windows looked forlorn
instead of expectant. The house that had always spoken of possibilities struck her tonight as a giant pile of
things undone. The feeling she'd fought off since she'd
signed the sale papers rose up huge and undeniable. It
was clear now that she'd bitten off far more than she
could chew.

I need to think this through.

She knew, as strongly as she recognized the truth,
that she needed time and space away from Jesse and
Gordon Falls in order to do that.

Charlotte stood in the hallway, half paralyzed with
indecision, half desperate to do something. She tried to

pray but she had no idea what to pray for. *I need something to do, Lord. I can't just stand here.*

With no visible path, Charlotte simply kept doing the next thing that came to mind. First, she turned the oven on low and tucked the food in to keep it warm until her hunger returned. Then she put the kettle on to make a cup of tea. While she drank the tea, she opened up her laptop and booked the flight to Vermont. Then, in what felt like the first clear thought of the night, she packed her bag to head back to the Chicago apartment. It'd be easier to catch a cab to the airport from there, and she needed to be gone when Jesse got off duty.

She picked up the cat carrier Melba had brought for Mo and opened the door. "If we leave now, we'll be in Chicago a little before ten. We'll figure out tomorrow when tomorrow comes." Astonishingly, the cat walked right in as if he thought that was a smart idea. What more encouragement did she need? She was packed and turning onto the highway before an hour had passed.

Chapter Fifteen

Jesse winced as the emergency room doctor wrapped the plastic splint around his swollen ankle. "Is it a bad break?" He'd seen the X-ray and could guess, but he wanted confirmation.

"I've seen worse. If you stay off it—and I mean really off it, no weight on that ankle for three days until the swelling goes down enough to put a hard cast on it—you'll be back in action in six weeks."

"Six weeks?" Jesse moaned and let his head fall back against the examining bed, listening to its paper cover crinkle in sanitary sympathy.

The doctor peered over the top of his glasses. "You could be off crutches and into a walking cast in three or four weeks if it heals well. But if you push it and try to go faster, you could end up needing surgery. You may need surgery anyway." He peered again at the bandage on Jesse's leg. It covered a nasty gash just above the break. "Come back tomorrow to get the dressing changed. We'll see how the swelling has gone down by then. Ice every twenty minutes, ibuprofen for the pain, keep it elevated, you know the drill."

Chief Bradens pulled aside the curtain, looking weary. "Another down. What the flu started, that porch railing finished. I'm going to have to call another department to send a few guys to hold us over until some of the others are back on their feet."

"Sorry." Jesse knew injuries were part of the job, and no one could have foreseen that the porch railing wouldn't hold when he tripped and fell into it. Some small part of him—the part that keenly remembered Charlotte's prayer for his safety not hours before—knew he was fortunate not to have been more badly hurt. Still, a larger and angrier part of him was ticked off at all the trouble this break would cause.

"Come on, Sykes, it's not your fault. I'm just glad you'll be okay to come back eventually."

"Sure, in mid-August."

"More like September, actually," the doctor cut in. "You'll need another two weeks of physical therapy after getting the cast off to get back into enough shape to go out on call."

"And let's not even talk about my time off the job," Jesse moaned. Mondale wouldn't take kindly to having to call someone else in to finish his jobs. Someone else working on Charlotte's cottage? And the loss of income? Even with insurance, it would set his plan for the launch of Sykes Homes back a month if not more. Tonight was turning out to be a lousy evening on every front.

"Let's worry about that tomorrow and get you home." Chief Bradens began the paperwork while Jesse hoisted himself up with the pair of crutches that would be his constant companions for the next few weeks. "Have you got someone who can help you out tonight?"

His mom would be here in minutes if he called. Even

Randy, busy as he was, might find a way to stay overnight if asked. Only Jesse didn't want any of those people. He wanted Charlotte. Despite everything that was getting tangled further between them, the urge to do his recuperating in that overstuffed old plaid chair in the corner of Charlotte's living room came over him like a craving. He'd even put up with Mo to spend his days sitting on that chair watching her putter around the house with that elated, decor-planning look on her face. Go figure.

That option, however, was off the table for now if not forever.

"I'm set," he hedged, knowing the chief himself would find someone to stay with him if he wasn't convinced Jesse had it covered. Right now he really wanted to be alone with his frustration. "Just get me home and I'll deal with the rest." His car was still at the firehouse, and he didn't think he could drive it, anyway. One of the guys could bring it over later.

He and Bradens hobbled out to the chief's red truck, the radio still chattering in the dash with all the usual post-incident communication. It had been a small fire, a holiday fish fry spilling over onto a back deck, more smoke and mess than any real damage. Only the deck was old and rickety, as Jesse and his left tibia had soon learned. Those mishaps—the ones that were so infuriatingly avoidable—made Jesse angry even if he didn't end up hurt. If people would just bother to repair things like stairs when they broke, or—better yet—call in someone who knew what they were doing instead of trusting structures to a lethal combination of lumber store supplies and an internet tutorial. As every paramedic in the department knew too well, sometimes "do-it-yourself" turned into "hurt yourself" or "hurt someone else," as tonight well showed.

"It's late." Chief Bradens sighed, looking at the digits on the dashboard clock.

"It's so late it's early," Jesse managed to joke, pointing to the "12:25 a.m." with a strangled smile.

"I hope we get a quiet night from here on in," Chief Bradens said, breaking his own rule. It was a standing joke at the firehouse that hoping aloud for "a quiet night" nearly always guaranteed the opposite. The holiday incidents and short-staffing had really wiped the chief out.

"I hope we get a quiet weekend," Jesse added. "We need a break." He caught his own unintentional joke and laughed, glad to see a weary smile come to the chief's face, as well. "Well, a different kind of break, that is."

They drove to Jesse's apartment in tired silence, listening to the back and forth of the radio chatter slowly die down as the department settled in. The guys on duty would be up for another hour cleaning and restocking before they got to go home to their families. Nights like this were hard under the best of circumstances, much less when they were short of staff, as the GFVFD currently was.

They pulled into the driveway of Jesse's duplex. "I guess it's a good thing you have the first floor." Chief Bradens nodded to the pile of Jesse's turnout gear in the truck's backseat. "I'll take your stuff back to the firehouse for you."

Jesse opened the door and put his good foot—now sporting a paper hospital bootie, since he'd gone in wearing fire boots—on the sidewalk. He angled the crutches out of the truck and stood up. Everything hurt.

Chief came around the car. "You're sure you'll be okay?"

"Fine." He'd keep his cell phone nearby and call Mom if he needed anything other than the ten hours of sleep he currently craved.

He was fishing in his pocket for his house keys when the beeper went off and they both noticed the radio in the truck spouting a crackle of commands. "Not again," Bradens groaned.

If the chief didn't look so drained and his own body didn't hurt so much, Jesse would have made some crack about Bradens jinxing the night with his hope for quiet. Mostly he just shook his head as the chief hoisted himself onto the passenger seat to grab the radio handset.

"Gotta go. Smoke at 85 Post Avenue."

"Go," Jesse said, turning toward his house. "I'll be fine once I..." He halted, frozen by the facts his tired brain had just this moment absorbed. Then Jesse spun around as fast as his crutches would let him, only to see Bradens's truck speed away, lights blaring as the firehouse siren sent up its second wail of the night.

85 Post Avenue was Charlotte's cottage.

Chapter Sixteen

It no longer felt like home.

That was the single, constant impression Charlotte's Chicago apartment left her with as she rattled around the dull white box of a dwelling. A month ago she'd found the urban apartment dripping with character, but now it felt sadly ordinary. Impersonal, even, despite the fact that it still contained many of her personal belongings. Even the addition of Mo didn't seem to liven up the place. How could a stuffed full apartment feel more vacant than a half-empty cottage?

When she'd pulled out of the driveway in Gordon Falls, she'd doubted the wisdom of that purchase. Now, back in Chicago, she recognized it for what it had become: her home. Sitting in her favorite chair in her Chicago apartment, she still felt uncomfortable and out of place. She wanted to be in Gordon Falls. She wanted to *live* in Gordon Falls for more than just weekends and vacations.

It didn't seem possible—at least not any way that she could see right now. *I want to be there, but there isn't a job for me there. Is there one that I've missed? Lord, why are you opening a door so far away when You've knit my heart to Gordon Falls? Is it because I need to be away from Jesse? We're not good for each other, even I can see that, but my heart...*

Charlotte curled up under a lush afghan, welcomed Mo onto her lap and began to make two lists. One list held ideas for jobs she could do in Gordon Falls or one of the neighboring towns—"make do" jobs like marketing for the local hospital or some other company, office work or finding online work she could do from home. None of these felt at all exciting or motivating. The second list held all the arrangements—like finding a moving company or renting a storage facility— that would be necessary if she went to Vermont. Both lists left a sour taste in her mouth, and she abandoned the task in favor of knitting with Mo purring beside her until she dozed off.

The loud ring of the apartment's landline phone woke her, clanging from the single receiver in the kitchen. She bumbled her way to the phone, the alarm of a middle-of-the-night call fighting with the fatigue of her difficult day. Mo tangled around her feet and she almost tripped twice. Her answering machine was kicking in by the time she lifted the receiver. "Hello?"

"Charlotte, what on earth are you doing in Chicago?"

"Melba?" How had her friend even known to call her here? She hadn't told anyone she was leaving. She'd planned to call Melba in the morning, but she knew if she talked to Melba before she left, her friend would have talked her into staying over. She needed to be farther away from the cottage than the Bradenses' house. "I decided to come to my apartment. What's wrong?"

Charlotte heard Maria crying in the background.

"I only tried this number because you didn't answer your cell phone. Charlotte, it's the cottage. One of your neighbors smelled the smoke and called the fire department."

Charlotte fumbled for her handbag, knocking a tote bag to the ground and sending Mo scurrying back out of the kitchen. "The cottage is on fire?" Panic strangled her breath and sent her thoughts scattering. "The cottage?" she repeated, as if that would help the news sink in.

"I don't know any details yet. No one knew where you were."

She found her cell phone and saw three missed calls—two from Jesse and one from Melba, not to mention multiple texts from both of them. All within the past ten minutes. She'd set the phone to Vibrate during dinner with Jesse and hadn't turned the ringtone back on. "I drove here earlier tonight." Charlotte sat down on one of the tall stools that fronted her kitchen counter. "My house is on fire?" Tears tightened her throat. She couldn't stand to lose something else. She just couldn't.

"Not fully, and the guys have it under control. Clark said it was mostly just smoke but he called me when they didn't find you in the house." Her voice jostled as if she were bouncing Maria to try and soothe the crying child. Charlotte squinted at the cell phone screen to see that it was nearly 1:00 a.m. "I'm so glad you're okay. I've been praying like crazy since I couldn't reach you on your cell phone."

"My house is on fire." She couldn't think of another thing to say. "My house. My cottage." She began stuffing everything back into the tote bag she'd knocked off the counter. "It'll take me hours to get there. Oh,

God…" It was a moan of a prayer, a plea for clarity where none existed.

"What if you took the train? Maybe you shouldn't drive."

She couldn't wait for a train. And she surely wouldn't sleep anymore tonight. No, the only thing for it was to head back to Gordon Falls and pray along the way for safe travel. "No, I don't think there's one for hours anyway. I'll call if I need help to stay calm, and I promise I'll pull over if I need to rest." *My house is on fire.* Her brain kept shouting it at her, making it hard to think. She was supposed to be the calm head in a crisis, the problem solver, but none of that felt possible now. "I'll be on my way in ten minutes." She reached into the fridge and stuffed the last three cans of diet cola—a faster caffeine source than waiting for the coffeemaker to brew—into the tote bag. Mo, in a move she knew no other cat owner would probably ever believe, calmly walked into his carrier as if he knew they were getting back into the car. "Call my cell if you learn anything more, okay?"

"I will. Stay safe, Charlotte. The cottage is important, but you're more important than all of that. Don't speed, and call me if you need me. I'll talk to you the whole way in if you need me."

The cell phone buzzed on the counter. Jesse's information lit up the screen.

"Where are you?" his voice shouted over a lot of background noise, including sirens.

"I'm in Chicago. I just talked to Melba."

"Chicago? What are you doing there? I went nuts when they couldn't find you in the house."

There was so much noise behind him. The thought

of Jesse standing outside the cottage watching flames eat her house made it harder to fight off the tears. She sat down on the stool. "How bad is it?"

"Not as bad as it could have been. If you had been inside…" Someone barked questions to him and she heard him pull the phone away from his ear and answer, "No, no, I've got her on the phone right now. She's in Chicago. Yeah, I know."

"I'm coming." She was desperate to see the cottage, to know how badly it had been damaged. The 160 or so miles between Chicago and Gordon Falls felt like a thousand right now.

"I would." His voice was unreadable over all that noise. Did he say that because he would have made the same choice? Or was it so bad that she needed to be out there as soon as possible?

"Whoa, Sykes! Ouch! How'd that happen?" She recognized the voice as one of the firemen but couldn't begin to say which one.

"Hey, not now, okay?" came Jesse's quick reply. His voice came close to the phone again. "You be careful driving. Things are under control here, just try and remember that."

What did he say just now? "Jesse, are you okay?"

"I'm fine. Just rattled, that's all. The cottage and everything. Call me when you get to the highway exit." He paused before adding, "I'm glad you're okay. Really glad."

She heard emotion tighten his words and felt her own chest cinch with the awareness. "I should be there sometime before four." She took a minute to breathe before she asked, "Jesse, what aren't you telling me? Is the cottage gone? Just tell me now—I need to know."

"The cottage isn't gone. Looks like mostly smoke and water damage. I didn't get close enough to know anything more than that."

Not close enough? Jesse had been brought in on duty tonight. Why wasn't he in the crew that went to her house? "But I'd have thought you—"

He cut her off. "Just get here. The longer we talk now, the longer it takes for you to get on the road. I promise, I'll be here when you pull in and I'll answer all your questions then."

"But what—"

"Look, I've got to go. Please promise me you'll drive safely, and you'll pull off if you get sleepy."

She had a gallon of adrenaline running in her veins. "No chance of that. I've got a bunch of Diet Cokes besides." She had to ask. "It's going to be okay, isn't it?"

"Yes."

She wanted him to turn on the charm, to launch into that irresistible persuasion that was his gift, to sweep her up in that bold confidence he had, but really, how could he? A phone conversation in the middle of what might be a disaster couldn't do that. The only thing she knew that could do such a thing was prayer.

"Jesse?"

"Yeah?"

"Pray for me? I know it's not really your thing, but God will hear you anyway, and I'll feel better knowing you're asking Him to keep me safe until I get there." It was a drastic thing to ask, but if this wasn't a time for drastic measures, what was?

"I'll give it a shot."

That was all the foothold she needed. "Okay. Mo and I are on the way."

"Wait…you have the cat with you?" He sounded surprised.

"Evidently he likes car rides."

He pushed out a breath. "I had the guys scouring the neighborhood for the beast. I thought he was a goner, or at the very least ran away." He actually sounded relieved. "Glad to hear he'll live to torment me another day."

Even on the phone, even faced with disaster, he'd managed to pull a smile from her—one just large enough to get her on her way. "See you soon."

Every single bone in his body ached. His leg injury was down to a dull fire thanks to the pain medicine, but Jesse felt the sorry combination of wide awake and exhausted pound through his muscles and thud in his brain.

He should go home. It was feat enough that he'd hobbled all the way here on his crutches—it wasn't that long a walk but still, that had to have been damaging. He should take himself back to his apartment and at least make an effort to get some sleep.

Only he couldn't. He sat on the curb, his splinted leg sticking out in the deserted street atop his crutches in a makeshift attempt at "keeping it elevated," staring at the cottage. He was trying to make the place feel like his cottage, striving to muster up the sense of ownership he'd privately claimed before Charlotte came along. It wouldn't come. This was Charlotte's place, and two things were currently driving him crazy.

One, that he needed to make it Charlotte's perfect place—wonderfully, uniquely hers.

Two, that no matter what he told himself, no matter

how "unserious" he claimed to be about that woman, he couldn't stand the thought of her gone.

What had swept through his body when he realized Chief Bradens's radio was crackling out orders for Charlotte's cottage was sharper than fear. It was the bone-deep shock of loss. A loss that wasn't about bricks and shingles, but the woman who'd come to invade his life. He'd told himself it was better to keep things cool, to play their mutual attraction the way the old Jesse would have done. Only he couldn't. She'd done something to him. He'd told himself that his balking over her rental suggestion was just the legendary Sykes ego, a refusal to live in the house over some sore-loser impulse. That would have been a good guess for his personality a month ago. That wasn't it, though—he'd bristled because he hated the idea of the house without Charlotte inside, even temporarily. Somehow he knew—had known since the beginning in a way he couldn't comfortably explain—that she belonged there. Living there instead of her seemed just plain wrong.

Sitting there, feeling something way beyond sidelined, Jesse added two more items to the list of things that were bugging him:

Three, that he couldn't help with the cottage. Normally, Jesse wasn't the kind to rush in toward a fire. There were guys like that, firemen who were nearly obsessively drawn to a crisis, driven by an inner urge to save the day that made ordinary men heroes. He'd never felt that pull—until tonight. It buzzed through him like a ferocious itch that he could only watch from the sidelines. It gave him nothing to do.

Which brought up number four: Charlotte's request that he pray. He could no more help her get here from

Chicago than he could march into that cottage, and the sense of helplessness crippled him worse than his leg. The prayer she'd requested was the only thing he could do for her...but he wasn't sure how. He was not a praying man. He wasn't opposed to the idea—he took some comfort in the prayers Chief Bradens or Chad Owens or any of the other firefighters had been known to offer, and he found himself drawn to Charlotte's prayers of grace over their dinners. Still, none of those people had ever directly asked for prayer from him. It was like being told to use a complicated new tool without being given the owner's manual.

Only, was it complicated? Charlotte never made it look like anything more difficult than breathing. Prayer seemed to come to her like singing came to him—something that just flowed out of a person.

Singing.

Jesse searched his memory for a gospel song. He owned nearly every recording Sam Cooke, Aretha Franklin and Bobby Darin ever made, not to mention Ray Charles and Smokey Robinson. One of them had to have a gospel song in there somewhere.

He couldn't remember the title of the song, but his mind recalled Sam Cooke's mournful voice singing, some song about Jesus and consolation. That's what Charlotte needed. And so, after a guilty look around to see if there was anyone who could hear, Jesse began singing the couplets he remembered. Charlotte needed consolation to return to the assurance she'd first proclaimed to him: *God is never late and He's never early; He's always right on time.*

He kept on singing, letting the words soak into his own tangled spirit as he remembered more and more of the lyrics, letting the song undo the knots in his shoulders and the grip in his chest that wouldn't let him breathe. Letting him know that it might not be a bad thing that he felt so bonded to her, and her alone. Slowly, he felt his own words form—not out loud, but like a sigh inside his head, a breath waiting to be exhaled.

"She knows You're there, God. Give her consolation." With something close to a grin, he switched the lyrics so that they were about Charlotte, about her knowing there was consolation. She ought to be halfway by now, closer to Gordon Falls than Chicago. Exhausted as he was, he felt his heart rate pick up at the thought of seeing her soon.

Why was he so frightened of being serious with Charlotte—why be scared of something that had already happened? Getting serious with Charlotte was no longer a proposition; it was a fact. A done deal, whether he was ready for it or not. *I'll sing you home, Charlotte. I'll sing you prayers to bring you home.*

He began improvising a little bit on the melody, stretching it out into long phrases he imagined could cross the miles between himself and Charlotte, bonding them further, reaching into that little blue car as it made its way through the dark. "Charlotte knows You're there. She knows there's consolation."

Do I?

The question from somewhere in the back of his brain startled him so much he bolted upright. *Do I know God is there?*

It was the "know" part that brought him up short. He didn't not believe in God, in the grace of Jesus forgiving sins. He liked to think God was around, working in the world. He'd certainly seen what it did for the lives of people he knew. But did he know, really know in the rock-solid way Charlotte seemed to? The way Charlotte would need him to? The way that offered the consolation he felt himself lacking?

It was then that the title of the song surfaced out of his memory. "Jesus Wash Away My Troubles." It could not be coincidence that of all the gospel songs recorded by all the Motown artists in history, that was the song that came to him on this forlorn street corner in the middle of the night. *You are. You're there.* Jesse felt the astounding sensation of his soul lifting up and settling into place.

He looked around, feeling...feeling what, exactly? *Transformed* was such a dramatic way to put it, but no other word came to mind. He felt lighter. Looser. In possession of a tiny bit of that peace of Charlotte's that pulled him in like a magnet.

This was what made her the way she was. What made her able to ride through life with that indescribable trust that everything would work out in the end, and the courage to leap into situations without hesitation. It was the exact opposite of that drive he had, the one that made him plot and plan and scramble to bend life to his advantage. He'd never trusted that things would work out, because he'd never had anything to trust *in*. But he did now.

Consolation.

He felt consoled. Nothing in tonight's circumstances had changed—the cottage was still a wreck, his leg was still broken, the next six weeks up in the air and all of it beyond his control.

Yesterday's Jesse would be gnawing on his crutches by now. Tonight, he felt absurdly okay with it all.

All of it except the fact that Charlotte was not here. The sting of her absence, the bolt of ice down his back when he thought she might be harmed, the unsettling power of his need for her—those things weren't consolation. They were powerful, a bit wonderful and a great big hunk of terrifying.

Okay, God, this is me, doing the prayer thing. No songs, not someone else's lyrics, just me. And I'm asking You—begging You—to bring her home safe. Keep her head clear enough to drive or smart enough to pull over if she's too tired. I'll wait if I have to. But I figure You already know that I don't want to. Just keep her safe, because I can't. Not from here. That's going to have to be Your department. You get her here and I'll take it from there.

He sat there on the curb in the fading darkness of near dawn, listening to the steady drip of water off the cottage. They hadn't soaked the house, but even a small fire like the one tonight called for a fair amount of water, and firemen never had the luxury of being careful with their hose. He sang all the verses he could remember from "Amazing Grace"—Aretha Franklin had a dynamite ten-minute version on one recording he owned—humming in the parts where he couldn't remember the words. He was segueing into Ray Charles's "O Happy Day," feeling the beginnings of a second wind, when his cell phone rang.

He grabbed it like a lifeline, a gush of "Thank You" surging from his heart when he saw Charlotte's number on the screen. "Charlotte?"

"I just got off the highway. I pulled over on the shoulder on Route 20 to call."

Jesse was glad she was only ten minutes away. She

sounded weary. "You're almost here. I'll be up by the floodgates, waiting for you." He wanted to hold her, to give her every ounce of support he could before she saw the cottage.

She guessed his strategy. "That bad, huh?"

"No, not really. It's all fixable from what I can see. But you have to be so tired."

"I am. You must be, too. This was your second fire of the night and you weren't even supposed to be on duty."

Jesse saw no point in giving her the details yet. She'd see the crutches soon enough. "No worries, Miss Taylor. This is what I do. Get back on the road and I'll see you soon."

"Okay." If she hadn't already been crying, she was close to tears. Who wouldn't be in her situation?

Jesse pocketed the phone, picked up his crutches and hobbled toward the floodgates humming "O Happy Day."

Chapter Seventeen

Charlotte worked it out, somewhere west of Rockford. The force of her own idiocy had struck her so hard she'd nearly had to pull over and catch her breath.

She had set her own house on fire.

She'd left the oven on with the paper bag and tin containers of food inside to keep them warm. The greasy nature of Dellio's fries made them downright addictive, but probably also made them something close to kindling if left unsupervised. *Father God, I burned my own house down. How could I have been so foolish?* She wanted to ask Jesse—had tried to, in a roundabout way with her repeated question of "How bad is it?"— but she knew he'd never say. Not while she was driving. He'd save the lecture for when they were face-to-face. *Why did I have to leave right then? Why couldn't I have been sensible and waited until morning or at least until I was calmer?*

Part of her knew the answer: what she felt for Jesse was frightening her. She wasn't ready to love a firefighter. She wasn't ready to accept the life that she saw beat Mom down over the years. Needing someone who could be yanked away from you on a moment's notice? She didn't think she could handle that. Hadn't she already proved how poorly she handled that? The facts that Jesse didn't have a relationship with God—and seemed to have trouble with relationships in general— were just the icing on the cake.

She wouldn't worry about that right now. Right now she would just get to Gordon Falls, fall exhausted into his arms, thank him for saving her house and praying her safely here, and let him save her for now. The rest of it would have to wait until she could think straight. Charlotte pulled off Route 20 and sighed out loud when she caught sight of the familiar green floodgates that marked the official entrance into Gordon Falls.

The sigh turned into a panicked yelp when her headlights shone on Jesse. He was standing on a pair of crutches with a bandage over one eyebrow, and a splint on one leg.

He'd been hurt. And he hadn't told her. Had he been injured fighting the fire at her cottage? A dozen thoughts slammed together in her head as she threw open the car door and raced up to him.

"You're okay!" He reached out to her as much as the crutches would allow.

"You're not!" As much as she wanted to melt into his arms and cry buckets of tired tears, the shock of seeing him injured wedged between them. "You're hurt. What happened? Why didn't you tell me?" It was as if the omission of that detail let loose a deluge of her own panic, and everything she'd been holding in check the entire drive came gushing out of her in a choking wave of sobs.

"Hey." He tried to grab her but she darted out of his

grasp. "Hey, I'm okay. I didn't think you needed the extra stress of the news on the drive."

She noticed the bloody bandage on his leg above the splint and felt a bit dizzy. In her mind she heard her mother yelling at her father. The one night he'd been seriously injured—a stab wound in his shoulder—he'd simply waltzed in the door with his arm in a sling and Mom had gone through the roof. Now she knew how that felt. "You were hurt and you didn't tell me? You were hurt fighting the fire *at my cottage* and you didn't think I could handle knowing? So it's bad enough that I started the fire, so why add to my guilt? Is that what you think of me?" Some part of her knew she was being unreasonable but she couldn't stop the spiral of panic and guilt that wrapped itself around her.

Jesse managed to grab her arm, the force of his grasp startling her out of the tailspin. "Look at me. Charlotte, *look at me.*" His eyes were fierce, but in a protective way. He pulled her toward him. "I am fine." He spoke the words slowly, clear and close. Charlotte latched on to them like an anchor line. "I'm hurt, yes, but I'm going to be okay. We're both going to be okay."

She didn't see how any of this was going to be anything close to okay. She started to shake her head, but Jesse tugged her closer, crutches still under both arms, and held her close.

"You're here. You're safe. That's what matters." He let the crutches fall against the side of her car, holding her face in his hands. "I went nuts when I realized it was your house. I would have run there in my bare feet if it weren't for this." He wobbled a bit, standing on one leg, and she helped him hop over and sit on the hood. "When they couldn't find you…"

His words struck her. "You were hurt at the first fire?" It was still awful, but the weight on her chest eased up a bit. She looked at his leg. "What happened?"

"I tripped and fell into a porch railing. The railing was in bad shape, so it gave way and I went down. Kind of hard."

Only Jesse would make light of something like that. "And…"

"Broken tibia and sixteen stitches."

She put her hands to her mouth. "Oh, wow. That's bad."

"Well, it's not the 'put some dirt on it and walk it off' kind of thing, but I'll be all right." His hands came up to her hair. "I was worried about you. I was close to banging down your cousin JJ's door and getting one of those corporate helicopters her husband uses rather than forcing you to make that drive."

She knew Jesse would have, too. She hadn't imagined what had sprung up between them; it was real. "Alex doesn't run a huge corporation anymore, you know that."

"I just kept thinking about you all alone on that dark highway, tired and scared. For a guy's first prayer you sure picked a doozy. I'd say 'baptism by fire,' but I think that would be in poor taste."

Charlotte touched the bandage over his eye. His eyes. He could never fake what was in his eyes right now. It was no trick of entertainment; it was deep, true care. "So you did pray?"

"Of course. You asked me to. I couldn't work out how at first, so I just started singing whatever gospel song I could remember. It got easier after that. I just tried to believe as much as I know you do, hoping it would rub off."

"Did it?"

The warmth in his eyes ignited further, and she felt his hands tighten around her waist as she stood next to him beside the car. "Yeah, it did. I couldn't help you from where I was, but I began to feel like God could. Like He would." He looked down and shook his head. "I don't know how to explain it, really."

She lifted his chin to meet her eyes. That wasn't just warmth or care, it was peace. "No explanation needed. I get it. And I'm glad." The peace that had momentarily abandoned her—or had she abandoned it?—returned bit by bit. She allowed the strength of his embrace to seep into her, felt his head tilt to touch the top of hers and leave a handful of tender kisses there. Real. True. Trustworthy.

"You may not be so glad in a few minutes. The cottage is a mess. It's still there, it didn't burn, but there's a lot of damage."

She cringed. Her beautiful cottage—undone by a burger and fries with a side of stupidity. "I started it. Oh, Jesse, the fire is my fault. The oven..."

He tightened his grip on her. "I know. Clark told me they found the Dellio's tin in the oven. Or what's left of the oven." He put his face close to hers. "We'll get through it. Just..."

"Just what?"

His entire face changed, the fierceness leaving to reveal a heart-stopping tenderness. "Just don't leave. Don't go to Vermont, Charlotte. I don't want you to go. You belong here. You belong with me. You know you do, don't you?"

She knew how much it cost him to admit that, to make the request, and the last piece of her heart broke open for this incredible man. "I want to, but how?"

"I don't know yet. But if God is never late and He's never early, then maybe He's never wrong. I'm pretty new at this, but you told me yourself you felt like God led you here. It's got to still be true. We'll just have to figure out how to trust that."

Jesse's work with the GFVFD put him in the position of dealing with friends and neighbors after a fire, so he should have been used to this. None of that explained how his heart drummed against his ribs as he rode in Charlotte's little blue car, crutches banging against his shoulders, frustrated that he was forced to let her drive.

The damage on the outside wasn't especially visible in the predawn light, though there were *some* signs. The loose front railing had given way when knocked by one of the firefighters, and it lay propped up against the side of the cottage. The bushes Charlotte had just trimmed after months of neglect were trampled, and there were divots and gashes in the front lawn, scraggly as it was.

He caught her gaze as she turned off the ignition in the driveway. "See, it's still here. Not even a window broken. You should realize how fortunate you are." He wanted to reassure her, bolster her up before she saw the inside. He'd not been in there yet, but he knew what to expect. He dreaded watching her eyes take in the overwhelming sooty blackness he knew would cover her home.

"Yeah, I know." She said the words for his benefit, her tone hollow with disbelief.

He grabbed her hand, needing to make her understand. "Your neighbor called when she heard your smoke detectors go off and she didn't see any lights come on in the house. If it had become fully involved in open flames, I don't think you'd have much of a cottage left." He tried to put it into the terms that would mean the most to her. "You're blessed, Charlotte. It could have been so much worse."

Her grip on his hand tightened. "You put those smoke detectors in for me."

"And boy, am I glad." There was no way he was going to let her sleep in that house without the best smoke detectors he could get. It was the one extravagance he endorsed without a hint of guilt. He couldn't help drawing the connection between that urge and her current safety. He knew Charlotte wouldn't call that coincidence, and it was starting to sink in that it wasn't. He'd been placed in Charlotte's life right at this time. *God is never late, and He's never early; He's always right on time.* "Come on, let's get the first look over with. It gets better after that."

She hesitated, one hand still white-knuckled on the steering wheel. "What's in there?"

"I don't know. I haven't been in yet."

"Yes, but you know what to expect. Tell me what I'm going to find."

Jesse took a deep breath. Perhaps this was the least he could do—lessen the sensory shock so that it didn't hit her like a brick wall. He pulled her hand into his lap and stroked it softly while he kept his tone low and calm. "It will smell bad—at least for now. It's good that you don't have a lot of furniture in there yet." He thought of the little plaid chair where he'd imagined resting his leg. "Most of the textiles might need to go or be professionally cleaned."

"All my yarn and fabrics are still in Chicago. And my china, too—well, most of it." Her grappling for positives unwound his heart.

"Yep, that's good. Most of the kitchen will be covered in black soot and probably some whitish powder from the extinguishing agent. Probably some of the dining room and hallway, too. None of the windows are broken, so that's good, too."

"My new sink and faucet are goners, aren't they?"

"Maybe, maybe not." He gave her hand a final squeeze before he let go and opened the car door. "There's only one way to find out." When she winced, he added, "I'll be right beside you, Charlotte. Now and all the way through this."

Before he could get himself out of the car, Charlotte grabbed his shoulder and gave him a tender kiss. If there had been any resistance left in him, the need he felt in that kiss dissolved the last trace. The small, insistent longing to make her happy swelled into a consuming urge. He returned her kiss as if he were sealing a promise. *I will see you through this. I will stand by you.*

"Thank you," she said, their foreheads still touching.

He started to say, "You're welcome," but the words weren't near adequate. Instead, he kissed her again, hoping his touch spoke more. "Okay." He forced a grin and a wink. "Enough necking in the driveway. Let's get the hard part over with."

Her hands were shaking as she pulled aside the yellow tape that held the door shut. They'd had to break down the door. "Oh well, I was thinking about a new front door anyway."

"That's the spirit. Ready?"

"No." She managed the smallest slip of a smile, a weak and wobbly thing that still looked breathtaking on her.

"Want me to go first?"

She pushed back her shoulders and raised her chin. "No. I can do this."

You can. I know you can. In that moment, Jesse knew she'd come through this even stronger. Chief Bradens said he could always tell which people would beat the fire, and which people would let the fire beat them. In this case, Jesse could see it, too. Charlotte wouldn't let this keep her down for long. Jesse felt his heart slip from his grasp as she stepped across the threshold.

The acrid scent of smoke hit them with a force that was almost physical as he followed her into the house. Her hands went up to her face. "Oh, Lord, help me." It wasn't a casual expression—it was a heartfelt plea to heaven. Jesse, to his own surprise, felt a similar plea launch up from his own heart—*Help me help her.*

The front hallway and living room weren't as bad as they could have been. Thin black film covered everything, but he'd seen far worse. In the gray-pink light of dawn, it was as if the room had been poorly erased; everything blended together in a smudge of colorless dust. He made his way over to the windows and began opening them up. He'd go through the house with Charlotte and open every working window until the worst of the smell had eased up a bit. It would feel like progress to her, and he knew all she really needed was a first foothold.

He heard a whimper and turned to find her staring at the plaid chair, now damp and smudged with soot. He could tell her something optimistic, but he owed her the respect of honesty. "You'll have to trash it. I'm sorry."

She hugged her elbows and shrugged. "It was so perfect." It was true. She'd grown ridiculously attached to that chair ever since the day she'd brought it home, half hanging out of the hatch of the tiny blue car. It had made him wonder how it hadn't fallen out on the way home and why she hadn't asked him to pick it up in his truck, which would have held four such chairs easily.

"You'll find another perfect one. Maybe a pair this time." He wanted to swallow the words back—a pair?— what kind of dorky misplaced romantic comment was that?

Opening two more windows, Jesse made his way to the kitchen, taking care not to slip on anything with his crutches. He was due back at the hospital in three hours, where he would have to explain why he had not, in fact, done anything close to "take it easy and keep it elevated." The last dose of painkillers had worn off and his leg was throbbing.

"Oh." Charlotte's word was more of a gasp. "It's ruined. It's all ruined."

Jesse went over to one of the blackened cabinets, which looked like someone had set a dozen cans of black spray paint on the stove and triggered them in every direction. The new stove was a total loss, as were the cabinets directly above and around them. He had kissed her up against one of those cabinets. Every scorched corner of the room held a memory for him.

Even more so for her. Charlotte was pacing around the room, hands outstretched as if she needed to touch everything but couldn't bring herself to do so. "Everything is covered in black."

He opened one of the cabinets, wanting to show her one thing that hadn't been blackened. The interior wasn't scorched, but the plastic containers inside were slumped into melted, distorted forms. Her teapot lay in pieces on the far corner of the kitchen floor. The mason jar that had held his flowers the first time he'd brought them for her lay cracked with a big chip out of the top. One chair lay sideways on the floor, a leg bent in on itself and smeared in black. Footprints and smudge marks covered the once cheery lemon-colored linoleum floor she'd wanted so badly to keep.

"I did this." She stood in the center of the room, losing her battle to the returning tears she'd been trying so hard to fight off since the floodgates. "I'm so stupid to have done this."

She wouldn't hear any argument he might make right now. So Jesse did the only thing there was to do. He leaned against the counter for support, and pulled her to him. He let her cry it out, holding her tight and singing "Jesus Wash Away My Troubles," with his eyes closed and his heart wide open.

Chapter Eighteen

⌒

"Charlotte! Charlotte, where are you in here?" Melba's shocked voice called from the hallway.

"Kitchen," Charlotte called out, then sniffed and wiped her eyes with the corner of the zip-up sweatshirt she'd been wearing. Already it had black streaks on it, the fabric beginning to give off the tang of soot and smoke. Her eyes stung from more than the on-slaught of tears.

"Look at this place. Thank heavens you're safe." Melba's hug somehow brought everything into full reality, making Charlotte instantly exhausted. She needed to sit down but didn't have a single clean spot to do so. "Clark told me it wasn't as bad as it could have been, but it looks awful enough to me."

Jesse seemed to sense her weariness. "Let's go out onto the back porch. There's still a lot of smoke and soot in here, and I could use a dose of fresh air."

"And Mo. He's yowling in the car, you know."

"I forgot about Mo!" Charlotte rushed to the car to find a disgruntled Mo protesting his neglect from the backseat. In the emotion of the past hour, she'd not even remembered he was there. She pulled him from the carrier, keeping one hand on his collar. "Oh, big guy, this isn't a place for you to be inside right now. We'll get you set up in a little while, but I need you to stay put." Guilt over Mo piled on top of her grief and stress over the house. "This isn't much of a new home, is it? It'll get better, I promise." She found some strong yarn in one of the bags in her trunk and tied it to Mo's collar. "The back porch is the best I can do for you right now. Be nice to Jesse, okay? He's done a lot for us and he even went looking for you."

She walked around the side of the house, wincing at the dark streaks around the kitchen window and wondering if they would wash off or if she'd have to repaint.

She walked up the back porch steps, Mo still in her arms, to find Melba had pushed open the back door and propped it wide with a sooty box of books. Jesse had maneuvered himself into one of the porch's bistro chairs. He looked exhausted and uncomfortable.

"Clark told me you were hurt in the first fire," Melba was saying to Jesse, as Charlotte practically fell into the other chair and settled Mo on her lap. "It's broken, huh?"

Jesse nodded, one eye on Mo. His regard toward the animal had softened a bit. Charlotte was so touched that he'd gone in search of "the little beast" before he knew Mo was with her in Chicago.

Melba settled herself on the porch steps. "I was worried sick, Charlotte. I wished you'd called me when you got into town."

Charlotte leaned back in the chair, fatigue growing stronger with every minute. "You were asleep. You had Maria to tend to. I knew Jesse was waiting." Charlotte yawned. She'd been up for almost twenty-four hours now, and it was taking its toll.

Within seconds, Melba had her "mother face" on. "Have either of you slept at all?"

"Not exactly." Jesse yawned the words, although they had more of a wince quality to them. He hadn't said anything about the pain he was in, but it was obvious he hurt. Badly. The bandage on his leg was starting to grow pink at the center.

Melba stared at Jesse's bandage and splint as well, coming to the same conclusion. "Clark's dropping Maria off with JJ and Alex. He'll be here in ten minutes. Charlotte, you're coming home to shower and sleep at our house while Clark takes you to your apartment to do the same, Jesse. Clark's dad is skipping church to come pick you up for your hospital appointment at ten-thirty and deliver you back home. I should tell you, Chief George has orders from Clark to tie you to your couch if that's what it takes." Melba's father-in-law was fire chief before his son took over the job, and Charlotte knew George now served as an unofficial guardian of sorts to the firehouse. Jesse could use that kind of support right now.

"I don't think I have the strength to argue with that," Jesse said, shifting his weight tenderly. "Charlotte needs to sleep."

"So do you," Charlotte added, a surge of gratitude for all Jesse had done in the past hours welling up and threatening a new bout of tears. "You've probably done a million bad things to that leg in the last eight hours."

"I haven't exactly kept it rested and elevated, if that's what you mean." He held Charlotte's eyes for a long moment. "I had other priorities."

"These firemen," Melba chided. "They think they're invincible." She walked over and stood over Jesse. "Where are your pain meds? Your antibiotics?" She was on full mother alert now. Charlotte had seen it when Melba was caring for her ailing father. It was not wise to mess with Melba when she was in caregiving mode.

"Back at the apartment." He had the good sense to look sheepish, like a kid caught skipping his chores.

"A fat lot of good they're doing you back there."

"Yes, I hurt. Everything hurts. I need my medications. I'll go home with Chief and I'll keep my doctor's appointment—after some sleep. Okay, Mom?" His half-exaggerated pout told Charlotte he was nearing the end of his good humor, and so was she.

"It isn't like we can do anything right now except air the house out anyway." Melba planted her hands on her hips. "I'm going to go see how many windows I can get open."

"You'll need my help on some of those." Jesse made to rise but Melba pushed him back down.

"I'll do just fine. And what I can't get open, Clark will. You sit tight, both of you." She fished around in her handbag until she produced a pair of granola bars. "Eat something." Then she disappeared back into the house, a few expressions of her dismay echoing from the mudroom and kitchen.

Jesse sighed and tore open the wrapper. "She's a total mom now. Like someone threw a switch inside her, you know?"

"She's always been the caregiving type. It's why she came here to take care of her dad." Charlotte tied the other end of Mo's yarn leash to the porch railing and went over to kneel at Jesse's feet. "How are you, really?"

Mo, after giving Charlotte a "you gotta be kidding me" glare and swatting once at his makeshift leash, sauntered over to brush against Jesse's good leg. With a small "harumph," Jesse reached down and ran one hand over the cat's fat back. They were making friends after all. "I wasn't kidding. I hurt. Everywhere, it seems."

Charlotte noticed a bruise on his forearm and some scrapes on his knuckles. The risks of what he did clashed with the care she felt for him. It was an awful tug-of-war inside her, and she was too tired to endure it. She couldn't think of anything to say other than "I'm sorry."

He ducked his head down to meet her eyes. "It's not your fault."

It was the wrong thing to say. Tears welled up in her eyes and she nodded back toward the house. "Oh, this most definitely is my fault."

"The usefulness of that debate right now aside, my leg is not your fault. Firemen get hurt. It comes with the territory. Always has."

And that was the problem, wasn't it? "Have you been hurt before?"

She watched Jesse start to give her some wisecrack answer, then stop himself in favor of the honest truth. She was glad he didn't try to brush this matter off—it was important. "Not this badly. Mostly cuts and bruises. I chipped a tooth once. Usually I'm a pretty careful guy."

"What happened, then?"

A hint of a smile reached the corners of his eyes. "I had an argument with someone I care about. Something about Vermont, but it's all kind of fuzzy right now." He leaned down toward her. "I meant what I said, Charlotte.

I don't want you to go. I know it's not my decision and I can't tell you what to do, but I don't want you to go to Vermont. Even for a year. Even for a month."

Charlotte touched the bandage, the splint. "I don't know if I can do this. I told myself I'd never do this."

"I told myself I'd never do church, but I prayed so hard tonight I thought God Himself would drop His jaw in surprise. Maybe it's not as hard as we think."

Charlotte let her head fall on Jesse's lap, feeling Mo curl up beside her. "Maybe it's harder. Maybe we're kidding ourselves."

She felt Jesse stroke her hair. "I'm not saying God allowed your house to burn, but what if He knew it would take something this drastic to get us together?"

She angled her head up to look at him. "Are we together?"

"That depends on whether or not you need to go to Vermont." There was a cautious pleading in his eyes that broke Charlotte's heart wide open.

"I don't know," she admitted. "I want to stay here, but I don't know if I can."

"We can find a way. I believe that."

She let his confidence bolster her own. "I believe you."

Clark's voice came from the mudroom doorway. "Okay, kids, it's time for bed."

Jesse frowned. "And *he's* become a total dad."

Jesse held up his hand as he sat on the exam table. "Don't start on me, please. Chief George has been laying into me for the last twenty minutes." Chief George hadn't been fire chief for over a year now since his son

Clark took over, but no one had ever stopped calling him by that name.

Dr. Craig crossed his arms over his chest. "Let's just say I don't agree with your definition of 'keeping off it.' You didn't help yourself last night."

"Well, no." George, after his brisk lecture, had been amazingly supportive once Jesse opened up about what happened to him in the heart sense, and yes, in the soul sense—although it felt weird to talk about his own soul—during that long wait on the curb outside of Charlotte's cottage. Truth be told, Jesse was still grasping for ways to understand what had happened last night and this morning, much less explain it. He just knew his life had made an important turn.

He was glad Chief George seemed to understand. The former chief had unofficially adopted every single guy in the firehouse—and many of the married ones. The GFVFD was his family, even though he was only Clark's actual father. More than once in the conversation, Jesse had been stung by the thought of what his life might have been like if he'd had a father as supportive as George Bradens. He was pretty sure his own dad loved him; it was just that Dad's love came with so many requirements before it was paired with approval. Jesse always felt as if he had to earn his father's affections, whereas George seemed to be so generous in giving his—even if it came with a lecture or two.

"He didn't help himself at all, medically," George asserted, placing a fatherly hand on Jesse's shoulder. "But let's simply say the evening evened out." George offered a wink. It made Jesse wonder if Clark had sent his dad for this task by convenience or by design. He'd tried to give Clark a sense of what the night had been for him, but he was far too tired to make much sense. Explanations and talent-show serenades aside, Jesse was pretty sure Clark could have been fast asleep and still have sensed the bond now strung between himself and Charlotte.

And what exactly was that bond? That song at the talent show had shown him Charlotte was different from any other woman. Even as he'd taken steps not to single her out, his gut was telling him he wanted to single her out. *Exclusive.* That wasn't a term Jesse had ever cared to apply to women before Charlotte. Did that mean he was in love with her? Maybe. Whatever it was, Jesse knew it was powerful and worth whatever last night had cost him. That didn't change the worry in the pit of his stomach at the doctor's scowl. His leg looked awful and felt terrible.

"It's gonna be okay, right, Doc? I mean, I didn't do any real harm." He knew he was fishing for reassurance.

Dr. Craig seemed in no hurry to give it. "I can't say for sure. You broke it on an angle. Any weight you put on it last night could have shifted the bones and made things worse. How's your pain today?"

He didn't want to admit how badly it hurt. "Well…"

"Son," George cut in, "there are three people you should never hedge your answers to, ever. One's your lawyer and the other's your doctor."

"And the third?" Jesse felt the punch line of a bad joke coming on.

"Yourself."

Okay, that wasn't so funny. "All right, it hurts a lot. The medicine takes it down to a dull roar, but I'm dying before I get to the next dose. And…I sort of skipped a dose overnight. I was out at the fire site and I left all the prescriptions back at my apartment."

Was the pop-eyed shock from the doctor really necessary? "You went to a fire scene last night?" His face went from surprise to annoyance to dismissal in a matter of seconds. "You hero types make my job a lot harder than it needs to be."

"I'd classify last night as extenuating circumstances, if that helps," George cut in. "Jesse did what he had to do. We can't change that, so can we just move on from what we've got here?"

It seemed as though Dr. Craig dropped any pretense of gentleness as he bent to examine Jesse's throbbing shin more closely. His leg had turned a startling shade of purple, among other pessimistic medical appearances, and Jesse fought the nagging sense that the night had cost him far more than he realized. Personally and professionally, he could take an enormous hit here.

"We'll need another set of X-rays to see if the bone has shifted, but given how it looks—" the doctor doubled his scowl "—and from what you've told me, I'd say we're looking at surgery. Maybe even pins or a plate."

Jesse slumped back against the examining table, all his bleary-eyed wonder at last night giving way to a rising dread. "It's just a break. People break their legs all the time."

"It's a bad break that you put weight on—all night long, evidently. I've half a mind to schedule you for surgery just so I can admit you right now." Straightening up, the doctor put his glasses back in his lab coat pocket. "Mr. Sykes, would your cooperation be too much to ask for here?"

"I'll be a good patient from here on in, Doc. I promise." He folded his hands on his lap, trying to look penitent. "Where do we go from here?"

Dr. Craig picked up a chart and began writing. "I can't cast you—the swelling hasn't gone down sufficiently. I'm sending you for X-rays. We'll change the dressing on that wound and then see what the X-rays tell us. You might get lucky, but I think you should be prepared for the possibility of surgery tomorrow morning." He put the brace back on, which made Jesse wince. "When was your last dose of painkillers?"

Jesse had yearned to swallow a double dose the moment he woke up from his nap earlier. The twenty minutes it took for the stuff to kick in felt almost longer than the wait for Charlotte to pull into Gordon Falls last night. This morning. Had it all really just happened? He felt as if he'd lived a year in the space of those hours. "Six this morning. I'm due. Believe me, I'm due."

George padded the pocket of his windbreaker. "I've got 'em right here."

"I'll have the nursing assistant bring you some water when she comes in to change the bandage. You'll want them—the boys in radiology aren't known for their tender touch." He closed the chart. "I'll see you back here afterward and we'll talk about next steps."

"Okay, Doc." Jesse tried to look cooperative and hopeful, but it was hard with his leg screaming at him. In five minutes he'd down those capsules without water if that nurse hadn't shown up yet. The pain—and his doubts—were beginning to make it hard to keep his trademark humor.

As the examining room door closed, George pulled his cell phone from his pocket and began tapping with youthful speed. "Time to call the cavalry." The former chief had taken to texting with enthusiasm; he sent more "Gexts"—as the firehouse had come to call the numerous electronic check-ins the man was prone to send—than most of the teenagers Jesse knew.

"Huh?"

"Church."

He'd heard stories about the ladies of GFCC swooping in to care for people, but he wasn't sure casseroles were what he needed right now. "You don't need to do that."

George kept typing. "Oh, yes, I do. We need to pray that leg into cooperation. We want those X-rays to show you haven't hurt yourself further by what you did last night. That's going to take prayer."

This was foreign territory. People praying for him? Him praying for himself? For Charlotte? The world had tilted in new directions overnight, and Jesse still wasn't quite sure how to take it all in. "Um…okay…I guess." It probably was going to take divine intervention to keep him off the operating table. "I'll be okay, though, if I have to go under." He rubbed his eyes, reaching for a way to explain his foggy thoughts. He looked at George. "I mean, it was worth it."

One end of George's mouth turned up in a knowing grin. "I agree. But I'm still lighting up the prayer chain for that leg of yours. After all, you're part of the church now."

He was part of a church. Jesse waited for that to feel odd, or forced, but it just sort of sank into his chest like a deep breath. "I guess I am. Not such a bad thing, is it?"

George's grin turned into a wide smile that took over the old man's entire features. "Best thing there is."

Chapter Nineteen

Charlotte found her way to the kitchen, hoping for a cup of steaming tea to face what was left of the day.

"Hey there." Melba looked up from feeding Maria. "They prayed for both you and Jesse at service this morning. Feeling better?"

Charlotte walked over to the sink and began filling the kettle. Did she even have a teakettle at the cottage anymore? What kind of person has a life that destroys two teakettles in so short a time? "Not really. Less exhausted, but now I feel like I have twice as many thoughts slamming through my head." She sat down at the table opposite Melba and Maria. They looked so peaceful and happy.

"You'll be okay, Charlotte. You know that, don't you?"

She ran her hands through her hair. Even with a long hot shower, Charlotte felt as though she still smelled of smoke. "It's a little hard to see today."

"Maybe today's not a good judge of everything. Clark says it takes two days for the shock to wear off, longer for some people." She looked at Charlotte with such warmth in her eyes. "You can stay here for as long as you need to. Really."

Charlotte knew she meant it, but Melba and Clark had played host to her long enough. She didn't want to stay any longer than absolutely necessary. They deserved to be a family on their own again. "Thanks. I know I need a few days to get my feet underneath me, but I've still got my place in Chicago."

That wiped the warmth from Melba's eyes. "I hate the thought of you being back there. I hate the idea of you going to Vermont even more. I know it's selfish of me, but I really feel like you belong here. Even with everything that's happened."

Charlotte didn't have an answer. Her brain felt far too clouded to think. She was grateful the kettle's whistle gave her something to fill the silence.

Melba settled Maria on her shoulder and began patting the baby's back to burp her. "You want to tell me what happened with Jesse last night? And don't say nothing, because it's all over both of your faces, not to mention what Clark told me last night."

Turning to her friend, Charlotte asked, "What did Clark tell you?"

"That Jesse went crazy with worry when the call came and they realized it was your cottage. That he ignored the doctor's orders and walked to the scene because Clark had already left. That he was frantic to know you were okay, and it was all the guys could do to keep him from trying to help."

Mo, who had thankfully made fast friends with Melba's cat, Pinocchio, darted into the room to weave his way around Charlotte's legs as she set the tea to steeping.

"And that he hobbled around the neighborhood calling for Mo when no one was found in the house." Melba stood up and walked over to Charlotte. "That man has it bad for you. And you have it bad for him."

"It's just that after the display at the talent show, and all he said about not wanting to get serious with any one woman—well, he didn't come right out and say that, but it wasn't hard to guess—I didn't know if I could trust his charm. I don't want to be dazzled."

"But he's gotten to you, and he cares about you—a lot, obviously. I know it's not perfect, but do you really want to walk away from that?"

"*And* he's a firefighter. I know that's okay for you, but—"

"And then there's the whole faith thing, and that's big, too—especially now that he's made the first steps, from what I've heard."

"That's just it. Those things are sort of working themselves out. And for the first part…what he told me, the way he treated me last night at the fire, you can't fake that. His heart is true, I know that now. Only, is that really enough?" She told Melba the entire story of Jesse's night, how he'd come to terms with the God she knew had been pursuing him since the night of the talent show. "It wasn't really God Jesse was resisting, it was his preconceptions of church and judgment. His father's been putting him down for years. That made it hard for him to grasp a Father who loves unconditionally, you know?" She remembered him holding her in the destroyed kitchen, singing a gospel song she'd never heard before but now felt engraved on her heart. What could be a deeper truth than that? "He has such a huge heart, Melba. It's been aching for grace for so long."

Melba started to get mugs down from the cabinet, only to stop and look straight at Charlotte. "Do you think you're in love with him?"

Charlotte leaned against the counter, squinting her eyes shut for a moment. "Shouldn't I *know* if I'm in love with him?"

"I think it slams some people clearly like that, but I think more often it is something that slowly takes shape. Like knitting with a striped yarn—sometimes you don't see what it really looks like until you get further along."

"The attraction is certainly there." Charlotte thought of the head-spinning serenade that had made it hard to breathe back at the talent show. "The man knows how to sweep me off my feet, Melba, but just because he can doesn't make him the right man for me." She poured the tea into the pair of mugs Melba set on the counter. "You know how impulsive I am. Vermont was going to give me the space to think about this. Maybe it still should."

"Are you running to or running from?"

"What?"

"It's something Clark always says. About jogging or even guys at a fire. People rarely get hurt running to something, but they often injure themselves running *from* something. If you go to Vermont, are you running to what could be a good job or running away from what could be a good man?"

Melba had managed to boil the whole storm of Charlotte's thoughts down to one piercing question. Was she really enthused about Borroughs's offer, or was it just an escape from facing the scary prospect of loving a man who risked his life for others? "I don't know. I don't even know how to figure it out."

"Maybe that's why you ought to talk to Abby Reed

this afternoon. She's coming by in an hour if you're feeling up to it."

"Abby?" Abby had a reputation as a notorious match-maker. If she'd taken Jesse on as her newest project, Charlotte didn't see how she'd lend any clarity to the situation. "What's she got to do with any of this?"

Melba's smile was sweet but a little secretive. "I think you'd better hear that from Abby herself. I'm going to go put Maria down for her nap. Why don't you go sit on the deck and just relax for a while. It's a beautiful day, and you need all the doses of fresh air you can get."

The next thing Charlotte knew, someone was gently tapping her on the shoulder as she lay slouched in one of Melba's back deck lounge chairs. She forced her eyes open. "I must have dozed off."

"I'll bet you needed a nap." Abby Reed sat down on the chair opposite Charlotte, a kind smile on her face and a bag of chocolate-covered caramels in her hands. "I know chocolate doesn't make everything better, but it makes most things better."

Charlotte sat up and accepted the bag, reaching in for one of the sweets. "I guess it pays to be good friends with the candy lady."

"Jeannie wants to help in any way she can. She's been through a fire, too, you know. She lost everything a while back, and she knows how it can pull the rug out from underneath you."

"I keep trying to remember I haven't lost everything, but it still feels like I have. There's soot over every-thing." She smoothed her hair out, thinking she prob-ably looked like a mess today. "The fire was my fault, you know—food that I left in the oven and forgot about.

I've made such a mess of things with my own stupidity. I used to think of myself as such a clever person."

"You're still a clever person. You're just a clever person in a tight spot. We've all been there. Gordon Falls is full of people who are great helps in tight spots."

Charlotte knew that. She could feel the pull of Gordon Falls's tight-knit community calling to her even before her house filled with smoke. "I'm not going to end up with a refrigerator full of church-lady casseroles, am I?" She winced. "I don't think I even have a working fridge anymore, much less a stove to heat them in."

Abby laughed. "You might. GFCC is good at crisis management with food. It's a universal church thing, I think. Jeannie will tell you one of the blessings of a crisis is all the help that comes to your side. I know it may not feel like it this morning, but I'm sure you'll come out of this fine."

"I'm not so sure."

"Then I'd have another caramel if I were you."

No one had to twist Charlotte's arm. When the delicious, sticky confection allowed her to talk again, she prompted, "Melba said you had something you wanted to talk to me about?"

Abby settled her hands on her lap. "I've had an idea for a while now, and before last night I was going to wait until the fall. Now I think I shouldn't wait. Charlotte, I'd like to ask you to consider running a new shop for me. I want to expand the store to open a full yarn and fabric shop in the space next to mine. I'm looking to knock the wall out between the stores and create two connected spaces—one dedicated to gifts and art, the other for crafting. Only I can't run the both of them—really, I don't want to. When Ben finally moves out, I don't want to spend my newly earned free time behind a cash register or in a stock room."

Charlotte's brain struggled to comprehend what she was hearing. "You want me to work for you? Open up a yarn shop next to your store?"

"I'd thought of it more as a partnership, but that was further down the road. I figure that's a bit much to take on right now. I'd mentioned it to Melba a while ago—just as an inkling I'd had when you first said something about job hunting at the knitting group—but when she told at church this morning that you were considering going to New Hampshire or wherever it was, I had a long talk with God about whether I might need to speed up my time frame."

"Vermont," Charlotte clarified, and then thought that was a stupid thing to say. She blinked and ran her hands down her face, reaching for a focus that she couldn't quite attain. "Not that it matters." She straightened up, planting her feet on the ground as if that would help. "You're serious? You're offering me a job? Here?"

"There are probably lots of details to iron out, but yes. I want you to know you have an option to stay here if you want to. I'm not at all sure I can match whatever you were making at Monarch, but—"

"I want to stay here," Charlotte cut in. She blinked again. "I don't think I even realized how much until just this moment. I don't want to go to Vermont." She held Abby's gaze, feeling a bit dizzy. "Thank you. I'm sure we can figure something out."

Abby's smile told Charlotte this was no pity offer, this was God at work, moving things to His perfect timing. "I'm sure, too. After all, we both know you are a very clever person."

* * *

Charlotte was sitting on his front steps by the time George pulled into Jesse's driveway. Jesse was glad to see a little more of the old Charlotte back in her eyes. That smile did more for him than all those painkillers.

"Well now, look who's waiting to take over nurse duties," George teased as he pulled the crutches out of his backseat while Jesse opened the passenger door. "Toss me your keys, son, and I'll get your front door open while you say hello to the lady."

Charlotte ran a hand down Jesse's cheek, and he felt his whole body settle at her touch. "Hello, you."

He leaned up and gave her a small but soft kiss to her cheek. She smelled just-showered; clean and flowery. It was like fresh air compared to the disinfectant-soaked doctors' rooms. "Hello to you, too." He stood up and tilted his head close to hers, closing his eyes and stealing another breath. "You smell amazing, do you know that?"

He felt her smile against his cheek. "Flattery just might get you better nursing care." She pulled away to eye him. "How'd it go?"

He'd have to tell her sometime, might as well get it over with on the front sidewalk. "Not well."

Alarm darkened her features. "What do you mean?"

He started making his way carefully to the front door. "I messed my leg up pretty badly. I'm going to need surgery. I have to be at the hospital tomorrow morning at some cruel hour." He tried to keep the anger out of his voice, but her eyes told him he hadn't been successful. George's "prayer warriors," as he called them, hadn't won this particular battle.

"Surgery? Oh, Jesse."

Somehow the worry in her voice just made it worse. Weren't church people supposed to get happy endings from God? His twenty-four-hour venture into faith wasn't going very well, even though George had spouted some platitudes about God still being in control. "I'm more of a Motown guy than a heavy-metal one, but it seems I'm going to get chrome-plated tomorrow. I get fifteen whole hours at home before I have to report for surgery." The further he got into his explanation, the less it seemed worth the effort to keep the annoyance out of his voice.

"I'm sorry. I know that's not what you wanted." She hugged her arms. "You should never have stayed out there waiting for me."

He stopped, nearly losing one crutch in his effort to grab her elbow. "I don't regret it. Don't you think that for a second, Charlotte. I'm just mad I didn't get a clean getaway, that's all."

"You're going to be okay," she offered, even though she had no way of knowing that was true.

He simply nodded, not having a good comeback for that one.

Once they got him settled on his couch, George ticked off a list of instructions to Charlotte and bid goodbye with a promise to visit Jesse tomorrow at the hospital. "Make sure he calls his folks," George ordered on his way out the door.

Charlotte pulled an ottoman up to the couch. "Want me to get your cell phone?"

"No." He took her hand, pulling her in for another gentle kiss. "Not yet. How are you? Did you go back over there?"

She smiled and brushed the hair off his forehead. Her fingers were gentle and soothing. He wanted those hands nearby when he woke up from surgery tomorrow. He wanted those hands nearby every waking moment. With a sort of slow-motion burst of light, he realized he loved her. Exclusively her, absolutely her.

"No. I slept most of the morning, and then Abby Reed came over to talk to me." Something bright danced in the corners of her eyes.

"That's nice." That struck him as a dumb response. "What'd she say?"

Charlotte took his hand in hers. It was much easier to push the pain out of his thoughts when she was near. "She offered me a job, Jesse. Evidently she's been thinking about expanding her business into a full-fledged yarn shop next door, but hadn't planned on doing it until the fall. When Melba told her this morning I was looking at a job in Vermont, Abby decided maybe it was time to speed up her time frame."

Jesse wished the pain medicine didn't sludge up his thinking so much. "A job? Here?"

The brightness in her eyes now lit up her whole face. "A job. Right here. We're still working out all the details but I think it's going to be perfect. I've always wanted to run a yarn shop—it's almost what I did with Mima's money. Now I can learn, only as part of another business and with a partner."

"Me?"

She laughed and slid off the ottoman to bring her face close to his. "No, silly, Abby. You'd be terrible as a yarn salesman."

He kissed her again, needing her close. "Nah, I'd

be great." He reached up to touch her cheek. "You're staying."

She nodded. "I think so."

Maybe George's prayer army had pulled off getting him what he truly needed after all. "What about...us?" He didn't think he could stand the thought of her being in Gordon Falls and not being with him. As he looked into her eyes, Jesse realized, with a crystal-clear shock of certainty, that he'd do whatever it took to be with her. Whatever it took. "I need us to be...us." He knew he wasn't being eloquent by a long shot, but the look in her eyes told him she understood. "Tell me what you need for that to happen." He'd never in his life placed someone else ahead of his own interests, never laid his own plans at the feet of someone else's needs. A fire rescue was one thing, but his whole life? How did that work? He was pretty sure faith was what made such a thing possible. Clark had said it before—even Charlotte had talked about it—but he'd never really believed it before now.

Jesse wanted to see certainty in her eyes, but saw honesty instead. She settled in against him, sitting on the floor and laying her head on his chest. "I don't know. At least not yet. I've got a lot of...baggage...in that department and I'm not sure how easy it will be to lay that all down."

"I'd leave it. The firehouse, I mean." He didn't even know that until it leaped from his mouth. He waited for the regret to come, but it didn't arrive. "It'd be hard, but I would."

A tender pain filled her face. "I don't want it to come

to that. It's so much of who you are. I don't know what the answer is, but I have to think there is one out there."

For the first time, waiting didn't feel like procrastination. "We've got some time here. I'll be off duty for a while after the surgery." He grinned. "Look at me, all silver lining and stuff. Maybe God really is always right on time. This is going to take some getting used to. I've got authority issues."

Charlotte laughed, and Jesse felt the hum of it against his chest settle somewhere deep inside. "I've noticed." After a long spell of staring into his eyes, she ran one finger across his stubbled chin and whispered, "I love you. I don't know when it happened, but I'm glad it did."

The glow in his chest had nothing to do with any prescription. "I know when for me. I mean, I didn't at the time, but looking back, I know exactly the moment."

"You do?"

He nodded. "Berry cobbler." Just remembering the moment doubled the glow under his ribs.

"Then?"

"The face you made when you dug into it? A man can only take so much. I lost it right then and there. I didn't know it yet, but that was the end of it."

Her face flushed. "So that's why that kiss pulled the rug out from underneath me."

It had yanked him way off balance, too. "I didn't work it out, though, until the fire. I figured it was just a great kiss…until I thought maybe you were in that cottage. When that call came and I didn't know if you were safe… And then later when I thought about you driving back all that way all alone…"

She lay her hand across his chest, and he felt the

warmth of her palm against his heartbeat. "Maybe that's what it took for both of us. All the stuff we thought we needed—lots of it is gone right now. Maybe that leaves more room for the stuff that really matters."

It was so clear, right then, what really mattered. He slid his arm around her shoulders and pulled her closer. "I love you. We'll work it out. Right here."

"On this couch?" Her laugh was soft and velvety against his cheek.

"It's a good place to start."

If he'd thought the kiss over the cobbler sealed his fate, he was dead wrong. The kiss she gave him now beat that one by a mile.

Epilogue

Ouch.

Jesse's head felt as if it had been stuffed with cement and he couldn't feel the tips of his fingers. His mouth was dry and something was beeping with annoying regularity off to his left. He forced his eyes open to a bright room.

"Hey there, hero."

It took him a minute to recognize the voice as Charlotte's. He rolled his head away from the beeping and saw her eyes in the glare.

"Welcome back."

He winced and grunted, no words coming beyond the dusty dryness of his mouth.

"Thirsty?"

He felt Charlotte's fingers feather across his forehead as he nodded.

She held a cup and straw up to let him drink, and he felt the cool water pull him back to life.

"You came through beautifully, Jesse. There's a plate in your leg now but it'll be okay."

Jesse recognized his mother's voice and turned his

head toward the foot of his bed, where his mother and father stood looking like twin parental pillars of worry.

"I always wanted to be in hardware," he choked out, the voice sounding as if it came down from the ceiling rather than from his own body.

"At the moment, you're in plastic. You get a fiberglass cast later." His father's voice filled the room, but without the edge it usually had. "You'll be back to your usual antics in a few weeks."

Not really. Jesse still hadn't figured out a way to tell his parents how drastically things had changed for him in just a matter of days. As he watched his mom's eyes dart back and forth between himself and Charlotte, it was clear she had caught on. Dad still looked a bit confused. "Maybe. Right now it hurts."

"I imagine it does."

"You always had a flair for the dramatic." Jesse turned to find Randy sitting on the guest chair. Randy was here. "Or should I say heroic?" He rose and offered Jesse his hand.

"That's me, your friendly neighborhood hero."

"That *is* you," Randy said, squeezing Jesse's hand. "You're pretty amazing. I may have to take back all my wisecracks about the firehouse." It was as close to a declaration of support as Jesse had ever gotten from Randy. "Let me know how I can help. I'll find the time." Jesse blinked hard, almost unsure he'd heard Randy correctly. The world really had been turning inside out lately.

"You will be off your feet for a while," Charlotte said. "George already has a schedule up at the firehouse for when your parents, Randy and I can't be there. And your church fan club will keep you in food clear through Thanksgiving if you need it."

"Why didn't you call us earlier?" His father's voice was tight with worry.

Jesse's first response was a knee-jerk "Why are you so concerned all of a sudden?" as the usual wound of his father's inattention roared to life. Only something made Jesse stop and look at his father's eyes rather than just react to his voice. He was genuinely concerned. It wasn't just the "Why do you do that firefighting thing?" Jesse always read into his father's inquiries. Today it looked more like "You were in danger." He wasn't quite sure what brought on the distinction. Had his father changed? Had even Randy changed? Or was it his ability to see his family that had altered?

An honest answer—instead of his usual wisecrack— came to him surprisingly easily. "I didn't really have time. And I knew I'd be okay."

"Oh, you knew, did you?" Mom did not look as though she shared that opinion. "Surgery is not my version of okay, son."

"I called you for the surgery part, Mom. And look at me, I'm fine." He wasn't fine—not yet, really—but he wanted that worried look to leave his mother's eyes. "Mom, Dad, Randy, this is Charlotte."

Charlotte laughed softly and his father smiled. "We had a chance to meet while you were getting your new hinges put in."

"So this is who bought the cottage," Dad said. His words hinted at more than a real estate transaction, and Jesse found himself wondering just how well his parents now knew his favorite customer. "I'm glad you weren't hurt in all that the other night."

"We have lots of work to do—" Jesse felt Charlotte's hand tighten on his "—but I think it will all work out in the end." She caught Jesse's eyes. The fact that she'd used the word *we* planted a grin on his face that had nothing to do with the postoperative painkillers.

Only he couldn't really help with the renovation work for now, could he? "Who are we going to get to help you finish the cottage?" He didn't really like the idea of anyone else working on that place—he liked to think of the project as his and Charlotte's alone.

"I think we can worry about that tomorrow. Chad Owens helped me call in a cleaning company that specializes in these things, and that will take a few days anyhow. And then there's all the insurance to be settled." She ran her thumb over the back of his palm and Jesse felt his eyes fall closed at the sensation. "We have time."

God is never late, and He's never early, Jesse thought as the fog began to fill his head again.

"What did you just say?" His father sounded baffled.

"It's something my grandmother taught me," he heard Charlotte's voice explain. "About how everything works out. 'God is never late, and He's never early. He's always right on time—His time.'"

"That's a lovely thought." His mother sounded pleased.

She's a lovely woman. I'm in love with her, Jesse thought to himself as he began to slip back asleep.

"You don't say?" Randy actually sounded amused. When had Randy learned to read minds?

"And I'm in love with you," he heard Charlotte whisper in his ear. "But we've got time for that, too."

"I think we'd better leave these two alone for a bit," came his mother's voice. "We'll meet you back here later to bring him home."

Jesse fought the fog to push his eyelids open. Charlotte had the sweetest look on her face. "I'm loopy," he admitted, realizing what had just happened. "But I still mean it." He brought his hand up to touch the delightful softness of her cheek. "I'm head over heels for you. Well, maybe just one heel at the moment."

She laughed. "One heel is enough. Though, I thought you were sweeping me off my feet, not the other way around." She parked one elbow on the bed beside him. "Your family is sweet. Your dad tries to hide it, but he's really worried about you. He cares, Jesse. He just isn't very good about knowing how to show it."

"I think they like you."

Her smile made his head spin. "I hope they do. I think they were onto us before your little pronouncement a moment ago."

"They'll have to get used to it sometime, why not now?" Jesse yawned and blinked. He needed her to know before he slipped away again. "I'm absolutely, one hundred and ten percent in love with you." The words were taking more effort to get out as the fog settled back in. "So you have to stay. You have to." He couldn't keep his eyes open any longer. "I need you. Stay, please?"

The last thing he remembered was the cool softness of her kiss on his forehead. "I know where home is now. I'm not going anywhere."

* * * * *

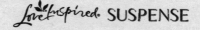

SPECIAL EXCERPT FROM

Love Inspired®
SUSPENSE

*A K-9 cop must keep his childhood friend alive
when she finds herself in the crosshairs of a
drug-smuggling operation.*

Read on for a sneak preview of
Act of Valor *by Dana Mentink,*
the next exciting installment in the
True Blue K-9 Unit *miniseries, available in May 2019*
from Love Inspired Suspense.

Officer Zach Jameson surveyed the throng of people congregated around the ticket counter at LaGuardia Airport. Most ignored Zach and K-9 partner, Eddie, and that suited him just fine. Two months earlier he would have greeted people with a smile, or at least a polite nod while he and Eddie did their work of scanning for potential drug smugglers. These days he struggled to keep his mind on his duty while the ever-present darkness nibbled at the edges of his soul.

Eddie plopped himself on Zach's boot. He stroked the dog's ears, trying to clear away the fog that had descended the moment he heard of his brother's death.

Zach hadn't had so much as a whiff of suspicion that his brother was in danger. His brain knew he should talk to somebody, somebody like Violet Griffin, his friend from childhood who'd reached out so many times, but his heart would not let him pass through the dark curtain.

"Just get to work," he muttered to himself as his phone rang. He checked the number.

Violet.

He considered ignoring it, but Violet didn't ever call unless she needed help, and she rarely needed anyone. Strong enough to run a ticket counter at LaGuardia and have enough energy left over to help out at Griffin's, her family's diner. She could handle belligerent customers in both arenas and bake the best apple pie he'd ever had the privilege to chow down.

It almost made him smile as he accepted the call.

"Someone's after me, Zach."

Panic rippled through their connection. Panic, from a woman who was tough as they came. "Who? Where are you?"

Her breath was shallow as if she was running.

"I'm trying to get to the break room. I can lock myself in, but I don't… I can't…" There was a clatter.

"Violet?" he shouted.

But there was no answer.

Don't miss
Act of Valor *by Dana Mentink,*
available May 2019 wherever
Love Inspired® Suspense books and ebooks are sold.

www.LoveInspired.com

Looking for inspiration in tales
of hope, faith and heartfelt romance?

Check out **Love Inspired**® and
Love Inspired® **Suspense** books!

New books available every month!

CONNECT WITH US AT:

Facebook.com/groups/HarlequinConnection

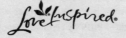 Facebook.com/HarlequinBooks

Twitter.com/HarlequinBooks

Instagram.com/HarlequinBooks

Pinterest.com/HarlequinBooks

ReaderService.com

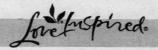
"Dating is so complicated."

"People are complicated, Noah. Every single person you meet
is dealing with something."

He asked, "How did you get so wise?"

"Never said I was."

"I'm being serious. How did you learn to navigate so seamlessly
through these kinds of interactions, and why aren't you married?"

Olivia Mae thought her eyes were going to pop out of her head.
"Did you really just ask me that?"

"I did."

"A little intrusive."

"Meaning you don't want to answer?"

"Meaning it's none of your business."

"Fair enough, though it's like asking a horse salesman why he
doesn't own a horse."

"My family situation is…unique."

"You mean with your grandparents?"

She nodded instead of answering.

"I've got it." Noah resettled his hat, looking quite pleased with
himself.

"Got what?"

"The solution to my dating disasters."

He leaned forward, close enough that she could smell the
shampoo he'd used that morning.

LIEXP0419

"You need to give me dating lessons."

"What do you mean?"

"You and me. We'll go on a few dates…say, three. You can learn how to do anything if you do it three times."

"That's a ridiculous suggestion."

"Why? I learn better from doing."

"Do you?"

"I've already learned not to take a girl to a gas station, but who knows how many more dating traps are waiting for me."

"So this would be…a learning experience."

"It's a perfect solution." He tugged on her *kapp* string, something no one had done to her since she'd been a young teen.

"I can tell by the shock on your face that I've made you uncomfortable. It's a *gut* idea, though. We'd keep it businesslike—nothing personal."

Olivia Mae had no idea why the thought of sitting through three dates with Noah Graber made her stomach twirl like she'd been on a merry-go-round. Maybe she was catching a stomach bug.

"Wait a minute. Are you trying to get out of your third date? Because you promised your *mamm* that you would give this thing three solid attempts."

"And I'll keep my word on that," Noah assured her. "After you've tutored me, you can throw another poor unsuspecting girl my way."

Olivia Mae stood, brushed off the back of her dress and pointed a finger at Noah, who still sat in the grass as if he didn't have a care in the world.

"All right. I'll do it."

Don't miss
A Perfect Amish Match *by Vannetta Chapman,*
available May 2019 wherever
Love Inspired® books and ebooks are sold.

www.LoveInspired.com